PRAISE FOR NANCY GEARY'S NOVELS

Being Mrs. Alcott

"The best book I've ever read about a woman in search of herself."
— **CHRISTOPHER MOORE, bestselling author of**
The Stupidest Angel **and** *Fluke*

"Beautifully told . . . A touching and moving portrait of a woman you will grow to love and deeply admire. Geary does a superb job."
— **GirlPosse.com**

"An engrossing tale . . . thoughtful and entertaining."
— **Bookloons.com**

"Compelling . . . The author does an excellent job of bringing Grace Alcott's plight to the attention of the reader [and] with character portrayal . . . Highly recommended."
— **BestsellersWorld.com**

Regrets Only

"Fascinating . . . a taut plot, complex characters, and smooth dialogue that make for a great read."
— **LINDA FAIRSTEIN**

"A likable heroine, and Geary's blending of a psychological thriller with classic police procedural produces a crime novel with appeal to fans of both genres."
— *Booklist*

more . . .

"Strong scenic detail and a winning heroine."
— *Kirkus Reviews*

"Highly recommended."
— TheRomanceReadersConnection.com

Redemption

"Wonderful . . . a remarkable achievement . . . A new star has appeared in the galaxy of contemporary crime fiction."
— NELSON DEMILLE

"A well-told tale . . . from one who knows the dark secrets simmering beneath the shiny surface of society . . . an entertainment of the highest order with wildly engaging suspense and brilliantly drawn characters. I loved it."
— LINDA FAIRSTEIN

"Wonderful . . . totally captivated me from page one to the jaw-dropping ending. Absorbing, with gripping characters, nonstop suspense . . . I couldn't put it down!"
— CARLA NEGGERS, author of *The Harbor*

"A suspenseful tale . . . Geary is a wonderfully mordant observer of the rich gone awry — her books are funny, sharp, and stylishly written."
— SALLIE BISSELL, author of *A Darker Justice*

"A lyrical novel . . . gently and perceptively written . . . Geary has a refined talent for exposing the dark edges of all too human characters and the ripple of violence in their lives. *Redemption* will captivate you."
— LYNN HIGHTOWER, author of *High Water*

Misfortune

"Geary keeps the pace racing."
— *People*

"Few writers succeed in describing the world of the American aristocracy or how they truly live. But Nancy Geary has authentic voice. She knows this world. What a great first novel!"
— OLIVIA GOLDSMITH,
author of *The First Wives Club*

"An irresistible read, both because it takes you behind the hedges of blue bloods in the Hamptons and because it's a compelling mystery that keeps you guessing whodunit and whydunit until the final page. A stylish and expert debut."
— JANE HELLER, **author of *Sis Boom Bah***

"Riveting . . . haunting, compelling, and beautifully written . . . Geary's astonishing first novel reads like a cross between Scott Turow and Edith Wharton. I couldn't put it down."
— AMY GUTMAN, **author of *The Anniversary***

Being Mrs. Alcott

NANCY GEARY

WARNER BOOKS

NEW YORK   BOSTON

For my mother, Diana Michener,
with love and thanks

Copyright © 2005 by Nancy Whitman Geary
Reading Group Guide copyright © 2006 by Hachette Book Group USA
All rights reserved.

Warner Books

Hachette Book Group USA
1271 Avenue of the Americas
New York, NY 10020

Visit our Web site at www.HachetteBookGroupUSA.com.

Printed in the United States of America

Originally published in hardcover by Hachette Book Group USA
First Trade Edition: July 2006
10 9 8 7 6 5 4 3 2 1

The Warner Book and the W logo are trademarks of Time Inc. Used under license.

The Library of Congress has cataloged the hardcover edition as follows:
Geary, Nancy.
  Being Mrs. Alcott / Nancy Geary.—1st ed.
    p. cm.
  Summary: "A Cape Cod housewife deals secretly with an illness and confronts losing
the home that has been the cornerstone of her family life."—Provided by the publisher.
  ISBN 0-446-53220-7
  1. Housewives—Fiction. 2. Cape Cod (Mass.)—Fiction. 3. Home ownership—
Fiction. 4. Married women—Fiction. 5. Secrecy—Fiction. 6. Sick—Fiction. I. Title.
PS3557.E228B45 2005
813'.6—dc22

                                                                  2004030851

Book design and text composition by Le3G McRee

ISBN-13: 978-0-446-69756-9 (pbk.)
ISBN-10: 0-446-69756-7 (pbk.)

Acknowledgments

I thank Jamie Raab for helping me to grow. This book could not have been written without her encouragement, support, and thoughtful editorial suggestions. Thanks to Ben Greenberg for his helpful comments during the early stages of this story, to Laura Jorstad for her careful copy-edits, to Sharon Krassney for managing the details, and to Tina Andreadis for her publicity efforts, energy, and friendship.

Many thanks to Pam Nelson, Levy Home Entertainment, and the Get Caught Reading at Sea crew for their tremendous support of my work. And thanks to Barb Garside at Webbtide for her meticulous attention to my Web site and constant good cheer.

Thanks to everyone at Nicholas Ellison, Inc., for their dedication and commitment. I thank Abby Koons for her hard work, unfailing support, and optimism. Thanks to Jennifer Cayea for all her foreign rights work on my behalf. And, as always, I remain deeply indebted to Nick Ellison, who has believed in me since we first met and has yet to lose faith. I thank him for encouraging me to take risks, offering a safety net, and always answering the telephone.

I am forever grateful to my wonderful friends. Thanks to Amy Kellogg and Missy Smith for their advice, patience, laughter, and help. Despite our distance, they have supported me more than they know. Thanks to Susan and Craig Hupper, who have welcomed me into their family for holidays and vacations and come to my aid when I needed it most. I appreciate their concern and their wonderful company. And thanks to Ann Espuelas for all the conversations about writing, cooking, love, life, and raising little boys. I cherish our friendship.

For her patience and prayers, I thank the Reverend Lynn Harrington. Her spiritual and practical advice guides me, and her friendship gives me strength. Thanks to Anne Testa for her overwhelming support, and to Donna Lutton and Maryann Kann for their kindness, generous assistance, and encouragement. I am blessed to be part of the St. John's community.

I could not have survived the past year without the love and support of my extraordinary family. I thank my mother, Diana Michener, for her compassion and help. She has shown me what it is to be a parent long after her daughter has left home. Her grace, elegance, intellect, and creativity inspire me. I thank Jim Dine for his patience and pragmatism. Together, their love and advice have kept me safe. I thank Natalie Geary for her friendship, support, and care. I admire her courage; I rely on her help and pediatric advice; I am eternally grateful for her love. Thanks to Ted Geary, Jack and Dolly Geary, and Daphne Geary for their encouragement and good humor.

And I thank Harry, my greatest blessing and darling son. Because of him, I never wonder why.

Being Mrs. Alcott

The Present

Prologue

Undergarments are like seasonal slipcovers; they need to be replaced every six months." Her mother, the late Eleanor Montgomery, had issued this directive so many times over the years that it had become a mantra. And Grace remembered it perfectly now. "God forbid an accident befalls you and someone you don't know should discover you or attempt a rescue." She'd even received the instruction on her wedding day over three decades before, as she'd been arranging the thin diamond tiara amid her golden curls. That time, her mother had leaned forward so that her own handsome face shared the mirror with her daughter's, opened her chestnut eyes wider than usual, and whispered, "Imagine if there were a stain!"

Every first of June and September, Grace had heeded her mother's warning and purchased all-new brassieres and underpants. She'd never had the courage to raise the obvious question. She'd simply accepted that worrying about impropriety after death was just as worthwhile as worrying about it ahead of time. And today of all days, she didn't feel like gambling that a corpse couldn't be embarrassed. Not after Dr. Preston's news.

Over the years, she'd always selected the same Swiss brand, the same cotton fabric, and the same colors. She bought three matching sets in white and three in nude. At one point just around her fiftieth birthday, she'd debated black, but ultimately rejected it as impractical. So her choices remained uninspired, but the lingerie was well made and feminine without being tawdry. When she'd moved from Boston to Cape Cod four years before, she'd found a small shop in Osterville that carried exactly what she'd been able to find at Neiman Marcus in Copley Place. And so the tradition continued uninterrupted, the new undergarments being folded neatly into the top drawer of her bureau along with a fresh lavender sachet, and the old being wrapped in a paper bag and discarded in the kitchen trash.

But this month she'd been distracted. Preoccupied as the engine of her taupe sedan idled at the exit to the covered parking lot at Massachusetts General Hospital, she'd suddenly realized that today was the fifth of June, and that the task hadn't been accomplished. Something in the parking attendant's face had reminded her even as her hand trembled reaching into her purse for change to pay. Perhaps it was the girl's youth, the freshness about her smooth chocolate skin and neatly braided plaits, that conjured a sense of optimism. Grace wouldn't be wasting money. Regardless of what might befall her, in whatever state she might be found, she wouldn't compromise now.

Although she made her resolution to adhere to her biannual ritual, she hadn't been able to face Mrs. Worthington, the proprietor of A Woman's Elegance: Discerning Lingerie for the Discerning Woman. White-haired Mrs. Worthington had a small, neat shop on Main Street with lace curtains in the storefront window, a powderpink, upholstered slipper chair in the dressing room, and a large plaque proclaiming her membership in the AARP above the register. She'd offer to model some formfitting, curvature-slenderizing, tuck-the-tummy lingerie, despite the fact that Grace had no hips or stomach to hide. Or she'd produce an absurdly suggestive nightgown they both knew Grace wouldn't consider. Each time this happened, Grace would smile politely and shake her head. Then Mrs. Worthington would return the garment on its quilted hanger to the rack with a look of disappointment on her face. "It's never too late to add a little spice to your life."

Normally, Grace welcomed the familiarity, the camaraderie, but not today. She feared Mrs. Worthington might be able to read her face as clearly as if her forehead flashed a newsreel. She didn't want to be questioned. She didn't want to risk breaking down, bursting into tears, falling to her knees, losing control of herself. All she wanted was fresh underwear.

And so she'd ended up at the ghastly Cape Cod Mall, a place no sane person would ever want to visit, let alone patronize. But she'd wanted anonymity, and Filene's had a lingerie department.

The sprawling cement-block building was unmanageably huge, and as the automatic doors swung open she wondered for a moment whether she could lose herself inside. Had she found an abyss off Exit 6 that would swallow her whole, leaving nothing but her parked car outside as the only trace of her existence? The thought of poor Bain struggling in that circumstance almost made her laugh. She could not imagine her husband attempting to find her here. Elegant Bainbridge Forest Alcott II, in his blue blazer, golf shirt, white trousers, and driving moccasins, had rarely crossed the Bass River since he'd retired to Chatham. He'd stayed east of Exit 9, enjoying the peaceful off-seasons and the social summers, lowering his handicap from an eleven to an eight, admiring the harbor view, and swimming laps in his heated pool. Navigating this parking lot would be traumatic; a venture inside the mall to retrieve his wife would be hell, perhaps a worse hell for him than letting her disappear.

Filene's was nearly empty. At two o'clock on a Friday in early June, the lunchtime shoppers were gone and the summer hordes hadn't arrived. She read the store directory and navigated the escalator only to wander through tightly spaced racks and racks of leisure wear and weekend wear, designer sections filled with brands of which she'd never heard. She stopped to examine the clothes: bright-colored business suits with faux pockets and handkerchiefs sewn in, coordinated tops with large bows at the neck, slacks that came with attached gold-buckle belts, loosely woven acrylic sweaters, and acid-washed jeans. It seemed a sea of colors and textures and labels, an array of merchandise priced at $99.99 or $59.99 or two for $79.99. Finally, she spotted pajamas off in the distance and homed in on her destination. She knew then she was close.

Forty-five minutes later, Grace now stared at the Formica counter where she'd piled her six packages of Jockey for Her. It was an odd choice, especially given her allergy to horses. She'd never worn underwear that came sealed in plastic, but she couldn't find her usual brand and the package said these were cotton, or at least mostly so, give or take a small percentage of Spandex. Plus the model on the front with a towel around her neck and her bottom tilted toward the shopper looked alluring. Would that sex appeal rub off, hide her varicose veins and tighten the loose skin that draped from her backside? She wished she could envelop her whole body in a single transforming garment, a youth-producing unitard, anything to turn back the clock, even just to yesterday.

The checkout girl with an artificial stripe of red hair down the middle of her otherwise brown locks swiped her American Express card twice without success. "The magnetized strip must have gotten wet," Grace offered weakly, even as she sensed that there might be a more

ominous explanation. And so the girl, whose badge iden-
tified her as KIM, called for authorization.

After reading off the account number, Kim seemed to
be placed on hold. Several minutes transpired. To pass the
time, the girl picked at something in her teeth with her
long black fingernail and then stared at the underside of
the nail in an effort to discern what the particle was.
Finally, she said, "Yeah. Okay," as she glanced at Grace
with a stern expression. Replacing the receiver, she
opened a drawer under the counter, removed a large pair
of black-handled scissors, and cut the plastic card in two.

"What are you doing?" Grace asked, even as she realized it was too late.

"You want the halves?" Kim extended a hand.

"I . . . I," she stammered.

"They told me to do it. Amex isn't a credit card."

She felt dizzy. Bain dealt with all the bills. He'd always
kept the checkbook, never delegating the task to a secretary or assistant even when he had one. He liked organization. He liked the control that came with knowing
exactly what came in and what was spent. Although she
knew there were problems—he'd explained as much in
urging her to be careful with her personal expenditures—
she never would have expected something so dire.

"I've been a member for decades," she pleaded, as if
Kim held the power to change a corporation's mind. *Membership has its privileges*. What kind of a promise was that if
it was revoked at the tiniest hint of difficulty?

"You've still got to pay on time."

Grace felt as though she might collapse. She looked
around, wondering who else had witnessed her humiliation.

A heavyset black woman waiting patiently behind her
with an armload of merchandise smiled knowingly. "You
should think about a MasterCard."

"Yes. Yes. I'm sure you're right." She stared at the two pieces of her credit card, which Kim had placed on the counter in front of her. She remembered clearly the day Bain had given it to her just after they were married. It had been linked to his, two cards on the same account, the sort of permanent convenience a husband and wife should have. Now the scissor cut separated the *t*'s from the rest of her last name, the name she'd taken from her husband along with the card.

Alco. It sounded like a cleaning service or a dog food.

She grabbed the halves and slid them into the interior pocket of her purse. "I'm sorry for the inconvenience," she managed to say. "It won't happen again."

❧

The mall's interior was a mass of fluorescent and neon bulbs reflecting a glare onto the black floor tiles. Grace stared at the industrial-strength planters, each potted with some species of palm willing to grow without a hint of natural light. The piped-in overhead music mixed with a blare of sound from a nearby record store. Leaning against a planter for balance, she watched as a gum-chewing couple walked by, the girl seemingly oblivious to the fact that her boyfriend had his hand down the back of her pants.

"Noooo. No." She heard a high-pitched wail.

A mother dragged two crying children toward the exit. With a look of utter desperation, the woman in a shirt with a plunging V-neck and jeans that hugged her wide hips yanked on their small arms even as they both collapsed to the floor. "Just wait till I tell your daddy how bad you are," she snarled. "You'll be sorry then."

Her threat only made the little girl with light brown hair and dirty knees scream louder.

"I've a mind to spank you right here and now, you little brat."

The mother released the arm of her son and, with her free hand, slapped the girl on the side of her head. The small child looked up, momentarily silenced. Her cheeks were streaked with tears.

The girl sniffled several times, wiped her nose with her T-shirt, and then took her brother's hand. They shuffled just in front of their mother, who had lit a cigarette even though prominent signs throughout the mall proclaimed that smoking was prohibited. The mother swatted at the girl's head several more times as they slowly moved toward the exit.

Grace felt the sudden urge to sweep the crying girl and her sibling up in her arms and comfort them both. A daughter. A healthy little girl, who needed a bubble bath, a glass of warm milk, a bedtime story to make her sadness go away. Perhaps *The Lonely Doll* since she resembled its sweet heroine, Edith, and could think the book had been written about her. She could tuck her into the canopy bed with a feather duvet, adjust the little angel night-light, and pull the pink-and-yellow-flowered drapes. Grace could share the nightly ritual she craved, the simple tasks of which she'd dreamed, with this little stranger.

Didn't this unkempt woman realize how lucky she was?

But instead Grace walked away. There was nothing she could possibly do to help, and no doubt publicly embarrassing the mother would only exacerbate the situation when they were behind the closed doors of their two-bedroom Cape.

She tried to distract herself by staring at the window displays of the variety of low-end shops. Athletic shoes. Plastic beach tumblers. Sun visors and caps. Fragranced candles in tub pots.

"We need more tests. It's too soon to tell anything con-
clusively. Why don't you take the weekend, talk to Bain,
and call me on Monday? I've scheduled an appointment
with a specialist, but it's not until Wednesday." Dr. Preston had a calm, collected tone, the sort that reminded
Grace of voice-overs for investment commercials. There
was a certain reassurance in such low male timbres. *Your
retirement fund is safe. Your husband will take care of everything.
You'll live to be a hundred.*

Staring at the series of X-rays on the light board that
hung on the wall, she didn't believe a word.

Grace stepped through the entrance of Victoria's Secret
and was consumed by the sweet-smelling perfumes, the
bordello lighting, the salesladies with curled hair and
black dresses. Tucked into alcoves along the pink-striped
walls were nightgowns, shorties, pajamas, and bathrobes
in all styles, colors, and sizes. Satin push-up bras and lace
thongs dangled from plastic hangers. Throughout the
store, scantily clad dummies modeled styles that would
make a Vegas dancer blush. She wondered whether this
display was designed to appeal to the women who would
wear such garments, to attract the men who wished they
would, or to titillate the prurient browsers.

Round tables were piled high with panties. Size small
was on top. Grace reached for a single pair of red underwear with lace covering the entire front.

She stepped up to the cashier and handed a twenty-
dollar bill to the attractive blonde with full lips.

"Will this be all?"

Grace did not reply.

"If you buy two, you get one free," she said in a chirpy
voice.

She stared again at the wisp of fabric. "No, thank you."

One was quite enough for her purpose.

Part One

1967–1968

Chapter One

A visitor's first impression of Harvard Square was that of a hippie swarm. On any given day—but especially between September and June—the educational cross-roads was a mass of guitar-playing, candle-lighting students who had managed to corner the bead market despite the marijuana haze in which the days disappeared. Women wore loose skirts, sandals, no bras, and even less makeup. Men wore beards.

But amid that swarm, there were plenty of young women just like Grace Montgomery, attractive students of art history, English literature, and landscape design, who preferred Lilly Pulitzer to tie-dye, and who wouldn't consider ingesting anything more intoxicating than a glass of Fumé Blanc. These women were intent on getting a proper education and graduating with a good degree, a process made slightly more exciting by the prospect of meeting an eligible bachelor along the way. Each wanted a husband, too, and preferably one with no facial hair.

Grace had come to Harvard Square in the fall of 1964 from across the river, the only daughter of Eleanor and William Montgomery of Chestnut Street. As most of her peers had done, she'd applied and received admission to Radcliffe and Barnard. She chose to remain in Cambridge, heeding her father's advice. "You can concentrate on your studies without the distractions of Manhattan.

That city could swallow alive the most sophisticated of New England girls and you, my dear Grace, are not one of those. I don't want to imagine your fate once you were to cross the Willis Avenue Bridge."

William's reservations about his daughter venturing beyond the borders of Route 128 had been well founded. She hadn't gone to boarding school or even summer camp. Despite her classic beauty, her lithe figure and heart-shaped face framed in blond curls, shyness got in the way of accepting dates, and she'd had no experience with men. She wouldn't have attended her senior prom except that her second cousin agreed to escort her.

William had never publicly acknowledged her inno-cence, but it was there in her face, her childlike enthu-siasm reflecting off her porcelain skin.

Plus she seemed so happy in Boston. She liked the quaint brick sidewalks of the Back Bay, the beauty of the Public Garden and the Charles River, Brigham's ice cream and the Red Sox.

Most of all, there was no reason for her to consider leaving because no other place in the world could repli-cate the lively atmosphere of 37 Chestnut Street. Her father's work as an economic consultant to public and pri-vate institutions alike, and his brief term as undersecre-tary to the Cuban ambassador, meant the Montgomerys had an array of personal friends and professional col-leagues, and the family's elegant town house was a gath-ering place for what she'd been raised to think of as the best of Beacon Hill society. Her parents did more than their fair share of entertaining professors, business leaders, political strategists, philosophers, and even the occasional out-of-towner. Grace passed many an evening lying on the floor of her attic bedroom, listening to the hum of voices several stories below her and staring at the night sky through the window in the small gable. Whether it was improvement of the Emerald Necklace of Boston's urban parks, fund-raising for Children's Hospital, or acquisitions for the Museum of Fine Arts, these adults shared intense conversation while consuming Eleanor's overcooked flank steak washed down by the contents of William's ample wine cellar.

Upon her fifteenth birthday, she was invited to join in her parents' soirees, to hear firsthand the intellectual debate, and to add her own opinions so long as she'd thought them through. Although she rarely availed herself of this opportunity—by high school she had friends and dreams that consumed her time—there were certain evenings amid her parents' company that she would never forget.

It had been a Thursday in August. Grace had graduated that spring from the Windsor School for Girls, and had already begun to pack her trunk for her impending move to Cambridge.

The cherrywood table was set for only seven, a small gathering by Montgomery standards. Lace place mats, starched white napkins, and an array of glasses accompanied each place setting. Light from the taper candles reflected off the polished silver pepper shaker and footed salt dish. To Grace's right was a visiting professor of political science from Columbia, a relatively young man in a tweed blazer and an ascot who emitted a strong odor of sandalwood. On her left was the assistant rector at Christ Church in Cambridge, who was under consideration for a faculty appointment at the Harvard Divinity School. It was between these gentlemen that the "Vietnam situation" was transformed from an issue seemingly to circulate in the air as she walked to the Charles Street T-stop into something tangible in her conscience.

Eleanor had forgotten about the pumpkin dinner rolls warming in the downstairs oven, and a faint smell of charred bread permeated the room. Politely ignoring it, the professor opined about the political instability in the region and the need to control communism. "Congress was absolutely justified. Johnson needed the Gulf of Tonkin Resolution. We've got to stop this aggression."

In terminology she didn't completely understand, he then expounded on Truman's Cold War policy. "We don't want to have to put his domino theory to the test."

The minister disagreed. His voice was gentle but firm, and his bushy eyebrows seemed to dance on his forehead as he spoke. "Imperialism as a goal cannot be justified."

"You saw what the North Vietnamese did to our destroyers."

"Because we have no business there."

Eleanor lit a cigarette, to which William didn't object. "The images are so haunting. You must remember that poor monk last year? I can't imagine what it feels like to self-immolate," she offered.

"The war is immoral," the minister persisted. Grace somehow expected him to add *Amen*, but he didn't.

"Immoral," the professor scoffed. "That's the kind of language that colors the debate, that makes people afraid to be honest. What war is ever moral? The Crusades were supposed to be, and they were the bloodiest massacres in history."

Grace listened intently, turning her head left and right to watch each man as he spoke.

"Why should we pick up the mess the French left behind?" her father asked as he poured more wine and settled into his chair. "They lost the fight—even with our assistance—and now we're supposed to correct the situation. But I ask you, if they no longer care, why should we?"

Eventually her eyes grew heavy, and Grace excused herself long before the debate reached a conclusion. But as she lay in her bed in the moments before sleep overcame her, she mused again over what a complicated matter the war seemed to be. That her brother, Ferris, would return to college instead of enlisting only muddied the issue. There had been no discussion of his deferment—at least in her presence—but she wasn't sure that meant her parents disapproved of the war. Although from what she'd deduced, Ferris seemed to be drinking his way through his four years, her parents put the highest premium on education. It wouldn't surprise her if, in their view, the South Vietnamese simply had to wait for him to obtain his bachelor's degree before they could enjoy his aid.

All these thoughts spun around in her mind, keeping her awake, and she only managed to quiet the noise by remembering that her opinion didn't matter anyway. The men in Washington would determine the right course of action.

❧

Radcliffe as a choice for college held additional appeal to Grace beyond its proximity to home. Ferris was a junior at Harvard by the time she arrived, and a very popular one at that. While still at Windsor, she'd visited him regularly and met many of his friends. They were confident, striking, articulate young men who seemed so worldly, so experienced, and so very, very handsome. As she wandered the elegant brick-and-ivy campus, gazing up at the myriad clock towers each set to chime a few minutes apart, it was difficult not to be impressed. These men could do anything to which they set their highly intelligent minds.

So it was no great surprise that she fully believed Bainbridge Alcott when he informed her that he planned to write "the great American novel." He made his proclamation as they sat on a plaid blanket on the Esplanade with a crew race along the Charles River as their backdrop. It was the fall of her junior year and their second date. Grace had spread out her carefully made picnic of egg salad sandwiches, cold roast beef, carrot sticks, and homemade shortbread before them. For his part, Bain had surprised her with a bottle of champagne, which he'd popped as she'd cried out with delight. Perhaps it was the heat, perhaps it was the company, but one plastic cup's worth had gone to her head.

"I'm going to be the next Salinger or Scott Fitzgerald. I may sound immodest, but I assure you that most would agree." Bain leaned toward her and rested his palm over hers. "I'll write a novel that makes people look at themselves, really examine who they are. I want my words to be a mirror—even if the readers don't necessarily like what they see. If the intellectuals—America's only true aristocracy—can't make a difference, then we're quite lost as a civilization."

His touch excited her.

The portable radio crooned a hit from the summer of 1960, "Itsy Bitsy Teeny Weeny Yellow Polka Dot Bikini."

"The world looks at America as the land of opportunity," Bain continued. "People can come from nothing and make a fortune, thereby changing their place in the social caste. But we also have to recognize the inherent gifts of those whose families have succeeded for generations."

She tried to concentrate, but her mind wandered to the idea of a very small bathing suit. Perhaps she should get one. She'd always worn a one-piece, the kind with a skirt attached.

"This is not an issue of luck. Cream does rise to the top. My novel will focus on those differences—the attributes of a chosen few and the need for the rest of our country to accept gainful employment in factories or on farms and stay the course. That's a proper division of labor, healthiest for any economy."

She didn't bother to question him. It all sounded fine, or at least as if he'd figured it out. His words blurred into the music as she focused instead on his chiseled features and deep blue eyes.

Everything about him was perfect. A senior, he was a member of the AD club, the son of a North Shore family, and fifth-generation Harvard. His great-grandfather had endowed a chair at the medical school. They'd met at a party for the *Crimson*. She hadn't planned to attend and hadn't been invited, but a group of nice girls from her dormitory had convinced her to come along with them. "Anyone's invited. It's not like that at all," Melody Berkowitz had explained.

Eileen Baker from Swampscott, who lived in the room across the hall, stepped forward. She had an hourglass figure, which her clothing tended to accentuate. "Writers for the *Crimson* have a reputation, if you know what I mean. It should be fun. What other plans do you have, anyway?" she had asked, adjusting Grace's headband in a maternal way. "You won't meet any men sitting in a dorm room on a Saturday night."

She'd been introduced to Bain almost immediately. He was editor in chief and the obvious host of the evening. But his smile alone had been enough to keep her glued to his side, and she'd allowed herself to hope from the moment he first took notice of her. He smoked a cigar and discussed a piece he'd almost had published in *Life* magazine, an article he'd submitted urging the nation to stop the protests, support its president, and get behind a full-blown war against the North Vietnamese. Sadly, the magazine's editors had rejected it. "Barely," he explained. "They thought it was brilliant."

Life magazine.

At the end of the evening, he'd offered to drive her home. She reluctantly declined. She'd come with her girlfriends. It wouldn't be right to leave them behind. But his offer was very kind, very kind indeed.

He'd given her a puzzled look, a mixture of confusion and disappointment, which she understood later but didn't at the time. He wasn't a man accustomed to rejection. "Would you care to join me for a coffee tomorrow? There's a great place in Central Square. Turkish I think it is."

A coffeehouse seemed exotic, and a Turkish one even more so. In accepting his invitation, she kept to herself that she didn't drink anything with caffeine. Fuel oil would have been palatable for the pleasure of his company. And it had been that brief date—an espresso and a shot of brandy for him, with a sip of the house blend for her—that had led to the picnic on the river. "We won't feel so rushed if the waiter isn't looking to clear our table," he'd said. He would pick her up at one.

"Pull!" The sound of a coxswain on the Charles River caught her attention, and she looked up to see several sculls speed by. Even from this distance, it seemed as though she could make out the biceps on each oarsman as he dipped his oar, pulled it through the black water, and lifted it for only a transitory moment to put it back into position. The synchronization was hypnotic.

"Eileen tells me you're going to the protest rally tomorrow night."

She turned to gaze back at Bain, who reached for the Moët to refill her cup.

Eileen Baker? That was odd.

Grace recalled that Eileen had been filled with questions about Bain when they returned from the *Crimson* party, but she'd perceived her dorm mate's curiosity as friendly excitement, shared giddiness. Eileen knew *of* Bain but hadn't had the pleasure of being introduced at the party. Or so Grace had thought. So when had they had the conversation to which he now referred? It must have been within the past twenty-four hours. Grace had only just agreed to attend.

"Several girls from my English class want to go. We thought we should go together since none of us knows what to expect." She forced a smile, suddenly recalling his article, the almost published piece in *Life*. Hadn't it had a pro-war premise? She faulted herself for not remembering details with more accuracy.

"Grace, you aren't honestly against this war, are you?" His face looked concerned, but his tone was stern. *Honestly* sounded as though it came with the full weight of the Ten Commandments. *Thou shalt not protest the war in Vietnam.*

She paused, not knowing exactly what to say. Pro-war, anti-war; she'd hardly thought all the arguments through in her head. But she did understand that American soldiers were being killed—lots of them—and all because of a country so far away, she wasn't sure she could locate it on a map. "It seems to me more appropriate to let the indigenous people decide what kind of government they want to have. Isn't that why we had the American Revolution?" She hoped her pronouncement didn't sound stupid.

"The North Vietnamese don't want a democracy. That's the whole point." He took her hand in both of his and gently kissed the top of it. "Now, promise me you won't go and that you'll leave decisions about the war to people who know what they're talking about."

She stared at the hand that had just experienced the softness of his lips against its skin. What would a real kiss feel like—his lips, his teeth, his tongue against hers? Despite a smattering of male companions and even one gentleman who might have been considered a "beau" during part of her sophomore year, physical intimacy still remained a mystery. On the threshold to her dormitory, she'd offered her left cheek or given a tentative kiss to her date, but these were acts of politeness, nothing more. She'd heard what other girls were doing and knew her reticence and lack of experience made her different. But she hadn't yet figured out what to do about it.

Now it appeared Bain was set to change that for her.

He picked himself up and moved next to her. As he sat beside her with his legs outstretched, she could feel their hips touch and his thigh against hers. He put his arm around her and drew her to him. She wished she'd had a mint, or wished she hadn't yet taken a bite of egg salad. It didn't seem the most romantic of foods to have in her teeth. But she'd waited nearly twenty years for this moment, her first real kiss, and decided to put the lunch menu out of her mind. She closed her eyes in anticipation. Or was she supposed to watch?

As she was debating how best to handle the matter, he turned her face toward his and kissed her, pressing his lips against hers, then gradually opening his mouth and exploring her with his tongue. It was long and wet and wonderful and he tasted of raw carrot. She never wanted it to end, and when it did, she wobbled slightly.

He laughed and gently kissed her cheek.

Should she kiss him back? She wasn't sure, and blushed instead.

He reached both arms around her and gently laid her back onto the grass. His face was inches from hers, and their chests were pressed together. She could feel his weight, his chest expanding with each breath. They kissed again and again and again.

When they finally sat upright, she felt dizzy. Her lips tingled and her heart pounded.

Bain reached for a slice of roast beef, rolled it into a

tube, and took a bite. Then she thought she heard him mumble, "I couldn't possibly propose to a war protestor, now could I?"

Maybe she'd misheard, given the thoughts swirling in her head from the kisses and the champagne, the sunshine, and his presence. But whether she'd heard correctly or not, it was enough to change her mind.

She'd never been all that committed anyway.

Chapter Two

You'll like the life of a writer's wife. I'll be home all the time. We can have lunch together and romantic after-noons when I have writer's block and can't work. You can come with me on my book tours. Maybe you'll get to see a real radio interview."

She didn't need convincing. From the moment he'd pro-duced the small square box—silver, with SHREVE, CRUMP & LOW lettered in black—she'd agreed. The one-carat royal-cut diamond in a gold basket setting jumped from the satin cushion onto her thin finger. Unbeknownst to her, he'd already asked her father's permission, which had apparently been granted with a great deal of backslapping and uncorking. She liked that he'd followed protocol.

Engaged and overwhelmed by the full excitement of planning a wedding, she was easily persuaded by Bain that there was no sense postponing intercourse until after they were married. "Pretty soon we'll be living in the same house, anyway."

"But . . . but what about—" She cut herself off. Birth control wasn't a subject to be discussed with a man, not even a fiancé. Why hadn't she been prepared? She'd somehow expected that her mother would give her some advice, or, if not, that the gynecologist would have made some suggestions in this area. Clearly, she would have to muster the courage to ask.

"Don't worry. I've got all that under control." Bain reached into the pocket of his khaki trousers, produced a square package, and handed it to her.

She stared at the gold condom wrapper, which made a crinkling sound as she held it in her hand. She didn't dare ask how it worked. If he owned one, she assumed he could operate it.

Bain smiled. "It's not wrong, remember. You're going to be my wife."

That night they surprised her parents with a visit home. Losing her virginity in her own room, her own bed, seemed less tawdry than locking themselves in a dormitory room or finding a motel off Route 1. She wanted to lie under her eyelet bedcover, stare out her window, and imagine life as Mrs. Alcott while Bain held her in his arms. But she knew there was a mountain to climb before she'd enjoy the bliss of evening's end. As much as she wanted to please him, as much as she wanted everything to work as it should, she was terrified.

"We're in luck," Bain whispered when her parents announced that as pleased as they were to see their daughter and future son-in-law, they had plans: a benefit dinner for the Boston Symphony followed by a concert of Brahms sonatas. William hummed the opening measures as he escorted Eleanor out the door.

Alone, Bain poured her a glass of sherry. He'd found the bottle in her father's library and taken two cut-crystal glasses from the breakfront cabinet in the dining room. She put Ferris's *Meet the Beatles* on the record player, the album he'd left behind when he moved into his own apartment on Marlborough Street. That it had been released more than four years earlier made it completely out of date to his trendy ear.

They sat together on the edge of the bed, neither one knowing what to say. She wished she had a satin nightgown, something long and clingy. She wanted to be Nora Charles with high-heeled mules and a mink stole and a cigarette holder. Instead she wore an A-line light blue skirt and a sweater set.

Bain reached for her sweater and started to undo the top buttons.

She couldn't bear to look, couldn't bear to help, and wished he would turn out the lights. She fingered the piqué fabric that rested on her slim thighs.

"Grace," he said softly. "We're not the first two people in the world to have sex. And we won't be the last."

She coughed and instinctively covered her mouth.

The Beatles sang at a near-hysteria speed, a beat too fast to set the right mood. She regretted her choice. Perhaps Peter, Paul and Mary would have been better.

Then he spoke again. "This isn't rocket science. Relax. It'll be easier if you're not so tense."

I love you. I want you. You're beautiful. Something along those lines would have sufficed.

Closing her eyes, she reached for what she assumed was his belt buckle and fumbled to undo it. Somehow the logistics seemed overwhelming. What was she supposed to do when she undid his pants—reach inside? What if he was already erect? How big would it be?

"Couldn't we just get undressed and get under the covers?" she finally asked. Her voice sounded more pleading than she'd intended.

He nodded, perhaps relieved by her suggestion. He got up and walked to the other side of the bed. She heard the crackling sound.

With her back to him, she folded her clothes neatly on the chair and then slipped beneath the soft sheets. She felt his whole body. Naked. It was more startling than she'd imagined.

He rolled on top of her, but propped himself up so she would not feel the bulk of his weight. He kissed her forehead, then her cheek, her neck, her chest. He licked her nipple and sucked gently. She felt a tingle and closed her eyes, waiting. After a few moments of awkward adjustments, and a quick stab of pain, he was inside her. His hips moved rhythmically, as if he'd practiced. Within moments, they'd accomplished the task.

"Was that so bad?" he said, as he gently kissed her ear.

"No." Then she added, "Thank you," because she couldn't think of anything else to say.

⊱⊰

"My work is sure to be sold abroad, you know, published in translation," Bain had explained to William. "Important American fiction always is." Bain smiled a presidential grin and took a sip of his port.

"It's difficult for me to imagine that the Europeans are turning to us for great literature," her father had replied.

They'd been having dinner with her parents. Bain had just graduated; their wedding was imminent. The meal had been planned to finalize details, but minutiae bored him. After agreeing to make Ferris his best man, Bain quickly managed to change the topic from centerpieces and seating arrangements.

"The best part is that Grace and I will travel the world together," Bain said, appearing to have missed the irony in William's remark.

"You assume a great deal of success," he replied. "Most of the writers that Eleanor and I know have professorships, too, a steady income to pay the bills. Perhaps I overstep my bounds, but I might remind you that marriage requires a certain degree of stability."

"I can't wait to travel," Grace chimed in, wanting to redirect the conversation. Bain didn't like to be challenged, and her father was coming precariously close. Just because her parents exalted academicians didn't mean it was the profession for everyone.

"You'll get lots of it, I promise," Bain said, smiling at her. "That is, so long as you don't get locked into some menial employment as a corporate assistant that keeps you from being an attentive wife."

Grace didn't recall whether her father had agreed with the statement, or even whether he'd had a thought about his daughter's career. Surprisingly, neither her mother nor her father had even questioned her decision not to return to school in the fall. She didn't need a degree to be a spouse.

Being an attentive wife. She remembered Bain's words as the minister of Trinity Church now read their marriage vows. Love, honor, obey. Attentive wasn't on the list. But she would nurture and cook and dress the part. Bain was the genius; he was to make the mark on society. Nothing she could do could ever compare.

He lifted her veil.

It was gauze held on her head by a diamond tiara with a slight train, her mother's choice, as was almost everything about the wedding, right down to the pale pink spray of roses that made up her bouquet. She would have preferred white peonies. Given her preference, she also would have had a much smaller gathering, a lunchtime service instead of evening, and an informal reception in the small garden behind her parents' town house. But the Montgomerys had friends and colleagues, and the Alcotts had friends and relatives, so anything less than two hundred was out of the question. That number meant a gathering at home was impossible. They needed a hotel ballroom with all the institutional elegance that accompanied it.

She glanced down the aisles at the bouquets attached to

each pew with a white gauze bow, and then scanned the sea of faces. So many of them were unfamiliar, even several of the women who now dabbed at their eyes with handkerchiefs. For a fleeting moment, she had the odd sensation that they'd gone to the wrong ceremony, and that strangers were now witnessing their union.

Then she spotted her mother and knew she was in the right place. Without expression, and certainly without shedding a tear, Eleanor sat absolutely straight and motionless in the front row. She wore a pink silk suit, a large matching hat, and a string of pearls. Since it was June, Grace knew she'd purchased new underwear. Not for the occasion but because it was that time of year.

Bain brushed at her veil to make sure it was out of the way, then leaned forward and pecked her lips, surprising her with his speed. She'd expected the first man-and-wife kiss to be long and dramatic, a Hollywood sort of kiss where, with his arms wrapped around her, she would lean back almost parallel to the floor. After the kiss, he'd pull her upright in a great sweeping motion. But none of that came to pass.

Perhaps he didn't want a public display of affection.

The crowd applauded. She could see Ferris over Bain's shoulder. He caught himself in a yawn and forced a smile.

The organ struck the opening bars to Mendelssohn's Wedding March. Bain linked his arm through hers and escorted her out. She wondered if he, too, was as eager as she for the reception to be over, for the party to end, and for them to be alone in their hotel room, sharing a room and a bed all night for the first time in their lives.

⌒⌐◌

They took a monthlong honeymoon, traveling to London, Paris, Madrid, Rome, and Venice. The days were a blur of activity, of long walks through winding streets, of visits to museums. Bain had everything planned — itineraries and meals and time allowances at each destination. When she lingered too long at a store window or a statue, he took her hand and pulled her away.

At night they both rushed through meals, skipping appetizers and dessert, eager to return to the solitude of their luxurious hotel room. Bain was insatiable, and for her, too, lovemaking improved. "It's all about practice," Bain explained as he orchestrated her movements, repositioning her body, urging her to explore with her hands and her tongue. "By the time we return to the States, you'll be a pro."

Finally, lost amid the down pillows and sateen bedspread of her five-star hotel, with the noises of the street, the buzzing sounds of motor scooters, honking cars, and animated voices coming through the open window, a warm shudder of joy emanated through her body. She let herself go and allowed a cry of bliss to escape her lips.

As he lay beside her, she slid her hand under the covers and touched the wetness between her legs, a mixture of them both. This was what it was to be Mrs. Alcott, and she felt closer to Bain than to anyone in the world. It was a feeling she wished she would experience every day for the rest of her life.

❦

In London, Bain was fitted for three custom suits. Standing in the haberdashery, they stared at row upon row of fabric bolts, rich wools and gabardines, flannels and cashmeres.

Over Grace's objections, Bain selected a navy and a gray pinstripe, along with a black wool. "You'll look as though you belong on Wall Street," she said. "Why not an elegant smoking jacket or a cashmere blazer? Isn't that more suited to the life of a writer?"

Bain held her chin in his hand, tilted her face toward him, and kissed her forehead. "My romantic," he said with a smile. "I hope you never lose your flair for the dramatic."

She didn't know exactly what he meant. In silence, she watched the experienced tailor with his mouth full of pins and a tape measure draped around his neck pull and pleat the soft fabric to envelop Bain's frame. With a white crayon, he marked where the buttons should go.

"You should have them by the end of September, depending upon customs in America," the tailor said.

"I may need them sooner," Bain replied. "I'd like to receive them by the time I return home at the end of this month."

"You can get by in your pajamas for a few weeks," Grace teased.

Bain ignored her. Handing the man an additional twenty-pound note, he said, "Make sure they are there by August thirtieth."

In Paris, they strolled through the Jardin des Tuileries. The view was breathtaking, the majesty of the Louvre behind them and the grand esplanade opening before them. By a marble-edged pool, an elderly man in a beret and a striped shirt stood smoking. Beside him, his collection of wooden sailboats and pushing sticks was assembled neatly in a cart. Bain paid a franc to rent a red-painted one, and Grace marveled at how weightlessly the small craft floated across the water, leaving a ripple of wake behind it.

Sprinkled throughout the garden were artists with portable easels, palettes of oils, and cans filled with paint-splattered brushes. Their canvases reflected the scenery: the pond with its colorful array of boats, a man scooping *glace framboise* out of a small ice cart, a child with a balloon, a lady on a bicycle. But one canvas in particular caught her eye. It was of two figures, a man with good posture in a light blue polo shirt and a young woman beside him in a lilac sundress and matching hat. She looked at the painter, a man about Bain's age in black pants and a gray smock, and smiled. He'd captured them — Mr. and Mrs. Alcott — as they stood admiring the Parisian landscape.

"Look at that canvas," she whispered. "It's us. We have to buy it."

"Is that what you'd like?" Bain asked.

"Yes," she replied, circling around him. She wanted to skip. "A memento of this glorious day, this wonderful honeymoon, a reminder that I am the luckiest woman in the world." She stopped in front of him, leaned forward, and kissed him gently. "And it can be our first piece of art."

"You're being generous to call it that. More like our first bad investment in something with no intrinsic value. Let's hope it's the only one of its kind that we ever make." He squeezed her hand.

With that, Bain approached the painter. They spoke briefly, the artist clearly struggling in broken English. A few francs exchanged hands, and the man removed the canvas from the easel, making gestures to handle it carefully since it was still wet.

Bain presented it to Grace. "For you, my darling."

"What did he say?"

"Believe me, he was quite thrilled." Bain glanced back over his shoulder at the man, who was packing up his paints into a worn leather bag. "Let's hope we never get to a place where I'm selling a day's worth of work for less than twenty-five dollars."

"Don't worry for a moment. I can live on love alone," she added, playfully.

He raised his eyebrows. "I'm glad at least one of us can."

❧

Their last evening abroad, they sat together at the Club del Doge sipping Campari and soda and staring out at the street lamps reflected in the black water of the canal.

Grace had spent a good part of the afternoon packing, leaving each trunk and suitcase in its place by the door of their hotel room. The valet would come in the morning and bring everything down to the water taxi that had been ordered for eight. Bain hadn't helped; he'd received a series of telegrams and withdrew to the business center to place overseas calls. He hadn't mentioned the nature of his business, or why it was so pressing that it couldn't wait for their return, but she knew it had to be important. He wouldn't take time away from her unless it was. Maybe the editors at *Life* were offering him an opportunity. Maybe now that a full-scale war was under way, they were reconsidering their rejection. And so she comforted herself in his absence by folding his clothes and packing them between layers of tissue. Each shirt, each pair of boxer shorts, each belt, now had a distinct memory, an association. In the course of thirty days abroad, she felt as though she had learned everything about him.

Bain ordered another round. The waiter returned with the drinks and handed Bain a leather folder with the bill discreetly tucked inside. In a few minutes, they would retire to their opulent room with its tasseled drapes and ornate furniture, but they were both tired and content to sit a while longer.

The Gritti had been her favorite of all the hotels in which they'd stayed. She leaned back in her chair and fingered the strand of pearls around her neck. "Venice is as magical as I'd dreamed," she murmured.

Bain sat forward, as if startled by the sound of her voice. "I've good news to share."

"Of what?"

"I've taken an analyst position at the Bank of Boston," he announced. "I wired my acceptance today. That's what all the time and fuss was this afternoon. But I wanted to make sure everything was lined up, the contract signed, so that I could surprise you tonight. I'll start upon our return." He reached for his wallet. "It's a prestigious appointment and a lot of money."

"But . . . but what about . . . your writing?" She struggled to speak.

"Grace, you and I both know that was unrealistic. If I had any doubts, all I needed was this honeymoon to make certain. I've seen how happy you are, how you delight in nice hotel rooms and fancy restaurants. I want to be able to give that to you forever, to take care of you—you and the family I fully expect we'll have, if we don't have one started already." He winked, no doubt referring to their disregard for birth control since their wedding. "And I want to do that *now*. We're young, and it's not responsible to rely simply on what our parents may give us, or on an inheritance we won't see for years." With that, he presented her with a small velvet box. A pair of diamond earrings sparkled from their padded liner.

"They're beautiful," she said, shocked. "But you shouldn't have. The last thing I need is a present. The trip, this time with you, you've spoiled me already."

"With the salary I've just been given, this was the least I could do," he said, grinning.

Her eyes filled with tears, and she looked away.

"What's wrong?"

"I just . . . I . . . ," she stammered. "I can't bear that you gave up your dream for . . . . for . . ." She couldn't bring herself to finish the sentence.

He took her hand. "Sweet Grace, you must trust me. It's not only about money. It's about stability, building a foundation for us. It is for the best or I wouldn't do it." He lifted her chin and gazed into her eyes. "Besides, the struggling-artist thing is seriously overrated."

⤴⤵

She pretended to watch the movie offered in the first-class cabin of the American Airlines flight to Boston. It avoided conversation.

She pulled the synthetic blanket up to her chin and stared at Sean Connery as 007 on the small screen. In her mind, she replayed all the conversations they'd had about his career. Beside her, Bain read *The Economist* and sipped a small glass of champagne.

A Bank of Boston employee, a financial analyst. No writer's block, no romantic lunches, no book tour, and no cardigan sweater.

She fingered the diamond studs in her thin lobes. She knew he meant well. She knew it was at least in part for her, for the children they would have. That's what he'd said. She might tolerate the uncertainty of a writer's life, of a decision to follow his dream, but he was putting his family's interests first. That was what a good husband was supposed to do.

Perhaps it was the prudent course to take. But it was the first of many decisions he would make alone that would change the course of her life.

Chapter Three

They hadn't been home a week when Eleanor Montgomery passed away at the age of forty-five wearing a fur-
trimmed satin bed jacket over her faded hospital gown.

Breast cancer.

Although she'd complained of fatigue in the months
leading up to her daughter's wedding, Grace had had little
sympathy at the time. She, too, had been anxious and
overtired. The planning and preparation was exhausting
for everyone.

Now Grace felt stupid and selfish. She had yet to say
the diagnosis—the ultimate cause of death—aloud.

"It had metastasized. She'd known in May, but didn't
want to tell you, didn't want anything to spoil your big
day or interfere with your plans with Bain," William
explained to Grace. "She knew if you realized the severity
of her illness, you wouldn't take a honeymoon. She
wanted you to experience Europe." He dabbed at the
corner of his eye with a handkerchief. "There was nothing
anyone could do to help her."

They sat together in the library on Chestnut Street with
a fire going even though it was early September. Grace
had selected the damask wing chair, Eleanor's favorite
seat. She wanted to feel her mother's presence, to breathe
in the faint smell of her perfume on the upholstery.
William slouched on the settee with his elbows resting on

his knees. Every few minutes, he ran his fingers through his thinning hair. "She was a courageous woman. Damn courageous," he mumbled.

Grace stared into the flame. The log popped.

The past few days had been a blur. William had met them at Logan Airport and informed them on the drive into town that Eleanor was already hospitalized at Dana Farber, and would not be released. It could be hours, could be a week, but her life was coming to a rapid end.

They hadn't gone out to see her that first night. They were both jet-lagged. Grace had needed a good night's rest to calm down.

All she could remember after that was the Green Line from Park Street out to Brookline, watching streets lined with brick apartment buildings and the shops of Coolidge Corner through the window. Out in the morning and back in the evening for six straight days. The hospital was huge and anonymous. Nurses and doctors came and went from her mother's bedside, checking blood pressure and monitors and intravenous drips. Occasionally, William excused himself and went into the hallway to converse with one or the other of them, but she wasn't privy to the conversations and found she had nothing to ask.

She'd wanted the first weeks of her married life with Bain to be different. She'd looked forward to collecting his shirts from the laundry, and checking off the list he'd made of items to purchase at the hardware store. And yet she hadn't cooked a meal or even unpacked. Instead she stared at her mother, nearly lifeless from the heavy doses of pain medication that William insisted she receive.

Once during the week, Bain had visited. He stood at the rail of Eleanor's bed and graciously kissed her hand. But for the most part, he was consumed by his new job.

Otherwise, one day at Dana Farber was much like the next. Ferris paced the halls and smoked in the visitor lounge. He seemed to welcome the opportunity to get doughnuts and replaced the uneaten stock on the windowsill with a fresh box every few hours. Together, they watched them grow stale.

When six o'clock came, William removed a silver flask from the breast pocket of his blazer, held it toward his wife as if to toast her longevity, and took a swig. Then he lay back on the makeshift cot set up in her room, adjusted the pillow behind his head, and read aloud from *Dr. Zhivago*. Shortly thereafter, Grace gathered her sweater and purse and said good night, leaving her parents behind in the fluorescent glow of hospital lighting.

Then Eleanor died, leaving her family with little to do besides sit, grieve, and wonder what life would be like without her. She and William had worked out the arrangements for the memorial service weeks before. Eleanor herself even called the caterer and the florist—the same ones she'd used for Grace's wedding.

Ferris now prodded the fire with an iron poker, releasing a few sparks. He dropped his tool to the floor, leaned against the mantel, and sipped what Grace surmised was his fourth or fifth vodka for the evening. It wasn't yet seven o'clock. She considered speaking up— Eleanor certainly would have—but decided against it. A stiff drink might help her, too, if she were to allow herself the indulgence. Anything to numb the dull ache she felt in the pit of her stomach. Her mother was gone.

"I thank God she got through your wedding," William said. "It kept her alive. She didn't want to try the chemotherapy that had been suggested because she feared she'd lose her hair. 'You don't expect me to be bald at my own daughter's wedding, now, do you?' she asked me." He shook his head. "Not that it mattered. At best she might have bought herself a couple of weeks, and a couple of weeks of hell at that. But it was typical of her. She was a very stubborn woman."

Ferris mumbled something in agreement.

"I must say that she was very pleased with your choice in Bain. I am, too. He's a good man. He'll be a good husband over the long haul. She wanted the best for you — for you and for Ferris."

Her father's words were comforting. Eleanor had thrown her last energies into the rite of passage that had transformed Grace from being a daughter to being a wife. No one could find fault in anything about the ceremony or reception. It had gone like clockwork. She closed her eyes, remembering her mother's stoic posture, her elegant outfit, as she sat in the pew. She'd even danced with Bain, or rather they'd performed a series of awkward gyrations while the band covered a Jimi Hendrix song with an irregular beat. Who would ever have known she was so sick?

She couldn't be angry with her parents for not telling her the truth. They'd wanted to protect her from a horrible reality, and their plan had worked. She could never have gotten married if she'd known her mother was dying. She could never have had such a celebration. It would have amounted to a dire portent.

Instead, Eleanor had selflessly and successfully launched Grace into a new sea. Bain would guide her course and bring her safely into harbor. Her life was transformed; she had different priorities, different frames of reference, and different responsibilities.

Ferris had no one. William was alone now, too, and she needed to do whatever she could to help them. She wouldn't forget that they needed a woman to tend to them, and she vowed to check on them both at least once a week. Her father might welcome a Sunday-night dinner invitation. Perhaps Bain could take them both to a Red Sox game. He had a way of making everyone feel better.

But she had Bain. He was on his way back from work and would be arriving at 37 Chestnut Street at any moment. When she'd called that afternoon to tell him that Eleanor had passed, he'd promised to come as soon as he could. He knew she needed him. "It'll be all right," he'd said. His voice had been soothing. "I know you'll be brave."

She rested her hands in her lap and leaned back in the chair. The room reflected her mother's good taste—a Chippendale sofa, an Oriental rug, a game table with turned legs and four matching chairs, silver candlesticks on the mantel and an oil seascape framed in gold above it, family photographs in silver frames mixed in with the leather-bound volumes that filled the bookshelves. This library felt as established and permanent as a well-tended perennial garden, something that could withstand life's worst storms. It was what every proper family needed—a comfortable, tasteful home in which to make memories—and she vowed to create such an environment for Bain and for their family, if they were fortunate enough to have one.

The creation of a home. A man's castle. By being Mrs. Alcott, she would survive this pain.

1972

Chapter Four

The sprawling Cape with its doghouse dormers and weathered-shingle roof faced out to sea. From the master bedroom where Grace now stood, she could see out across the Oyster River to the peninsula of Hardings Beach. Amid the beach plum and marsh grass, a lighthouse and camp at the easternmost tip of the beach marked the channel, the entrance to Stage Harbor and the exit to the Atlantic Ocean. Next stop, Portugal.

"That lighthouse is privately owned by a family that's been in Chatham for years. And they don't like trespassers," the Realtor had warned. "But I think it's available for private parties if you ever want a change of scenery."

The thought was absurd. She would never grow tired of entertaining in this house with its paneled living room, open stone fireplace, and a dining room that could easily hold twenty for sit-down. There was a flagstone terrace with the water as a panoramic mural. And there was room enough for two to sit on the widow's walk and admire the sunset. She and Bain could grow old together on that perch.

Grace tried to open the mullioned windows, but they were swollen stuck. The paint on the sills peeled. The air contained a hint of mildew. She turned around to face the empty room with its wide-pine floors. The walls, too, were bare but for a few picture hangers. She imagined it repainted with curtains and a matching spread on a queen-size bed. To the right was a dressing area and closets large enough to live in. The bathroom had his-and-hers sinks, a separate tub and shower, and a bidet. That the leaking toilet had stained the carpet was incidental. It could be replaced in time. Eventually, it could be as grand a room as the ones they'd stayed in on their honeymoon.

Home. The first home she'd ever owned. And it had good bones, as her father would say. Everything else was window dressing.

Bain's career at Bank of Boston had been a whirlwind. Promotion after promotion had landed him as the youngest vice president in the history of the company. His success thrilled him despite the long hours and frequent business dinners. And Grace managed to keep herself busy with a pottery class, charitable work, and visits with her father, who'd accepted an appointment as a professor emeritus at the Harvard Business School.

Although she'd hoped for a baby by the time of her second anniversary, the third year had come and gone without a pregnancy. Still, the passage of time wasn't alarming. She was only twenty-five. And Bain seemed convinced that success would be theirs. "Don't be ridiculous," he'd admonished her the few times she'd mentioned their bad luck. "There's nothing wrong with either of us. We just have to be patient." With that, he had rubbed her stomach and kissed her on the forehead.

As the months passed, though, he must have seen the disappointment on her face. That was when he made his announcement.

It was a Friday evening, unusually hot for the end of April, and their apartment felt stuffy. She'd spent the day polishing all seventy-two pieces of their Hamilton silver pattern, plus serving spoons, meat forks, and ladle, and the smell of Wright's Silver Cream lingered.

Bain read the *Globe* with his feet elevated on a hassock. She perched beside him and handed him two scoops of lemon sherbet in an etched-glass bowl. The set of six had been a wedding gift from her aunt Ida, her father's sister, and didn't match any of their other china.

"We need a country home. A retreat," Bain announced, as he took the bowl from her. "I want a house on the ocean."

Grace was startled. Their apartment was small and, more importantly, rented. Shouldn't they buy a primary residence first?

"Why buy here? Who knows if we'll stay? With my work, we could well end up in New York or Philadelphia. This is hardly the hub of the financial world. But we can always come back to a summer home."

"You think we'll leave Boston?" Grace asked.

"Gracie . . . relax. You know I'm never going to do anything you don't want, or make you live somewhere you don't want to be. But right now, I'm talking about a great place on the water. You can have a garden. We can swim. We can take sun. It means we can get out of the city on weekends and during the heat of the summer. It'll be a place for the two of us to really be together without the hectic pace of the city. Think long walks, canoe rides, picnics, seashells, and rum drinks." He took a spoonful of sherbet and smacked his lips. "Virtually everyone in my position at the bank gets away. It's a lot healthier for the mind and body. No one can keep up the pace that I do without a physical and emotional break, a change of scenery."

"Where are you thinking of going?"

"The Cape. There's still good values. We could get a lot for our money."

At least he'd said *we*.

"Cape Cod?" Grace knew nothing about the area. "Wouldn't Nantucket or Martha's Vineyard be better?" She'd prefer a more established resort destination. Plus she liked the idea of an island. A ferry ride, windswept dunes—it all seemed romantic.

"Doesn't make sense. Maine doesn't, either. You know, Edgartown, Bar Harbor, these places are already discovered. But for fifty thousand dollars in Orleans or Osterville or Chatham, we could have a dream home. Wouldn't you like lots of land and plenty of rooms with great views?"

Fifty thousand dollars. "That's an awful lot of money."

"Leave the finances to me. Let's just find you a house you love."

And they had. After several weekends of looking at real estate, they'd chosen Chatham, a quaint village at the elbow of the Cape. It had several half-decent restaurants if they wanted to dine out, an exclusive tennis and beach club where they had connections and could be well on the way to membership by the following season, and an established Episcopal church. The house had two acres, a split-rail fence covered in rambling Cape Cod roses, and a mooring if they ever decided to invest in a Boston Whaler. The beachfront actually came with the house.

"Massachusetts is one of the few states in the nation that allow for private ownership of the sand in front of a house!" the Realtor had exclaimed.

Grace shared her delight. Her own beach, seaweed, sea glass, bottles, and whatever else washed up on her shore.

Bain did all the paperwork for their mortgage and attended the closing. Afterward, he'd presented her with a key to the front door.

The drive down the Southeast Expressway and out to Exit 11 of the Mid-Cape Highway took less than two hours.

As Grace now studied the upstairs, the long hallway, the study, the three bedrooms—two with an adjoining bath and one with its own—she thought about colors and fabrics and furniture. She wished Eleanor were here for advice. Decorating was a challenge, and she didn't completely trust her own taste, but the prospect excited her. No doubt Bain would offer his opinion if she needed help.

Her father would give them the twin cast-iron beds from her room on Chestnut Street and the pair of quilts. They had an extra chest of drawers in an alcove in their apartment that could be put to use. That would fill one room. But there was still a lot to buy. Fortunately, there was no rush. She and Bain needed little but each other to manage.

She skipped down the back stairs and walked through the house in search of her husband. Moments later, she came upon him in the living room. He stared out the bay window toward the ocean. Standing behind him, she wrapped her arms around his waist and kissed the back of his neck. "This is magic. I don't think I've ever been so happy," she said.

"Those bushes are going to block our view in a year or two," he remarked. She stepped to his side and followed his gaze out to where a mound of beach plum danced in the middle of the lawn, the purplish pink blossoms moving in the salty breeze.

"I can prune them easily if you'd like."

He glanced at her with an odd expression. "That's a temporary solution at best. These things grow like weeds. I'll get someone out here to rip them up."

Weeds. Hardly that. In the short time she'd spent on the Cape, the beach plums had come to seem quintessential to life here, such a part of the landscape that they staked a stronger claim than that of any new homeowner.

"Get a notepad and we'll go through each room to

figure out what has to be done. This place is more of a mess than I remember. The furniture that was here apparently hid a lot of blemishes. I see evidence of water leakage in several spots, and I have the horrible feeling we are going to need a new roof sooner than I calculated."

She stared at the warm wood paneling, the wide floorboards, and the dozens of windows. The room had beautiful proportions and a fundamental elegance. It could be perfect with no more than a couch and a coffee table. Or they could keep it bare and use it as a ballroom, dancing alone to the music in their heads like Daisy Buchanan and Jay Gatsby. If a drop of rain came through here and there, it would only add to the romance.

She reached for him, wanting to embrace.

"Come on," Bain said, impatiently. "We're going to have to prioritize."

She smiled coyly. "How about we forget that?" She'd be happy to make love on the floor for the rest of the afternoon as a way to christen their home. "This is our first home together. Let's celebrate."

"We can see if there's any money to celebrate with after everything is fixed," Bain snapped.

She shrugged. The last thing she wanted on this special day was for them to have any kind of disagreement. "My bag is in the kitchen. I know I have a pad in there." As she walked away, she chastised herself. She needed to be more sensitive to his concerns. For all its charm, this house was a financial burden, and one that he shouldered alone. It was easy for her to be the dreamy optimist.

They walked slowly through every nook and cranny of the spacious home. He observed, frowned, kneeled to examine, and remarked about leaks and stains, cracks and chips, outlets that didn't work and evidence of carpenter ants, mildew and mold, windows that didn't open and doors that creaked. She took notes, trying not to be distracted by the beautiful views and the sun reflected on the ocean.

Two hours later, the list of imperfections completed, Bain sat on the bottom steps of the sweeping staircase. With an adding machine, he calculated the enormity of his investment and what it still might cost to bring his home up to his standards. His pencil marks and scribbles soon covered her pad.

Finally, she'd watched long enough. His stress was palpable. If he wanted to ruin the day buried in practicalities, it was his choice. The beach beckoned. Leaving him to his own concerns, she slipped outside.

The wind off the ocean had picked up, and whitecaps specked the harbor. The salty air was chilly. Scattered splotches of dark brown seaweed and dried sea grass covered much of the sand along the tidewater line. Grace left her sandals by the steps, wrapped a scarf around her head, and hugged herself as she walked toward the ocean. Then she stopped and turned west, her gaze following the setting sun. Never in her life had she seen such a beautiful spot.

A wiry-framed man in an oversize canvas shirt, rubber boots, and a large hat stood in about six inches of water. Bent over, he raked the mucky ocean floor. Grace watched as he dug, found specimens, measured the smallest ones against a tool that he had strapped to his belt, and dumped the clams in a wire basket.

Living off the land, thought Grace. There was something majestic about the fishing industry.

"This is private property."

It was Bain's voice, loud and stern behind her. Startled, Grace turned to face him.

"This is my property," he repeated.

The clammer didn't look up.

"I own this beach and you are trespassing. If you don't leave at once, I will call the authorities."

Grace's heart pounded. She couldn't bear a confrontation, let alone one on the first day. For all she knew, the clammer didn't realize the house had been sold. Maybe the prior owners had given him permission. Besides, what difference did it make? They would be driving back to Boston in a few hours. Despite her suggestion, Bain refused to camp out in the empty house. They wouldn't be at the beach. And with the work that Bain wanted done on the house, it might be weeks before either of them had another moment by the sea. She'd be too busy consulting with contractors and electricians and plumbers.

Bain had moved forward to where the tide began to recede. In his khaki trousers, blazer, tasseled loafers, and socks, he looked ridiculous. He belonged back in their apartment on Louisburg Square. She wished at least that he'd taken off his shoes and rolled up his pants.

"Don't make me call the police," he said.

At that the clammer straightened up, removed the hat, and allowed the long brown curls to tumble down over her shoulders. Grace had been wrong. The clammer was a woman and, judging from her face, not much older than Grace. She was attractive with a slight tan and rugged features.

Still holding her small rake, she rested her hands on her hips. "You may own this house, but your property extends only to the mean waterline, no farther. I'm below that— and have been since I got here. Besides, if you knew the law instead of spouting idle threats, you'd know that people are not trespassing if they use the beach for fishing, fowling, or navigation. Clamming—for which I have a license—is considered fishing for these purposes. The courts have come to the same conclusion time and time again around here. So go ahead, try and arrest me."

With that, she bent back over and jabbed her rake into the sand.

Grace looked at Bain, who stood speechless. His face reddened as he studied the clammer. She'd never before seen him stymied, and she struggled not to laugh.

"We'll see what my lawyer has to say about that," he mumbled as he retreated to the house.

Chapter Five

Neither of them had expected the Friday-night traffic, the congestion as Route 128 and the Southeast Expressway merged at Braintree, the bumper-to-bumper drive down past Hingham, and then the dead stop more than a mile before the Sagamore Bridge. But the lost hours were worth it. It was their first weekend in "Horizons."

The name had come with the house. Grace wasn't sure whether it exactly suited the place, nor did she like the idea that it forever associated the place with its prior owners, but Bain didn't want to mess with history. Besides, they'd have to come up with a replacement. "What else would you call a house on a bluff looking out to sea?" Grace's lack of an immediate response sealed its fate.

"Horizons, Horizons," Grace murmured as they had pulled in the drive just as night was settling over the landscape. She wanted to get used to the sound.

Hyannis Bedding had taken her order over the telephone and delivered the full-size mattress, box spring, and Harvard bed, leaving them all on the back porch. Grace had brought a few stray hangers, sheets and towels, a bar of soap, a Revere Ware frying pan, a coffeemaker, and a teapot, along with the essentials to get them through breakfast on Saturday morning. She'd even remembered a mattress pad for Bain's sensitive skin.

They quickly went to work, lugging the bed upstairs and assembling its frame. Grace wanted the bed to face the window so that they could gaze out to sea in the morning. She envisioned sitting with an old-fashioned breakfast tray on her lap, sipping English breakfast tea, smelling a single rose in a bud vase, and staring at the lighthouse, the channel, and the boats beyond. Bain disagreed with that location. The furniture would fit better if the headboard—which had yet to be purchased—backed up to the window. "You won't be able to enjoy any view at night, when we'll be in here. The ocean is nothing but blackness."

Grace wanted Bain to be comfortable and acquiesced. Still, as she crawled between the butter-yellow sheets she'd purchased two days before from Bloomingdale's, she thought what a shame it would be not to begin her day with the sight of the sun reflecting off the water.

Bain slept fitfully, arose with the first light of morning, dressed without showering, and drove off in search of a *Wall Street Journal* and a *Globe*. She didn't have the heart to remind him that most shops wouldn't be open before nine on a Saturday morning. Left behind, Grace drank a cup of tea standing by the stove. She knew that the entourage of tradesmen with whom Bain had scheduled appointments would begin arriving shortly after ten. With any luck, she could take a brisk walk before Bain's return. She threw on a loose sweater and a pair of blue jeans and headed down to the beach.

The sand under her bare feet was cold and hard. She swung her arms, quickening her pace as she took in the morning. An egret at the shoreline gazed out to sea. Spindly-legged piping plovers scurried through the foam. Several seagulls picked at the remnants of a dead seal that had washed ashore. In the distance, she heard the rumble of a motorboat heading for the channel.

And then she spotted the clammer. She knew it was the same woman. She could tell by the floppy hat that reminded her of Paddington Bear. A red Ford pickup was the only car parked at the town landing. She'd never known a woman who drove a truck.

As she approached, the clammer glanced up from her raking, paused for a moment, and then waved in recognition. Such friendliness under the circumstances was surprising. Perhaps Cape Codders were a more forgiving breed than Bostonians, or at least more forgiving than she would have expected.

"Hello," Grace called out. She pushed her jeans up over her knees and stepped into the water. The cold temperature was a shock.

The woman laughed. "The air temperature doesn't heat this ocean into the sixties until late August. It's better to swim around here in October than June."

"I'll try to remember that." Grace watched a small fish explore her ankle as she gathered her courage. "I've been meaning to apologize for my husband and what he said to you the other day. He didn't mean to be rude," she blurted. "It really wasn't his intent. It's just . . . well, it's hard to describe. You see, we live in Boston, and Bain— he's my husband—is very busy. He works incredibly hard, long hours, that sort of thing. He bought this place as a sanctuary, to escape the city." She looked at the clammer, who stared at her with a blank expression. Perhaps she should have left the topic well enough alone, but now she was in too deep not to finish whatever it was she was trying to explain. She wasn't at all sure she knew herself. "All he wants is peace and quiet. That's why we came to Chatham in the first place instead of Nantucket or Martha's Vineyard. Boston is such a social place, wonderfully busy, but it can be too much, and he just wants to be left alone. And so, I think seeing you right here, so close to our house sort of . . . well . . . upset him. But it will pass. I know it will. As soon as he can start enjoying our new home, relaxing a bit and taking in the scenery, I know he'll calm down. He just wants his privacy respected." She forced a smile, hoping the clammer would join her. "And he didn't know the law," she added.

"You're the one who has to be married to him," the woman replied, dismissively.

The remark took Grace aback. She wanted to be married to Bain; it wasn't something she had to do. Plus she was just trying to make the woman understand why Bain had been upset. She wanted this woman to empathize, to not feel bad about them.

"I'm sorry, that was out of line. It's none of my business. What I should have said is *No apologies necessary.* I wasn't the politest person myself the other day." The woman smiled. "My name's Prissy Nickerson."

"I'm Grace Alcott." Grace extended her hand, but Prissy already had returned to her work and didn't shake it. "Prissy, that's a rather unusual name."

"It's Patricia, really. But who in hell wants to be called *Pat*? I get a bad feeling about that name. Must be the flat *A* sound."

Grace nodded. She didn't want to admit she knew several Pats, but they had bouffant hairdos, red nails, and wore Jack Rogers sandals. She felt quite confident that none of them knew how to dig for clams or would ever take an interest in learning. Clam chowder could be bought ready-made at most of the good fish markets and was on every menu in Boston.

Thinking to change the subject, Grace remarked, "Did you ever see *Gone with the Wind*? There was a Prissy in that, a young slave girl." She remembered all the characters in the David O. Selznick classic. If it wasn't her favorite movie, it certainly made her top two or three.

Although she, like Melanie, preferred the stability of Ashley Wilkes—and was proud that in real life she'd ended up with his counterpart—there was something awfully alluring about Rhett Butler. Perhaps if she'd been Scarlett O'Hara, she would have been happy to be spoiled by such a seductive man. It wasn't such a bad fate.

Prissy's eyes lit up. "I can't believe you remembered that. That's why I chose the name! Prissy was my favorite character." She stood back up and took several steps toward Grace. When she spoke again, her voice was animated and she gesticulated with her rake. "Do you remember the scene where Dr. Meade asks her to help deliver Melanie Wilkes's baby? She's got her hair tied back in a kerchief and wears a plum-colored dress. Anyway, she says yes, absolutely, she can do it. But when Melanie goes into labor and Scarlett tells her to help, Prissy becomes hysterical. She's scared about having lied, but she's more terrified about the baby, so she confesses."

"Yes, yes," Grace interrupted. "I do remember. She's crying, and she says, 'I don't know nothin' 'bout birthin' no babies.'"

"That's it! That's the line."

Both women laughed.

Then Prissy added, "That's me. I don't know anything, and I don't want to know."

"About babies? You don't?" Grace asked. "You don't want a child?"

Prissy shook her head. "Life is plenty complicated enough. I'm glad my mother did it, but that's about all I can say." With that, she stabbed the sand with her rake.

Grace watched in silence for several minutes. She couldn't imagine sharing that sentiment. For the past three years, she'd hoped every month. That a woman would choose to be childless was alien; for a moment, she wondered if Prissy was a transvestite. Or maybe a lesbian.

Who else would ignore her maternal instincts? "Are you married?"

"Yeah, although quite frankly I can't quite figure that one out, either. I was perfectly content to live together, but he's old-fashioned. He's never said as much, but I think he thought that having a marriage license would make us care more about each other. It always seemed to me, though, that you either do or you don't. All the official paperwork in the world doesn't keep a lot of folks together."

This was a curious woman. Even if Grace had such thoughts, she couldn't imagine sharing them with a virtual stranger.

After a while, Prissy paused in her work and extended the rake in Grace's direction. "Do you want to try?"

"Oh . . . I don't know. I don't know the first thing about how to clam."

"It's not hard, except for the strain on your back. But you can deal with that problem tomorrow. Come here."

Grace moved to where she'd been working. The two women stood side by side. This close, Grace realized that Prissy was several inches taller. Her height gave her a regal quality.

"First you look for airholes in the sand. They can be crabs or something else, but they're your best indicator. When you see them, start to dig. You need a rhythm, keep it gentle. You don't want to break the shell with your rake. When you think you've got something, dig in with your hands. Feel around with your fingers. You're looking for a round shape, ideally a couple of inches in diameter. Too small and you've got to throw it back. Fortunately, unlike lobster, bigger isn't bad. You definitely want to keep the jumbos."

Grace nodded, indicating she understood the instructions. She leaned over and began to claw, hesitantly at first, then gradually with more confidence, digging up darker sand as she went. The wet sand was heavy, and she found the work more difficult than she'd imagined. She raked and raked, finding nothing, pausing, looking for air-holes, and moving on, all the while listening to the gritty sound her rake made against the ocean floor. Then, after what must have been several minutes, she touched something hard. "Oh, oh," she exclaimed as she kneeled down, feeling the cold water seep into her jeans. She dug with her hands for a few seconds before her fingers grasped a round shell. She pulled it up. There it was: a perfect clam of adequate size.

"Look! Look!" she exclaimed.

Prissy smiled. "That's the one. You did it. Your first Chatham clam." She pointed to the wire bucket positioned half in the water.

Grace walked over and gently added her treasure to Prissy's catch. It sat on top of the pile, seemingly bigger and fresher than all the others.

"You want to keep digging? I have another rake in the truck."

Yes, she thought. She wanted to stay and dig all day and then invite Prissy back to make clam chowder in her kitchen for supper. Prissy could shuck the shells while she sautéed onions and peeled potatoes. They could share a glass of white wine and nibble Wheat Thin crackers. Clam chowder would never taste the same again.

But she couldn't. She had to get home. Alone. There was so much to do, and Bain would chastise her for being irresponsible.

"I can't," she said to Prissy. "Not today. But thank you." It had been a magical morning.

"Anytime."

"Are you here often?"

"Yeah. I like this area. The spot's pretty and the clams

tend to be plentiful. Must be something about the currents. I used to know how all that stuff worked. But the short answer is that, yes, you're likely to find me here just about every day of the season."

"I'll see you soon, then." Grace reached for Prissy's shoulder and gently touched the rough canvas of her jacket. Her first Chatham friend. She needed to be sure the woman was real.

&c∽

Back at the house, she found Bain upstairs. Their bed had been turned; it now faced the window. She could look out to sea after all.

"What are you doing?" she asked.

"I thought I might bring you breakfast. But you were already up and about. So instead I rearranged the room. You're right about the bed. It is better to face the sea." He gazed into the paper bag. "This one is supposed to be a Chatham specialty," he said, handing her a sugarcoated muffin that smelled of cinnamon, nutmeg, and ginger. "It's called French spice."

"French spice in Chatham?"

"You know the French came into Chatham through Stage Harbor. They landed here and fought the Indians right over on Champlain Road. I guess they left their muffin recipe behind."

Grace laughed. Bain did, too.

"Thank you," she said, taking the crumbled muffin from his hand.

Together they sat on the bed. She broke off pieces of the sweet cake and handed them to him. He ate some and fed her others, while she spoke of re-meeting Prissy and the joy of finding her first clam. As he listened, he exhibited none of his earlier hostility toward the local woman,

and instead seemed genuinely pleased that she'd con-
nected with Prissy. She'd been right; his temper had been
an aberration.

They devoured the French spice, then a blueberry, and
then a cranberry. When they were done, she wiped the
crumbs from his lap onto the floor.

"Breakfast with a view," he said, sighing. "I can think
of only one thing finer."

But she couldn't ask what. At that moment, the door-
bell rang announcing the arrival of the contractors.

1973–1974

Chapter Six

Sarah Eleanor Alcott was born October 26, 1973. If Bain regretted that their first child was a girl, he kept the thought to himself. That she had long legs and longer lashes, blue eyes, and pale smooth skin no doubt worked to her advantage with her father. Physical beauty in women mattered to him. The dark hair that shocked both her parents when they saw it matted against her newborn face quickly fell out. Within a month, blond curls replaced her baldness. By six weeks, she resembled a doll.

Although her disposition was not nearly as sunny as her physical appearance, Grace took it in stride. There was so much to learn and, without her own mother to teach her, she knew she made mistakes. Sarah's tears may well have been rooted in her own errors as she struggled to change a diaper without a safety-pin prick, to heat the bottle without scalding the formula, and to burp her daughter without applying too much pressure. Maternal skills required practice. The important thing was to maintain her patience even as her baby screeched with displeasure.

Still, it was disheartening that such a small creature harbored such a horrid temper and could make and sustain such an odious sound.

Occasionally, if Grace was honest with herself, she would admit her difficulties. The days of pottery classes, rearranging paperwork, and long walks on the Esplanade were over. When Sarah's face became red from screaming, it was all Grace could do not to call the fire department. Once or maybe twice she'd been forced to leave the baby in her crib while she retreated to the living room and tried to drown out the shrieks with the stereo. But even Mick Jagger at full volume was no competition for Sarah.

Most of the time, though, she managed eventually to quiet her daughter. Then a rush of relief would wash over her as she stared down at her precious baby. After all, wasn't this precisely what she'd wanted since the day she married? Pushing Sarah in a perambulator down Commonwealth Avenue, dressing her in a linen bonnet and the tiniest of baby booties, rocking her gently in her arms, the moments when her beautiful little girl cooed and smiled made up for all the hours when life seemed to have lost any semblance of order.

But when at nine months Sarah still wasn't sleeping through the night, Bain put his foot down. Grace looked haggard. She'd lost weight. They hadn't made love in more than a month, and when they had, she'd nearly fallen asleep beneath him. "This child is obviously too much for you to handle alone." He wanted a nanny.

Grace was dismayed. She didn't want help. She didn't want to share the mothering, even the difficult moments. Sarah was her joy, truly. She just needed a bit more time to get into a better rhythm.

"You've had nine months," Bain replied, firmly. "And if anything the situation has gotten worse."

"We don't have room," Grace offered, trying to keep the desperation she felt out of her voice. As it was, Sarah's crib barely fit in the study that doubled as a second bedroom. There wasn't an inch of available closet space for live-in help, let alone room for another bed.

"You'll move to Chatham for the summer. We have

plenty of space. If the woman can get Sarah on a schedule by Labor Day, we won't bring her back."

"You mean we'd go without you? What would you do?"

"I'll be just like every other husband and commute on the weekends. I can probably work my schedule so that I can spend Sunday night and drive up Monday morning. The guys with houses on Nantucket certainly cut back on their summer hours in order to make the ferry."

Grace couldn't imagine Bain by himself all week long. Who would buy his bran muffins or make his coffee? What would he do in the evenings? She dreaded the idea of being apart from her husband and living with a virtual stranger who would care for her daughter. The setup didn't seem right. They were a new family. She was now a mother, but she was still Bain's wife. She needed him. This was just a difficult phase, not one that required a separation.

"Grace, this makes perfect sense," Bain said in the voice she knew meant the decision wasn't open for discussion. "I'd rather have you for two good nights than continue in this manner."

She could think of nothing to say. His comment left her feeling as though she were an overripe peach, unsuitable for anything but composting.

"Just find someone by the end of the week before we both lose our sanity."

The next day while Sarah napped, Grace reluctantly contacted several agencies. The women on the other end of the telephone sounded perky and efficient. They wanted her data, and she could hear them typing in the background as she responded to their questions. All of them offered excellent candidates, women with years of experience as nannies, just exactly what she needed. But the agency fee was a percentage of the projected annual salary. The figure seemed way too high for someone who would only be in the Alcotts' employ for a season.

At the grocery store on Charles Street, Grace scanned the bulletin board. It was covered by an array of messages—a stereo and tape deck, a used Chevrolet, and a dining set for sale, housecleaning services offered, a local veterinarian promoting his new office. At the bottom in awkward scrawl was a listing for a babysitter. *Experienced grandmother. Good references available.* Ninety dollars a week and no hiring fee.

As soon as she got home, Grace called the number and spoke to Maryann O'Connor, who had a sweet voice and a Dorchester residence. A widow with seven grown children and twelve grandchildren, she had more experience than most professional child-care providers. "I'm sure we can agree that I've done my share of raising children—and I've seen it all," she said, revealing a tinge of an accent and a warm laugh. Plus she loved to iron, would do light housework, and could cook, too.

The next day, Mrs. O'Connor arrived for her interview. She wore a floral dress and her gray hair in a bun. She smelled of perfumed soap.

They shook hands, and Grace felt her thick, warm palm. The sensation made her want to ask for a hug.

Mrs. O'Connor followed Grace into the kitchen. Grace offered her a cup of tea and apologized for the disarray. Sarah had just had lunch, and her high chair, the floor, and several of the cabinets were speckled with pureed carrots and lamb. The breakfast dishes hadn't been done. "It's not usually like this," she said, sheepishly.

Sarah started to cry. No doubt her diaper was soiled, but Grace felt uncomfortable changing her with this woman watching. She didn't want to fumble or make a mistake. So she bounced Sarah up and down in her arms trying to distract her, or calm her, or just plain quiet her for a moment. Instead the baby vomited.

As Grace mumbled excuses, Mrs. O'Connor reached for Sarah, nestled her on her substantial bosom, and began to sing an Irish ballad. Without breaking the melody, she removed the soiled bib, ran a dishtowel under warm water, and wiped the baby's face. Sarah was silent. Then she smiled and cooed.

"You have a beautiful little girl," Mrs. O'Connor said.

Grace filled with pride. "Yes, we think she's very special."

"But I can see she's a lot of work. For a young mother, that is."

Grace nodded.

"Common wisdom is that boys bring the trouble, but I can assure you there are plenty of little girls who can wreak just as much havoc. You must be a tad overwhelmed."

"My husband thinks so."

"Ah, one of those," Mrs. O'Connor said, knowingly.

She rocked back and forth with Sarah still resting on her bosom. Grace watched, longingly. The platform actually looked like a cozy spot. She glanced down at her own paltry set of 32Bs.

"And he's not the most sympathetic to exhaustion, now, is he?" Mrs. O'Connor continued. "Men are all alike— babies themselves. You'll hear no complaints over making the children, but they don't much care for tending them. And they don't like any interference with their own attention."

This woman seemed to understand everything.

"Let me guess. He thinks you're too thin and complains that you've forgotten about his needs. I know how hard 'tis to be a good wife with a young one at home. And just wait until the siblings start arriving. Oh, Mother of God, that's when the complications begin. But let me keep my big mouth shut or you'll be too afraid to ever get back in bed with that man. And then I'll have talked myself out of a job for sure." She laughed again. "Don't worry about a thing. Now you go take a bath and freshen up, and leave this darling—and this mess—to me."

Grace nearly skipped out of the kitchen with the sounds of Sarah's giggles and gurgles behind her. Bain had been right. She did need help. Maryann O'Connor would get their life back in order. She'd care for Sarah, the house, and even Grace herself. She could hardly wait for her husband to come home so that she could tell him the good news.

❧

Mrs. O'Connor sat on the back porch in a rocking chair with Sarah on her lap. They were looking at a pair of robins that had settled into the lilac bush a few feet away. Sarah flapped her arms with excitement.

The summer had passed in relative bliss. Sarah loved the water and the sand, and spent hours sitting under a large umbrella with a plastic bucket and several shovels. Mrs. O'Connor was always at her side, clucking and tending, adjusting her sun hat, offering her snacks, and changing her diapers. Grace had filled several albums with pictures of her beautiful daughter's first days at the beach.

Without Bain during the week, Mrs. O'Connor's presence gave her considerable freedom. It took Grace less time than she'd expected to adjust to leaving Sarah behind, but Mrs. O'Connor encouraged her. At the end of the day, she escaped to the shoreline with a folding chair, a striped towel, and, on occasion, an evening cocktail and a Tupperware container of sliced cheddar and Wheat

Thins. She'd walk along the beach, take a swim in the cold
Atlantic water, and then find Prissy, who was often fin-
ishing her work in the low tide. Not only did Grace welcome the conversation, but it brought her considerable
pleasure that Prissy actually seemed to enjoy her company. She'd even put down her rake, come sit in the sand
by Grace's chair, and share her drink and snack.

"So, how's mothering going?" Prissy asked one evening
as she extended a rake in Grace's direction.

Grace shook her head. The novelty of clamming had
quickly passed; she was content to sit in her folding chair
and watch. She settled back against the mesh supports
and drank seltzer water from a plastic tumbler. "In all
honesty, I don't know how I was surviving without Mrs.
O'Connor. She's a godsend, truly."

"What did I tell you about babies? You should have listened to me instead of getting yourself knocked up."

Grace laughed. "What a way to speak!" Although she
could be crude, Prissy's blunt manner was part of her
appeal. "Besides, I find my husband irresistible." She
blushed, disbelieving that she'd uttered the words. There
was something about the presence of her friend that made
her normal inhibitions relax.

"Isn't it just in the Bible that sex and procreation are
synonymous? Last time I checked, you were entitled to
enjoy each other without ending up with offspring."

"Bain doesn't want to use birth control."

Even from a distance, she could see Prissy's raised eyebrows.

"It's just . . . I think it's a source of pride for him that we
might have a large family."

"Then you'd better train him to be an assistant nanny,
too. One won't be enough."

"That's for certain," Grace said, sighing. "It is hard
work, harder than I ever imagined. If I'm honest, I'm

exhausted most of the time. I had some notion that motherhood would be simple, constantly rewarding, and endlessly fulfilling. Who knew I'd be so wrong?" She forced a laugh. "I shouldn't admit it. I never could to Bain."

"Your secret is safe with me."

"Thanks." She scanned the shoreline. Two seagulls pecked at something in the sand. "Mrs. O'Connor really is a saint. I feel as though she's given me this great gift—a gift of time for myself, for our conversations, for even just going to the grocery store. I didn't realize before how easy it was to get a quart of milk. I pulled into the parking lot, jumped out, found what I wanted, paid, and went home. Now I have to get Sarah in and out of the car, then worry about whether she'll wet her diaper while I push her in the carriage, or if we'll lose her pacifier or her teething ring along the way. I panic if she starts to cry. Everyone stares at me as though I'm this horrible mother. I guess I now appreciate how simple life once was."

"Sarah will grow up and go about her business. You and Bain can have peace and quiet in your old age."

"If we get there is the better question. Her crying makes Bain absolutely crazy. Last Saturday, I thought he might walk out on all of us. We'd come back from a party, and I think Bain might have had one too many gin and tonics. We walked inside and heard screeching as loud as a siren. Even with Mrs. O'Connor's efforts to quiet her, nobody could sleep. I couldn't believe how long she lasted. It wasn't until after three that Sarah settled down."

"So don't let the woman go."

"No, I can't. I don't know where I'd be without her."

"Then make sure she signs a life contract, or at least a contract until your youngest child reaches maturity—something along those lines."

"She may not want to stay forever."

"Well, as I said before, don't say I didn't warn you."

Prissy paused, rubbed her forehead with a muddy hand, and then asked, "Why do you still call her Mrs. O'Connor?"

Grace considered the question. She hadn't ever thought about it. The days had turned to weeks. She and Mrs. O'Connor were almost friends; they certainly were familiar with each other. "She's older, sort of like a friend of my parents. You know, those people you knew as a child and always called *Mrs. So-and-so*, and then suddenly you're a grown-up, too, and yet you can't make the transition to call them by their first name? That's how it feels to me. As if I've known her forever but still can't call her anything other than her formal name because it was how we were originally introduced. She calls me Mrs. Alcott. I want her to know I have the same respect for her. And she's never said to call her Maryann."

"That's probably a distance thing, her way of maintaining boundaries."

"Yes, I suppose you're right. It must be hard not to become too attached." Grace shrugged. "I can't imagine raising someone else's child."

"It's a hell of a lot easier than raising your own," Prissy remarked.

~∽~

On the weekend evenings of July and August, Grace and Bain socialized. From the moment they'd purchased the house, there had been invitations: The neighbors, a slightly older couple with three children and a live-in housekeeper, invited them over for dinner; the minister from St. Christopher's and his wife took them out on a large sailboat for a tour of Morris Island. They'd been put up at the Chatham Beach and Tennis Club, a membership process that involved myriad cocktail parties and several hours of mixed doubles games. After only the first summer, Grace felt welcome in the community. And three years later, Grace and Bain Alcott were so ensconced that she no longer thought about their social life. It was simply a part of who they were.

Bain seemed pleased each week when he arrived on Friday evening to find her more tan and relaxed than when he'd left her the Monday morning before. "Thank God for Mrs. O'Connor," he'd say, laughing. "I wouldn't want to keep you too busy."

It almost felt as though they were on their honeymoon again.

"I don't want this life to end," she whispered one night as she lay beside him. Labor Day was only ten days away. Her linen nightgown and his cotton boxer shorts lay on the floor beside the bed. "It seems too good to be true."

Bain agreed.

And so that night they'd decided to keep Mrs. O'Connor on in their employ when they returned to Boston. Sarah was sleeping through the night. The woman could live in her own apartment in Dorchester, arriving in the morning and departing after the supper dishes were done.

❦

Now, watching Mrs. O'Connor and Sarah on the porch imitating the birds, Grace knew they'd made the right decision. She would tell Mrs. O'Connor that afternoon when she returned from the hairdresser. She knew the woman would be pleased. She seemed to genuinely adore Sarah. Grace would even offer a ten-dollar-a-week raise.

"I'll be back in an hour," she announced as she leaned over and kissed her little girl's head. Against her lips, the soft curls felt like down.

"When is Mr. Alcott to be expected?"

"I'm not sure. He'll probably call while I'm gone to say when he's leaving Boston. Depending on traffic, it's about two and a half hours after that."

"Shall I answer?"

Grace paused for a moment. Mrs. O'Connor didn't normally answer the telephone. She had difficulty with taking messages and had botched several numbers, causing Grace some degree of embarrassment. They'd even missed a cocktail party on account of a transcription error. But this would be Bain calling, and he'd been in a meeting when she'd tried to reach him earlier. "Yes, please. If you could tell him we're expected at the Marshalls' for drinks at six thirty, I'd appreciate it."

"Very well, then. Take your time. We'll be fine."

Chapter Seven

Grace had heard and seen the flashing blue lights even before she'd turned into her own driveway. *Mrs. O'Connor,* she'd thought with panic. Had she slipped? Had her heart failed?

An alternative scenario didn't occur to her.

A young policeman with sandy hair and strong arms blocked the door.

Grace paused to catch her breath. "Poor woman. Will she be all right?"

He didn't reply.

"You must let me in. I have to get my daughter. She's just a baby."

He turned his head to look inside but didn't move his body from blocking her way.

"Please," she said with more urgency. She envisioned Sarah left in her crib, no doubt screaming for someone to lift her out. Grace blamed herself. They'd asked too much of Mrs. O'Connor. She wasn't young, and she was a bit overweight. And the house did get hot by the late afternoon. "You must let me pass." She stopped speaking and waited for a reply, but none came. Then she realized. There was no sound of crying. There were no baby shrieks. "Where . . . is . . . my . . . baby?" She lurched forward, gasping for air. Suddenly all she wanted was to hear the abrasive infant screams that had worn down her nervous system.

The policeman caught her and held her steady.

She tried to step forward but felt the officer's hands gripping her upper arms. Stuck, she looked around. Through the open door, she could see Mrs. O'Connor slumped in an armchair. Two police officers seemed to be speaking to her. One of them—an older man—took notes in a spiral pad. The other paced back and forth on the Oriental rug.

She looked up at the officer who held her in a vise. His large mirrored sunglasses obscured his facial expression, and she found herself staring instead at her own distorted image: short legs, a thick middle, an oversize oval head. "What . . . happened?"

"I'm very sorry for your loss."

Loss, my loss, what loss? Why was he sorry? Even as her barometer of realization rose, she was confused. His words didn't make sense. The situation didn't make sense. She'd just been gone an hour. It was a hair appointment and nothing more. She hadn't been negligent. She hadn't been a bad mother.

Sorry for your loss, sorry for your loss, sorry for your loss, sorryforyourloss. The words echoed. She felt her legs collapse, and then the cool flagstone beneath her. The officer wouldn't let go, and bent over her, still gripping her arms.

"Give me my baby! I want Sarah now!"

Mrs. O'Connor's head turned toward the noise, and Grace could see her face, puffy and bloated, streaked with tears. Her hair was in disarray, and the front of her dress appeared to be wet. In her hands, she scrunched a white handkerchief.

The screen door creaked open, and two paramedics in short-sleeved uniforms appeared. The small shape on the stretcher was covered with a dark blanket and held in place by one of the safety straps. The second one dangled down, unbuckled, since the covered body lacked sufficient length to require its use.

Grace stared at the perfect mound, the form in silhouette. She tried to picture the sweet face and blue eyes and blond curls, but all she could see was blackness. She couldn't breathe. Her limbs didn't move.

She looked back at Mrs. O'Connor, sitting in her home. Their eyes met, and the nanny's mouth contorted in an expression of horror. It seemed to be a cavernous, gaping hole coming at her, opening and closing without uttering a sound. Her eyes bulged. It wasn't Mrs. O'Connor at all. It was a bloated fish wearing a dress, no doubt dripping salt water all over her upholstery. But then she saw the handkerchief that the woman had been holding. It waved back and forth, some sort of a truce offering. Maybe that was it. The war was over. Her vision blurred. It wasn't a piece of cloth at all. Grace was mistaken. The grouper in her armchair was holding a dove, and was about to release the bird in her library.

Grace sank back against the policeman's legs. She prayed for this moment to end.

꧁꧂

An assistant in the public relations department of the Bank of Boston recommended an event coordinator. Bain spoke to her briefly on the telephone, checked with a reference, and hired her. Pat Jeffries drove down the next morning to plan the memorial service. She wasn't bothered by the fact that it was a Saturday.

"We'll keep it simple, elegant," the woman said as she produced a leather binder from her attaché case and began to take notes. "Appropriate for a child loss."

Not *a* child loss, Grace wanted to scream. Not any

child. Not even *the* child. Sarah. Sarah Eleanor Alcott. Her only baby. Her daughter.

She started for the stairs. She needed to lie down. Maybe if she could just bring herself to fall asleep, she would never again awaken. Or if she did, maybe this nightmare would be over. She closed her eyes, remembering the weight of her daughter as she held her in her arms.

"You have my deepest sympathy. My company's, too. It is just devastating. Absolutely devastating," Pat offered. Her voice was flat, corporate, as if she were announcing to the outside directors that profits were down this quarter. Maybe that made her a professional, but to Grace it seemed hard-hearted. What kind of woman could make a career out of child funerals anyway?

Turning to Bain, Pat added, "I'd recommend we do this as quickly as possible. Monday at the latest. It will be best for both you and your wife if the formalities are over, and you can have privacy to grieve."

Monday. Two days away.

≈≫

Pat filled St. Christopher's Episcopal Church on Main Street with baskets of pale pink and white flowers. The handles were tied with pale pink satin ribbon. She coordinated with the minister, arranged the order of service, and had programs printed quickly. Although the script lettering was difficult to read, each scroll was tied with a pink ribbon. "Done by hand," she explained, justifying the per-copy price.

She hired a caterer to prepare finger sandwiches and petits fours, nothing too heavy. "Especially in cases like this, nobody eats," Grace heard her whisper to Bain. "An adequate liquor supply is the way to go."

The white casket lined with white satin was twenty-four inches long. That meant it was small enough to rest on the altar.

Pat selected a dark suit for Bain with a white shirt and gray tie. Although the suit was back from the cleaners, Pat re-pressed it herself. The clothes were hung on a special rack, with tasseled loafers and gray socks lined up in front. Grace wondered whether the woman planned on buttoning his shirt and zippering his fly, too.

Sunday evening, Grace found Pat going through her own closet. That was the last straw. "Please leave," Grace said matter-of-factly.

"Your husband wanted me to make a choice for you," she explained, defensively. "So that you wouldn't have to think about it tomorrow morning."

"Well, that's very kind. You've provided quite an excellent service. But I gave birth to Sarah. I am her mother. And I can damn well figure out what to wear to her funeral all on my own."

It was the first time she'd ever cursed at anyone. But it felt good. She hated this woman, this stranger who had come into her life to take control of her daughter's death. "I want you out of my bedroom. I want you out of my home. Now." She half smiled, relieved that she'd spoken her mind.

Pat did walk out, but she also reported Grace's conduct to Bain, who appeared in a few moments.

"I know you don't want her here. I don't, either. But that's because neither of us can bear to face the reason that she's here. We couldn't have managed this without her, Grace," he said. "She's trying to help. You don't have to be rude."

Rude! That emotion hardly began to capture how she felt. Anger, rage, despair, they were all just words.

And because Mrs. O'Connor was gone, the real culprit

couldn't be blamed. Grace couldn't vent her fury, couldn't shake the nanny until her eyes rolled back in her head or pound her with a Belgium block from the driveway, couldn't scream and curse at the person who had ruined her life. The experienced grandmother with fine references had virtually disappeared in the back of a police cruiser along with her suitcase and travel bag. All she'd left behind were her toothbrush and a pair of slippers under her bed, items that Grace would have thrown away, but she didn't want to touch them.

"I know what pain you're in," Bain said, his voice softening. He wrapped his arms around her and drew her to him. He gently stroked the back of her head. "I love Sarah and I miss her. She was my daughter, too. But we mustn't forget who we are. You won't feel any better by lashing out at Pat."

In other words, the event planner was just executing her orders, doing her job.

The consummate professional, she was kind enough to accept Grace's feeble apology.

⤫

Monday arrived, despite Grace's every effort to will it not to come to pass. It should have been dark with pelting rain, thunder and lightning. Or, if the weather were to more closely mirror her mood, a thick band of fog should have enveloped everything, making visibility impossible. She wanted the salty moisture to saturate the walls, the fabric, even her skin, anything to penetrate the overwhelming numbness. Instead, as if to taunt her, the morning was beautiful, sunny and cool without a cloud in the sky.

By nine thirty, station wagons filled the small parking lot of Children's Beach. She couldn't bear the sight of the mothers in shorts and bikini tops with their children and folding chairs, umbrellas, beach buckets, and bright-colored sand toys. Happy voices and giggling children wafted through the car window as they drove to the church. She would ask Bain to take a different route home, one that didn't take her along Stage Harbor Road.

Bain parked in front of the church, just behind the hearse that waited to transport Sarah to the cemetery for what had been called in the obituary a "private burial." The term seemed redundant. As much as Grace wanted to follow her daughter's coffin into the earth, to dive behind it as it was lowered down into the hole, Sarah would be buried with only the stuffed pink rabbit that Grace had tucked into the casket beside her cold body.

At the curb, there were several orange cones to keep tourists from taking the coveted spot on Main Street. Bain cut the engine, alighted, and then came around to her side. He opened the passenger-side door and helped her out. She stood, blinking at the sun as her eyes adjusted. Mourners mingled on the flagstone path leading to the church entrance. One of them smoked.

A woman approached quickly, taking small steps in her high-heeled shoes. It took Grace a moment to place her. They'd met the previous summer at a Stage Harbor Yacht Club newcomers' party. All she recalled was that the short, squat woman with bright pink lipstick was an avid sailor. She was the club champion in some class of boats or another.

"I just don't know what to say." The woman spoke in a voice that had a slightly Southern twang. "I am so sorry and you have my sincerest condolences. My husband, frankly, was so distraught for you and Bain that he couldn't bring himself to attend. But his prayers are with you both."

Grace remembered the husband, Barney, and his pants

with anchors appliquéd on them. He didn't strike her as the type to be distraught over much of anything. On a beautiful Monday morning in late August, that man with his salt-and-pepper hair and double chin was no doubt teeing off the seventh hole.

"Yes, indeed. We're both praying for all you Alcotts."

All. Try just two.

"This must be hard, so hard," the woman, who professed to lack words, continued without even a pause for breath. "And you're handling this so beautifully. My God, I don't know how you do it. You even look good. Trust me. Jackie Kennedy just lost the award for most grace under pressure."

Grace couldn't listen. She tried to speak, to utter some pleasantry to dismiss this person, but when she opened her mouth she thought she might vomit.

Turning away rather abruptly, she saw Prissy in the corner of the courtyard, alone. Her hands rested on the back of a weathered bench that had been given in memory of some other family's lost member. She looked clean and formal, almost unrecognizable in tailored slacks, a fitted cotton sweater, and leather sandals. Her hair was pulled off her face in a thick braid.

Her sympathy-filled walnut eyes rested on Grace. In a few long strides, she came over, threw her arms around Grace's neck, and embraced her. "Despite all my stupid comments, I know what motherhood—and what Sarah— meant to you. And it's got to hurt like whale shit. I am so sorry," she whispered as she held her friend tight to her chest.

Grace felt the weight of her body fall onto Prissy. She'd been almost silent for two days, but suddenly she wanted to take Prissy aside to confess, to tell her everything, to explain all the details that the paper left out: that she had told Mrs. O'Connor to answer the telephone because she needed to coordinate with Bain; that the woman had left Sarah in the bathtub when she heard the ring because she wanted to follow her employer's instructions; that her baby girl had drowned in the time it took for Bain to explain that he was delayed at work and that, if he wasn't there by seven, Grace should go to the Marshalls' without him; that her baby should still be alive.

As if reading her mind, Prissy murmured, "It wasn't your fault." She squeezed her tighter and their bodies swayed ever so gently from side to side. Grace could feel the heat emanating from her friend's tanned skin. She wanted to be down at the beach, watching Prissy clam as she sat in her folding chair and sipped from a glass of iced tea. If only she were there now instead of here, standing with a black-clad crowd on a beautiful August day. Then she could lull herself into thinking her daughter was up at the house, sleeping perhaps, or nibbling on a cracker. If only.

Bain touched her arm. "We have to go in."

The memorial service. She couldn't dream it away.

"Thank you for being here," she said to Prissy as she struggled to hold back her tears. "Thank you for being."

Bain led her down the aisle. Gripping her arm, he steered her through a sea of unfamiliar faces. Every Bank of Boston secretary seemed to have shown up, no doubt wanting an excuse to take the day off and drive down to the Cape, an easy holiday. The service would be over by noon.

Grace took her place in the front pew next to her brother. She could hear his breathing. Ferris's face was red, no doubt a result of the Bloody Marys he'd ingested on an empty stomach shortly before leaving for St. Christopher's. "I'm on a liquid diet," he'd remarked, adding more pepper and stirring the vodka and tomato juice with a celery stalk as he declined the buttered English muffin she'd offered.

Bain sat on her other side, his gaze fixed straight ahead. He'd said little all morning, and she worried about his seeming calm. He'd mastered the necessary motions — drinking black coffee, getting dressed, and driving to church — but his face remained expressionless.

Grace wished her father were here. But he had agreed to lead a delegation of economists, urban planners, and engineers to Vietnam, and was at that moment somewhere meeting heads of state and other policy makers. She doubted that he'd received her telegram informing him of Sarah's death; even if he had, there was no way he could have returned in time for the funeral. Still, she couldn't help but feel his absence. His first — perhaps his only — grandchild was gone.

As the minister proceeded down the aisle reading about resurrection and life, she glanced behind her and scanned the crowd. She wished Bain had agreed to let Prissy sit with them in the front row, but he'd been adamant. She wasn't family. She wasn't entitled to a reserved seat. And now Prissy was nowhere in sight.

"O God, whose beloved son did take little children into his arms and bless them," the portly priest said, addressing the congregation face-on. "Give us grace, we beseech thee, to entrust this child, Sarah, to thy never-failing care and love . . . "

In the arms of Jesus Christ, Sarah was lifted to eternal life in a better place. The image was soothing. Her baby was safe. Her little girl was at peace.

She reached for Bain's hand and held it in hers. The fingers were limp, and his palm was slightly clammy. He didn't respond at all, and she wondered if he even realized she was touching him. But she refused to let go.

Then somewhere through the service, after the minister had read a Gospel passage and had given a brief, uninspired homily, she felt her husband's fingers tighten in her grasp. The pinkish skin of his knuckles lightened as he gripped her, not too hard, but enough to get her attention. There was desperation in his touch.

She looked over at him. He didn't turn. Still staring at the altar, he whispered, "I have you." A tear ran down his cheek.

"And you always will," she replied as she wiped it away with her handkerchief.

Those words were what she needed to hear. He didn't blame her. Even childless, he still loved her.

Grace closed her eyes and pictured Sarah, her diapers protruding from the sides of her swimsuit, her curls peeking out from beneath the pink gingham sun hat, and her smile as she flicked sand with her yellow plastic shovel. She would hold on to this memory, as she held on to him.

⇥⇤

The caterers had washed the last of the glasses and boxed up a few remaining hors d'oeuvres.

Shortly before the final mourners departed, Pat, too, took her leave. "I've seen a lot of sorrow in my line of work, and I offer a single piece of advice for what it's worth," she'd said, standing by the front door. Her voice was uncharacteristically somber. "Celebrate life."

"We'll try," Bain had said, shaking her hand vigorously. "Thank you for everything."

Then the woman had turned to Grace. For the first time in two days, Grace could see that Pat was tired. There were circles under her eyes and, once her lipstick had rubbed off, the lines and cracks on her lips showed. "If you don't go on with your life and make the most of it, Sarah's brief time here will have been for nothing. Don't do that to her, or to yourself."

For twenty dollars a head, the event planner threw in a platitude or two along with the watercress sandwiches, miniature crab cakes, and Sauvignon Blanc. Grace had felt the urge to strike her.

With that, Pat headed down the brick walkway to the waiting limousine, the one that Bain had paid for.

The sky darkened, and Grace watched as Bain poured himself yet another gin and tonic and cursed the lack of limes. On another day, at another moment, she would have gone running into the kitchen to see if there happened to be one left, an overlooked lime tucked into the produce drawer of the refrigerator or hiding under a cantaloupe in the fruit bowl. But she had no energy for the search at this point—and no sympathy for his drinking, either.

They sat in silence.

She had almost dozed, almost surrendered to the sweet respite that sleep would bring, when she heard his voice. "That woman was incompetent. I told you to use an agency."

Grace sat upright, stunned.

"She didn't have credentials. Taking care of her own brood doesn't give her experience as a professional. In her family, the kids probably took care of one another anyway, so she could cope with her drunken, good-for-nothing husband. That's not child rearing. Bloody Catholics. They're all peasants."

Mrs. O'Connor. He was talking about Mrs. O'Connor, faulting her, and faulting Grace for hiring her. She didn't need to be reminded.

"You shouldn't have called," she murmured.

"How the hell was I to know the woman would leave Sarah alone in the bathtub? What kind of an idiot would consider doing such a thing? She should be locked up."

He paused and drained his glass. When he spoke again, his words were slightly slurred. "And where the hell were you, Mrs. Alcott? Oh yes," he said, mockingly. "Getting your hair done."

She'd never forgive herself for that. "I . . . I . . . I just needed to know when you'd be arriving, that's all. It was a mistake. A horrible mistake."

He leaned toward her, and the lines around his mouth looked hard and menacing. "Is that your view of our children? Of the sanctity of our family? Because I'll tell you something, and I'll tell you something right now. My family is not expendable. My children are precious and should be treated that way. I don't work as hard as I do—"

"Please, Bain," she interrupted, although her voice was timid.

I have you. He'd seemed relieved by that fact just hours before. Now she was his albatross. Having her was his view of punishment. "Please don't say that," she pleaded, although a part of her agreed with everything he said. It was her fault. She'd been so relieved that Mrs. O'Connor had taken charge, taken over the care of Sarah, their darling. She'd relished the freedom. But she loved Sarah. And she'd been a good mother. He couldn't take that away from her. "It was an accident. Even the police said—"

"Goddammit!" He hurled his tumbler across the room and it shattered against the bookcase.

Grace didn't intend to move, but she couldn't stop herself from shaking.

Bain slouched back into the armchair. "What have I done?" He put his head in his hands. His shoulders shook ever so slightly, but he made no discernible sound.

Grace didn't answer. She didn't know how, didn't know whether his question referred to his harsh treatment of her and was actually some sort of an apology, or whether he was asking himself why he'd ever gotten involved with her to begin with. At least with silence he couldn't get any angrier.

But this night, too, would pass. Bain couldn't be responsible for what he said. Neither could she. They were both in terrible pain.

Grace got up and went to bed. She knew she wouldn't sleep, but she couldn't bear silence and dreaded further conversation. She was about to shut off the hall light and then—from instinct more than from compassion—refrained. Bain might come upstairs. And she didn't want him to trip in the dark.

&c&

The clock showed a few minutes after three. Outside the night was black, and Grace could hear the wind through the partially opened window. She stood gazing out, but there were no stars and the moon was only a dim crescent millions of miles away. In the distance, she heard the rumble of a truck as it left the fish pier with its load.

Grace made her way down the hall. The door to Sarah's room was ajar, and, from the threshold, she stared at the white crib with its pink bumpers, the Beatrix Potter mobile dangling over one end, the diapers stacked in neat piles on the changing table, the Owl and the Pussycat music box on the edge of the dresser. Everything was neat and ordered. There was only one problem.

She leaned against the threshold and stared again at the perfect nursery, the painted bureau and canopied bed. They'd bought the bed shortly after Sarah's birth. With its pink ruffle and frills, thick mattress and spindled posters, it had seemed to be out of a fairy tale, the kind of bed where little girls would have only sweet dreams.

It took Grace several moments to notice that Bain was asleep on it.

The pile rug was soft on her bare feet as she crossed the floor. He lay on one side on top of the quilt with his mouth open and his knees curled up. He hugged a boudoir pillow embroidered with Sarah's date of birth.

Gingerly, Grace lay beside him and draped her arm over his chest. She could feel his side rise and fall with each breath. She pulled herself closer to him and pressed her legs up against the backs of his. He didn't stir.

She lay still, listening to his breathing. Maybe she, like Sarah, had become a spirit with no physical presence. Perhaps that was why he couldn't feel her touch. Perhaps she, too, had vanished.

Then, after what seemed like hours, she heard his voice. It sounded scratchy, disoriented, and far away. "Grace, is that you?"

"Yes," she replied, softly, and rubbed his cheek. The skin felt prickly. "Yes Bain, I'm here."

With a bit of an effort, he rolled over to face her. He pushed one hand underneath her, so that the weight of her back rested on his arm, and pulled her toward him. She smelled alcohol and the faint hint of cologne. "Forgive me," he whispered. After a few moments, he began to shake slightly, and she heard only his sobs.

"Forgive me, too."

Chapter Eight

Bain left for Boston that Saturday. He'd been away from work since Sarah's death, and throwing himself back into his business at the bank was the distraction he needed. He claimed he was leaving early on Labor Day weekend to avoid traffic, but Grace knew he was tired of the Cape, of its sadness and pain. The house on Sears Point seemed haunted by Sarah. Everywhere there were reminders of her life: a spittle stain on the library carpet, a plastic rattle mixed in with the scissors, Scotch tape, and letter openers in the desk drawer, a collection of rubber-coated spoons and plastic-handled cups in the kitchen cupboard, photographs of her smiling face and blond curls on every tabletop.

And Bain was no doubt exhausted by Ferris's presence, too.

Ferris had arrived the day before Sarah's funeral with a suitcase large enough to indicate that he was not an overnight guest. After a few days, Grace realized that he intended to see the summer close from a well-situated chair on the Alcotts' terrace overlooking the harbor. As a freelance journalist, he had plenty of time and no particular need to stay sober. Horizons, the house on the bluff, was the perfect resting spot. "I'm in between stories at the moment," he explained. "But put me to use."

In between seemed to be the operative term for his life, but

Grace refused to dwell on that. That he was handsome and had plenty of female attention but never married, that he was intelligent but didn't focus on a career, these were his choices. Although she'd worried periodically about him ever since their mother's death, there wasn't much she could do, and she knew better than to offer advice. As a brother, he'd always been devoted, and his support at this extremely difficult time truly helped her fragile emotional state.

He listened patiently as she regaled him with stories of the smallest details of Sarah's short life: her discovery of a ladybug, the first time she'd rolled over, the pale pink color of her tiny toenails, the way she had sucked on Grace's finger as if it were a pacifier. He sat with her again and again turning the pages of the albums she'd made, talking about photograph after photograph. He understood she couldn't accept the abrupt end, the picture one day with none to follow. Ferris knew without her having to explain that these memories were all she had left. By his conduct, by his responses, he indicated that he knew that they were her last treasures.

And it was Ferris who helped her pack up Sarah's room and move the carefully labeled boxes of toys, clothes, bedding, and furniture outside to await the Goodwill van.

Sunday evening after Bain had left, Grace had decided to prepare dinner. She hadn't cooked since Sarah's death—not even to boil an egg—and experimenting on her brother seemed a safe option. At the last moment, she'd invited Prissy, too, to ensure that she wouldn't back out and order pizza. "Feel free to bring your husband," she'd offered.

"Thanks," Prissy had replied. "But he's not the dinner-party type."

"This is hardly a dinner party."

"Anything more than him and me sitting around in our underwear makes it formal to him. But I'll be there."

Now the three of them sat on the terrace. She'd set straw place mats on the glass table, arranged over-opened roses and greens for a centerpiece, and made a potato salad with plenty of chopped onion and egg. They'd given up on the grill—the air was moist, and the charcoal didn't want to light—and cooked the hamburgers in a frying pan instead. Ferris mixed a large striped pitcher of Southsides.

The sun was setting. The sky was bright pink.

Grace had no appetite. After pushing her food around with a fork, she abandoned even the idea of eating and leaned back in her chair to admire the view. Ferris, too, seemed disinterested in food, but he continued to drink liberally. Only Prissy enjoyed the meal.

They had been sitting in silence for several moments when Ferris asked abruptly, "So Grace tells me you're married, but that your husband is a bit of a mystery."

"Ferris," Grace reprimanded. He'd asked her about Prissy twice in the last several days, and she'd been candid in her responses, but she'd expected him to be discreet.

Prissy coughed once either to clear her throat or cover her surprise. "My mysterious husband, is that what he is?" She looked at Grace. "I just never wanted to bore you."

"Well, if that's the case, do tell," Ferris prompted. "I can't imagine he's a total bore. What's his name?"

"Oscar, but he likes to be called Kody."

"Kody? There. That's unusual right off the bat."

"It means 'helpful,' which he is. You know, the handy sort."

"That must be nice," Grace mumbled. She envisioned Bain on the telephone to a contractor, carpenter, plumber, electrician, or landscaper virtually every weekend. What would it be like if he could actually deal with the problem himself?

"I think you can tell a lot about a man by whether he

can fix things or, better yet, make them from scratch. A combination of artistic vision and actual craft, skill, that's what you want. To make a long story short, we've known each other forever and been through a lot of ups and downs. I can't say everything's perfect all the time but he's my old sofa that I can't part with. And if something breaks, well, I know where to turn."

Can the man fix a broken heart, too? Grace wondered. She closed her eyes, wanting to imagine that Sarah slept in her Moses basket beneath the table.

"How did you meet?"

Prissy smiled. "We're your all-American story. We lived next door to each other in Hull—you know, just up the coast north of Boston—and our parents were friends. Our families had these awful cookouts. Our mothers both got all dressed up as though they were being presented to the president instead of standing around in the weedy grass of the backyard, and our fathers bought huge cigars that would take them all evening to smoke. There wasn't much money so it was a lot of barbecue sauce to make the meat edible, and wine that came in a terra-cotta jug. Kody and I shared a mutual disdain for the event. But it was the catechism class that drove me into his arms. Who wouldn't rather have fun in the janitor's closet with your pants down than study the stations of the cross?"

Ferris laughed. He, too, had never been one for organized religion, and Grace wondered what trouble he'd gotten into during Sunday services at Trinity Church. At least until he'd moved out, Eleanor and William had required attendance.

"When Kody decided to drop out of high school at sixteen, he urged me to quit, too," Prissy continued. "We ran off in his pickup truck. We got to somewhere in Nebraska before the cops stopped us for a broken taillight, figured out we were runaways, and called our parents. We went back reluctantly. My mother called me a slut to my face and told me I'd disgraced her—now, there was a joke, although you'd have to know my mother to understand the irony—and shortly after our return we left again. The Cape was a perfect destination: white sand beaches and privacy miles away from our parents. We've been here ever since."

"What about your parents?"

"I guess they gave up. Kody went back when his father died, but I haven't seen any of them since the day we left."

Grace was shocked. She couldn't imagine any rift that would divide a family forever. "Do you miss them?"

Prissy paused, and took a sip of her drink. "Yes and no," she said after a while. "I miss the sense of family, of a broader community. But I was relieved not to have the expectations, the artificial pressure. I wanted my own life. My mother made choices about what she wanted, and so did my father. But I didn't share those dreams. I didn't want a forty-square-foot lot, a house with vinyl siding, three kids, and a Buick. I didn't want to spend my free time sitting on the porch with rollers in my hair trying to figure out what everyone else on the block was up to. So in that sense, leaving was liberating." Prissy turned to Grace, reached out, and rested a palm on her arm. "We should be focused on you. That's what we're here for, to help if we can. And here I am babbling. I'm sorry."

"No, not at all," Grace replied. "It's nice to hear."

The words came out wrong. The story of ne'er-do-well teenagers and a broken family could hardly be considered a fairy-tale romance, but she had to admit she'd been curious about Prissy's past ever since they'd met. Although on more than one occasion their conversation revolved around Bain, her references to Kody had been sporadic at best. Most of all, though, the distraction was welcome. Even if the discussion ignored the horrendous loss that had brought all three of them to this place at this moment, anything to keep her mind off her gaping wounds was therapeutic.

"So now I see why you and my sister are such dear friends," Ferris said, sitting back and folding his hands in his lap. "You both chose the familiar over the mysterious. No doubt a wise decision. What our parents would call prudent."

She wouldn't have thought that Bain, a well-educated, highly successful man, and Kody, the fisherman, were comparable selections, but she did understand his point. The relationships, the backgrounds, the values were comparable. Neither she nor Prissy had married someone completely different. However, she resented the implication that the choice had been cautious, or boring. It wasn't how Grace would characterize her life. Perhaps Ferris couldn't imagine anyone settling down, being content with a routine and a community, having life revolve around a spouse, but that was what she'd wanted and that's what Bain had delivered. Apparently Kody had, too.

Prissy stared at Ferris for what seemed like minutes. Her expression was difficult to read. Was she sizing him up, evaluating his remarks, or shocked by his rudeness? Finally she asked, "Well, then, what about you? Aside from being Grace's dear older brother, what's your story?"

"That's a rather provocative question."

Grace thought she saw Ferris wink.

"You don't have to answer. But since you appear to be such a master of the mysterious, I thought you might be able to teach me something—impart a life lesson or something of that sort."

Grace had the odd feeling that she'd landed in the middle of a conversation that had been under way for hours. She'd never seen Ferris like this—inquisitive, flirtatious—or Prissy, either. They seemed so familiar. Perhaps they'd had too much to drink.

"My story . . . dear Gracie, help me out here," Ferris said, jokingly. "Let's just say Grace is the good girl in the family. She found Bain and they've made this lovely home, made a lovely—" He paused, letting his sentence hang. Nobody wanted to finish the thought. "I on the other hand just managed to get through Harvard several years back, a feat I still wonder about, but it's been rather a downhill slide since then. I write for *National Geographic* when they'll have me, and I rely rather heavily on my father's largesse. So far he hasn't let me down, but you never know when the well will dry up."

Grace felt uncomfortable. Talking about money, or the lack of it, was a sign of poor breeding, and his candor embarrassed her.

"What about a wife? A girlfriend? Or do you limit yourself to brief affairs in exotic countries?" Prissy leaned forward. "Do tell. Who's the woman of your dreams?"

Ferris laughed. He reached for the pitcher and refilled his glass and hers. Grace wanted to excuse herself, but couldn't think of a diplomatic way to exit.

"They've come, they've gone," Ferris sang. "There was one girl from Miami who stole my heart for a moment, but I got it back eventually."

Grace remembered meeting Selena once at the Montgomerys' house. Her appearance was striking. Part Cuban, she had long black hair, black eyes, and wore a salmon-colored nail polish that matched her ruffled blouse. Her family was some sort of nobility, and they'd moved to the United States when Castro came to power. Grace had admired her tremendous confidence as she spoke openly with William about politics. But after that evening, she'd never seen the woman again, and hadn't realized Ferris was so smitten.

"At the moment, you might say I'm in between passions."

"Ah . . . the gentler sex had better watch out."

Grace passed the potato salad to Prissy, who helped herself to a second generous serving.

They sat in silence as Prissy ate. Grace was about to get up to clear the plates when Ferris asked, "Does your Kody work?"

Prissy laughed, as if the question was unusual. "He's part owner of a commercial fishing boat, and his crew goes out to the shoals or Georges Bank. But often the destination is much farther—the Grand Banks off Newfoundland or even the Flemish Cap. He used to be gone for long spells at a time." She crossed her arms in front of her chest. "We're pretty used to living separate lives."

"What's the catch? Of his crew, I mean."

"This year it's been mainly swordfish, but he was into tuna for years before that."

"Hard duty," Ferris mumbled.

Grace couldn't imagine her brother stuck on a boat with a crew of other fishermen for weeks on end. He didn't have the emotional makeup or the physical tolerance. Bain didn't, either. Did that make them weaker or just different? Could Kody have begun to get through a day at the bank?

"I've suggested he start a contracting business," Prissy said, sighing. "More and more houses are being built around here, and there seems to be loads of money for new construction. Since he doesn't go out on the boat anymore, it would get him out of the house. Believe me, housebound with me is no treat. What's that joke? 'In sickness or in health but not for lunch.' It's just, well . . . we're kind of independent."

Separate lives.

"Why doesn't he go out on the boat? What made him stop?"

Prissy looked out at the ocean beyond them. She appeared to think for a moment before responding. "He's making a living without the hard physical labor. That's better for him at this stage."

Ferris raised his glass. "Cheers, then."

"To what?" Grace asked.

"Independence."

Prissy laughed again and raised her glass. When Grace didn't move, she added, "Come on, it's not a four-letter word."

"I want to toast to Sarah's memory, instead." Grace covered her mouth with her hand to try to hide the quiver in her lips. She couldn't bear to cry yet again. It had been less than two hours since she'd broken down in the kitchen. But that time, she had the chopped onions to blame.

"To Sarah, yes," Ferris said quickly. "To her memory, to her sweetness—"

"And to her amazing mother," Prissy interrupted.

"May her soul rest in peace," he concluded.

That the reference was ambiguous nobody questioned.

Part Two

Chapter Nine

T he passage of time had been kind to Grace. She could be thankful for that. Unlike with many of her friends, the decade barely showed in her face, and two more pregnancies had hardly altered the contour of her flat stomach.

Her first son had followed more quickly than most would have expected. Erin was born shortly before the anniversary of Sarah's death. Although at times the stares at her pregnant belly had felt oppressive — she could almost hear her friends gossiping that it was "too soon" — she'd wanted a family, had felt a desperate need to fill a void, and pursued it with an intensity that even Bain questioned, begging him to make love to her night after night at the right time in her cycle. She'd needed to prove something to herself, even if she couldn't articulate precisely what that was, and for once she didn't care about how it made her look. Although he'd talked about recovering, surviving the tragedy, and taking the necessary time to grieve, he'd complied with her wishes.

And she would never forget the expression of utter joy on his face when the nurse at Cape Cod Hospital held out the bundle in a blue knit cap.

"Congratulations. You have a beautiful baby boy."

Bain must have told her he loved her a hundred times that night. She'd done something right, something perfect. She'd given him a healthy child, his first son.

Grace insisted that Prissy be the godmother. She decided that even if Bain resisted, she'd stay firm. This mattered to her. Prissy had seen her through the loss of Sarah, and, more importantly, she'd kept her secrets: her confessions as they'd sat together that summer of the difficulties and frustrations of motherhood. That Prissy never reminded her of that—and never even remotely suggested that she was an unworthy or unfit parent— made her eternally grateful.

"Is she even religious?" Bain asked.

"I don't know exactly. But what real difference does it make? How much religious instruction did you receive from your godparents?"

"Mine?" Bain laughed. "I viewed Roger and Lauren Buttonworth as suppliers of gifts—primarily Christmas— and sources of cash on birthdays and Easter. Lauren did manage to find an enclosure card with a religious theme, a cross or some passage from the Bible quoted on the front. But that was the extent of the religious references."

"And you turned out all right." Grace smiled.

"I don't think the Buttonworths should be the model. The whole point is to find someone to promote the child's spiritual development."

"She has tremendous respect for nature, is in awe of its beauty, and believes in a creative force," Grace recited. She'd thought through this conversation in advance.

"Great. That and a membership in Greenpeace and we're all set to raise our son."

"Prissy is not a radical." Grace's forcefulness surprised even herself. "She's a dear person with good values and strong morals. I trust her completely."

What Grace would never articulate to Bain was that Prissy had taught her what little she knew of independence. If the woman imparted that and nothing else, she'd play an invaluable role in her son's life.

"All right, then," Bain said, acquiescing with a shrug. "That's who it will be. Just loan her something to wear for the service. Our guests will have heart failure if she shows up in tie-dye or one of her clamming hats."

∽৯৯

That evening, Grace went down to the beach with Erin Montgomery Alcott bundled in a striped cotton blanket. She held him tight against her chest and hunched her shoulders, protecting him from the cool wind.

Prissy looked up and smiled as they approached. Dropping her rake, she walked to where they stood at the waterline and admired Erin's round face, pink skin, small hands, and large eyes.

"He's beautiful," she said. "Absolutely perfect. Fine work, Mrs. Alcott."

Grace could tell from her tone that she meant it.

"Would you be his godmother?" she blurted out. She'd meant to ease into the discussion, but she'd been too excited to worry about timing. "It would mean so much to me."

Prissy's eyes widened. "I . . . I don't know what to say. I'm flattered, but you know I don't go to church. I can't believe Bain would approve."

"We don't care. And he already has."

The water lapped up onto the sand, covering their feet. It was colder than Grace expected, and she hopped from foot to foot.

"Then I'd be honored." Prissy rubbed the tops of Erin's fingers as they clutched his cotton blanket. "Your parents may not know what they're getting you into, but we'll celebrate all the same," she cooed.

Grace felt relief. "I'll let you know as soon as we get the church service planned."

"What?"

"Oh, it's not a big deal. Baptisms are usually part of the regular Sunday service, and then we'll have a lunch or something casual afterward."

"Are you crazy?" She spun around with her arms extended. "Look where we are! Look at this ocean. Look at this spot. If this natural beauty isn't a sign of God, then nothing is. You've got the purest, best water in the whole world right here, and much more of it than you need to do the job. What's a routine service and a bunch of folks stuffed into pews and waiting for it to be over going to add?"

"But—but—" Grace looked down at the bundle in her arms. Erin had fallen asleep. She needed to protect him. She wasn't sure what she believed about original sin, but if he had it, she wanted to cleanse him of it. Could something homemade do that?

"Come on, you say the words—whatever it is you want to hear, whatever prayers, whatever magic, make something up—and we'll christen him in Stage Harbor. With that auspicious beginning, he'll grow up to be the loveliest man the world has ever known."

Was that true? Grace wanted to believe Prissy; wanted to be inspired, too. Her excitement was infectious.

"I'm sure John the Baptist would approve."

Grace waded out into the water. It was cold and clear, and she could see a horseshoe crab crawling along the bottom. A few more steps and she felt dampness on her shorts. She turned back toward shore as Prissy bounded in behind her, splashing water and singing "Amazing Grace."

They could have a proper baptism for Bain's peace of mind later. Maybe even get someone from his office to be the godparent for that one, someone in the proper suit and lace-up shoes. If he wanted, she'd make watercress and salmon sandwiches. Friends could bring silver teething rings in Tiffany boxes and stand around admiring the sleeping baby.

But this was the moment that truly mattered. She squeezed Erin tighter. In the salty Atlantic water, they could all seek repentance and renewal. She was ready.

❧

Hank was born three years after that.

She'd been right. Starting over was what they'd needed.

Until both boys were strong swimmers, nobody except for her gave them a bath, or took them to the beach, or even filled a bucket to bob for apples. She'd almost harbored a reluctance to let them play outside after a rain if the puddles were more than a quarter inch deep.

But her diligence paid off. Erin and Hank passed safely through their infancy and toddler years, and into childhood. Grace actually looked forward to their adolescence. Perhaps then—when they were nearly grown—the worries would subside. Perhaps she would finally be relieved of the burden of waking up in the night to make sure that they were still breathing.

The family settled into an apartment on Beacon Hill with a balcony off the living room, a partially obstructed view of the Charles River, and a much-coveted parking space at the Brimmer Street garage. As the boys grew up and had longer school days at the Advent School, Grace turned her attention elsewhere. Primarily, her focus returned to her home on the Cape. Not to say it had fallen into disrepair. But she'd had projects and ideas in her mind that she'd simply lacked the time to execute. And one of them was to install a rose garden, a traditional English design that would forever transform the

Chatham house. She would build it as a living tribute to Sarah.

The idea started with books: dozens of picture books on specimens and varieties, followed by more technical volumes. But self-teaching wasn't her strength, and she'd decided to return to Radcliffe to finish her degree. A year later with a number of landscape design credits earned but still shy of a diploma, she dropped out of school for the second time and began to execute her vision. She'd mapped out the paths and beds for a twenty-by-thirty-foot garden. She'd interviewed masons from all over New England and finally found the perfect Scottish gentleman from Jamestown, Rhode Island, who could build the stone walls and lay the brick walks. It had taken him several months—and several cost overruns—to finish the work, but the result was exquisite. She'd left the installation of the right mixture of floribundas, David Austins, and hybrid teas for herself. By working in the soil, planting, feeding, and fertilizing, she'd create a beautiful garden worthy of symbolizing her daughter.

After the children's academic year ended in June 1987, Grace brought the boys to Chatham for ten glorious weeks of vacation. By that summer, Erin was old enough to ride his bike to the yacht club, and he spent most of each day there, practicing his knot work, cleaning the boats, and racing his Sunfish. She loved the collection of freckles that appeared around the bridge of his nose and the blond streaks that the sunshine brought to his hair. He was happy surrounded by his friends and well adjusted according to the club staff, the gentle, good-natured sort of boy who painted flowerpots as Mother's Day gifts or brought pieces of sea glass up to the house to leave on the windowsill in the kitchen. Erin was her living proof that she could be a good mother. If only he could sail with a banner attached to his boat. She wanted everyone to know.

That summer, Bain had convinced her to hire a mother's helper, a college girl who could make meals for the children, run errands, and babysit. Neither of them wanted to admit that their social life had suffered, but there was no doubt that it had. Because Grace was often too reluctant to leave the boys, many invitations had been declined. For others, elaborate ruses of sudden stomach viruses or too much sun had been devised at the last moment. If their friends were to piece together all the illnesses, they might conclude that the house on Sears Point was plagued.

"You've hardly seen anyone but Prissy. Just get some help so we can start to live normally," Bain insisted.

Rachel, the strawberry-blond nineteen-year-old, arrived with a small duffel bag and a guitar. She'd completed her freshman year at Leslie College, where she was studying to be an elementary schoolteacher, and her parents had a home in Barnstable, only five exits west on the Mid-Cape Highway. On her day off, she could go home. After two weeks, she'd learned the routine, and the boys seemed to like her. Or so Grace thought.

She'd left the hatchback of the station wagon open so that the tubs of roses she'd squeezed in the back wouldn't overheat. It had been a long day of exploring nurseries and garden centers in search of specific varieties, and she couldn't begin to unload the car before she'd used the bathroom. Public restrooms harbored too many germs to fathom, but five hours on the road left her nothing short of desperate. She threw open the screen door and hurried inside.

From the toilet in the small powder room off the kitchen she could see outside. There was a soccer ball on the lawn, and Rachel and Hank were engaged in some conversation. Hank was sweaty, red-faced, and dirty-kneed. Rachel stood a few feet away from him with her

arms dangling by her sides and her shoulders slouched. As
Grace opened the window to try to overhear their interchange, she saw Hank make a fist with his pudgy hand,
run toward Rachel, swing, and sock her in the stomach.
The girl took a step away and covered her midsection with
her arms.

"I don't need to listen to you," Hank screamed, his face
reddening even more. "I pay you. Remember? You're just
my em-ploy-ee." He strung out the word. "You have to do
what I say. My father knows how to handle you if you
don't."

Rachel burst into tears and covered her face with her
hands.

"Hank!" Grace called in alarm through the window.

Hank turned toward the sound of her voice. A look of
surprise crossed his face.

"Don't ever use that language or that tone of voice."
She pulled up her pants, flushed, and hurried outside.

By the time she got there, Hank was dribbling the ball.
Rachel was still standing precisely where Grace had last
seen her.

"Hank, I want you to come back here and apologize
right now."

"Why?" he asked without stopping his game.

"Because you were rude and unkind."

"It's only Rachel." With that, he kicked the ball, and it
disappeared over the knoll in the lawn. Hank broke into a
run after it.

"Hank! Hank!" Grace called, but she knew it was useless. Turning to Rachel, she held out her arms, offering an
embrace. Rachel didn't move. "I apologize. I don't know
what's gotten into him. I hope you'll forgive him."

Rachel didn't speak for a moment but rubbed her nose.
"Yeah, yeah sure," she said finally in a voice utterly
lacking in conviction.

Grace felt her heart begin to race. *Please don't leave because of this,* she wanted to plead. "Why don't you take the rest of the day off?" she offered instead. "I hate to see you upset. You could go home if you like and come back on Friday. And when you come back, perhaps we should discuss a raise. I know this work is difficult." She hoped her generosity might soothe the poor girl's injured feelings but even as she spoke, she knew what would happen.

So it was no great surprise when Grace noticed that Rachel's duffel bag and guitar were gone, too.

❧

"What would you do if you were me?" she asked Prissy.

Her friend had stopped by the house to drop off a basket of Wellfleet oysters, and the two women stood together at the sink washing the sand out of the shells and shucking them.

"I'm the wrong person to give advice."

"Please, you've spent time with Hank. You know him."

"I know both boys, sure, but not like you. You're the mother. You've got to decide what's best."

Grace glanced over at Prissy, who remained focused on the task at hand. "I don't know what's best, that's the problem. I still can't believe he acts the way he does." Here she was again, confessing to her dear friend how she'd failed basic parenting. She hadn't been able to raise a boy with manners. She hadn't managed to teach him about respect. "How do I talk to him? Should I discipline him?"

"Oh please, Grace, kids don't get sent to bed without supper anymore. That's a cruel throwback to *our* childhood."

"But I don't want him to be a spoiled child. You've got to help me!" Grace begged. "I can't believe I'm doing a terrible job again."

Prissy turned off the running water and pulled the rubber gloves off her hands. "I can't tell you what to do, that's the point. I can't begin to be a mother. Raising a child is the hardest thing in the world. In some ways, how the person turns out is completely dependent on you, the values you impart, the experiences you give, and in other ways it's completely beyond your control. It's genetics. There's nothing you can do. I'm not saying anything new—it's the old nature-versus-nurture debate—and I'm certainly not telling you anything you don't know. But my point is that you're trying. And you're doing the best you can. You'll figure this one out like you've figured out the rest. You've got tremendous courage, Grace. Don't sell yourself short."

"I don't know how to change him."

"Maybe you can't. But he's got a father. Why don't you get Bain's input? Maybe it's time your husband actually got involved in child raising."

Her suggestion sounded accusatory, which Grace supposed was the design, and she felt instantly defensive. Bain was a committed father. He worked hard to provide for all of them, and he stepped in when there was a serious problem. But he expected her to smoothly manage the day-to-day issues, and she'd accepted her role without question. It was the normal division of labor between man and wife.

Now she didn't know how to respond.

"He wanted these kids as much as you did. Let him help with some of the tough calls, the times when it's not so fun to be a parent. You can't do everything alone, and, frankly, you shouldn't have to. Being your husband's wife and being the mother of two boys are two very different roles." Prissy smiled.

Once again Prissy was right. Although Grace welcomed her position as Bain's wife—it was as comfortable to her as her own skin—navigating the uncharted waters of raising children together still seemed foreign.

She wished that Prissy could speak to Bain. She had a way of focusing issues. Where Grace waffled, struggling with words and concepts, being inarticulate and deferential, Prissy had strong views and had an even stronger ability to communicate them. She would challenge Bain to pay attention and to act.

But it would never happen. Bain largely avoided Prissy and would never tolerate a lecture from her on his conduct. This reality washed over her, leaving sadness in its wake.

Why was it that Prissy saw so clearly what Bain did not—that their sons needed an actively engaged father, not just a financial provider? Had she been more honest, more candid about herself and her family with her friend than she was able to be with her own husband? That had never been her conscious intent. The marital bond was supposed to be the very strongest, the steel belt of love, respect, and shared secrets. Nothing and nobody else was supposed to compromise that. So what had happened to them?

❧

She didn't have the courage to tell Bain about Rachel's departure over the telephone. It was too complex a conversation. She feared Bain would blame her for Hank's failings, or for inadequate supervision. Something. His rudeness was no doubt her fault.

But Friday night arrived. It was cool for July, and Bain lit a fire in the library. The family supper had ended without incident. Hank and Erin scampered off to watch television, leaving their parents to after-dinner drinks and conversation.

Bain seemed relaxed as he sipped a cognac and smoked on a thin cigar.

Grace took a deep breath, trying to think how to explain. She wished he would sense her apprehension and ask what the problem was. But that wasn't Bain's way. In fact, she wasn't sure he'd even noticed that Rachel was gone.

"Hank was very rude to Rachel," Grace finally said. "Beyond rude. He hit her. She may be working for us, but he has to learn that he can't treat people that way."

Bain raised one eyebrow.

"He told her to listen to him because he was paying her a salary or words to that effect. I was so upset by that time—I'd already seen him punch her for no reason—that I . . . I . . . I'm not sure I even remember the details. But the point is, Bain, we have a problem, a serious problem, if our nine-year-old has that sort of attitude."

"It was one incident."

"No, Bain. Not one." She closed her eyes. "You don't hear the harsh tones, the dictatorial commands he uses. 'Get me my tennis racket.' 'You clean up.' 'You're stupid,'" she imitated. Instructions to be polite, requests for *please* and *thank you* fell on deaf ears. And Hank was only nine. She hated to think what kind of a man he'd grow to be. "He's not a baby anymore. He certainly should know what's acceptable and what is not by this age."

The air in the library was suffused with cigar smoke. The fire crackled. She stared at her husband. His bemused expression revealed not the slightest hint of concern. Why wasn't he willing to agree with her? She'd fantasized that they would stay up late into the night talking through possible solutions and devising ways to correct what was obviously going wrong. They could be supportive of each other and collaborate as parents. But instead, he wanted to ignore it.

"Rachel was in tears. I don't expect she'll come back."

"Well, perhaps you should have found someone with a slightly thicker skin to begin with," he replied without a moment's hesitation. "My guess is that hormonal girls aren't the best babysitters."

"Bain, I hardly think that hormones—"

"Oh, Grace, relax," he interrupted. "You act as though we're raising a monster. Hank's a normal nine-year-old boy. I'm not saying he should hit—of course not—but you can't get around the reality that boys are physical. They're aggressive. It's going to happen. But he'll outgrow it. As for his comments—" Bain chuckled momentarily. "Frankly, it may not be the worst thing in the world that he knows his place in life. And hers."

She gazed down at the grain of the wood on the wide-pine floors, and then studied the neat pile of the woven rug. She wanted the patterns to distract her, anything to avoid facing what this conversation revealed: that Hank's attitude wasn't such an anomaly; that his behavior was learned; and that his tutor was closer to home than she would have wished. Which meant that if changes were to be made in the way her children were raised, she was going to have to do it alone.

But what if, as Prissy had said, it was genetics, a hard-wired sense of entitlement and arrogance? Did that mean that there was nothing she could say or do that would make any difference? Then why struggle to raise a family, to impart values and morals? After birth, children could be let wild, and they would turn out exactly the same. For a moment, she imagined Hank and Erin running through the cedar swamp in loincloths instead of corduroys, shredding small animals for food, the Tarzans of Cape Cod.

She wasn't willing to accept that reality, at least not yet. They would grow up to be Alcotts—good, decent, hard-working men like their father—if it was the very last thing she did. Raising the next generation was what she was supposed to do.

1993

Chapter Ten

A quarter century, my darling. And you look as lovely as the first time I laid eyes on you. Happy anniversary," Bain whispered as he handed her a flute of champagne and then stepped past her into the living room.

She took a sip. From where she stood in the library, she could watch Bain. He moved smoothly with the air of confidence that came from financial and personal success, shaking hands, offering a joke or a liquid refill, and back-slapping his way through the crowd of gatherers.

The whole thing had been a mistake.

"Great place," a heavyset man said.

He raised his tumbler in her direction. Dark hairs wrapped around the gold ring on his finger, and his black briefs showed through his white trousers. She had no idea who he was.

"We're fond of it," she replied with a smile, trying to make conversation. "It's been our home now for quite some time."

"I wish me and my wife had been smart enough to buy into Cape real estate back in the seventies. You sure could get something for just about nothing. But then again, that wife isn't my wife anymore so I probably would have lost it anyway. Divorce will kill you if something doesn't get you first." He laughed. "Anyways, it's a great party.

Thanks for the invite," he added, moving on into the crowd.

She never wanted so public a celebration of their anniversary. She'd pictured a small dinner, close friends, the children, a simple meal at a table set under the scrubby pines on the bluff, but as soon as she'd raised the issue of a party, Bain had seized on the opportunity to make it a business affair, a way to entertain potential clients for his new endeavor, Alcott Savings & Loan. "You should be thrilled. You can hire the best caterer and serve the finest champagne. It'll all be tax-deductible."

Maybe. But she didn't want such flash. It didn't feel right. In fact, his career change hadn't felt right. Much to her disappointment, he'd left the Bank of Boston, abandoning the slow but steady corporate climb with health benefits and retirement contributions for the promise of a financial windfall. That she liked the security and stability of his position as vice president wasn't relevant. He was on a mission. "There's real money to be made out there."

"We're comfortable now," she'd said, even as she knew that neither her words nor her feelings had an impact on his career.

"And we'll be more comfortable later. I'd like to retire while I'm young enough to still enjoy it—but I won't do that on a salary with an incremental annual raise and a measly year-end bonus."

So there it was. And one of the immediate ramifications was that on this special day, many acquaintances and even more total strangers mixed with a few of her Chatham friends. People spilled out onto the patio and across the lawn. Bain had sent most of the invitations, letting his secretary address them. Although he referred to his guests as "money people," judging by the rapid rate of consumption this evening, none of them had eaten in weeks. The overweight men held soggy cigars between their thick fingers while they stuffed down mushroom caps and shrimp cocktail and oysters. Their young-enough-to-make-a-statement wives, one of whom stuck her wad of chewing gum under the ledge of the bookcase in the library, mainlined white wine.

Grace checked herself in the mirror. She wore a chartreuse gauze blouse and white pants, matching flats, and a scarf tied around her loose ponytail. The outfit seemed off—too collegiate, too young. No one would ever accuse her of looking old, but tonight she felt that way.

Forty-seven. She quickly did the math. She'd passed midlife long before, unless she planned to make it to ninety-four.

By the bar at the entrance to the living room, Hank and two of his friends stood in silence. Hank had so far managed to avoid the awkwardness of teenage years. He was lean but not gawky, and his complexion remained free of the horrid acne that smothered the faces of several of his friends. Grace had persuaded him to change his clothes; he now looked every bit the respectable Chatham youth in a clean pin-striped buttondown and khaki trousers. Compared with his friends, who hadn't bothered to shed their black T-shirts with unrecognizable rock bands on the front and tour dates on the back, he made her proud.

The light from the bay window reflected off the green glass beer bottles they held in their hands. Underage drinking caused some alarm, but there was plenty of room for all the boys to sleep over—and sleep off the alcohol before their parents could notice. She didn't want to be the killjoy.

Hank tilted the bottle back, took a long swig, wiped the foam with the back of his hand, and burped. His companions laughed.

She turned away. Why on earth had she ever agreed to this party?

"Would you care for one of these, Mrs. Alcott?"

The voice surprised her. A waiter in black pants and a black T-shirt smiled a flash of white teeth and offered a platter of shrimp cocktail.

"No. No thank you," Grace replied as she stared down at the mound of peeled pink bodies and orange shell tails. Freshly grated horseradish garnished the well of red cocktail sauce in the middle of the arrangement.

"They're going fast," the young man said.

"Everything seems to be," she murmured.

The waiter didn't move. She looked up. He seemed frozen with his platter extended. Was something the matter?

"I'm Jesse," he said after a moment more. His voice hummed. Then he leaned toward her. "Hey, congratulations. I hear this is twenty-five years. Your husband's a lucky man. He's got the hands-down best-looking woman here." He nodded to emphasize his point.

"You're very kind," she said, hoping he wouldn't notice her blush.

Although he wasn't what she considered her type, she couldn't deny she found him attractive, in a tawdry sort of way. He had prominent features that seemed exotic, or at least ethnic, and dark hair that he'd slicked back with a scented gel. The T-shirt outlined his well-developed pectoral muscles.

"Just observant." He made a clicking sound with his tongue.

She stared at his mouth for what she knew was an inappropriate length of time, but she couldn't turn away from his full lips and strong jaw. Who was this person? Then she remembered. "Whatever do we pay you to say such outrageous things? No doubt not enough," she said, sounding more flirtatious than she'd intended. "You'd best be getting back to work, hadn't you?"

"Whatever you want. You're in charge." He winked as he forged his way into the living room, balancing the platter on his right hand.

This unexpected exchange made Grace feel dizzy, and she leaned against the wall for balance. The boy was half her age. And this was her anniversary. But she was still sorry that he was going about his job, passing and refilling platters. She would have preferred his company to whomever else she was likely to find this evening.

She rested her flute on the windowsill. More champagne was out of the question. Her thoughts were already running amok.

Through the window Grace could see Erin in the rose garden holding hands with Marley, his "friend," as he called her because he claimed that *girlfriend* sounded derogatory. Erin was the more handsome of her two sons; he'd inherited Bain's square shoulders, long torso, and natural grace. She wished he'd trimmed his hair for the occasion; his wavy locks almost reached his shoulders. But at least he'd made the effort to come.

What had been the great surprise, though, was that he'd arrived with Marley, a freshman from the University of Vermont with a freckled nose and long strawberry-blond hair. This evening she wore a white tank top that didn't properly obscure her dark nipples, along with a flowing batik skirt. Grace observed the gaze of several men linger as Marley strolled through the party. In fact, several women stared, too, though no doubt for different reasons. Eleanor would have called her a "free spirit." Grace wasn't inclined to be so generous.

Erin now leaned toward Marley and licked her ear. She giggled and pressed her body into his. Although they were alone at the moment, the conduct still seemed too intimate, too sexual for something out of doors. Marley then licked him back, and Grace thought she spotted a flash of silver on her tongue.

That was quite enough.

She stepped outside, purposely interrupting the romantic interlude, although neither of them seemed the least bit embarrassed.

"You're good to come home, Erin," Grace said, extending a hand. "It wouldn't be the same without you." And then, so as not to exclude Marley, she added, "And you were very kind to accompany him."

Marley giggled. It was an odd sound, rather like hic-cups.

"Well, Dad sure has a strange way of making us feel welcome," Erin responded. "In case you weren't aware, he's been totally unreasonable about the sleeping arrange-ments. He wants Marley in the downstairs guest room. That's bullshit."

"Please don't use that language."

"Marley and I sleep together at school virtually every night. Why should we pretend the situation is different here?"

Grace looked at Erin's stern expression and then glanced at Marley, who smiled and giggled, again. Finding the whole situation stressful, Grace had missed whatever it was about Erin's conversation that was amusing.

"Please, let's leave it alone." There wasn't any point revisiting what had been an already dreadful exchange between Bain and Erin earlier in the day. Bain had a temper and harbored no reluctance to let it show, espe-cially with the boys. But Erin was gentle by nature. His elevated tone of voice and steadfast determination had shocked her. She'd broken up the argument by pleading with everyone to get ready for the party. Bain seemed to have forgotten about the unpleasantness, but apparently the same could not be said for Erin.

"You know how your father is," she said. "Formalities matter. They matter to us both. We know we can't control what you do when you're not here, but this is our home."

"It's my home, too."

"I'm sure Marley's parents would feel the same way," she said, ignoring his remark.

"Actually, they don't."

Why hadn't she anticipated that response? She felt increasingly annoyed at this strange girl and now at her family, too. Perhaps they were all lovely people and she was being horribly judgmental, but, then again, Marley's mother had made no effort to teach her daughter about appropriate dress or, apparently, social proprieties. She hoped Erin's fascination would be short-lived.

"Buzz and Mom are crazy about Erin," Marley offered.

"Excuse me?"

"Buzz is her dad," Erin explained.

Buzz. What happened to *Daddy* or *Dad* or *Father* or even *Papa*? More to the point, when had Erin *met* her parents? Even during summer school, didn't he require permission to leave campus? *Focus*, she said to herself. *Focus on the issue at hand.* Her eighteen-year-old son and his girlfriend wanted to share a bed—and presumably have sex together—in her house.

That was out of the question. This overpierced, moralless girl and her family might corrupt her son in Vermont, but not here in Chatham. Whatever in God's name it was that the stud in her tongue was designed to achieve would have to await the drive back north.

"I'm sorry. Your father said no; that has to be the final word. Please try to understand. And help us celebrate this day instead of being angry." She forced a smile, hoping he would return it.

Erin was grinding his teeth.

"Erin," she coaxed. "It's only one night." She debated

stating the obvious—that Erin could sneak down the back staircase to norgle with this floozy once Bain had retired—but even she couldn't bring herself to utter the suggestion aloud. Why did he insist that their overnight bags go in the same bedroom?

"It's hypocritical," he said. His tone was flat. "You just refuse to stand up to Dad and his old-fashioned morality. You've always taken the path of least resistance and hidden behind him."

"I beg your pardon."

"You didn't hear me? Should I repeat myself?" Erin barked.

"No . . . I . . . That's not true," she stammered in her confusion. She waited for Marley to giggle but no sound came. The girl appeared to grapple with some sort of itch inside her nostril.

"Of course it is, and you know it. If this were your house—on your own without Dad's judgment or temper—you wouldn't give a shit. Just because you've been chained to him the last twenty-five years shouldn't change that."

The words stung. "Don't swear in my presence," she said again because she couldn't think of a proper retort. Her head was spinning. "You're being very rude." She struggled to hold back tears.

"I thought more of you, Mom. I really did," he said as he took Marley's arm and headed inside.

Grace's hands trembled. She wished she hadn't left her champagne flute on the windowsill after all. She needed something to calm her frayed nerves. She closed her eyes and took a deep breath, hoping a moment of peace could rejuvenate her spirits. But all she could imagine was the dark-haired, full-lipped waiter leaning toward her with his platter of shrimp.

She opened her eyes and strolled through the rose

garden, her labor of love. All but two bushes were in full bloom; the remaining had buds waiting to open, and the bushes abounded with an array of pink, red, peach, coral, yellow, and white. Their simple, timeless beauty was what she loved most. That was why she'd chosen them as Sarah's memorial flower. Roses had been cultivated and adored for centuries and would outlast them all.

More than anything in the world, she wished Sarah were here now to share this day, as well as each of the ones that had preceded it, and every single day that lay ahead. Her daughter wouldn't have sworn at her or accused her of being weak. Her daughter wouldn't have insulted her at her own anniversary celebration. Sarah would have had the grace and dignity to make a toast in honor of her parents.

She walked to the opposite end of the path to where her favorite rose was planted. She reached out to touch the beautiful blooms and buds. The creamy white petals of 'Honor' were soft, and she pulled one from its flower to roll between her fingers. *A quarter of a century of marriage.* It was hard to believe that she'd been Mrs. Alcott for more years than she'd been Grace Montgomery.

How did she feel? It was a question she rarely allowed herself to ask because there was little if anything to be done with the answer. What had she expected? Her husband was a good provider, faithful and decent; her sons were healthy; her home was beautiful; she had friends, interests, plenty to keep her busy. That was a full life, wasn't it? It was more than enough to make most ordinary women happy, and there was certainly nothing about Grace Alcott that made her extraordinary. So there was her answer.

Then why was she spending her anniversary consumed by the thought of a twenty-five-year-old waiter making ten dollars an hour to feed her guests? All this ruminating had to stop. She'd never be able to eat—or even look at—a shrimp again.

"Grace." She heard a voice behind her.

Startled, she turned to see Prissy. Her golden tan accentuated the wrinkles on her forehead and around her eyes, but otherwise she looked as lovely as ever.

Prissy raised her bottle of Heineken. "Cheers. I'm incredibly proud of you for making it this far," she said with a smile. "Let's just say I never could have."

"You've made it longer."

"But not in the way you have," she answered mysteriously.

"I'm thinking maybe I should consider your way."

Prissy laughed but said nothing.

Then Grace added, "I didn't think you'd come."

"We go back a long way. And good friends are hard to come by." She took a sip of her beer. Then, seeing that Grace's hands were empty, she offered her the bottle.

Grace raised it to her lips. The alcohol tasted bitter.

"What are you doing out here alone?" Prissy asked. "Didn't you notice, the party's in there?"

Grace didn't reply.

"I can hardly blame you. Cocktail parties and I are not a match made in heaven. In fact, if you won't be offended, I'm going to be going. I really just came to give you a hug and offer congratulations."

"Tonight I could use condolences."

"It's all relative."

They both laughed. The familiarity felt comforting.

Prissy smiled, stepped forward, and wrapped her strong arms around Grace. Standing in the rose garden with her old friend, Grace began to cry. Prissy's presence, her gesture, her kindness were all too emotional. She wasn't exactly sure why she wept: for Sarah, for the memorial service when Prissy had done the same thing, for the times they'd shared, for the years that had passed, for Erin and Hank and Marley and the boys in rock-band T-shirts, for her disappointment, for the house that was now full of Money People she didn't know and hoped she'd never see again, for the party she hated, and for the fact that all the hors d'oeuvres and liquor in the world couldn't make it palatable.

"Please don't leave me here," she mumbled. Her words were muffled by Prissy's shoulder.

"What?" Prissy stepped back. Noticing Grace's teary eyes, she grabbed hold of her arms and shook her slightly. "What's going on?"

"I just . . . it's not . . . I can't." She didn't know how to reply and struggled to pull herself together.

"I'm not going anywhere." Prissy's smile seemed to illuminate the darkening sky.

Grace sighed with relief. "Let's go to the beach," she said in a conspiratorial tone. "Let's get away from this dreadful event."

"The beach? Now? Won't Bain be furious if you leave?"

"Maybe. But my guess is that he may not notice. He's doing what's known in the industry as business development, and for that he doesn't need me. His attention is on his corporate guests. I'm not even sure he's said hello to most of our friends. The caterer has everything running quite smoothly as far as I can tell. And I need a swim." She smiled, pleased with the prospect. "Make that a skinny-dip. I almost had a moment of overheating."

Prissy looked skeptical. "With these people? Do tell how you managed that?"

"I'll tell you at the beach."

"You can't skinny-dip now."

"If we walk down past the town landing, no one can see us from the patio," Grace replied, feeling animated at the prospect.

Prissy laughed. "You're crazier than I thought."

"Oh, please, if someone at this party needs to gape at a naked, forty-seven-year-old body that has produced three babies and has the varicose veins to show for it, they can be my guest."

"Look, you don't have to convince me. I'll never see any of them again," Prissy replied. "That is, except for you . . . and maybe Bain if he lets me in the driveway after this escapade."

"Yes. The Big Maybe." They both laughed again. "Don't forget to grab Ferris on your exit. He must be beside himself with boredom by now. Speaking of which, I haven't even seen him. Perhaps he's lost in the savings-and-loan morass."

"Close. Try passed out on the chaise in your guest room."

Grace blushed. Ferris's alcohol consumption, especially in public, was an embarrassment. She needed to speak to him, but it would have to wait for another time. No doubt it would take him the rest of the night to sleep off whatever he'd consumed. "Let's go," she said, wanting to forget. "I'll leave through the back door. We can meet at the dock in a few minutes." Grace's growing excitement was displacing the sorrow of moments before. She wanted to sit with her friend and talk and laugh, swim in the cool salt water, watch the darkness fall and stare at the stars, leave Bain to deal with the drunken teenagers and the sleeping arrangements. "I'm beginning to think that who-ever said it's important to live life with no regrets, never truly lived," she said as she disappeared around the side of the garden.

❦

Only a few cars and a pickup truck remained in the driveway when Grace wandered up from the beach with a towel wrapped around her. She carried her clothes in a bundle, a now empty bottle of champagne that she'd taken with her when she left, and two crumpled paper cups. Sand clung to her feet and water dripped from her hair.

The lights glowed in the house, and she realized once again how beautiful it was, the simple architectural lines, the weathered shingles, the well-proportioned rooms. For all the time they spent in Boston, this place was home.

Inside, she could see silhouettes moving about; a few remaining employees of the caterer were wiping counters, gathering rumpled napkins, and attending to the last details before departing. She could hear voices wafting across the lawn. Her favorite waiter came out the kitchen door carrying several racks of rented glasses, but she looked away. She'd behaved badly enough already.

Alone, Bain smoked a cigar on the patio. A cognac glass rested on the table in front of him, but he didn't touch it. As she stood debating what to do, what to say, how best to apologize, Bain waved.

"I was wondering where you'd gone," he called.

His good nature surprised her. She'd expected a reprimand, something along the lines that she'd disappointed him by ditching her hostess duties. It had been a big night for him and for Alcott Savings & Loan, and she'd no doubt spoiled it to some degree.

"Look at you," he said with a smile. "I suppose this is your way of letting me know it was a rotten party, and I ruined our anniversary." He shrugged. "I don't know what I was thinking ever letting most of those people in our home."

"It wasn't so bad," she said halfheartedly.

"Let's see how fast we can forget it, shall we? If I promise a romantic dinner for two at the Chatham Bars Inn, could we have a real celebration tomorrow? Or better yet, why don't you drop that towel and come sit with me?"

"Oh, Bain," she scolded. "The caterer is still here. And our children are, too." She didn't want to spoil his playfulness by inquiring how the sleeping arrangements had been resolved.

"Actually, they're not. Hank is spending the night at Troy's house, or so he said. And Erin and his girlfriend left."

"Gone?"

He nodded.

"What time?"

"I don't remember."

"They were going to drive all the way back to Vermont?"

"I presume so. I didn't ask."

Grace felt a pang of dismay. Her elder son had left without giving her a chance to explain. He'd drive all night harboring the notion that his mother was a coward. She wondered whether he'd even taken a moment to look for her to say good-bye.

"What about Ferris?"

"He's out for the night. He did come down a little while ago and made a Bloody Mary, but disappeared back upstairs. When I went to check, he was asleep in his clothes on top of the covers."

"Poor Ferris."

"He'll be all right. He just needs to learn the concept of moderation." Bain extended his arms. "Come here," he said.

She sat down on his lap and let the towel fall open.

He rubbed her stomach gently, then cupped her breasts

in his hands and kissed her shoulder. "Thank you," he said, speaking softly. "Thank you for putting up with me."

She twisted around and stared at Bain, the familiar features, the subtle lines along his forehead that had arrived over the last decade, the slightly graying hair. In some ways she knew him better than she knew herself. And yet he still remained an enigma. She never would have anticipated this display of affection, not after she'd defected to the beach. Perhaps he'd read her mind and knew what she needed on this night more than anything else. Perhaps he knew her better than she realized.

She kissed his nose. "Thank you," she replied. "Thank you for making me your bride." And for the first time all evening, she meant it.

2002

Chapter Eleven

W hat in the world is he doing?" Prissy asked, positioning herself beside her friend with her hands on her hips.

Grace couldn't take her eyes off the backhoe rolling slowly along the driveway. Just to the right of the house, it turned and veered off the gravel. A few yards in front, Bain stood beside a man with a hard hat, who beckoned the enormous machine with an orange flag.

"He's putting in a pool."

"A swimming pool?"

Grace nodded. The gesture was almost invisible.

"But where? You don't have the setbacks. Most of this property is wetlands."

Grace closed her eyes, not wanting to answer. Speaking the location out loud would make it all too real. But the arrival of the backhoe meant the destruction was imminent. Its huge rubber tires had already left deep grooves in the neat lawn.

"Where is it going to go?" Prissy repeated.

"In the rose garden."

❦

How had life changed so much in less than a decade? At times her honeymoon, her few months with Sarah, Hank's and Erin's childhoods, her life as the corporate wife of a

Bank of Boston executive seemed so vivid that it could have been yesterday, or a week or a month previous; at other moments these same memories were distant, faded. Her children were grown, married. She was a grandmother to Erin's two; Hank and his wife, still babies themselves, were expecting their first. A whole generation had elapsed.

Had she actually worn a green leather suit to the dinner when Bain won an award for the highest volume of new investments for the year? That must have been 1972 or 1973. Long ago the suit had been donated to the thrift shop at St. Christopher's, and no doubt bought by a teenager as a costume for a seventies party, but she still remembered the compliments she'd received from the president's wife. "So chic, so stylish, you put the rest of us to shame." Bain had overheard the praise and beamed with pride.

That her wardrobe had changed was the least of the transitions. Business success hadn't been theirs since Ronald Reagan left office. Despite Bain's efforts, nonstop work, and considerable experience in the industry, his savings bank went the way of most and closed just eighteen months after it opened its offices in a lovely brick building on Beacon Street. In an attempt to salvage what capital he could, he'd auctioned off the office equipment, safes, and copiers before closing the doors to the single branch of Alcott Savings & Loan.

He'd been way too late to ride the tide that had brought riches to so many; the scandals in the banking industry had brought in extensive regulations; the climate wasn't right; the government had destroyed opportunity. He'd offered the reasons more as explanation than excuse to virtually anyone who would listen. It had nothing to do with his financial acumen. His reputation wasn't tarnished.

So he put that endeavor behind him and slept for nearly a week.

But a series of consulting jobs met with similar fates. Bain had a reason for each of the departures—nothing seemed a "good fit," as if a job were a pair of tassel loafers—but at some point Grace had to wonder if he would ever be the right size. This man who'd done so well, who'd climbed the corporate ladder swiftly and seemingly effortlessly, struggled. Was he now virtually unemployable? It was a question she would never ask, or at least not ask aloud.

"I've decided to write the novel I should have written when I was at Harvard," he announced to her one afternoon. "We'll have that life we once dreamed of: time together, travel, and the joys of writer's block. Remember?" He smiled.

He was fifty-seven. Grace knew he couldn't bear to start over. The world was a different place. He didn't understand the Internet. They hadn't even been able to figure out how to sell a pair of andirons on eBay, and so had given them as a more-valuable-than-usual Christmas gift to Hank and his wife for their home in Natick.

Early retirement seemed the best solution, and writing allowed him to think he'd made a choice. He wasn't a failure; he was moving in a different direction, finally fulfilling the dreams of his youth. It even sounded romantic.

Grace had never been much involved in their finances. Bain took care of all that. But she knew enough to know that much of what he'd saved for that eventuality—his retirement—was a casualty of the many failed business experiments. He'd needed capital from somewhere, and he'd had faith in himself. They'd already refinanced their Boston apartment with its views of the Public Garden. So it was no surprise that shortly after his pronouncement, they sold their city home, took the remaining equity with them, and drove over the Sagamore Bridge to become year-round residents of Cape Cod.

Grace registered to vote and volunteered on the First Night Committee.

A representative from the Chatham Newcomers' Association paid a visit. The plump woman who'd arrived by bicycle almost choked on her shortbread when Grace mentioned they'd owned the house for thirty years. "Why, you should be welcoming me!" she'd exclaimed awkwardly.

And then came Bain's growing obsession with the pool.

She knew he wanted to make a statement, to indicate to their neighbors and friends that his retirement had been a choice; that they were as financially comfortable now as before. A forty-thousand-dollar capital improvement would be just the ticket to publicize their solvency.

But in her mind the price was impossibly high.

"We live right on the ocean. We have our own beach. Why would we ever need or want a pool?" she'd protested as she handed him a turkey sandwich and some Cape Cod Potato Chips. She'd watched him all morning, wandering around outside with a survey map, a yardstick, and some stakes.

"You're the hardy one. That you can swim in sixty-five-degree water is something I love about you. But I want the luxury of laps in eighty-degree peace and quiet—no boats, no seaweed, no fish, and no sand. I guarantee you'll come around as soon as it's in." He unfolded his paper napkin and placed it on his lap.

"It's not safe, Bain," she added. "You don't need me to remind you of that. What about the children?"

Both Erin and Hank brought their families to the Chatham house. It was a beautiful vacation spot—a destination—and under the guise of a reunion, the boys availed themselves of her hospitality, her organization, and her housework. Better than hotel service, and it was all free of charge. That much of her time was then spent driving to the fish market, picking up produce, unloading the dishwasher, and vacuuming up sand dragged in from the beach bothered no one. She didn't want to seem bitter or resentful. Her boys worked hard and deserved a break. And it was one of the few times each year that everyone was together. Still, it would have been nice if once—just once—they'd arrived with a bottle of wine, a small bouquet, or a bag of scented soap as a hostess gift.

But neither their selfishness nor the amount of housework had any bearing on the issue of the pool. To that her objection was deep-seated, visceral. Her grandchildren were still small, not yet swimmers. It would be years before all of them would be comfortable around a pool, and with parents who were hardly vigilant, it was an accident waiting to happen. She'd be paralyzed with fear—just the thought of installing a pool filled her with panic—and forced to spend the entire visit as lifeguard. She imagined herself in night-vision goggles patrolling the perimeter in case an Alcott toddler opened the gate. Housekeeping, meals, socializing, everything about their life would shut down for the duration of the visit. She wouldn't rest until the grandchildren were safely buckled into their car seats en route home.

"It's too dangerous, much too dangerous."

"We'll get a good latch on the gate, I promise. And I'll go to Ben Franklin and buy extra sets of floaties. Besides, the kids won't be infants forever. Millions of people with small children have swimming pools, and nothing happens except that everyone enjoys themselves."

Millions of people haven't lost a baby to drowning, Grace thought. And flotation devices were not the solution. Why didn't he see that he was building a gunite coffin? She couldn't stand such a visual reminder in her own backyard, and couldn't manage with the fear that history might repeat itself in the next generation.

"We're not millions of people," Grace muttered, feebly.

Bain took a bite of his sandwich. "My dear Grace, if only our boys had inherited your neuroses, they'd stay away from here to keep their children safe. Then we'd have some peace." He chuckled and picked up a chip between his fingers. Before biting, he added, "My guess is that much to my dismay the pool will only be a further enticement for them to come visit. And you'd like that, now, wouldn't you?"

Grace moved back to the butcher-block island and stared at the sliced turkey in its plastic wrap, the head of iceberg lettuce, the jar of mayonnaise, and the two slices of whole wheat toast she'd made for her sandwich. She had no appetite and couldn't bring herself to put all the ingredients together, anyway. Instead she screwed the top back on the Hellman's, giving it an extra twist to secure it. Looking at the blue label, she realized she'd forgotten to buy low-fat.

What *had* her boys inherited from her? Was it anything more than blue eyes, lean bodies, and good teeth?

As far as she could tell, Erin wandered aimlessly through life. For the past few years, he'd managed to stay in one place—somewhere outside Putney, Vermont. That was a feat in and of itself, and as close to something per-manent as he was likely to come. He'd done odd jobs and God-only-knows what else to earn a living. Last month, it was a maple sugar company, which Bain had sent him a thousand dollars to start. So he spent his days tapping trees and talking with the people at Ben & Jerry's, trying to get them to develop a flavor involving pieces of pancake and syrup. He wanted some sort of inventor's fee, as well as an agreement to be the exclusive local supplier.

Before that, there had been an apiary, a project that came to an abrupt end after his weeklong hospitalization from bee stings. A job at the Putney General Store selling

Bag Balm and cans of Chef Boyardee preceded the honey production, as well as an administrative position at town hall sending out delinquent tax notices. From that he'd been immediately terminated once the assessor realized he'd sent a notice to himself.

Meanwhile his wife, Marley, studied "energy healing" and spent money they didn't have on equipment for her enterprise. According to Erin, a purple faux-leather massage table now filled most of their small living room.

Neither of them seemed to have much time for their children.

And then there was Hank, her baby. He was attractive, and had managed to parlay his good looks into a job as a rental broker with a real estate outfit in Wellesley, Massachusetts. "Clients love him," his female boss had explained on the one occasion they'd had to meet her. Perhaps she did, too. But he earned enough to live in a center-entrance Colonial in the neighboring, though less prestigious, town of Natick with his similarly attractive wife, Susan, who sported quite the collection of tennis whites and volunteered at the library. He'd recently called to inform them with a great deal of pride in his voice that he'd bought a BMW.

He was only twenty-five and yet seemed to have the curiosity of a brick. On weekends he did nothing, as far as she could tell from their conversations, other than attend a cocktail party or take a trip to the car wash. "Simonizing really helps extend the life of the paint," he'd mentioned more than once. "And you've got to keep the mag wheels clean." He didn't even play golf, and she couldn't remember the last time he'd mentioned a book he'd read, let alone an article.

It's genetics, Prissy had reminded her once before. Beyond her control. But the explanation seemed wildly unsatisfactory. Who were these boys? They lacked the ambition of their father, but they certainly hadn't inherited her sense of whimsy, either. Perhaps they'd been born of a mixture of DNA that belonged to a slug.

Nonetheless, she couldn't bear if anything happened in the pool. No one should have to suffer the loss she'd endured. If Bain insisted on installing a swimming pool, she'd buy the best safety cover manufactured and never take it off.

∞

The rumble of the engine and the cracking of branches brought her back from her ruminations. Grace watched as the giant claws of the backhoe scooped down and ripped open the earth, tearing up moss-covered bricks, soil, rock, and plants with each pass. She could see leaves and flowers and root-balls with masses of thin roots dangling, lost, looking for the lifeline of soil to grip that they could no longer find. The 'Honor' bush had its first white buds of the season waiting to bloom.

Why had she let this happen? Why had she given up, or given in? Why had she sacrificed the roses she loved for a swimming pool she didn't want and they couldn't afford? That Sarah's memorial garden was the casualty only added to the painful irony.

She looked across the yard to Bain, who stood beside the pool contractor watching the progress. Neither acknowledged her presence. Nor did they seem to notice Prissy, standing beside her with her arms folded across her chest and her jaw set.

"It was beautiful while it lasted," her friend said.

"Aren't we all?" she mumbled, but the mechanical roar covered her words. She watched as the huge metal arm plunged into the sandy soil once more.

Chapter Twelve

Frank Sinatra crooned Christmas carols, a Duraflame-assisted fire now blazed, and, after several failed attempts, Grace had managed to roast enough chestnuts to fill a small silver bowl. Miniature white lights, red velvet bows, and seashells adorned the blue spruce. The quilted tree skirt was covered by wrapped packages, each tied with dried lavender and gold pinecones that Grace had painted herself. Red poinsettias framed the hearth, and a slow-burning scented candle filled the living room with cinnamon.

The forecast had been for snow, but Chatham weather was unpredictable. The unrelenting rain had started early that morning. The weight of accumulated water made the pool's safety cover droop precariously, and Grace had double-checked that the French doors were locked. After her grandchildren arrived, she bolted the front door behind them. Feeling trapped was a small price to pay for safety.

Breaking with tradition, Grace had experimented with a turkey recipe from *Gourmet* magazine that involved an orange glaze and a sage-and-sausage stuffing. The picture of the shiny bird on a transferware platter had enticed her. In fact, she'd tried to emulate the entire holiday setting that appeared in the glossy pages, complete with red etched-glass goblets, silver chargers, and loose arrange-

ments of white flowers. *Casual family elegance,* the article
had labeled it. She wanted some of that, too.

But now as she lit the votives on the sideboard and the
tapers in the candelabra on the dining table, she felt
apprehensive about the change. Perhaps she should have
warned Bain that he wouldn't be getting corn bread and
apples—her mother's recipe—for the thirtieth time. Perhaps she should have checked with him before she'd purchased this array of mismatched antique china from
various shops along Route 6A. Maybe her family wasn't
what *Gourmet* magazine had in mind. Maybe casual elegance was an unobtainable goal.

She checked the place cards. She and Bain had done
the seating, but suddenly the prospect of sitting next to
Hank for the entire meal seemed exhausting. She made
the switch, giving him to Marley. That they had nothing
in common might keep them quiet, although that was no
doubt wishful thinking. She couldn't bear another holiday
ruined by discord over Hank's failure to recycle. It wasn't
fair for Marley to blame all of the world's environmental
problems on the unsorted trash of a single Natick resi-
dent.

She'd take Ferris as her dinner companion instead.
He'd called at the last minute to ask if he could share the
holiday. The confirmed bachelor never accepted her invitations flat out, hoping, perhaps, that a lady friend might
offer something better, an invitation to a weekend party
on the French Riviera or a wine tasting in the Napa
Valley. When nothing materialized, he'd call sheepishly to
see if there was still a place for him at her table.

Erin's children, India and Deshawn, were sandwiched
between their parents in the middle seats. India, the pre-
cocious four-year-old, made Grace nervous. She'd
announced on her last visit that she'd gotten her name
because she'd been conceived while her parents were

trekking in that country. It was bad enough to imagine
Erin procreating in a tent surrounded by Sherpas or in the
dirt on the side of some mountain. They shouldn't have
shared such details with their young daughter. But the
origin of India's name prevented Grace from asking how
they'd arrived at something African American for their
son. As far as she knew, neither parent had visited that
continent.

Deshawn was a small child even for two and would
need another Yellow Pages to bring him to the appropriate height. Staring at the makeshift booster, Grace
wondered why she'd never bought a proper molded
plastic one. Most of her friends had high chairs, spare diapers, and every other necessity for their grandchildren.
All she'd managed was to hang on to last year's directory
for an added three inches.

She'd expected to enjoy being a grandmother—all the
pleasure of children with none of the hardship, no discipline to impose, no bedtimes to enforce, no homework to
supervise. Her friends treated their grandchildren as if
they were visiting heads of state, anticipating needs and
planning activities. Instead she found herself resenting the
arrival of Erin and his clan and Hank and his family. It
was work: more meals to make, more beds to change,
more towels to wash. It wasn't right; it wasn't warm-
hearted. And, just as she'd done each time before her sons
had arrived with their families, she'd vowed to make it different.

On the twenty-third, when Erin and Marley showed
up empty-handed once again, she'd forced herself to over-
look their bad manners and to hold on to her determination to reach out to the children. She could be the
storybook grandmother. But India refused her offers to
read Beatrix Potter. "Animals in clothes are unnatural,"
she'd said. Nor would she help wrap presents or bake

reindeer-shaped cookies. Neither child wanted to look for seals along the coastline. Even her vision of the family together at St. Christopher's was shattered when Erin and Marley refused to bring the children to Christmas Eve services. "Organized religion is mind control," Marley declared emphatically.

When exactly had Marley gone from giggly freshman to arbiter of independent thought? Grace had wondered. Now all she wanted was for the holiday to be over and the house to be quiet.

Baby Henry, Hank and Susan's seven-month-old, could sit in his Toys "Я" Us rocker chair, or his bouncing swing, or his port-o-crib, or whatever other apparatus Susan had brought for him. Shortly after his arrival, he'd eaten, watched his Baby Einstein video, and done one round of flash cards. "Several studies show a correlation between this sort of early brain stimulation and higher IQ levels by second grade," Susan had reported as she'd unpacked one gadget after another. "And that's just where we want to be, right, Hank?"

Hank had nodded. It seemed quite clear he left the baby's brain stimulation to his wife.

"Wouldn't he like to open a present?" Grace had asked, timidly. "This is his first Christmas, after all."

Susan had glanced under the tree. "Thanks, but we've got plenty to keep him occupied right now. And he'll just suck on the wrapping paper." With that, she'd produced a box with musical squares from a duffel bag. "Come on, my little Mozart," she'd said in a saccharine sweet voice. "Let's compose."

The science of parenting. Grace had known nothing of the sort. Would it have been a comfort to her? She wondered. If she'd followed the expert advice and bought the right neurological stimulants, would her sons be different now? If they'd imitated musical patterns or recognized the letters of the alphabet at an earlier age, would they have grown up to be more considerate, more whimsical, more interesting men?

She remembered the days when she'd put them on a blanket in the sand and found small rocks and shells on the beach to keep them amused. Her sons had seemed enchanted, cooing and gurgling at the collection of natural objects. Once Hank had swallowed a pebble, but that passed without obvious complications. What happened to that simpler life?

As Susan directed and coached, Henry had struggled with the music box. Grace had hoped for his sake that he could fall asleep and have a few hours off from the unrelenting pursuit of excellence.

The food was ready. She lifted the lids of the covered dishes, inserted serving spoons into the sweet potatoes, turnips, and brussels sprouts, and stirred her cranberry sauce, wishing her dishes more closely resembled the picture instead of looking lumpy and overcooked.

Ferris appeared in the threshold and surveyed the room. His eyes were bloodshot, and he held on to the doorway for balance. "It's beautiful as always, Gracie."

"We're glad you're here," she replied. "You know you're always welcome, Ferris. I meant to tell you that when you called, when you acted as if you were imposing, but I got caught up in our conversation and didn't mention it. I hope that you would know that, that our home is yours, no advance notice required." She smiled.

Sweet Ferris, her slightly broken brother. His sweetness grew with age.

"Prissy's coming, isn't she?" he asked.

Grace pretended not to be taken aback. "I invited her and Kody, but she said they had other plans. Knowing how he feels about social functions, I didn't press."

"It would have been great to see her," Ferris said. His voice sounded wistful. "It's been so long."

"Yes, I don't know where the years have gone."

He didn't respond. She couldn't tell if he had something he wanted to say and was holding back, or whether his brain, already pickled in alcohol, had shut down after its previous thought.

It was true that ever since the days following Sarah's death, he'd seemed particularly intrigued by the clammer. Each time he'd visited, he'd made sure that Grace invited her for a meal, or that they had the opportunity to share a drink or a walk on the beach. Prissy seemed quite taken with him, too, and their conversation was always animated. Occasionally, one or both of them would make a remark that left Grace with the impression that they'd been in contact, perhaps even seen each other between his periodic visits to the Cape. She'd wondered, harboring suspicions, but tried her best to push the thoughts from her mind. That they were friends was fine—nice for both of them—but it couldn't be anything more significant than that. Prissy was a married woman. It had to be innocent.

She glanced at her watch. It was nearly three, later than she'd intended for the holiday meal. "Why don't you call everyone in for lunch?" she suggested.

Ferris started, apparently surprised by her voice. When she looked again, she could see him quickly wipe away a tear.

"Ferris, what is it? Is something wrong?"

He reached into his pocket, produced a handkerchief, and blew his nose. Then he folded it quickly. "Do you ever wonder about what might have been? The road not taken?" His voice cracked. "I'm sure I'm not right with my attribution, but wasn't it Robert Frost who wrote about the fork in the road?"

She nodded. "The one less traveled."

"Right. That's it. And his view was that the alternate road was better, or at least better for him. But I wonder not about which route, necessarily, but what happens when you get to the fork, the moment of decision. We made choices—consciously or not—so young, so early, and yet they affected the rest of our lives." He slumped back against the doorway, as if needing support from the wall. "I'm rapidly approaching sixty. And although I plowed through the fifty-year hurdle with little fanfare and no crisis, life was different then."

Wasn't one supposed to soar over hurdles as opposed to barreling through them? Grace thought of the Olympic track stars she'd seen on televison. They appeared to take flight over the barriers in their way. She wished her brother had that same ease.

"But I think about how easy it might have been to end up a completely different kind of person in a completely different kind of life," Ferris continued. "Why you and Bain? Why here in Chatham? Why am I alone as one more year comes to a close?"

"You've wanted to be alone," Grace said, although she knew her comment was unconvincing. Despite what Ferris said about choice, she'd long ago concluded that at least some of his fate was accidental. "You've never wanted a family or commitment."

"Maybe the right person never came along."

"Oh, please, you've been making fun of me my entire life. You wouldn't have wanted to settle down."

"Perhaps. But I admire you for it, too, and I'm terribly envious of that husband of yours."

They both smiled. Grace stepped toward him and gently stroked his cheek. "You know as well as I do that some of whatever life we make is deliberate and other parts are purely accidental. Then we try to undo some of the accidents and fail miserably."

"I try very hard not to dwell too much on the past," Ferris said, forcing a laugh. "*Been there, done that* seems to me a healthier approach." He glanced down at the floor. "But when I'm here, especially, I can't seem to help myself. This house is so full of history. I wonder about the chosen and the bypassed paths, the ones in my life and the ones in yours, too."

"It's never too late to change directions if that's what you want. Look at Dad," Grace said, trying to infuse the conversation with a lighter tone. It was Christmas, after all. She wanted to feel a sense of celebration or, absent that, at least of getting through the holiday without being too morose.

Her strategy worked. The thought of William's escapades made them both laugh. That he'd fallen in love with the neighbors' au pair, a young girl from Bordeaux who barely spoke a word of English, was shocking enough. But that he'd failed to mention it, had married her in secret, and had led a clandestine life for ten years was comical. It was only when they decided to sell the house on Beacon Hill and move to a château somewhere south of Paris that he'd confessed she was his bride. Although William had extended several invitations since he'd established residency abroad, neither Ferris nor Grace had managed to make the journey.

"Perhaps there's a lesson in that," Ferris replied. "Dear old Dad, experiencing the joys of Viagra."

Grace was relieved to see him smile at his own humor.

The sound of running feet broke the quiet of their interchange. India and Deshawn crashed into the gangly legs of their great-uncle, nearly toppling Ferris. Behind them came Marley, or rather Marley's enormous belly, judging by Grace's view. The woman was still a month away from delivering their third child, but she appeared ready to explode at any moment, a prospect she accentuated with her version of maternity chic—a Lycra top and skirt that barely managed to stretch around her. Even the contour of her protruding belly button showed.

Erin, Bain, and Hank brought up the rear.

"Susan's putting Henry down," Hank explained. "She said to start without her, which I recommend we do. By the time she gets through the required pre-nap reading, it'll be midnight."

ↄ৶ঌ

Grace and Bain needn't have bothered with the seating arrangement since, after proceeding through the buffet line, everyone sat where they wanted. Grace found herself between Deshawn and Marley, while Hank monopolized his father's ear at the far end of the table. Erin sat in a middle seat with India on his lap. Across from him, Ferris stared blankly at the wall, lost in thought.

"Inventory is definitely low, especially in the single-family and three-bedroom range. People are buying, not renting," Grace overheard Hank say.

"What about corporate transfers? They're always a ready rental pool," Bain replied.

"I hear you. But the transfers aren't coming my way. There are too many specialty firms doing that now." Hank emptied the bottle of Merlot without so much as a glance to see if anyone else's glass needed refilling. "My market is definitely soft. Frankly, it may be time to reposition myself. I'm thinking about mortgage brokering. Interest rates have gotten so competitive that even the institutional lenders are willing to pay to have customers brought in."

Grace wished she had headphones. She wanted to hear something invigorating, a Puccini aria or a Vivaldi sonata.

Her son the mortgage broker—no doubt an appropriate development to keep himself out of the unemployment line, but it wasn't what she would have ever imagined as a career choice.

Deshawn had fallen asleep in an awkward position with his head partially on her lap. She adjusted him slightly, repositioning his body so that her thighs served as a better pillow. His mouth opened, his lips curved in the circular shape of babies still accustomed to a nipple. She gently stroked his cheek and ran her fingers through his soft curls.

Blocking out the conversation, she focused instead on the warmth of Deshawn's body and the tinkling of silverware on the china plates. The candlelight flickered off the crystal and silver, and the red glass cast a warm sheen on the table. Her meal was a success; little remained in the dishes on the side-board. Self-congratulations were better than nothing, and since her family seemed to have forgotten that protocol, she silently offered up the finest of compliments to her own culinary expertise. She'd pulled off casual elegance whether anyone acknowledged it or not.

"So has Erin told you about our plan?" Marley's voice interrupted her musing.

"Why, no," she replied, feeling dread even before Marley began to elaborate. "What plan is that?"

"He's quitting his job, selling the business."

She rested her hand against Deshawn's back and felt his sides rise and fall with each breath. "Now? Just when his maple sugar company is starting to be profitable?" Grace vaguely remembered Bain relaying that news a few months before. The Ben & Jerry's deal had never materialized, but he had managed to sign a contract to supply a small candy outfit.

"Yeah." Marley rolled her eyes. "That took a while. Which might mean he could collect a couple of thousand for the whole kit and caboodle. We don't care at this point.

It's more important for him to be home with the kids than engaged in some capitalist venture that frankly is only going to result in a lot of rotten teeth."

"Home with the children," Grace mumbled, trying to keep the alarm out of her voice.

"Erin is so maternal. It's a beautiful thing."

"But—but—" Grace stammered. She wasn't quite sure what she wanted to say. Marley was supposed to be the maternal one. Erin was the father. What happened to the man as provider? What was either of them planning to live on, let alone their children?

She glanced down the table at Bain. He'd taken care of her. Even with their more recent financial pressures, she'd never really worried or wondered. He was in charge. Wasn't that what a husband was supposed to be?

Then it occurred to her. They would turn to Bain for help, as Erin had done so often in the past. But a thousand-dollar investment in his start-up company was a far cry from covering the needs of a family of five.

"How is your . . . your massage business?" Grace asked finally. *At least let there be one source of income.*

Marley shot her a stern expression. "I'm a healer, *not* a masseuse. And my practice has really blossomed. The bond with my clients is intense. I'm wondering how they'll manage in the few weeks I'm out with the new baby. Two of them want to come to participate in the delivery."

Virtual strangers watching the most intimate moment in someone's life? The thought made her stomach turn. "What did Erin have to say about that?"

"Actually, he was very receptive to the idea. India and Deshawn will be with us, too."

Grace scanned the table. There was nothing left to drink. "Ferris," she commanded. "Would you mind opening another bottle of the Merlot?" *As fast as humanly possible,* she stopped herself from adding.

Ferris, no doubt relishing the prospect of more himself, got up and disappeared into the pantry.

"So the plan that you mentioned is that you'll return to work and Erin will stay home?"

"Yes. We've both decided that stereotypical male and female roles are the product of a society we don't agree with. We want our children raised in an environment that nurtures their complete sexual identities."

Ferris returned with a bottle in each hand and one tucked under his arm. "What does that mean?" he asked. "I for one am very happy with two genders and, for the most part, people who choose one or the other."

"That kind of closed-mindedness is what Erin and I object to. We're all both male and female. We have masculine and feminine sides. It shouldn't be unmasculine to nurture or unfeminine to exhibit aggression or territoriality. The sides should be balanced in each person. The problem with current thinking is that the equilibrium is skewed. Just because someone has a penis, it doesn't mean that all he can do is play football and drive a truck."

"Yeah, but it probably also means he shouldn't wear a dress."

Ferris had uncorked all three bottles, and Grace didn't wait to be served. She reached for the closest one and filled her glass to the top.

"That's the kind of knee-jerk response that makes me sick about the world we live in. Remember, the labia start out as a penis and then shrink. So we truly are one sex."

"Not the last time I checked," Ferris muttered.

Grace covered her mouth to stifle a laugh. She appreciated that Ferris was willing to challenge Marley's dogma.

"Go to other cultures and you'll see a broader exploration and celebration of a universal sexuality. It's so Western to think of a man and a woman mating for life." When she said *man* and *woman*, Marley held up her hands and curled two fingers to make quotation marks. "Why not explore each other and those around us? If a man can realize his femininity by being with another man, or can make himself a better lover to a woman, what's wrong with that?"

Grace wasn't sure she'd followed the progression from balancing male–female traits to homosexuality. But watching Marley, the burgeoning mother, and Ferris, the consummate bachelor, debate the point was more humorous than she'd expected.

"*What* are you talking about?"

She looked down the table to where Bain and Hank sat with confused expressions on their faces. No doubt the well of real estate conversation had run dry, and they'd begun to eavesdrop.

"Marley is making the point that each of us is both man and woman," Grace summarized. The sentence sounded absurd. Maybe she'd had too much to drink, but she had the urge to lie on the floor.

"I'm only reminding Grace that she started out as a man."

With that Ferris spit his sip of wine into his napkin. Grace could no longer contain her laughter. Her shoulders shook, her body curled over itself, and she struggled to remain in her chair. Penile shrinkage, sex changes, energy healing; it was all too much. Ferris, too, was consumed by laughter.

Deshawn woke up and began to cry. Marley's attention returned to her plate of food. His shrieks grew louder and Erin came over, swept him up into an embrace, and paced around the room, gently patting his back. Within moments, he had quieted.

"What did I tell you?" Marley said through a mouthful of brussels sprouts.

"This is insanity," Bain muttered.

"No," Grace called out, still laughing as she stood from the table and began to clear. "Just casual elegance."

2003

Chapter Thirteen

Grace had made little progress in her attempt to knit a small blue sleeve. For no apparent reason, stitches dropped. She concentrated on her counting and still found the number coming up short at the end of the row. In order to avoid an imperfection, she had to then unravel, pick up the rogue stitch, and start again from that point. Her intent had been to finish the sweater by the time baby Henry had been born, but that milestone had passed more than a year before—and at the rate she was advancing, she would be lucky if it still fit him by the time it was completed. Perhaps she should have bought the pattern in a size suitable for a large toddler.

It was the first baby gift she'd made for any of her grandchildren, part of another renewed effort to fulfill a vision of her role that had yet to materialize.

Bain had the television turned to *Monday Night Football,* but he'd fallen asleep at halftime and hadn't awoken when play resumed. The voices of the commentators as they spoke about yardage and completions blurred. Although Grace wasn't listening and didn't follow the game, she welcomed the background noise. There was still plenty of testosterone in the room.

The telephone rang several times before she decided to answer it.

"Mom?"

Erin's voice surprised her. It had been weeks since they'd last spoken. Maybe more. She'd lost track of time.

"Are you all right?"

"Yeah . . . sure . . . why do you ask that?"

Because it's after ten o'clock at night and we haven't heard from you since I can't remember when, that's why. Catching herself from an exhibition of impatience, she asked instead, "How are the children and Marley?"

"Ah . . . okay. We're all okay."

"That's good to hear."

There was a long pause. She waited for a question to come from him. Perhaps he'd like to know how his aging parents were doing, something along those lines. Perhaps he could ask if the heat was working well. Did they need their elder son to come down and look after anything?

But he asked nothing. During the silence, she remembered what had caused their frisson: Marley and her accusations. She and Bain were responsible for the debacle in Iraq because they'd voted for George W. Bush in 2000. They might as well have abused the Iraqi prisoners at Guantánamo Bay, or at least helped the American soldiers out with the task. Didn't they see how people like them had ruined the country and destroyed its reputation abroad?

It was more of her political proselytizing. They should have been used to it, but as Marley's hostility increased, her comments grew uglier and more venomous. Bain was selfish and shortsighted like every other American. Grace was passive and noncommittal, just the sort of woman whom the sitting president relied upon to offer no resistance. Traditional family values to the Republicans meant the men had flag bumper stickers and the women shopped at Wal-Mart and cooked three meals with starch and protein.

All the while, Marley sat on their patio with her breast

exposed, nursing her third child, eating their grilled swordfish and drinking their rosé wine. When the evening ended, she planned to curl up in a bed made by Grace. There wasn't an ounce of recognition of that effort.

During the argument, Grace had perceived Erin's silence as his agreement and support of his wife. Only when Bain finally asked them all to leave—he'd had quite enough of being insulted in his own home—had Erin piped up, feebly urging his wife to apologize and begging his father to calm down.

The next morning, they'd left before Bain was awake. Erin hadn't been able to look her in the eye as he'd packed up the car and had hardly been able to say good-bye.

"Is there a reason for your call?" Grace now asked. Her own boldness surprised her. She wasn't in a mood to suffer through more silence. "I mean, it's nice to hear your voice, but it's just . . . well, you don't seem as though you're interested in much conversation."

She could hear Erin inhale on the other end of the line and wondered if he was smoking. "I need forty thousand dollars."

Had she heard correctly? "Forty? Why on earth do you need forty thousand dollars?"

"Don't act like I'm asking for the world."

He practically was. The downstairs powder room remained out of commission because Bain thought it might cost two thousand dollars to repair the plumbing, replace the fixtures, and redo the tile. That was two thousand more than they had, and now Erin wanted forty. "It is a lot of money."

"Look, I haven't paid the kids' tuition. It was due in July and the second installment was due in September, and now the school has our names posted as delinquents. But the kids love the place and they're getting an excellent education. You can tell already. India's working on letters, and Deshawn's done several great art projects, gluing beans and pasta swirls."

For that kind of money, India should have mastered the cursive alphabet and he should be using gold nuggets. But Grace didn't reply.

"If you and Dad pay, there's a tax deduction. Most of our friends' parents are doing it for them. Some federal program to benefit grandparents."

"Tuition for two children is forty thousand dollars?" India couldn't have been more than first grade. Was Deshawn even in kindergarten? How much could preschool cost? Why did he even put his children in private school if he couldn't afford it? And what about public education? She and Bain had spent a fortune on private education and it didn't seem to have done much for either Erin or Hank.

"The money's for the school and for day care. Marley's working a lot these days."

Forty thousand dollars; the sum seemed huge. Bain had bailed him out here and there—probably more often than she even knew—but never for this amount.

It wasn't possible. Just that afternoon, the town newspaper had published the names of those who were delinquent in their real estate taxes. *Alcott* topped the alphabetized list. Irate, Bain had called the editor directly and threatened a lawsuit for libel. "I don't care if it is a matter of public record! Who the hell goes down to town hall to review the records?" he'd screamed into the phone before slamming down the receiver. Then he'd turned to Grace. "This is great. Just great. Let's make a public spectacle of our finances. Be sure to cancel our subscription to that rag first thing tomorrow," he'd instructed.

She turned her attention to Erin. "And what about you? What are you doing with your time?" The questions came out before she could stop herself. Last she'd heard, he was the stay-at-home father, the liberated man. Then what was the baby doing in day care? Still, she wanted to apologize. She shouldn't have said it, not with that tone, not being so judgmental. But there it was.

"Let me speak to Dad," Erin said, ignoring her questions. His tone was flat.

"He's asleep."

There was a pause. "Ask him to call me tomorrow. I'll be around."

"Erin, I will tell your father to call, but I can tell you now that I'm quite sure we cannot loan you the money. I think . . . I think you should get a job."

"Coming from you that's just a tad disingenuous, wouldn't you agree? Have you ever worked a day in your life?"

Grace felt his words cut through her. She'd never heard such disdain in his voice. Her own son viewed her as worthless—too useless or stupid or lazy to find and hold employment. She took several quick breaths to restore her composure. When she spoke, her voice was softer than it had been before. "I was married before I even finished college, as you well know. Your father and I had a more traditional arrangement in our marriage than you do, and I didn't work because I was taking care of our children."

"Is that how you justify it?"

"Uh . . . I," she stammered. His harshness set her off-balance. "I'm not offering a justification." She spoke slowly, choosing each word deliberately. "I'm simply explaining the difference between your situation and mine. Your father and I made our own family. We didn't turn to his parents or mine for handouts."

"So what are you saying? I should have taken the corporate route like Dad, and sought out a woman who wanted nothing more than to be my wife? I like that Marley's got ambition and opinions and determination. I wouldn't want it any other way."

"Your wife is your choice. And the division of labor in your household is also your own business. But Erin, you need to take care of your family. Part of the responsibility of having children is providing for them. You're a grown man."

"And once you have children, you're always a parent. Has anyone reminded you of that? Parenting doesn't come with an expiration date."

She felt her eyes burn. She wanted a sip of water, something to clear her throat and prevent her voice from cracking. Her son's animus was shocking. And yet his perspective made her sad. She couldn't bear the thought that her son felt his parents had prematurely bailed out of their obligations.

Hearing Marley's voice in the background distracted her. She was talking to Erin, but he had covered the receiver and her words were muffled. Whatever instructions she issued, Grace couldn't hear.

When Erin spoke again, his voice was calmer. "Look, if you want to view this as a loan, that's fine with me. Take it out of my inheritance."

Grace felt the tears roll down her cheeks. Her lips quivered. *Rise above it,* her mother used to say to her whenever she was upset. *Take the high road. Disengage.* But this time she couldn't. She felt angry and hurt and dismayed and betrayed.

Finally she spoke. "We're not that old. And both your father and I—thank God—are in perfect health."

"That's not—"

"If I were you," she interrupted, "I would not be spending an inheritance in advance. Your father explained to me many years ago that relying on money after someone's death is a very bad way to live. Besides, in your case, your suggestion assumes you'll be getting one. That assumption may be incorrect."

Her ambiguity was deliberate. He was selfish and inconsiderate. She wanted him to think that he might be cut out. But she also knew there might well be nothing left.

There was a click on the other end. Her son was gone. The line was dead.

2004

Chapter Fourteen

W e'll take a reduced five percent commission given the listing price and the one-year exclusivity clause," Kay Webster said as she passed the document across the butler's table. The legal-size page was covered in print so small that even Grace, whose vision had yet to fade, needed a magnifying glass.

Five percent of two million was still a hundred thousand dollars. That seemed a high price to pay for taking people on a tour of her home, Grace thought. She'd wanted to sell it themselves, but Bain insisted. Realtors commanded better prices, knew the market, and knew how to contact potential buyers. Besides, he wanted to keep the sale quiet, and there was no way to privately sell a house at this price in a primarily second-home market without substantial advertising. It was a leap of faith already to trust the discretion of a broker. And judging from the number of brokers who had glad-handed them over the past months, news of the pending listing had already gotten around.

Now Bain produced a pen from the inside pocket of his blazer and signed where Kay indicated. Although Grace had expected to do the same, no one asked for her signature.

It was March, and outside the sky was gray. The three of them sat in the library. Bain had poured them all a sherry, but Grace hadn't touched hers.

"Now then," Kay said, leaning toward them and resting her elbows on her knees in a decidedly unladylike pose. "Let's talk repairs."

Grace cringed. Ever since they'd first discussed listing the house on Sears Point, the broker had hinted that certain improvements needed to be made: exterior painting, a partial reroofing, replacement of nearly a dozen broken mullions, possibly even a new linoleum floor in the kitchen. Those were considered cosmetic. What Kay didn't know was that one of the bathtubs leaked so badly that the Alcotts had stopped using it six months before, that the powder room remained out of order, and that the hot-water heater was on its last legs—they couldn't both shower within a four-hour time period.

But Bain resisted. Each of these investments cost money, money they didn't have. It was enough to keep up with mowing. There wasn't anything left over for non-operational expenses.

How exactly had they gotten to this place? Grace wasn't sure. But she didn't need a degree in finance to know that the market was down, the economy was in a recession, and what little they'd invested had lost at least some of its value. Bain had mentioned that companies were delaying issuing dividends, that their annual return was off by almost 30 percent, and that he was exploring other investment options. His Social Security was still several years away—and that would hardly cover the heating bill. So until something profitable materialized, they had no choice but to sell the house.

Calling it more than what they needed was his way of making clear that it was simply too expensive, too big, and financially unsustainable. But he had yet to mention the word *downsize*.

"You're going to get a great return on any of these investments," Kay continued. "People will pay for bathrooms and kitchens, not to mention curb appeal. The house will show much better with an exterior paint job." She took a sip of sherry. "And, Grace, you really should get those planters at the end of the walkway filled."

"This is hardly the time for flowers. I don't know what I could put in that would last."

"We're not concerned about longevity, just sprucing up the entrance. Stick in something artificial if you have to. I saw some half-decent silk roses at the Christmas Tree Shop the other day. From a distance, no one will be able to tell the difference."

Except that anyone who knows anything about plants will know that roses don't bloom on the Cape in March, Grace thought to herself. She glanced over at Bain, who seemed fixated on the pen he still held in his hand.

"Just sell it as is," Bain said without looking up. "This house is for sale in the condition that it's in. Period. And I don't want someone nickel-and-diming me after they've completed the home inspection. Make sure to tell people it needs work and that's why the selling price is two million instead of four."

"I really think—" Kay began.

"You heard me. You and I both know there's nothing on the waterfront anywhere near this price. We're practically giving it away because Grace and I don't want the headache of dealing with contractors. That's my position. Do you want the listing or not?"

Kay didn't move. Grace watched Bain with his jaw set. He would never admit to anyone that there wasn't any money for repairs. He would take the details of their precarious financial situation with him to the grave. Given the recession and rising property taxes, there were lots of homes on the market, but Grace knew that didn't take his shame away. Even now, he'd tried to keep the listing as quiet as possible. There would be nothing in the Multiple

Listing Service, no brokers' open house, and absolutely no advertising.

"Okay. I think you're making a mistake. A couple of calls and a bit of work and we could be looking at a much quicker sale, but I'll follow your lead. Remember, I'm on your side."

She gathered the papers up and replaced them in her black leather briefcase. Then she stood, removed her coat from the back of the chair, and swung it over her shoulders. "I'll call as soon as I can line up some showings."

∾

Neither of them saw Kay out. She knew her way around and would be in and out with potential buyers on her own. She could find the door.

Bain sat in his chair, holding his face in his hands. Grace stood in front of the fireplace. She felt numb. Their family home was for sale. But the silence between them was worse.

"Life certainly will be simpler with a home that's more manageable," she said, trying to sound optimistic even as the teacup in her hand shook. "Think how many hours you spend worrying about the lawn and the pool, the mice in the attic, and the shingles falling from the roof. All those worries will be gone, leaving much more time for—for—" She wondered how to finish her own sentence. What exactly would Bain do? As far as she knew, he hadn't written a word of his novel. Ever since his retirement, complaining about various problems with the house seemed to be his primary occupation.

"More time for us?" he said, looking up. His eyes were ringed in red.

"If that's what you want." She smiled.

"I didn't mean to impose a burden."

His words made her flinch. They hadn't grown apart, had they? She tried to remember the last time they had made love and whether or not it had been in this calendar year.

"Why don't you go upstairs and lie down?" she suggested. "I'll bring you a sherry." She sounded as though she were a nurse soothing the anxious patient with medication.

He glanced at his watch, no doubt relieved to see it was after five. "How about making that a vodka straight up?"

"All right then." She extended a hand and helped him to rise to his feet, then kissed him gently. His skin felt clammy beneath her lips. He shuffled toward the stairs, moving slowly, and for the first time that she could remember, she was conscious of his age.

Moments later, she carried a small square tray with his drink and a plate of sliced Havarti and crackers up to their bedroom. They'd both missed lunch and, given their current emotional state, would probably forgo a proper supper, too.

Bain stood by the window with his back to the room. The afternoon light cast a shadow, and his form with its beleaguered posture appeared in silhouette. He stared out to sea.

Grace put the tray down on the bedside table.

"I know how much you love this place," he said softly without turning around. "I never wanted to have to disappoint you. And look what I've done."

She wanted to say something palliative but resisted. He'd see through her feeble attempt to mask the truth. Selling her home left her sad and disappointed. She couldn't pretend otherwise.

But it was worse for him. He'd done everything in his power to avoid this moment. Judging from his haggard expression and the lack of sleep he'd experienced over the last weeks, just listing the house had taken a tremendous toll. And they were still possibly months away from an actual sale. How would they ever manage to get through that?

"We'll make a new home," she replied. "Moving off the water will make upkeep of any place easier."

Suddenly she envisioned a ranch-style home on a fifth-of-an-acre lot in River Bay with three bedrooms and a pressure-treated deck overlooking someone else's laundry line. Even that might be a stretch given the skyrocketing costs of Chatham real estate. The thought made her stomach turn. Storing their belongings and spending the rest of their days traveling in an Airstream held more appeal. At least there would be a sense of adventure.

"I worry for the boys, too. They see this as home base, as a place to bring their kids. It's nice for all of us."

That Bain chose this moment to be nostalgic seemed ironic. She wanted to remind him of how dreadful the family visits had been. Maybe they could laugh at those memories. What about the time Marley commented to him in front of their dinner guests that he had body odor? What about when India had spilled grape juice all over the antique settee and barged in on Bain in the bathtub to inform him of what she'd done? And then there was the last visit, when Hank brought some ungracious couple from Natick and they'd opened—and finished—Bain's bottle of Lagavulin? Bain, even more than she, had felt exhilarated when everyone had left.

Given this vantage point and the pending finality, he romanticized the experiences. He was the grandfather, the great provider and protector. Just as she had, he'd seen it as his role, and one that he never would have questioned. But the work, the worry, the strain had been the price.

"Please Bain, come lie down. It's been a long day. It'll be just our luck that after all this, nobody will buy it." She forced a laugh as she reached for his hand and pulled him over to the bed. He sat down, and she took off his shoes and loosened his belt. Then she fluffed the pillows behind him. He lay back, took a sip of his drink, and closed his eyes.

A cashmere throw that they'd bought in Italy on their honeymoon was draped over the end of the bed. She still remembered how she'd seen it in a shopwindow and exclaimed at the beauty of the blue-gray color. Bain had marched in and bought it for thousands of lire without a moment's hesitation. After they'd made love in the hotel room that evening, he'd wrapped her in it and held her tight to his chest.

Now Grace opened it and spread it over his body. Through the several moth holes, she could see the fabric of his shirt and pants. It was worn, and probably no longer enough to keep out the draft of early spring. She went to the closet, pulled out a synthetic comforter, and folded it at the foot of the bed.

Moments later, he still hadn't moved. She knew from his breathing that he wasn't asleep, but apparently he needed to pretend. Perhaps he'd drift off after she left.

She rubbed his back once more, kissed his forehead, and headed downstairs.

◈

Prissy's mesh basket was overturned and her rake thrown on the sand. As Grace descended the steps to the beach, she could see where the ocean floor had been turned and dug, but there was no sign of the clammer. The wind blew hard, and the salty air bit against her cheeks. She quickened her step, feeling panic creep into her neck.

"Prissy!" she called, scanning the dark water. She'd often wondered what might happen if a wave came up unexpectedly. If Prissy's waders filled, would she be pinned down? But even though the wind had whipped up a few whitecaps, there was no sign of any real surf and even less evidence of an undertow. Other than where it had been dug, the sand where the water lapped to shore was smooth and flat.

"I'm up here."

Grace turned toward the dune. Shielding her eyes with her hand to block the odd glare of light that came over the top of the high grasses, she spotted Prissy sitting cross-legged in the sand beneath a *Rosa rugosa*.

"Is everything all right?" she asked when she'd come close enough to speak without shouting.

Prissy laughed. "You mean because I'm not working? Yeah. It's fine. I was admiring the view."

Grace lowered herself down next to her friend. The sand was cool and still damp from the rain that morning.

"It doesn't get more beautiful than this," Prissy said, keeping her eyes fixed on the ocean that spread out before them both. The moorings were empty of boats, but a seagull perched on one. Together they floated up and down with the waves.

"If I could have a single image imprinted on my brain for all time it would be this: the Oyster River with Stage Harbor beyond, the water, the sea grass, the bird life. I saw a blue egret the other day and its wingspan had to be thirty inches. The puffins that come in the winter, the piping plovers that this town seems to have single-handedly saved from extinction . . . it's all magic."

"And each season is equally beautiful," Grace murmured, closing her eyes and imagining all that Prissy had described.

"I remember when Kody and I first moved here. I walked this little strip of beach and felt my senses had come alive. I've often wondered if I weren't here, if I had to leave, how life would be. How I'd manage once I crossed the Sagamore Bridge. This place has given me a sense of connection, belonging."

Grace glanced over at Prissy. Her eyes were filled with tears. What had prompted this introspection? Was it the thought that the Alcotts might leave? When Grace told her they planned to sell the house, she'd never suggested they might abandon Chatham; she didn't want to leave the area. They were simply downsizing, or half-sizing, whether Bain admitted it or not.

The best part of Chatham—the natural beauty of the landscape as the elbow of land bent out into the ocean— was free of charge. A grand house on the water was not required to admire it.

"You don't need to imprint it on your brain," Grace said loud enough for Prissy to hear over the wind. "It'll always be here. That's the true beauty. And so will we. With any luck, someone will bury us in these dunes."

Prissy slowly turned to face Grace. Her eyes looked possessed, her expression a mixture of bewilderment and pain.

It was an expression she'd never seen before. Grace knew instantly that she was hiding something. Prissy's secret eluded her, but something was definitely off, not right.

For now, though, with the wind in her face and the wetness from the sand seeping into her pants, she was too tired to explore whatever it was that was bothering Prissy or to force a confession. Like many of the changes she knew were coming in her life, she would face that, too, another day.

Chapter Fifteen ˙

Grace drove through the gates and up the long, winding driveway. An array of redbrick buildings and a few white clapboard houses covered the manicured lawns. If it weren't for the signs clearly marked ADMITTING, EMERGENCY, and OUTPATIENT, the sprawling facility that comprised McLean Hospital could have passed for a New England college campus instead of a treatment facility for some of the most seriously ill psychiatric patients in the area.

She parked in the lot, followed the arrow marked ADATC, and entered the Alcohol and Drug Abuse Treatment Center. After she signed in with the attendant at the front door, a buzzer let her pass inside. As directed, she sat in a faux-leather chair with wooden arms that was one of a dozen lined up along the walls of the alcove that constituted a waiting area. It was family visiting hour, the first time she'd been allowed to see Ferris since his admission the week before.

Grace had brought a *House & Garden* magazine to read, but it didn't take long before a shuffling sound made her look up. Ambling toward her was Ferris, wearing navy sweats and leather bedroom slippers.

Rising quickly, she ran to him and threw her arms around him. His body felt as though it might snap. His skin looked slightly yellow, and a shadow of facial hair covered his cheeks and chin. What had happened to him? It had been less than a month since they'd met for lunch on Newbury Street. She'd noticed his drinking. Had he had three or four martinis? But she hadn't paid much attention. He'd seemed animated and energetic, attributing his ruddy complexion to a week in Florida photographing wildlife in the Everglades and regaling her with stories of a dalliance he'd had with the manager of a crocodile farm. She'd had no idea he was so sick.

Then she'd gotten the call. He was hospitalized at Massachusetts General Hospital. He'd collapsed in the Public Garden and been admitted through the emergency room. The doctors diagnosed acute pancreatitis. He was lucky to have survived, but he could never drink again, nothing at all, not even nonalcoholic beer. So after his immediate medical condition was stabilized, he'd checked into McLean. It made more sense to go directly; he'd already been sober for twelve days before he walked through the doors of the ADATC.

"Thanks for coming," he said. His voice was slightly hoarse.

"Don't thank me. I love you," Grace replied. "I'm so glad you're all right."

He laughed. Then he linked his arm through hers. "There's a visiting room this way. If we're lucky, they might be serving juice and cookies. I'd forgotten how much I liked gingersnaps."

Together they walked to the end of the hall, made a left, and proceeded down a second corridor until they reached a vast room filled with furniture that had seen better days, blue-and-brown-plaid couches and chairs in makeshift seating arrangements. A television hung from the ceiling. Large windows provided an ample view of the parking lot as well as the emergency entrance to the building. The air smelled stale.

In one corner sat a gray-haired woman, who stared blankly out the window. Her bathrobe had fallen open, and the black T-shirt underneath clung to the rolls in her belly. Beside her sat a heavyset blonde who had fashioned a bizarre hairstyle using a series of combs. Neither appeared to say a word. As they smoked, they passed an already full ashtray back and forth between them.

Otherwise the room was empty.

A table by the entrance held a stack of paper cups, a pitcher of apple juice, and a plate of vanilla wafers. Ferris appeared obviously disappointed with the selection. He poured himself a cup of juice and offered one to Grace. Then he pulled two chairs together in front of a window in the opposite corner.

As Grace sat, she could see an ambulance pull into the turnaround. Its lights flashed, but the siren was off. One paramedic opened the back as the other wheeled a stretcher. She diverted her gaze, not wanting to see who was brought out, and reached for her brother's hand. It was cold and clammy.

"How's Bain?" he asked.

"Oh fine, we're fine. No need to think about us. You're the one who matters right now." She didn't want to sound anxious, but she was.

"Is he writing anything?" Ferris persisted.

"He's at his desk every day. I've never seen such discipline." That was only a partial lie; he did spend several hours every day bent over a notepad. But instead of creating great literature, or even something that fell short of that, he tracked expenses and calculated capital gains, real estate taxes, and depreciation. The American novel had been the lost dream he now refused to discuss. She hated to mislead her brother, but she couldn't bring herself to confess the truth. "I can't comment because I haven't seen any of his work."

"Hummm," Ferris murmured. "Glad to hear it. I've been wondering how things were going with him. It's a bloody hard business . . . And what about you?"

"Me?" She avoided his eyes. "It's just like you, Ferris, to be concerned about everyone else when you're here in a . . . a . . . hospital. Why don't you tell me how you are?" She still clasped one of his hands in hers; the other palm she rested on his thigh as she leaned toward him. "What do the doctors say?"

"I assume I'm better than ever. Nobody's told me otherwise. Fact of the matter is that the so-called therapists and psychiatrists say little to nothing. I'm spending money I don't have to sit around in small groups talking to myself and to the other nut jobs in here."

She was confused. "But . . . but aren't you—"

"That's therapy. The shrink sits and listens, and probably thinks about the date he had last night with the night nurse from Ward B while the rest of us blather on about our problems."

It sounded strange and not particularly productive, but Grace had no experience with psychiatry.

"The odd part is," Ferris said, staring out the window, "I think it does help. The first group I went to made me feel as though I'd stepped into the *Star Wars* bar. I remember thinking, *What am I possibly going to say to these weirdos?* I asked myself why I would ever discuss my problems with total strangers, serious misfits who'd clearly had more than their fair share of problems already. *What can these people possibly do to help me?* And yet when I got there and listened to other people's stories, to their traumas and sorrows, well . . . we're not so different as we think."

"That's wonderful," she commented with artificial enthusiasm.

"I haven't stopped to think about what I was feeling in

a very long time. Losing my health and my freedom has made me do that."

"And you're not drinking?" She wanted some reassurance. She wanted some sense that this place was ensuring her brother's physical safety.

"Around here they ban shampoo if the alcohol content is more than two percent. So in answer to your question, there's nothing for me to consume even if I wanted it."

"Which I can't imagine you do, given all that's happened."

"Oh, Grace, the eternal optimist. I love that about you." He patted her hand.

They sat together in silence. Ferris's leg began to jiggle, and she watched his heel bounce up and down at an abnormally fast rate. After a moment, he seemed to notice it, too. "Perhaps we should walk. They won't let me outside, but you can get plenty of exercise pacing these corridors. Believe me, I know. I've been wandering back and forth for the better part of the last four days."

Arm in arm, they strolled the halls. Ferris was frail and the pace was painfully slow, but she felt relieved. Her brother had been saved from his own destruction just in the nick of time. Now he was getting help.

"How long do you expect to stay here?" she asked.

"I'm not sure, exactly. No doubt my insurance will run out at some point and they'll kick me out."

"You should come down to stay with us after that," she said, realizing as she spoke that she didn't know where she'd be, or whether there would be an extra room. But she couldn't tell him that. She wanted everything on the outside to be just as it had always been. And the Chatham house was part of that normalcy. "I don't want you to be alone."

Ferris smiled but said nothing. They covered a few more yards.

"Do you really think that's why you got sick? Because you didn't allow yourself to feel?" she asked after a while.

"I think I got caught up in the pace of my life, my day. Obviously, booze was a big part of that, but I never paused. I never asked myself, *Ferris, what's making you happy today, or unhappy? Why are you drinking?* Instead I just kept going, never stopping, and drank myself numb so I didn't feel. I expect you're the same way. Not with alcohol but . . . I mean, we were raised not to acknowledge emotions. Look at Mother. She wouldn't even admit she was dying."

Grace didn't respond. She'd never viewed Eleanor's decision to hide her illness from her children as a sign of weakness. Instead she'd interpreted it as a show of self-lessness, courage, and inner strength. She'd kept up appearances for the wedding, for Grace's benefit.

"It would have been much harder for our mother to have to face us all, talk about the fact that she was going to go, than to pretend life was normal until the very final moment. I'm coming to realize it's a lot harder to be angry or hurt than it is to feel nothing. It means you have to come to terms with all the disappointments and wrongs and sorrows—all the feelings I've lived my whole life trying to avoid."

Grace was surprised. She'd assumed he was content with his lot in life, his independence, his more-than-interesting work. *Disappointment* and *sorrow* weren't two words she'd ever have thought of in connection with her brother. Apparently she'd been naive.

"We're both dreamers, you and I. We were raised that way. Mom and Dad created the perfect house in the per-fect society, a world of the mind—but not the heart. It was hard not to grow up thinking the rest of life would be sim-ilarly interesting and basically gentle. No one taught us to deal with passion, or even suggested there was such an emotion. And the flip side of that is everything that hurts."

"Oh, Ferris, I'm so sorry," she said. She wasn't sure she understood exactly what he meant, but she knew he was suffering.

He stopped and turned to face her. "We don't need to spend this time together talking about the past. I have six groups a day to help with that."

"Isn't it better to talk to me instead of strangers?"

"Not according to what they tell me in here."

"Don't be ridiculous. I'm your family." She nudged him gently. "I want to help. I remember last Christmas dinner where you talked about the paths not taken. I should have realized it was your way of telling me that you were hurting. I'm so sorry."

"Please don't apologize." He smiled and she could see the grayness of his teeth. "You've never been anything but kind to me. You are a dear soul."

"But I'm only your sister, so I fear it doesn't count."

He smiled again. Then, as if a snuffer had extinguished the last flame of found happiness, his expression flattened.

"The problem I've had is that I wasn't able to give up on the one path that I did want to take but couldn't. The road was blocked, or maybe the pothole was too deep. But the forces stopping me were beyond my control." He leaned against the wall, seeming exhausted. "Dear Grace, I don't want you to think badly of me." Dropping his gaze to the floor, he added, "Or your friend."

"I don't know what you're talking about, but I'd never think badly of you. Ferris, I love you, and I always will. No matter what. There's nothing you could say or do to change that."

When he lifted his eyes, they were filled with tears. He spoke slowly. "I wanted to marry Prissy. I wanted to spend my life with her. But she wouldn't have me."

Grace should have been shocked, but she wasn't. Instead she felt a sharp pain in her side. She'd known all along. Every sign was there. She just hadn't wanted to see it, hadn't wanted the complications. She thought of the evening before at the beach; she'd known then that Prissy had a secret she couldn't bring herself to share. But she hadn't made the connection to Ferris.

What a coward she'd been not to try to help them both. "What happened?"

He slid down the wall, tucking his knees up as he went, until he rested on the linoleum. Grace looked around wondering whether anyone would object, but nurses, social workers, and case managers passed them without even a sideways glance. She kneeled beside him.

"Prissy was so different, so strong. I think she liked the idea of me—the Boston Brahmin, the liberal, who lived in the world of the mind," he said, self-mockingly. "For her, I was a lively distraction. But at the end of the day, she wants a man who comes home from a hard day of work with a pound of fresh fish for the grill and then fixes a clogged drain or cleans a gutter." He snorted, and the sound startled Grace. "Maybe I'm selling Kody short. Maybe her husband is a great guy. And maybe the best thing about him is that he is simple and kind and predictable."

"You're all those things."

He shook his head. "No, Grace. I may be to you, but that's because we're so alike. Who wants to find faults in himself? All of us fantasize about the exotic, and Prissy was that for me. When I first met her, I thought she seemed wonderfully coarse with a great, dry sense of humor, and self-confidence without the slightest pretense. I'd never met anyone like her. Then I realized it wasn't a passing fancy. It sounds crazy but there was something very appealing about her bluntness. She wasn't educated;

she couldn't debate the philosophical fine points of Nietzsche. She ate with her hands half the time. But she was alive and vital and knew what she wanted and that was very sexy. And so I hung on."

Grace knew exactly what he meant. How many times over the years had she admired Prissy for her directness, for her disregard of social mores, for her fierce independence?

"How long have you been . . . ?"

"There were times when we didn't see each other for a month or more. But our involvement lasted thirty years, if you can believe it."

Since Sarah's death. The anniversary was rapidly approaching.

"Occasionally I'd rebel, go off and have some torrid moment with a woman I barely knew. Then it was even worse after that because Prissy never seemed to mind. She had no jealousy. She never got angry. I guess because she was married, she couldn't get involved in what I did when I wasn't with her. But for me it felt as though she didn't care, as if what we had wasn't particularly special, so she could take me or leave me. I was the broken-wheeled truck that the kid in the sandbox was happy to share so that he could keep the camouflage jeep all to himself."

"Did she know you wanted to marry her?"

"Maybe it was just a fantasy. I'm not sure how it ever would have worked, the melding of her life and mine, but we'd talk about it, sometimes joking and sometimes serious. I was going to move into her small Cape and photograph shorebirds, or she was going to come to Boston and study oceanography, or sometimes we both dreamed of moving away someplace totally new—San Diego was high on the list for a while. And before I knew it, thirty years passed. It's amazing to me how much a dream can sustain you if you need it to." He reached for her hand and squeezed it. "You built something real in that time, Grace. My life's been an illusion. You and Bain made a life together, raised a family, created a fabulous home for all of us to enjoy. You've been there for each other, always."

"It hasn't been perfect."

"But it's been permanent."

Was that the trade-off? She and Bain had a solid, enduring foundation. They shared a history, memories. But she, too, couldn't remember the last time she'd paused to ask herself how she felt, and she doubted Bain had, either. As Ferris had found, it was easier to be numb.

She turned her attention back to him. "Does Prissy know you're here?"

He was silent for several minutes. When he spoke, his voice was so soft that Grace strained to hear. "She does."

"What will happen when you leave?"

"She doesn't want to see me. She's pleased I'm not drinking, though. Told me she couldn't imagine me not three sheets to the wind, but she suspected I'd land on my feet. She knows I can always impose on you."

Grace coughed. Again she thought to tell him the house was for sale but couldn't. It seemed too much to add to his burden. And, she reminded herself, he could sleep on a roll-away couch if she had nothing better to offer. "After thirty years that's all she said?"

"She needs to know whether she stayed in her marriage because of me or in spite of me. Now she wants to see if she can salvage a future with Kody. I wouldn't be at all surprised if they disappear. I don't think she wants me to find her."

"Prissy's not going to disappear," Grace said, more to herself than her brother. She wanted to believe it, wanted to believe that her best friend wouldn't just leave without saying good-bye, especially given the pain she'd caused.

But Grace realized how hollow her conviction was. Despite all the time they'd spent together, all the conversations they'd had, and all that Prissy had seen her through, the clammer had never once confessed her deep, romantic involvement with her brother.

And then it hit her. Had the friendship been a ruse? Had Prissy maintained the relationship because it was useful? Ferris spent time in Grace's home; it made it easy for them to see one another. Stringing Ferris along had been what mattered, and Grace facilitated that process. She'd assisted her friend with hurting her brother. And now Ferris had been discarded. She felt sick.

"The last time we made love was on the beach in front of your house. It was her idea; she practically pinned me down." He laughed at the recollection. "Even in being strong and assertive, she was incredibly feminine. Bain would chide me for being a convert to the feminist cause, but she taught me a lot about women and about how incredibly stupid stereotypes of weakness and strength are."

Grace leaned over and gently kissed his cheek. He sounded so wise, and yet appeared so fragile. She wondered why it took a near-death experience and isolation in a psychiatric hospital to bring out such self-awareness.

"I remember that night looking up at the stars," he continued. "I was holding Prissy in my arms, and feeling as though I wanted time to stop at that precise moment. Have you ever felt that? As if life is so good, so perfect, that you can't bear for it to go on? If I had died then, I would have died with joy."

"There will be more joy, I know that." Grace squeezed his hand.

Ferris closed his eyes for a moment. When he opened them, tears ran down his cheeks.

They sat together in silence until the nurse informed them that visiting hours were over, and Grace would have to leave.

"I'll come again tomorrow," she assured him, but he shook his head.

"It was enough that you came today."

∽

Grace knew when the telephone rang at four in the morning that Ferris was dead. Bain answered and spoke to the doctor as she hugged a pillow to her chest to stifle her sobs. Someone had smuggled in a fifth of vodka. He'd drunk the entire thing, then broken the bottle and slit his wrists.

"How come he hadn't been monitored? Don't you have a suicide watch?" she heard Bain ask.

He wasn't considered a high risk. He'd been sober for more than two weeks, was an active group participant, and showed no signs of depression. The unanimous clinical opinion was that he was on the road to recovery.

"How'd he get the bottle?"

Nobody knew for certain. The only visitor recorded on the log that day was Mrs. Grace Alcott. In fact, she'd been the only visitor since he'd been admitted.

"What happens now?"

The director informed Bain that Ferris had left instructions in his room that he wanted neither a funeral nor a memorial service. Nonetheless, the disposition of his remains was Grace's decision. She was his next of kin.

Before hanging up, Bain said it was all right for the hospital to dispose of his clothing and toiletries. What remained of his personal effects would be forwarded to Chatham.

Ferris died intestate with virtually no assets. Despite

what he'd claimed to Grace, he had no medical insurance. The hospital would take a lien on what little there was.

Two days later, a yellow envelope arrived from McLean, containing a copy of Byron's *Don Juan*, a well-worn address book, and a brief hand-scrawled note outlining his last wishes. "If, Grace, you could be so kind as to arrange cremation and sprinkle my ashes on the beach, I would be forever in your debt." In a postscript, he added, "Don't be sad for me. I had a good run, not as good as it might have turned out, but a good one nonetheless."

Part Three

The Present

Chapter Sixteen

Cars were stretched out bumper to bumper. As she stared out at the metallic snake, red brake lights glared back at her. "Suicide Alley"—the single-lane section of the Mid-Cape Highway between Exits 9 and 11—had come to a standstill. The congestion was unusual for this time of year, even for a Friday. If traffic was an indicator of the summer to come, it would be deadly.

She put the car in neutral. Bain had spoken to her several times recently about not "riding" the brakes. She was wearing out the brake pads, and they would need to be replaced. Idling, the engine rattled. Her brakes might last, but she apparently needed a new muffler. She wondered if she'd done something to exacerbate that problem, too.

Grace rolled down the window and was greeted by a rush of hot air and the smell of exhaust. There were actually little ripples visible through the windshield, just like in the movies. She pictured herself between Thelma and Louise driving too fast through the desert, the camera offering a panorama of the Badlands in front of them, and the thought made her laugh aloud. Why did intense heat make waves? When Erin and Hank were young they'd asked that kind of question, and she'd never been able to answer. Fortunately for her, neither of her boys had persisted in pursuing the information, and both were easily distracted by other activities.

She leaned back in her seat. The digital clock on the dashboard showed that it was after four. She'd been absorbed in her own thoughts and didn't have a clear memory of what had happened in the hour since she'd left the mall. She glanced over at the Victoria's Secret bag on the passenger seat. Perhaps that was what happened to women who bought red lace underwear. They lost themselves in daily life.

Or perhaps sitting in traffic reliving the high and low points of life was what happened to women who were given certain medical diagnoses. They stopped being aware of their surroundings and disengaged with the world. They focused on memories both good and bad, the blending of one year into the next, because they had to look backward. When time was running out, they couldn't think about the next minute or hour or even day. The loss of it would be too devastating.

She had to talk to Bain. That conversation was to precede anything that was to happen on Wednesday. Dr. Preston had delineated the sequence of events. Talk. Then tests. Discuss medical options, including surgery. Then begin a course of . . . of what? He'd called them protocols. Chemotherapy and radiation, she wasn't sure which would come first, and he hadn't been more specific. "It's too soon to have this conversation, Grace. We need more information."

She wanted to skip the intervening steps. She thought of the Monopoly game she'd played with the boys over the years, and imagined drawing a small orange Chance card from the top of the pile. *Do not pass Go. Do not collect $200.* A direct line. Only in this case, she couldn't pay fifty dollars of blue, green, or yellow funny money and avoid her jail sentence.

She didn't want to spend the summer sick. Fourth of July to Labor Day was supposed to be the glorious time, the ten-week stretch that sustained year-round Cape residents during the cold winter and bleak spring. Invitations to cocktail parties and lobster bakes had already started to arrive. She put them up on the fabric-covered board that hung in the kitchen and looked forward to the chance to pull herself together, select and wrap a hostess gift, and get out of the house. The mood was supposed to change with the arrival of relatives and visitors. Summer was supposed to be festive. Life was supposed to be easy.

And yet at this moment she dreaded Fourth of July more than ever, dreaded the start of high season, when television commercials would be filled with images of backyard barbecues and summer clearance sales. She couldn't face the routine, the flag-flying nostalgia, and the mundane conversation about the joy of summer that came with America's birthday. How many holidays had passed where the day had followed precisely the same pattern? It was part of the Alcott tradition.

She, Bain, Ferris, and the boys walked to Main Street and found an opening in the crowd from which to view the parade. She preferred the Shore Road end where the parade began, but Bain liked the intersection of Main and Cross Streets. He was convinced that the lawn in front of the Methodist church afforded the best view. The boys didn't care where they sat as long as they didn't have to sit with their parents. They searched the crowd for a friend and quickly settled in with his family.

They watched the clowns throw candy and the Helping Hand dogs-in-training try not to be distracted by the noise and crowd. The gravel and paving company truck pulled the Miss Eel Grass float on which the unsightly princess in a seaweed skirt undulated to a boom box tune. The hook-and-ladder intermittently blew its siren, and the Minute Men dressed in traditional garb marched and played. It was supposed to be the simplest, the best of holidays, a celebration of America's independence, waving cheap nylon flags and sweating in the sun.

For the past twenty-eight years, the Alcotts had gone to the same postparade party. Andy and Cindy Briggs with their five children and manicured home on Champlain Road seemed the perfect family, the kind that relished togetherness and tradition. The annual event was something out of a Norman Rockwell painting: egg-toss games and water-balloon fights, dogs nibbling at the hors d'oeuvres laid out on folding snack tables across the lawn, pitchers of Bloody Marys and lemonade, children dressed in red, white, and blue. The Briggses included everyone — the tradespeople they paid so well and the sailing instructors from the yacht club, as well as their friends and family — a democratic affair over which Cindy presided, seemingly effortlessly.

Each year Grace had brought a platter of cheese cubes and crackers. When the boys were teenagers, she and Bain also contributed a case of beer, or a couple of bottles of wine — something for the collective alcohol consumption. Not that the Briggses needed anyone to contribute anything. It was a gesture.

The noises of the day were a blur of laughter, shrieks, cheers of encouragement, and more laughter. The occasional newcomers to the gathering were simply absorbed into the rituals, so there was little by way of introductions or explanations. The conversation ranged from the weather and the wind to any recent decisions by the zoning board of appeals or the Historic Business District Commission. Everyone was comfortable, relaxed in the knowledge that no particular effort was required unless they were part of a relay or a tug-of-war.

These were her friends, her neighbors. She was as welcome there as she was anywhere. So why had she felt more and more like an outsider, a voyeur? The last several years, she'd barely mustered the energy to attend, and could well have slept through the parade beforehand if it hadn't been for Bain's insistence. He liked the habit. Routine was a huge part of who he was. And he liked that the ever-successful Andy Briggs was one of his oldest friends.

She'd wanted a change, although not the one that this year would bring.

This year Ferris was gone. By the Fourth of July, Bain and everyone else would know that she was sick. Their friends would look at her with pity, not knowing what to say. Someone would offer to bring over a casserole, some concoction of noodles and canned soup with Ritz crackers crumbled on top to add crunch, a dish that could serve a double purpose if she happened to experience a glue shortage. Maybe the minister at St. Christopher's would quietly pull Bain aside to ask if he wanted to talk about planning. The floral designer might slip him her card, and casually mention how beautiful hydrangeas are in August.

Perhaps the teller from Wachovia Bank would call the next day to see if they needed anything. Employee-of-the-month for the past six, she was an attractive woman in her midforties. From her perch on her stool behind the counter, it was easy to look down her low-cut blouse and see her lacy brassiere underneath. No doubt if she called the Alcott residence, she'd mention that her husband, the owner of a local waste disposal business, had run off with the hospitality manager at Ocean Edge. She was now an eligible divorcée. And under the terms of her settlement agreement, she had free trash removal for as long as she lived in Chatham.

Grace cringed. The last thing she wanted was to have her health, their circumstances, and Bain's future the subject of cocktail-party gossip and speculation.

When he was a widower, there would be plenty of attention. She'd read in the obituaries column of the *Har-*

vard Alumni Bulletin that Art Walters, class of '67, had died, leaving behind his widow, Eileen Baker, Radcliffe '68. The name had jumped out at Grace. Although they'd lost touch, Grace remembered Eileen's interest in Bain from the night of that first *Crimson* party. Had nearly forty years passed? Perhaps Eileen and Bain could reconnect, empathize, and share each other's loss.

Bain would need attention when she was gone, and she wanted him to have it. She hated to think of him alone. But until she died, she'd prefer to think she might have his undivided attention, or at least as much of it as she'd always had.

That thought—the quantity of Bain's attention—made her laugh aloud again, and she felt lucky to be on a single-lane highway. Otherwise someone stopped in traffic beside her might have looked in, seen her intermittently chuckling to herself, and thought she was insane. *Precisely the kind of person who shouldn't be given a license,* she could almost hear the fictitious driver think.

The line of cars had barely advanced. Up ahead, she could see the sign for Exit 11—Chatham/Brewster, Route 137. Her exit, the one she'd taken time and time again, the road she knew so well that she could drive off the ramp with her eyes closed.

But the numbers on the digital clock flipped and she wasn't getting closer.

The rearview mirror showed a line of sedans and wagons and SUVs that extended back into the distance. Wedged in the middle, she was trapped.

She turned on her blinker, twisted the steering wheel as sharply as she could, and inched her way over to the right. As the tires rolled over the drains on the edge of the pavement, the car vibrated. Then she was onto the grass. She drove another several feet forward, rolled up the window, and cut the ignition.

This car is neither abandoned nor broken. Please do not tow, she wrote on a piece of notepaper. *It is not stolen, either,* she hastily added. She stuck the makeshift sign in the window and illuminated the hazards, but then turned them off. She didn't want the battery to die and didn't know how long it would last with the lights flashing. Then she grabbed the Victoria's Secret bag and pushed the power-lock button behind her.

As she walked away from her sedan, it occurred to her that she might not return, although at some point Bain would decide he needed it back even if she didn't.

⤮

"Where in God's name have you been?" Bain shouted as she opened the door. Before she could answer, he continued. "Do you realize what time it is? We've got a showing tomorrow morning."

Grace glanced at her watch. It was nearly seven. She'd been walking for three hours, covering a distance of more than eight miles from where she'd left the car. Her feet, legs, and back ached. Her hands were swollen.

"Kay stopped by briefly this afternoon. She wanted to speak with you. I don't know why you won't get a cell phone."

So that it can be disconnected, too? Grace thought. She didn't want to raise the issue of the American Express card. Perhaps she'd leave the two halves on the breakfast table and see if he noticed.

"What did Kay say?"

"She's bringing a couple who have been looking for property in Osterville for more than a year, but they haven't found anything and are willing to consider Chatham. Kay says they're very qualified. My guess is he's some sort of finance person, hedge funds maybe, or a trader. They've got a child."

Grace stood perfectly still. *Talk to Bain,* Dr. Preston had insisted. How was she to do that? He had been obsessing all day about some family he didn't even know. He hadn't bothered to ask how her doctor's appointment went. He hadn't noticed that she'd come up the driveway on foot.

"What time?" she asked.

"What?"

"What time are they coming? What time is the showing?" She forced her mind to concentrate on the source of Bain's agitation.

"Nine."

"On a Saturday morning?"

"Look, these people are Kay's clients so she wants to accommodate them. If they buy it, she won't have to split a commission. Which means maybe she'd take less from us. In any event, it's a good development. We need to keep the pressure on."

"But we don't even have an offer."

Bain reached into his pocket and produced a scrap of paper. Staring at the felt-tip scrawl, he appeared puzzled by what he'd written down. After a moment, he handed the note to Grace. "Here's what she wants us to do. Flowers, cleaning. I'm sure you can decipher it. I didn't know who to call."

She glanced down at the note, which Bain must have scribbled as Kay issued instructions. There was something about removing the dead Christmas tree that they'd thrown behind the garage, filling a vase or two, disposing of the empty boxes they'd piled on the back porch, turning on the heat overnight to get rid of the mildew, and emptying the dishwasher.

"Oh, and here," Bain said, handing her a bottle of what appeared to be cologne. "Kay said to use this in all the rooms tonight and again tomorrow morning before eight. She said it makes the place smell like summer, whatever the hell that means."

Grace looked at the label. *Parfum d'ambiance.* It had come from 34 Boulevard Saint Germain. She held it in both hands as if she were rubbing a genie bottle, wishing to be transported to that precise store in the middle of Paris instead of left in her Chatham kitchen holding a bottle of imported room freshener.

Bain's car keys lay on the island in the center of the kitchen. He picked them up and spun them on his finger. "We're out of vermouth. I'm going to the Epicure before it closes. Maybe you can get started on that list."

Suddenly Grace didn't want to be alone. She didn't want to be stranded while her husband went to town to replenish his liquor cabinet. She didn't want to be left behind to try to patch up the mistakes in the house. An astute buyer wouldn't miss the water damage, the peeling paint, or the leaking toilet just because there was an arrangement of delphiniums on the dining room table or because the air smelled of tuberose.

"We haven't seen each other all day."

Bain raised his eyebrow. "Look, we're running out of time. Nine o'clock will be here before we know it. I'll be right back."

He let the screen door slam behind him.

She wondered how long it would take him to notice her car was gone.

Grace slipped out the back door and cut behind the side of the house. The salty air had made the steps to the beach slick, and she held on to the railing as she descended. She didn't want to face Bain's return, his inevitable questions, and her feeble explanations. She wasn't losing her mind; she'd just lost her patience in the traffic. Kenny, the nice man from the Mobil station, might not even charge to give him a ride back out to the Mid-Cape to retrieve the sedan.

But she knew Bain when he got in this state. He wouldn't understand. He wouldn't find an ounce of humor in the blisters on her heels or the note she'd left on the dashboard. The fact that he was out of vermouth wouldn't help.

And she wasn't in the mood to have Dr. Preston's talk at this moment. Not tonight. Not until after the showing. No, she wouldn't talk to Bain until after they knew whether an offer was coming, and if it was, maybe she wouldn't say anything until after the house closed. But by then it would be too late to make any real difference. So perhaps she wouldn't have the talk at all.

Maybe Bain and Dr. Preston could talk later, after she was gone. They could recap.

At this rate, she'd be able to convince herself of anything.

The sand soothed her feet, each step massaging her sore arches. At a surprisingly brisk pace, she headed toward the town landing. The sky was turning a deep pink rimmed in purple as dusk settled over the Oyster River. She looked toward the tide line, expecting to see Prissy hauling wire baskets of clams up to her truck.

But the beach was empty. The landing was, too.

She scanned the shore again and then the edge of the dunes. Why did it have to be tonight of all nights that Prissy had finished early and gone home?

She'd avoided the beach the last six weeks since Ferris's death. She had plenty of excuses—she was in mourning for her brother; she was readying the house for sale—but if she was honest, she just hadn't known what to say. Prissy was entitled to make a choice, and Ferris hadn't been what she'd wanted. Still, Grace had somehow expected that Prissy would call or write or offer something by way of condolence or explanation. It was her responsibility. But there'd been no word.

Now she felt angry. Maybe it was learning of her own mortality, or maybe it was something simpler — being stuck in horrible traffic — but she wanted to confront her friend and wanted to know why. She wanted to understand, if such a thing were possible. Even more than that, even more than her anger and sorrow and confusion, she wanted life to be like it was before . . . before Ferris was dead . . . before she was sick . . . before her home was gone . . . before she'd known the truth. She wanted her tidy existence back. She wanted to be able to sit with the friend she'd had and confess how very scared she was.

"Where are you?" she called into the wind.

A seagull squawked. Turning, she saw it lift off from the beach, flap its wings several times, and then coast across the river to disappear in the sea grass on the other side. Another followed close behind.

She grabbed handfuls of sand and buried her face in her palms. The granules scraped her skin.

"I don't want to be sick!"

She tore at her blouse, pulling it over her head only half unbuttoned, and stumbled out of her pants as well as out of her more-than-six-months-old underwear and bra. The cool breeze on her naked body made her shiver. Her nipples were erect from the cold, and goose bumps dotted her thighs. Her hair blew in her face, and then stuck to her wet cheeks, blocking her vision. She started to run, kicking sand as she went. Slipping on a clump of seaweed, she struggled to maintain her balance without halting her progress.

Finally she felt the frigid water on her calves and

hurled herself out into the black tide, belly flopping into the channel. The shock made her muscles ache. She dipped her head under and felt the salt burn her cheeks. Resurfacing, she gulped air.

Rolling onto her back, she treaded water and stared up at the sky, then twisted around to face the salty blackness again. Swallowing a mouthful, she coughed and sputtered.

She swam out a few strokes. The middle of the channel — midway between the shore she'd left behind and the spit of Hardings Beach on the other side — was where she'd be sure she couldn't reach down and touch the sandy bottom with her toes.

She wanted to let the sea envelop her. This was the place she loved. This was where she'd sought solace before. It made sense for this water, the same water that had baptized Erin and swallowed Ferris's ashes, to take her diseased body and deliver her to peace.

Perhaps she should have done this long ago. A part of her had never survived Sarah's death.

The sun had set and the sky was dark. She could see nothing on shore but a single light. Judging from its location, it could be her bedroom. She hoped she wouldn't wash ashore to be discovered puffy and bloated and blue. Bain didn't need that. It would be better for everyone if she sank to the bottom and never returned.

Eleanor and then Sarah and now Ferris were gone. Would they all be reunited in the hereafter? It would be a welcome consolation for the loss of their presence that she'd suffered during her lifetime.

Then she thought of Hank and Erin. She wondered how they would take the news of her death. Maybe they'd look after their father; maybe they could be supportive and loving, or maybe not. Everyone always said it was much better to have a daughter during a tragedy.

Now was the moment. She gulped again, struggling to get the thick seawater down her throat. Having the ocean in her as well as around her was what she wanted. And yet even as she swallowed she knew this couldn't be the end. She couldn't follow in Ferris's footsteps. As much as this seemed an appropriate place and an appropriate moment for her death, with the smell of the sea, the feel of the cold wetness, and the sound of the wind, she'd never, ever felt more alive.

 ◈

The telephone was ringing as she opened the front door. Either Bain had not yet returned or he was upstairs in the bath and had decided not to get out. The ringing persisted.

She reached for the receiver and instantly regretted her decision.

"Mom, it's Hank. I can't believe that you're selling our home."

Our home. She knew his choice of words was deliberate, but the house hadn't felt collective since the boys had been children. They'd been gone for so long and, despite the summer visits with their families, never did anything to indicate they cared about the place. She couldn't remember a time that either of the boys had pulled a weed or fixed a broken screen.

Hank was babbling about his industry. She focused.

"You've got it on the Multiple Listing Service. Did you honestly think I wouldn't find out?"

A puddle had formed underneath her feet. She could feel cold water running from her hair down her back. She felt silly standing naked and wet holding the telephone, and wished she hadn't abandoned her clothes at the beach. What if the propane company or the UPS truck made a late-night delivery? It had been known to happen.

"Real estate listings are computerized. I can access everything. I could be looking at property in California. When did you do this?" Hank was yelling now.

She shrugged and closed her eyes. She and Bain hadn't wanted to tell the boys, hadn't wanted to have any discussion about finances or reasons. It was none of their business.

Keeping her voice steady and controlled, she announced, "We put the house on the market in March. There hasn't been an offer. We recently lowered the price, and allowed the broker to list it on MLS," she said matter-of-factly. *Lowered the price* was an understatement for a five-hundred-thousand-dollar reduction, but Hank didn't need to know details. "I think there will be some advertising, too, so don't be surprised."

"Gee, thanks for telling me. Now I won't be." His sarcasm was obvious.

"It's quite possible the right family won't come along. This is a quirky house. We've loved it, but it's not for everyone."

There was a pause before Hank asked, "March? We were there for Easter."

Bain had been adamant about maintaining secrecy, and they'd blocked out the holiday weekend with the Realtor. No showings. No calls. If someone was truly interested, they could come back after the family departed. As it was, there hadn't been a nibble.

He continued. "Have you had a lot of showings?"

"No, not really. A few. There is one tomorrow," she said, remembering. She glanced around the room. Where was Bain?

"Did it occur to you to ask how I felt about it? We were

just making plans for the summer. I was thinking we'd come down for the first two weeks of August."

Hank seemed awfully young for two weeks' vacation. Bain would never have dreamed of such a prolonged period away from the office at his age. He hadn't been gone that long even when Sarah died. Wasn't there work to do? A career to advance?

"Susan was thinking of staying for an extra week after I leave. She loves the beach."

We all do, Grace thought. Instead she just mumbled, "Oh."

"But apparently now our home may not still be in the family. What are we supposed to do?"

She hated his snide tone of voice. *Perhaps you should purchase this house yourself and we can come as your guests,* she wanted to say. *Then Susan can make sure the sheets are clean, there's fresh soap in the linen closet, and ripe peaches and plums for snacks. And you can pay the real estate taxes and come up with the cost of a new roof.* But she knew such thoughts were absurd. Her two sons could no more buy out their parents than run for president.

"Maybe you should think about Maine. I hear rentals are more reasonable."

"This is my profession," he said, ignoring her. "I might have been able to give you some advice."

Hadn't he abandoned the Wellesley rental market and become a mortgage broker several years before? Obviously, her information was outdated. Then again, she was only his mother.

"The least you could have done is talked to me before you listed it. It was both embarrassing and awkward at the office. Try explaining why your parents don't give you the listing for your own house."

Again the collective possession. Then she understood. He was upset because he wanted the brokerage commis-

sion. Even though his office wasn't on the Cape, local brokers could show it and he'd still be entitled to 2.5 percent
with little or no effort. First free rent. Then free cash. It
had absolutely nothing to do with nostalgia about the
family home. Money. It was all about money. He wanted
some more from his parents.

"When exactly were you planning on telling me?"

She wasn't sure how to answer. She and Bain had
avoided that subject. "When we moved out, I suppose,"
she replied. At least she was honest. She had expected to
give them a forwarding address.

There was silence on the other end.

She wiggled her toes in the puddle. The edge of the
area rug was wet, too. "I'm going to have to go. I've made
a bit of a mess here. Do send Susan my best! Little Henry,
too," she said with a forced cheeriness. "I'll tell your father
you called. Bye-bye." Before he had a chance to respond,
she replaced the receiver. She could justify a quick good-
bye. It was different from an actual hang-up on her son.

She stared at the telephone, wondering whether it
would ring again. He hadn't asked why, or where they
planned to go.

Hearing footsteps, she turned to see Bain. In his arms,
he held her bundle of clothes and a plastic bag from the
liquor store. He eyed her naked body, then the puddle.

"It's not what you think. I went for a swim," she said.
Her tone sounded apologetic. Although incontinence
might come, it hadn't happened yet.

He dropped the clothes and bag onto a chair. "It's
June. The water can't be above fifty-eight."

There had been so many times in their life together that
his precision, his attention to the smallest detail, had been
a source of tremendous comfort to her. Hearing him now
estimate late-spring water temperature made her smile.

He removed his sweater and draped it over her shoulders. Then he rested his hands on her shoulders. "You're going to get yourself sick. And that's the last thing we need right now."

She leaned her body against his and breathed in his familiar scent. "How did you know to go to the beach?" she whispered.

"The gate on the stairway was open. I just had a feeling I'd find you there. Instead I found your underwear." He patted her bare behind. "Go take a hot shower. And I'll make you some soup. I saw a can of that escarole flavor you like in the pantry."

She looked into his eyes, wanting to speak, but words didn't come. She nodded.

"And I assume at dinner you'll let me know what happened to your car." He smiled. "With the way you've been acting today, I fear I may be in for quite a story."

❧

The gray light of the full moon illuminated the bedroom. Even though she had pushed off the covers and wore only a thin nightgown, Grace felt weighted down. Her breathing labored with each inhalation. She wasn't getting enough air. Beside her, Bain lay on his back, his mouth agape, faintly snoring. She rearranged the pillows and flopped against them. When sleep still didn't come, she rolled back and stared at the spiderweb of cracks that covered the ceiling.

"We'll need a biopsy," Dr. Preston had said as he pointed to what appeared to be her right lung. The dark shadows of the X-ray made it difficult to see exactly what he meant, but he'd already explained that there was a lump in her breast. It was the size of a grapefruit, although in medical jargon every lump seemed to be grapefruit-size, that particular citrus the universal standard of measurement. She'd never heard someone say that a tumor had the diameter of an orange or the dimensions of a lemon, the weight of a pomegranate or a small avocado.

He'd consulted his prescription pad. "You've got an appointment scheduled on Wednesday with a doctor named Belafonte—like the singer."

She pictured a man in a white coat with tan skin, white teeth, and graying hair. Steel drum music would be piped into the operating room.

"He's terrific. We've known each other for years. You're going to like him."

She didn't need more friends. In fact, if the doctor was stern and rigid and scientific, it might be easier. She could subject her body to whatever probing and cutting he needed to do, listen to his diagnosis and prognosis, and then go about her business. A kind doctor, a hopeful man, was harder to dismiss.

"He's over at Dana Farber."

Dana Farber. Cancer. The terms were synonymous.

It was the same place that her mother had died.

Dr. Preston had leaned forward, rested his elbows on his desk, and given her an earnest look. "I know this comes at a particularly difficult time. But as I explained before, we shouldn't rush to conclusions. It could still be nothing. However, you do need to talk to Bain."

"If it might be nothing, let's wait until you tell me for certain," she'd replied. Her voice sounded foreign and far away, as though it were emanating from a tape recorder in the back of the room. "I don't want him to worry. He has a lot on his mind right now." She stared behind him. A blond woman with glossy lips and a red-and-white-checked blouse smiled from the five-by-seven silver frame on his credenza. The Mrs. Doctor Preston was attractive. There were no cancerous fruits growing in her breasts.

That kind of woman didn't even have a pimple. She wondered if they were happy. "How long have you been married?" she asked. It was the first personal question she'd ever put to Dr. Preston.

He looked confused, glanced over his shoulder to the photograph, and then nodded in recognition. Yes, he did have a wife. There she was on his credenza. "Brook and I married in '94." He turned his attention back to Grace. "Bain needs to be involved. There may be decisions to make."

Decisions. They were Bain's forte. She dabbled in decision making—after all, she did go to the grocery store and choose what to cook for supper—but she'd spent fifty-eight years without having to make any momentous choice. She'd gone along with his decisions, endorsed them and supported them without expending too much intellectual energy wondering whether she actually agreed. To render a decision meant she had to have an opinion of her own. Suddenly she liked that idea and wanted to tumble it around in her mind until it came out smooth and shiny.

"Now's the time," Dr. Preston had prodded.

She'd nodded.

When she'd left the hospital that afternoon, she'd vowed not to return. That would be her first major choice, and it had seemed a good one. To coin Ferris's phrase, she'd had a good run. Other than a few weeks in bed with Lyme disease, she'd experienced fine health. Now she didn't want more days driving back and forth to Boston, sitting on a plastic chair watching nurses shuttle up and down the hall checking clipboards, tying and untying hospital gowns, waiting for the X-ray, wondering what was wrong, imagining the worst, listening to Dr. Preston's feeble efforts to be optimistic.

Lying in bed, she made small circles on Bain's chest

with her palm. This evening had been the first and only time she'd had a suicidal moment, a brief indulgence that had been as transitory as the changeover airport on a one-stop flight. And tonight had ended as many had before it: with soup and a slice of toast on a tray in front of the news, Bain half reading *The Wall Street Journal* and half listening to the parade of horrors that filled the broadcast, and her shutting off the light behind them both when they went up to bed.

She glanced at the clock on her nightstand. Four A.M. The showing was only a few hours away.

As she'd stepped from a hot shower earlier in the evening, feeling relaxed for the first time she could remember, Kay had called. Her voice had seemed more abrasive than usual. "I'd say they're definitely interested," she'd announced as though the tea leaves were a challenge to read. "They already had me fax a copy of the survey to their attorneys in Manhattan. That's a very good sign. And they prequalified for something much more substantial, so you don't have to worry on that end."

Grace reached over and ran her finger along Bain's cheek. He twitched but didn't awaken. The lines in his forehead deepened.

Thirty-six years they'd been married. She'd never been with anyone else, and, as far as she knew, he'd been faithful, too. She welcomed his familiarity—the comfort of his body and the predictability of his character. Those feelings were real whether or not she was dying.

She thought of a story Bain had told her years before. A colleague of his at the Bank of Boston was diagnosed with prostate cancer. His wife, a professor at Boston College, had resigned from her position to care for him and tend to his every need. After six long years in and out of hospitals, traveling the country in search of the best care, he met with his doctors. He was disease-free. His prognosis was excellent. He'd beaten it. His wife and he went out for a five-star dinner to celebrate and splurged on a bottle of Cristal champagne. The next day he filed for divorce. No one could believe it. "If I was going to die, it didn't matter," he'd explained. "But since I'm going to live, the last thing I want is to be with her."

Grace couldn't imagine a life without her husband, and for a moment she felt selfishly relieved that she would be gone first. Never before had the order of death occurred to her. Now she understood why people wanted spouses who were substantially younger. It was as close to a guarantee as possible. Nobody wanted to be left behind.

What would happen to Bain? He seemed strong, much less dependent upon her than she on him, but maybe that was nothing more than the roles they'd established, the rhythm they'd fallen into since the day they'd met. And maybe she was underestimating herself. She took care of him; she'd raised their children; she'd run the household. Replicating her efforts would be a challenge for him.

She didn't want him to be scared. She couldn't bear for him to be lost. Her mind raced with all the information she needed to impart to him: that colored and white clothing needed to be washed separately; that whole coffee beans should be stored in an airtight container or kept in the freezer; that adding a touch of olive oil to the boiling water prevented spaghetti from sticking together; that he needed to buy all-new boxer shorts and undershirts every six months.

She rolled toward him and kissed his ear. Then she reached between his legs and felt the warm softness of his flaccid penis. She held him in her palm and gently caressed him. He stirred. After a moment, he adjusted the covers, slipped his arm under her torso, and pulled her toward him. He rubbed her hair, her shoulders, and her back. Without opening his eyes, his mouth found her lips.

It was then that she made what might be her final decision. She would take whatever remaining weeks or months she had to teach him to be self-sufficient. But the less Bain knew about her condition, the less time he had to worry, the happier their remaining days together would be. By keeping her own secret, by sparing him the pain, she could show him how much she truly loved him.

Chapter Seventeen

Hurry, Grace, we've got to leave," Bain called upstairs as he stood by the front door. It was five after nine and the broker would be arriving any moment with the well-qualified, very interested buyers.

Grace looked at her reflection. Her skin had a yellow tinge, but the dimming bulb in her wall sconce did, too. She leaned toward the mirror. When had those lines appeared, the crow's-feet at her eyes and the deep grooves around her mouth? What was age, what was disease, and what was perception? Lost in the warmth of Bain's arms the night before, and consumed by the passion they'd shared again this morning, she'd felt no older than she had on her honeymoon. Now she wanted to bottle the feeling.

"Grace!" she heard him call again. "They're driving in now!"

She grabbed the bottle of *parfum l'ambiance* and spritzed the air several times. The sweet odor filled the bathroom—not what she would call the smell of summer, but at least it masked the mildew. They'd forgotten to turn on the heat as Kay had instructed.

Still pulling on her barn jacket, she descended the steps just as the front door opened. Bain seemed to have frozen on the threshold.

"Oh, my, this is a surprise," Kay said, obviously displeased. "We did say nine."

Behind her stood a young couple. The man was tall
with broad shoulders, dark hair, and generically handsome features. He wore what Grace assumed was his version of country attire—twill pants, an oilskin jacket with a
corduroy collar, and short leather boots. But for the two
cell phones and beeper prominently attached to the front
of his belt, he could have been on his way to either a
pheasant shoot in the Czech Republic or a photo shoot for
Barbour outerwear. His wife had strawberry-blond hair
pulled back in a ponytail, a long thin face, and lips outlined in a plum-colored liner. Even in her stiletto-heeled
boots, she was short.

Ignoring Kay and Bain, the woman reached into her
lizard purse and produced a Palm Pilot. Fascinated, Grace
watched as she held the pointer in her French-manicured
fingertips and began entering information of some sort.

"Yes, yes, we're sorry. The morning got away from us,"
Bain apologized.

Grace blushed. She looked down at the floor, hoping
the source of their delay was not made too obvious by her
rose-colored cheeks. What would this young couple think
of two people who could have been their parents making
love before breakfast? What would her own children
think? She almost laughed.

Bain extended his hand. "I'm Bainbridge Alcott. This is
my wife, Grace."

"May I introduce Jay and Robin Marx," Kay cooed.

Robin paused in her data entry to smile and nod.

"How long's it been? You two living here," Jay asked
with more than a hint of a Long Island accent.

"More than thirty years," Grace said. "We bought our
home in 1972. We've raised our family here."

Bain looked at her with a perplexed expression.

Robin seemed to find that information worth noting
and plucked quickly at several keys with the wand.

"And would you say the place is well maintained?"

"That's an assessment you'll have to make for yourself," Bain replied, coolly.

"Looks to me like that roof needs some work."

"Why don't we let the Alcotts go about their business and we can take a look around?" Kay suggested. She gestured with one arm, seeming to want to swoop the Marxes inside. "The grounds are fabulous. There isn't a property with this waterfront anywhere." As she stepped past Bain and Grace, she gave them a stern glare. "It's a gracious family home for a remarkable value."

As Kay spoke, Grace watched a paper airplane fly out through the partially opened window of a navy-blue Range Rover parked in the driveway. Moments later, the side door opened and out stumbled a small child, wearing a Burberry-plaid driving coat. A Hispanic woman quickly climbed down, grabbed her arm, and pulled her up from the gravel.

"Mommy!" the child screamed, flopping down again.

Robin seemed to spin on her stiletto heels. "Juanita, I told you to keep her in the car."

"I'm sorry, Missus Robin, but she no want."

"You have to make her stay. Mr. Marx and I are busy. That's why you're here."

The little girl continued to cry. Juanita squatted next to her, whispering words of comfort. "No cry, Isabelle, come, come."

"Might I suggest," Grace began, stepping toward the nanny, "that you take her down to the beach." She kneeled beside them both and addressed the child. She was a beautiful girl, perhaps five but maybe a year or two older, with large blue eyes, fair skin, and brown curls. Although her cheeks were streaked with tears and her hands were dirty from the driveway gravel, she had an angelic quality. Her crying stopped.

As she looked back at the child, an image of Sarah flashed before her eyes. This little girl might be raised in her home, in her bedroom overlooking the Oyster River. She might grow up riding her bicycle to the Stage Harbor Yacht Club and listening to Friday-night band concerts on the village green. Then she'd have the wedding Grace dreamed of for Sarah under a huge tent spread across this very lawn. And if somewhere down the road Robin Marx got sick, her daughter would be there to take care of her. It wasn't fair.

"There is lots to look at and possibly some shells to collect. Do you like seals? If you look very carefully, you can sometimes see their heads in the water. Or what about seagulls? They're a lot easier to spot."

Isabelle stared at her, silent. Her lip quivered.

"My children liked to look for sea glass. They imagined it was special treasure. Would you like to do that?"

She nodded.

"The easiest way to get there is just down those stairs." Grace gestured to Juanita.

The nanny looked nervously at her employer. Grace followed her gaze and saw Jay and Robin Marx, Kay, and Bain all staring at the three of them standing in the driveway.

"Fine, take her," Robin directed. "But don't let her get dirty or wet."

Jay and Robin disappeared inside, and Kay shut the front door.

"Thank you, senora," Juanita said to Grace as she took Isabelle's hand and led her in the direction of the steps.

Behind her, Grace heard Bain start his car. The engine rattled for a moment before turning over. He let it idle to warm up, even though the day was mild. Although the plan was to drive out to Exit 11 and retrieve her car, pick up a few things at the Stop & Shop on Route 137, and then have a bite of breakfast before returning home, she didn't want to leave. She felt as though Kay were the National Guard forcing her to evacuate, and she refused. She'd be like those few brave men and women she saw on television whenever there was a serious hurricane or tornado, the ones who decided to sit in their homes and ride out the storm, the ones who preferred to risk death in familiar surroundings, in the places they loved, rather than flee to some overcrowded, converted school gymnasium.

Grace walked down the drive and picked up Isabelle's paper airplane. Its flight had been short; it had crashed into the lawn just a few yards from the Range Rover. The airplane was colorful. Unfolding it, she realized it was the listing brochure for her home. She stared at the pictures of her dining, living, and bedrooms, the pool, and the water view. "Recent price reduction on this gracious waterfront home ready for your personal touch. Eager sellers, this one-of-a-kind property won't last," the brochure read.

Horizons. This home had a personal touch. Hers. And the brochure was wrong again. The property would last. It would outlast her.

"Come on, Grace." From the driver's seat, Bain had leaned across and opened the passenger's-side door. She balled the brochure and climbed in beside him.

Bain didn't look at her. Instead he drove, staring straight ahead at the road. She could see he had tears in his eyes. "I'm not moving off the asking price," he said as they took a left onto Battlefield Road. "Not one dollar. Not one penny. Not for *those* kind of people."

⚬⚬

The house felt different to Grace when she returned, as if she'd been vandalized. There had been other showings but she hadn't met the potential buyers, hadn't had to interact, hadn't engaged with whatever children they might have had. They'd stayed anonymous, which was better for her. Now she could envision the interlopers.

She walked into the library and stared at the spines of dozens of books facing out from the shelves, the photographs of her, of Bain, of the children in tortoiseshell frames, and the knickknacks she'd acquired over thirty years. What had the Marxes noticed? Had Robin and Jay been to the same piazza in Venice where she'd taken a picture of Bain surrounded by pigeons? Had they paused at the pastel portrait of Sarah hanging over the mantel and wondered where that charming girl was now?

Looking around, she realized how many of her secrets this room held, how much evidence of the life she'd led was on display. That the Marxes were privy to this was a violation.

The house echoed with the sound of her hard soles on the pine floors as Grace ran to the kitchen. She pulled out more than a dozen plastic bags that she stored under the sink, then rushed back to the library and began pulling items off the shelves. She grabbed photos, the Limoges box of a birthday cake that Bain had given her when she turned thirty, the collection of arrowheads that Erin had found in the backyard, the first edition of Edith Wharton's *A Backward Glance* that she'd found in a rare-book shop in the West Village, everything personal, everything other than the coffee table picture books of Cape homes and gardens that almost everyone had. All this she stuffed into the bags. She worked quickly and carelessly, shoving things in haphazardly. If her home was now public, she wanted them out of public view. Never again would the Marxes or anyone else get to come in and learn about her life.

She paused in her efforts only when Bain entered the room.

"What are you doing?" he asked, although the answer was obvious. He fingered one of the full plastic bags that sat on the sofa and checked its contents. "You should wrap the frames in tissue or newspaper or something. They could break," he said matter-of-factly.

"I just wanted to get them off the shelves," she replied. "I can't bear to feel so exposed." She squatted and hugged her knees to her chest.

"I know, I know," Bain said, his voice soothing. She felt his hand on her back. "I was right behind you." With that, he sat on the floor next to her.

"This is awful," she said, sighing. "Those people were awful. I don't want them in our house." She knew that her words only made it worse for him, more shameful and humiliating, but she couldn't help herself. This house wasn't a Palm Pilot project. It was a labor of love. She'd rather have the walls collapse around her than turn it over to someone else.

"If there were some way I could avoid this—avoid this for you—you know I would. But . . . but this house doesn't make sense. We both know that. Not now and no time soon, or at least no time that I can see. It doesn't mean you won't have a nice home, and you'll always have me. We have each other."

She couldn't bear to reply. She couldn't bear to point out to him how wrong he was.

❧

"There's a message for you from Dr. Preston," Bain said later that evening as they sat down at the dining room table. They'd spent the remainder of the afternoon working to sanitize the library, the living room, and their bedroom. In a matter of hours, they'd eliminated almost every display of who and what they were. Bain brought boxes from the porch, and together they'd carefully wrapped everything that mattered. But the fact remained that the house still felt like them—the faint smell of Grace's perfume and Bain's cigar smoke lingered in the walls, and no *parfum d'ambiance* could displace it. Even the sofa cushions seemed to sag with the weight of their frames.

They'd lived there for so long that they couldn't get rid of themselves even though they tried.

Grace had prepared supper, or rather she'd taken the pasta-and-lentil salad that they'd bought ready-made and put it in a serving bowl. She'd been so distracted that morning at the Stop & Shop that she hadn't noticed what a strange combination of foods it was as she'd spooned it from the salad bar into a plastic container. But the $6.49 dinner would have to suffice.

"Didn't you see him yesterday?"

"Him? Who?"

"Dr. Preston. I thought that was why you went to Boston. Didn't you have an appointment with him yesterday?"

The day before, Friday, already seemed light-years away. With her anger and sorrow over the Marxes, she'd almost allowed herself to forget. Dr. Preston was no doubt calling on a Saturday to check on her progress with Bain, progress she hadn't and wouldn't be making. For once she wished her doctor could be less attentive.

"Did anyone else call?" she asked, ignoring his question. Neither of them had bothered to check the answering machine when they'd returned after the showing. And the phone hadn't rung since they'd been home.

"Hank. He said he's coming for lunch next week. He

wants to discuss the house." Bain put his napkin in his lap and stared twice at the farfalle dotted with brown spots of beans before digging into the mound with a serving spoon. Then he took a bite. "What is this?" he asked as he chewed longer than a usual mouthful required.

"I'm not really sure," Grace replied.

He furrowed his brow as if debating whether a second bite was worth the effort. "Why did you tell Hank it was for sale?" Bain said after a moment, the tone of his voice more serious.

"He already knew. He called me yesterday because he'd seen the listing on his computer."

"Well, just for the record, it's none of his business. This house isn't his." Bain stabbed unsuccessfully at the pasta with his fork, but the gummy bow-tie shapes slathered in oil and beans escaped him.

"He and Susan were planning to come for August. If the house is sold, he needs to change his plans." She remembered her conversation, the irritation she'd felt as she'd spoken to him.

Was it possible that he'd been more reasonable than she'd allowed? He'd relied on them being there. She might feel as though she was being taken for granted, but wasn't that a fair premise, one that her son should assume to be true? Did a child ever attain an age where parents didn't have to be there for him?

"Maybe the Marxes need an adopted son and would welcome his company. Henry could play with that sweet girl, Isabelle." Grace forced a smile. She felt her stomach turn at the thought and pushed her plate away.

"Unlikely," Bain muttered. He put his fork down and took a sip of the Merlot she'd opened for them. "Not bad. What is this?"

"A bin special of some sort. I'm not sure." It was a cheap Merlot, but it didn't taste as bad as she'd expected.

"Look, I don't want to have lunch with Hank," Bain said. "I don't want to get into reasons with him. And the last thing I want is a discussion of our finances."

"Do you think we should get it over with? Tell Erin and Hank what's going on and why? We're going to have to do it eventually." She couldn't exactly imagine the conversation; it was not the type of dialogue with which she was familiar. But she thought it might alleviate some of the pressure, especially the pressure on Bain. "What's the point in carrying on a charade?"

"A charade? Is that what you think this is?"

"I made a poor choice of words."

But there did seem to be an implicit agreement with both boys that nobody spoke of anything that mattered. She thought of the last conversation she'd had with her brother. Maybe they all wanted to be numb; silence facilitated that. Feelings couldn't be experienced without some degree of candor.

"I don't want to talk to them now. It's about privacy and respect. If we open up discussion on why we're moving, the next thing you know he'll ask to see my will. He'll want to know what he's getting."

A Last Will and Testament. Grace shuddered. She hadn't thought of that, of the necessity of having one. Then again, what was really hers to give away? Everything she had, everything she owned, was hers because of Bain. How he disposed of his dwindling wealth after his death was his business.

"Maybe I need to explain to Hank that it's time he looked out for himself and took responsibility for his family. I made that decision long ago. Remember when I took the job at Bank of Boston?"

She nodded. How could she forget?

"He shouldn't be waiting around for you and me to

die. He shouldn't be planning to bankroll his life with an inheritance. And we may outlast him," Bain said, smiling.

She tried to return his smile but felt dizzy.

"Now, are you going to answer my question about Dr. Preston or leave me in the dark?"

Grace looked down at her plate and poked at her pasta. "American Express canceled my card today." She spoke slowly and softly, knowing she was using the only bit of information she had that could distract him from further pursuing health issues she couldn't bring herself to discuss.

Bain steepled his fingers and pressed his thumbs into his eyebrows. He said nothing.

She regretted her tack. In an effort to distract him, she'd delivered a harrowing blow. Sharing Dr. Preston's news wouldn't have been any easier, but it wouldn't have been so shameful to him.

"Never mind," she said, rising to clear the dishes. "A woman I met said I should have a MasterCard instead. I hear it's much better."

Bain gave her a perplexed look.

She pretended not to notice, poured the last of the Merlot into his glass, stacked their plates, and propped the bowl on her forearm. "Do you want dessert? There's some of that lemon sherbet, or a Fig Newton?"

"No. I'm not hungry."

As she turned to leave, she heard him add, "Thank you, Grace. You're the only woman I can imagine who would be so kind about this disaster. I don't know where I'd be without you."

⚯

Grace was changing out of her knit suit when she heard
the knock on the door. They'd been home from church
less than fifteen minutes. She didn't want visitors; she
wanted lunch.

Bain opened the door, and she heard Kay's voice pierce
the late-morning silence. "I knew you'd be here, so I didn't
bother to call. That's what I love best about dealing with
churchgoers. You all are so regular."

"What is it?" she heard Bain ask.

Still undressed, Grace walked to the threshold of her
bedroom. She could hear clearly down the stairs.

"I've got an offer. It's a good one," the broker squealed.
"In fact, it's their best offer. That's how the Marxes
phrased it."

"What's that mean?"

"It means they don't want to negotiate. Take it or leave
it. One million three, cash. They'll close in a month. They
want to be in by August."

Grace held on to the top of the banister for balance.
She strained to hear Bain's response, but then realized he
wasn't speaking. The voice was still Kay's.

"The offer's open until midnight tonight. I'll tell you
right now, in this economy, you're not going to do better.
High-end houses around here have been on the market for
months, even houses that needed no work. Let's be realistic. This is the only offer we've had, and the house has
been listed since March."

Midnight. They had less than thirteen hours to make
the momentous decision.

Grace's mind raced. After payment of the brokerage
commission, the two mortgages, and the capital gains tax,
there would be little left over. River Bay was looking more
and more inevitable.

Bain didn't hesitate. "I'll take it."

Chapter Eighteen

Located out on a peninsula of land, the clubhouse of Eastward Ho enjoyed a spectacular view of Pleasant Bay. Although technically part of East Orleans, its members preferred to consider it one of the loveliest spots in Chatham. The golf course had an impressive history and a challenging architectural design, but what drew Grace to the place was its majestic setting. She was perfectly content to walk the course beside Bain, taking in the feel of the salty air on her face and watching the wind-filled sails of boats gliding on the water.

Tonight the sky had darkened to a foggy gray. The knobby pine trees along the edge of the rocky cliff and the pristine ocean beyond made for a picturesque backdrop to the evening's festivities inside the clubhouse. No wonder so many members rented the space for their personal celebrations.

Andy and Cindy Briggs's youngest child, Amanda, had gotten engaged. Word had it that the pink diamond on her slender finger was more than two carats. And with Cindy's usual flair, an engraved invitation announcing an engagement party had arrived just ten days after the fact.

"Weren't we at the club last year for her graduation?" Bain had remarked as they'd driven along Crowell Road. They'd been late, and Bain drove a little too quickly on the winding road in his effort to make up time. "Mount Holyoke, wasn't it?"

"Yes," Grace had replied, remembering the lavish celebration for what she'd understood had been the girl's modest academic performance. That she'd gotten the diploma to frame and hang in four years was all that mattered. It had taken Hank five to get through the University of Colorado at Boulder.

"I must say it did surprise me that none of the Briggs kids went to Dartmouth. Andy is head of the trustees, after all. He must give that institution millions. Just goes to show money can't buy everything."

Not nearly everything, she'd thought.

Because the party was well under way, they'd had to park at the far end of the lot. Beside the car, a seagull pecked at a broken clamshell.

The noise of happy voices spilled outside as they climbed the steps and entered the foyer. Nearly the whole area was taken up with a long table piled high with gifts. Most were wrapped in silver and white, although a few obvious robin's-egg-blue boxes remained bare. Grace added her contribution—a boxed set of cocktail napkins and matching coasters—to the pyramid. Somewhere en route from the car, she'd lost the card.

"I'd hate for them to think we brought nothing," she said to Bain in urging that they go back out and look for the small white envelope.

"Just forget it. You can tell her what happened when you see her."

Amanda would never remember given all the excitement of the evening, but she acquiesced. By the time the girl worked her way through her thank-you notes, it might not matter whether one was sent to Grace or not.

She and Bain moved toward the reception and paused at the entrance. The large square room was filled with people of all ages, the guests a sea of summer shades of yellow, green, and pink. It gave her no small amount of delight that Lilly Pulitzer was back in style, as though the world had come full circle just in the nick of time. She could wear the wrap skirts she'd bought in college and feel chic, or pretty chic so long as the lights were dim enough to mask the toll that age and wear had taken on the fabrics.

She gazed about the room. Young waitresses in white oxford shirts and black knee-length skirts wove deftly in and out of the colorful crowd offering food, collecting glasses, and bringing refills. On the mantel were enormous bouquets of lilacs in white marble urns, and along one wall were photographs of the bride- and groom-to-be: Amanda as a seven-year-old with her front tooth missing; Barnaby Hodges in his Dartmouth varsity lacrosse uniform; a studio portrait of the two of them that had been submitted to *The Chronicle* along with their announcement. She'd noticed that the column held a place of prominence in the rows of newsprint.

Cindy Briggs saw Grace and Bain and quickly made her way to greet them.

"Andy's lost," she said, smiling. "But please get a drink, have a bite to eat, and relax. We're so glad you're here. The music will start in a little while."

"How festive!" Grace exclaimed, meaning it. She and Bain hadn't danced together in years. Maybe she could get him to spin her at least once around the floor.

"That's Amanda's doing, not mine," Cindy replied, tilting her head in her daughter's direction and rolling her eyes. Amanda stood beside the mantel surrounded by a group of girlfriends. "It's not a party without rock and roll."

Her Fred Astaire and Ginger Rogers fantasy quickly faded.

"Has Amanda known her fiancé long?" Grace asked. She remembered that at the graduation party, Amanda was with Chad, one of the yacht club sailing instructors. Andy had failed in his efforts to hide his displeasure.

"Four months. In this day and age it seems like a second, but it was love at first sight, truly. And I have to remind myself that Andy and I were engaged after only a few months, too. We got to know each other as we went along. And here we are thirty-three years later marrying off our baby. Maybe all the waiting and living together that kids do nowadays takes away too much of the mystery. Where's the fun?"

Grace thought of her own romance. She and Bain had met less than a year before the day they walked down the aisle.

"I look around at all these young couples getting divorced and I wonder if it's because they can't adapt. They live together, they try to iron out every wrinkle in the relationship ahead of time—who gets the blue toothbrush, who keeps their clothes on the right side of the closet, and who gets the first crack at the Sunday crossword. So much advance planning and then they can't adjust to the inevitable changes in a marriage. I don't know about you two, but Andy and I were so relieved to share a bedroom and not have to lock the door that we didn't complain about the little problems. We were able to get through the tougher times. I think it made our marriages more resilient, wouldn't you agree?"

Resilience. It sounded like an admirable quality in a mattress.

Cindy didn't wait for a response. "So that's my way of saying I have absolute confidence in Amanda and Barnaby. They are adorable together. She's old-fashioned—dying to be a wife and set up a home, but not about to do it without the vows—and the ring, which by the way is a beauty. Barnaby has very good taste. And believe you me when I tell you that he is the man of that family. But again, that's just fine. Andy still wears the pants in our marriage." She smiled and leaned toward them, adding in a conspiratorial tone, "Except when it comes to this wedding. I'll make those decisions. I told him the day they announced their engagement, 'This is a mother's dream so you stay quiet and get ready to write the checks.'" She laughed.

"When is the big day?"

Cindy's eyes lit up. "June seventeenth. You'd better save the date. We'll have it at the house here, and we want to make sure all our old Chatham friends are with us. It will be a true Cape reception, a shell motif on the invitations, a lobster bake for the rehearsal dinner, bridesmaids in cranberry."

What Sarah might have had and what Grace would have wanted. She suddenly felt sick to her stomach.

"So put it on your calendars now. I won't take no for an answer."

Next summer. Grace couldn't think that far ahead. Then again, she wouldn't have to.

"I may even impose on you to put up some of the groom's family. Apparently he's got all these British cousins who are planning to attend. How would you like a houseful of strapping young Henley types?" Cindy poked Grace's side. "You see, Barnaby's mother is English. She couldn't be sweeter, and her accent is to die for. She met Barnaby Senior when he was over there as a Rhodes scholar. What can I say? The whole family is attractive, brilliant, and successful. We are so lucky." She paused, perhaps to take a breath, and rested her hand on Bain's shoulder. "Now I'm stopping you from getting to the bar. Please, go celebrate. Help us celebrate. After you get a drink—and I highly recommend the margaritas—

introduce yourself to Barnaby. He's over there." She
pointed to a tall boy in Nantucket red khaki pants, a pale
blue oxford, and a navy belt with green anchors appliquéd
on it. He had wavy blond hair and a young face. But for
his extraordinary height, he could pass for twelve.

"He's terrific," she said, flapping her hands to gesticu-
late. "Andy's so crazy about him, I fear our own boys may
get jealous. He thinks his future son-in-law is a substantial improvement on his own flesh and blood." Cindy
laughed. "He's joking, of course, but you can imagine."

"I see Barnaby is a Dartmouth grad," Bain remarked,
pointing toward the photograph of the lacrosse player.
"That must help."

"You hit that face on the nose," Cindy said, laughing
again. "Nothing beats the green!" With that, she glanced
over Bain's shoulder, spotted the arrival of another couple,
and cooed, "Damon, Sally, how super of you to come all
this way. You are too dear!"

❦

The band had been playing for more than an hour.
Although some of the tunes were familiar, most made
Grace realize how long it had been since she'd turned on
the radio. Contemporary rock and roll to her was the
Pointer Sisters. The music of this generation baffled her,
and she remembered a brief conversation she'd had with
Hank years before about a group called Smashing Pump-
kins. The name had conjured an image of pulp and seeds
and devilish-looking carvings adorning a stage, but Hank
had only laughed at her response and told her they were
awesome. What did she know about music anyway? She
and Bain still listened to Frank Sinatra.

When the lead singer suddenly announced a "golden
oldie" and started his rendition of "You Belong to Me,"

Cindy and Andy and most of their other guests took the floor. Grace turned to Bain, hopeful. Even if she couldn't gyrate as fluidly as the others, she still yearned for Bain to take her hand, escort her to the dance floor, and lead her effortlessly around the perimeter.

He took her by the elbow. "Let's see if we can find a quiet spot," he said, leading them away to the farthest corner of the vast room. But it wasn't to dance alone. He cupped his hand to his mouth and whispered in her ear, "How soon do you think we can leave without seeming rude?"

She didn't have a chance to answer before Bob Lockerby approached. In his late seventies, he had a ruddy complexion and a shock of white hair. Holding himself steady with a mahogany cane, he nodded a greeting.

"Evening, Bob," Bain said.

Although he'd lived only a few houses away since before they'd even visited Chatham for the first time, they'd never known Bob well. He neither entertained nor accepted many of the invitations that came to him. Rumor had it that he might be homosexual. That he was single, impeccably dressed, and had a red dining room contributed to the suspicions.

"It's a lovely party," Grace added.

"So what made you decide to sell?" he asked abruptly.

What Travels Faster—Gossip or a Racehorse? That had been the topic of an eighth-grade essay she'd written at the Windsor School. If she remembered correctly, the assignment had been designed to deal with symbolism. Now the issue was real.

Grace glanced at Bain. She expected him to startle, to express some sort of dismay at the fact that their accepted offer was part of the public domain only hours after the fact. Instead he seemed to have resigned himself to the inevitable.

"We got an offer we couldn't refuse," he replied. "And it's really too much house for Grace and me anyway."

Bob raised his eyebrows but said nothing. Did he know the price, too? Was that it? Anyone who'd lived in Chatham for a week, let alone three-quarters of a century, would know the value of real estate, would know that the Alcotts had one of the best parcels of land around, and would know that the house had been given away.

"The boys come less and less. It's really a waste," Bain added in further justification.

"You of all people. I thought you would be around here forever," Bob mumbled. "The Alcotts on Sears Point seemed about as permanent as the lighthouse on Shore Road."

"Times change," Bain said. His voice sounded beleaguered.

"That's for sure."

Everyone stood in silence. The moment was awkward. "Well, on behalf of those who remain, I've got to thank you for selling it as is. It's still hard for me to believe the Elliotts are subdividing. Now, that's a crime if there ever was one."

Bain nodded in agreement. The Elliotts had twelve acres on Stage Neck. Much to the dismay of the neighborhood and over considerable objection, they'd received approval for a six-lot subdivision and had already cleared to put in the road. There was no explanation except pure greed. As far as anyone knew, they were as rich as they'd ever been. Martha Elliott was driving a brand-new Mercedes convertible and Herb boasted that he was traveling all the way to Finland to discuss the commission of a Swan 65.

Then again, Grace knew from her own experience that appearances could be deceiving. In fact, she might conclude that appearances were designed to be that way. Bain had installed a swimming pool rather than acknowledge their financial downturn.

Thinking of the Elliotts, Grace wondered what she would have done if the possibility of selling off land could have allowed her to stay. Would she have agreed to the building of a house that would block her view of, or her access to, the water in order to earn enough from the sale of the land to be able to stay in her home? Could she have tolerated such a jarring change and remained? It was an option so many people seemed to take, but for better or for worse she was glad that their lack of acreage had precluded it.

"So where are you headed?" Bob asked.

"We haven't decided," Grace said.

Simultaneously Bain replied, "Palm Beach."

Palm Beach. They'd never discussed leaving Chatham, let alone moving to another state. They'd visited Florida several times on business for Bain—Palm Beach and Naples and Boca Raton—and even though they'd stayed in the most elegant hotels, they'd both hated it, the ugly highways and strip malls, the flat topography and oppressive heat, the smell of taco stands and suntan oil. There had been one happy moment that she could recall. She'd been lying by the pool at the Ritz-Carlton reading a book and Bain had surprised her by placing a chameleon on her brightly patterned bathing suit. They both watched in amazement as the poor creature's coloring began to change. But a makeshift science experiment hardly justified establishing a residency.

"Tax laws are certainly better," Bain added.

Grace looked at the floor. She closed her eyes and listened to the music, the sounds of footsteps on the dance floor, the background rumble of conversation. She knew what Bain was doing, publicly at least. He couldn't stay in a place where everyone would realize that he'd lost what they'd had, that he wasn't an adequate provider, that he couldn't be the financial equal of his peers, that at this point he'd be lucky to get a job as Andy Briggs's butler. That truth would be impossible to hide when they moved from their enviable home on Sears Point to a Cape in West Chatham or a new subdivision on the Harwich line, or when the new owners began to talk about the terrible condition of the house and all they had to do to make it habitable.

But older people retired to Florida. That's what they did. So if he went there, no one would question the decision. He wouldn't have to explain. He wouldn't suffer humiliation or scorn. He'd climb aboard a flight at Logan and fly off into the sunset, leaving his possessions to follow in an interstate moving van.

He wasn't even sixty yet. If he hadn't taken early retirement, he'd still have five years to go. She tried to imagine Bain settling into his new locale, a two-bedroom condominium with a distant view of the Intracoastal, the kind of high-rise with a marble elevator, a doorman in a short-sleeved shirt, and an assigned parking space in a covered lot. She tried to imagine his reincarnation as an aging Jimmy Buffett fan drinking a frothy mixture with an umbrella in the glass or the fourth in a bridge group of men wearing white leather shoes.

It wasn't Bain. A transformation didn't seem possible; he was who he had always been. But Florida did hold one appeal. He could rewrite recent history—and, without her, there would be nobody to correct him.

Bob nodded and pursed his lips. "Sure, good choice. I got to admit, the winters around here are getting to me, too."

She could tell Bain struggled to keep his voice sounding casual. "January and February are brutal. Much worse for Grace than for me, but we travel as a team. Plus we're thinking of spending summers in Portofino. You know, a little European atmosphere to keep us all young."

"Sounds like you've got it all figured out," Bob said, shifting his cane to the other hand. "I envy you, Bain. That life sounds pretty darn good to me. You should let some of us in on your secret."

Bain smiled and put his arm around his wife. As he squeezed her, she knew he was hoping for one thing: that this story would travel as fast as the news of the house sale, and neither of them would have to explain anything again.

Chapter Nineteen

Grace stood over the stove, poking at the scum that had congealed on the top of the cream of asparagus soup. She'd planned lunch for twelve thirty, but Hank was late by more than an hour. The salad she'd dressed had wilted, and the baguette slices were hard. Her meal was ruined, not that she cared. Neither the presentation nor the taste of food mattered, and most smells made her nauseous.

Had it been only four days since she'd learned of her illness? Her physical condition couldn't have changed much in so brief a period of time, but knowledge had changed everything. Being conscious of her disease made her body ache in a new and eerie way. She imagined the worst—hungry black cells gobbling her flesh, and evil signals flashing through her neural systems. Destroy. Destroy. Destroy. She wished she could shed her skin like the magical seals of fairy tales and slip into the sea as a free spirit or a transformed mermaid.

The pantry door swung open. "Where the hell is he?" Bain said as he stepped into the kitchen. He glanced into the pot on the stove. "Is that soup?"

Grace nodded. "It needs to be reheated. That layer on the top will disappear, but I thought I'd wait until he gets here."

"I don't get it."

"Well, the heat melts that—"

"Not the soup. I meant the whole thing. This meeting, this lunch was at his insistence. You think I wanted a confrontation to discuss a decision that doesn't involve him?" Bain shook his head, disgusted. "You know what's particularly interesting to me?" he asked, reaching into a box of Wheat Thins and popping a cracker into his mouth.

"What's that?"

"A couple of years ago when I tore that ligament in my ankle and was on crutches, remember?"

"Of course."

"I heard you on the phone to Hank, to Erin, too. I heard you several times asking them to come visit. You wanted them to 'bolster my spirits.' Those were your words."

Grace felt a rush of heat in her face. She hadn't realized he'd overheard her pleas. Bain was a decidedly bad patient, and she'd thought the boys could help.

"Funny thing is, I don't remember anyone showing up. No doubt they had a million excuses, were too busy with family and kids and whatever it is they do to waste time. But it still interests me that a Monday in June is suddenly free and clear. I guess when he's got a personal stake in the outcome, he can find the time."

"Maybe we can all have a pleasant visit. It has been quite a while." She forced a smile.

Bain glanced at his watch. "You'd think he'd have the courtesy to be on time."

"I could try his cell phone. He might be stuck in traffic."

"On a Monday morning coming south?" Bain raised his eyebrows. "I doubt it. Susan probably insisted he finish his flash card sequence with Henry. '*Parents* magazine says that if the father participates in the exercise, the child has a sixteen percent greater chance of retaining the information,'" Bain said, imitating Susan's high-pitched voice. He shrugged his shoulders. "What is with those two?"

"They're doing the best they can, I'm sure," Grace said, not necessarily intending to defend them. Bain was right. Hank was incredibly selfish and self-absorbed. But she did empathize with Susan. She was struggling to make all the right decisions for her son, just as Grace had tried to do for Hank. She hoped her daughter-in-law would have better success. "Parenting has changed a lot. It's more of a science, a skill, than it was in our day. Maybe that's not such a bad thing."

"With the way she pressures that kid, he'll either be the next Einstein or a serial killer."

"Bain, what a way to speak of your own grandson."

"I'm only voicing an opinion. But mark my words. He'll snap one of these days. Run the lawn mower over a cat or something."

"Oh, stop. She's just encouraging him to reach his full potential. Maybe he'll be president someday."

Bain raised his eyebrows. "No matter what she does to the kid, he's still Hank's son."

Just then they heard the sound of tires on the gravel. The time had come. Grace turned the knob on the stove and relit the burner while Bain went to answer the door.

❧

They'd been at the table for several minutes without anyone saying a word. Before lunch, Hank had toured the house. Although his remarks had been casual, his swagger had been territorial, and Grace had the distinct impression that he was marking his turf.

"Didn't Grandpa give you this when I was born?" he asked as he stood before an oil portrait that had been done by a protégé of John Singer Sargent. It was an elegant painting of a man in tortoiseshell glasses perched on a stool with a green glass and brass lamp glowing on a table behind him.

"No," Bain replied. "He did not. It was given to me and I had it in my office for years."

Grace understood Hank's insinuations, and she didn't disagree with Bain's method of responding, although the truth was somewhere in the middle. It had been a gift from her father, and it had been given around the time of Hank's birth, but Bain had adored it and kept it with him at work until his recent retirement. Neither of them had considered it then or now as a gift to Hank.

The dance had continued as Hank wandered from room to room, asking questions about origins and making an elaborate mental inventory of what his parents were likely to take with them, what Erin might want, and what he could rightfully claim.

His conduct reminded her of an article she'd read years before, an exposé on an estate resolution gone amok, when the heirs of a household went through the entire mansion with color-coded stickers—one color for each grown child—and marked what they wanted just a week after their parents' deaths. As to be expected, the valuable antiques got numerous stickers, but what was shocking was that one heir put a round red sticker on the half-used roll of toilet paper in the master bath, while a blue sticker was attached to an opened box of cornflakes in the pantry. The newspaper had used the apt term *vultures*.

Now, as she listened to the clink of soup spoons against the bowl rims, Grace stared at the tablecloth, noticing a small stain just to the right of her plate. She wished she could remember when it had gotten there, but she couldn't even remember when she'd acquired this particular cloth. It might have been years before. She wanted the irregularly shaped brown mark to have come from a dinner with Ferris. Back in those days, she still cooked.

Perhaps in his animated conversation, or his enthusiastic way of gesticulating, he'd dripped his fork or accidentally hit the edge of his plate, and gravy had dripped onto the fabric.

She missed Ferris. Thinking of him made her think of Prissy, too. She wondered if there would ever be a time again when she didn't associate one with the other.

If he'd never met Prissy, Ferris's life might have followed a completely different course. He might not have been so restless or unstable. He might have fallen in love or even married. All it would have taken was the slightest change of direction. An entire life might have evolved in a different way. A better way. He might still be alive.

It was horrible to think that one choice set forth a sequence of events that rolled inexorably to a horrid end. If she'd never befriended the clammer, if she hadn't made the introduction to her brother, if both of them hadn't come to her aid after the tragedy of Sarah's death, Ferris might be here now. In fact, if she'd never hired a nanny, if she hadn't cared about her hairstyle for a cocktail party, then Sarah would be here now, too.

She wanted them both. She'd be able to talk to Sarah, to explain her fears, to ask for her care. And she'd be able to ask Ferris for advice. Then he could smile and tell her everything would turn out all right in the end. *Doesn't it always?* She imagined his voice. His lies.

Was a life simply the accumulation of consequences that resulted from a single choice? Looking at hers, it was easy to identify the source. Everything stemmed from Bain. It was impossible to even imagine what might have unfolded if she'd never attended that fateful party at the *Crimson.*

"You're making a mistake to take the photos away." Hank's comment interrupted her thoughts. "A house shows better with personal effects on display," he said, breaking a slice of bread in two. "It makes the place feel livable."

"Your mother was more concerned about privacy."

Hank gave her a baffled expression. "Privacy? You're selling the house."

"That doesn't mean we're on display," Bain insisted.

"We're selling walls, windows, floors, a roof," Grace added, wondering when Bain might mention that they'd accepted an offer. Although she'd decided to leave that announcement up to him, it did seem surreal to discuss the manner of showing the house when the showings had accomplished their purpose.

"Absolutely right. Not our lives," Bain said, obviously pleased with her remark.

Hank glanced down at the spoon in his hand. Then he rested it on the side of his dish. "Part of selling a home is convincing the buyer that they want your life. They need to think they're buying into a myth of something else, something better. That's the point. If I were the broker, I'd insist you put them back."

"Well, you're not."

"You don't need to remind me of that, Dad."

She passed him the salad bowl.

"You need to understand that what you're doing is very upsetting to both Erin and me. We may not have been vocal enough about that before, but I'm here to tell you now. Erin wanted to come, too, so that I wouldn't be speaking for both of us. He feels as strongly as I do about the house, but he couldn't make it."

"A sure sign that something's important, setting priorities," Bain mumbled, although Grace knew he was relieved that he didn't have to face both sons at once.

"I would think you'd cut him some slack given the mess he's in. You couldn't honestly have expected him to leave home under the circumstances."

"What mess is it this time?" Bain asked.

"You don't know?" Hank looked from his father to his mother. He leaned back in his chair and crossed his arms in front of his chest. His smug expression indicated he was quite pleased to have information that they didn't. "Marley's moved out."

"When did that happen?" Bain asked without a hint of alarm in his voice as he dipped his spoon into his soup.

"About two weeks ago."

"Two weeks!" Grace felt her pulse race. Her son's wife had left him and she hadn't heard a word. Her mind flashed to Ferris, the despair she'd seen on his face and the sorrow she'd heard in his voice the last time they'd been together as he'd spoken of Prissy and her decision to say good-bye. She couldn't bear for there to be such pain again. "Is Erin all right?"

"Look, Ma, I didn't get into details with him. Our conversation was mostly about the house. We all know that woman is weird. Look at the crap she talks about—faith healing and pansexuality. It's BS if you ask me. For all I know, she's finding herself and will come back after there's been some revelation in a week or two. Erin's a lot better off without her."

"That's not for us to say," she replied, although her voice sounded foreign. "Where did she go?"

"I don't know. I don't think Erin does, either."

"People don't just disappear!" Grace heard the desperation in her own voice. Images of Ferris and Prissy swirled in her mind. Now Marley was gone, too. "What about the children?"

"They're with Erin. Marley walked out on the whole kit and caboodle. She even left that mangy dog she seems so attached to. The mutt slept in their bed." He made a face to indicate his repulsion.

What character trait allowed people to simply walk

away from everything they'd known, everything they'd made, and everything they'd loved? Did the past haunt them, or could they truly purge themselves, as if a giant vacuum cleaner had consumed their memories in a single whoosh? Marley and Erin had been together since freshman year, nearly half his life. For better or for worse, it had been his choice, her choice, a choice they'd made together.

She thought of Erin, alone in his tiny house, trying to care for three small children while navigating around her purple healing table. Maybe he could feed the children on it. Faux leather cleaned up nicely.

"Why didn't he tell us?" She might have done something to help, although at this particular moment she couldn't imagine what. She chastised herself. The distance—the estrangement—was her fault. After the school tuition conversation, her telephone calls with Erin had been more brief and distant than ever. Making excuses about how they needed to be with Marley's family, he hadn't come for Thanksgiving or Christmas. Maybe Marley hated her in-laws and that's why she'd left. Maybe she'd had it with the whole Alcott clan. Maybe Erin didn't say anything because his parents were responsible for the breakup. Maybe Erin hated his parents, too.

"I have no idea." Hank took a bite of salad. "It wouldn't have done any good."

"We're his parents." The sentence seemed as lifeless as Grace felt. She reminded herself of all that she kept secret from her sons, and even her husband. Why would she have expected Erin to be more open or forthcoming?

"Have you any idea what happened?" Bain asked.

Hank nodded. "Probably what always happens: People realize they've spent years together, still aren't happy, wonder if they ever were, and start looking for something else. Even if they don't find it, just the thought that it might be out there, and that they might be missing something, is enough incentive."

Grace looked at her son, wondering whether he'd arrived at that theory from personal experience.

"It's astounding to me how many people Susan and I know who are getting divorced or having affairs. A life together like the two of you have is becoming extinct. Your marriage is a relic." He laughed.

Bain did not.

The image was apt: a fossil with the flesh and blood gone but the skeletal imprint remaining, an enduring marriage captured and preserved in layers of sand and rock. Some archaeologist could come along in a thousand years and dig it up, mount it in a museum as a testament to longevity, and students could ponder what it might have looked like when it was alive.

"Susan has her opinions on the matter, believe me. I think it's about plain old boredom. But my advice to Erin was to contact a good lawyer. I could see that woman being vicious if she wanted to be."

Grace felt the urge to get up from the table and call Erin immediately. But as soon as she made the suggestion, she could see in Bain's eyes that it was out of the question. He did not want to be alone with Hank and forced to face Hank's real concern, which wasn't his brother. "You can try him this evening, after the kids are in bed," Bain offered.

But Grace felt agitated, and so instead got up to pour coffee from the carafe she'd set out on the sideboard. As she placed a cup and saucer in front of Hank, she noticed that the handle was chipped, and a replacement was impossible. The china pattern had been discontinued years before. Since she'd been in its registry, Shreve, Crump & Low had sent her a notice to that effect.

The pharaohs of ancient Egypt had been buried with belongings they'd need in the afterlife. Maybe the broken demitasse, another relic, would be an appropriate object to insert in her coffin.

Hank took a sip and grimaced slightly. "Look, despite what else is going on, you two need to understand that Erin and I are strongly opposed to the sale of this house. We want you to take it off the market immediately so that you won't be liable for a commission if a ready, willing, and able buyer comes along. The last thing you need is to be sued for five percent of the sale price."

"This is not your decision to make," Bain said, sternly. "This is my home. I'll decide when it's time to leave. And that time has come."

Grace avoided Hank's gaze. Bain's comment—his distinct use of the singular—had registered with her, too, but she didn't need her son reminding her of that.

"The decision is shortsighted."

"You're wrong."

"We've grown up here," Hank insisted. "Chatham's been our home our entire lives. It's been central in our children's lives."

His sentimentality surprised Grace, and made her wonder if she'd underestimated him. Perhaps she'd been wrong in thinking that his anger stemmed from a missed opportunity to sell the house. Perhaps he had formed an attachment born of history, memories, and a sense of family.

"You can't just decide on your own to dump this place."

"I don't intend to," Bain replied.

"So why sell?" Then, as if the idea had only just occurred to him, he added, "Are you in financial trouble? Is that the problem?"

Bain was silent.

"If that's the case, if you can't afford this place, we really need to talk, because . . . well . . . Erin and I feel that there's been some serious miscommunication."

"I don't know what you're talking about."

"Look, Dad, let's cut to the chase. I've seen the listing. You're selling at what is arguably way below market price. You're virtually giving the property away. If you're under that kind of pressure, you have an obligation to disclose that to us."

"Don't talk to me like that. I am not a publicly traded company issuing an annual report. I have no disclosure obligations—to use your phrase. I have no obligations whatsoever to you or your brother." Bain's face reddened.

"You're not being fair to us," Hank said. His voice bordered on shrill. "This is our inheritance."

The word seemed to echo.

Bain leaned forward. When he spoke his voice was low and controlled. "I can do whatever I damn well please."

Grace felt dizzy and drained her coffee in the hope that the caffeine would stabilize her senses. Hank had found Bain's Achilles' heel and driven in the sword. Whether or not it was fatal, the family relationship could never be the same. She knew that. They all knew that.

"I mean . . . this house is your legacy. You know . . . to pass on." Hank stammered. "Erin and I appreciate that. We really do. It's an incredible asset."

"Let me give you one piece of advice," Bain interrupted. "It's one thing you may want to remember, a lesson I learned and took to heart years ago, years ago when I decided to go to work as a financial analyst. It was an important lesson, one that has stood me in good stead." Bain paused for a moment as if to collect his thoughts. "Don't sit around waiting for your parents to die to make money. It's both unattractive and impractical."

It was the second time in as many days that Bain had alluded to that fateful decision from years before, his decision to abandon his artistic dreams for money and for the ability it gave him to provide for his family. He'd done that job, and done it well. They'd all been the beneficiaries until this moment when, needing to provide for himself in the last years of his life, he'd ordered a fire sale of the family home. Despite his rage at Hank and his frustration at the situation, Grace realized how deeply Bain meant the advice he offered. It was a lesson that came from a man who wanted to spare his son the shame that he'd experienced, and the humiliation she knew he'd felt when he'd accepted the Marxes' offer.

"Dad, this isn't about waiting for anyone to die. All I'm saying is that you're being impulsive and . . . frankly . . . stupid. This house is a one-of-a-kind property."

"Then I suggest you get to work so you can buy it back." Bain struggled to maintain composure.

"It is ours. That's the point," Hank continued. "Save it for us. We shouldn't have to buy anything back."

"That's where you're wrong. The house is already sold. We'll be out by the middle of July. You and your brother can come down, pick over our belongings, and grab as much as you can of all that won't be coming with us. Maybe that can satisfy your appetite for a few years, while you give me a chance to grow really old." Bain pushed his chair away from the table and stood. "Let me make one thing perfectly clear. I have no intention of leaving this fine earth anytime soon, so I'd advise you to find another source of revenue. Now, if you'll excuse me, I've had quite enough of this gathering."

Grace watched him turn and walk out of the room at a slower pace than she would have expected given the conversation. His shoulders stooped slightly. She realized that he'd lost weight, and his pants sagged.

Hank didn't move. She, too, remained in the last place she wanted to be: at the table, across from her son, and without her husband.

"Is this what you wanted?" he asked after a few minutes. His voice had softened; he no longer spoke with an accusatory tone.

"It . . . it makes sense for us. This house is too big, too much to manage." Grace struggled to parrot Bain's excuses.

"But it's your home, too, our home. Don't memories mean anything? Isn't a family's history important? You were the one who always talked to us about rituals."

"That's true. I did." She paused, thinking. "But I've come to the conclusion that rituals only matter if everyone is invested equally in them, in the tradition, in the spirit of a gathering. Rituals for rituals' sake—for the routine—are hollow, meaningless."

"So what are you saying? That what we did together as a family in this house didn't matter?"

She looked at him not knowing how to respond. Her eyes welled with tears. This pain, this ending, was not what she'd intended for any of them. Now she desperately wanted to change their destiny. She wanted Hank to be small again, small enough that she could take him into her lap and explain to him what was important. She wanted to be able to redo his history, to nurture him and help shape him into a different man, a man who would never have to ask that question, a man who would harbor no doubts about the meaning of his family, a man who wouldn't count his inheritance dollars before his parents were in their graves.

But she couldn't pretend or imagine or wish any longer. The family of her dreams wasn't the Alcotts. The argument with Bain couldn't be undone or the words taken back. Hank and Bain had both revealed themselves. And in Erin's silent absence, he had, too.

"I wish I knew," she replied, mumbling more to herself than to her son.

⌘

Bain and Grace sat on stools at The Squire. The local restaurant with its plaid carpeting and clunky wooden tables was crowded. Through the wall, Grace could hear the bass guitar of the band next door. Live music marked the start of the season at The Squire's adjacent bar, a boisterous watering hole decorated with license plates, a jukebox, several pool tables, and bouncers with biceps popping from their green golf shirts.

At the adjacent table, a toddler screamed. Not wanting to further embarrass the family, Grace didn't turn around, but she couldn't help listening. She heard a woman, presumably the child's mother, provide comfort by offering more ketchup for the french fries and the promise of dessert. Then a boy's voice, an older sibling, asked if he could have more, too. The mother told him he'd had enough. Ketchup was a condiment, not a food group. It was to be used in moderation. The boy protested. Tomatoes were vegetables. Didn't that count? Then he appealed to his father, but the man refused to come to his aid. "Look, Sam, I don't care what you eat, but your mother just said no so that's that. Next time you'll learn to ask me first."

The waiter set bowls of steaming clam chowder on the acrylic place mats in front of them.

Bain ordered another Bloody Mary and some more bread.

Grace opened the bag of oyster crackers and stirred them into her soup, but she couldn't bring herself to taste it. She put down her spoon.

With his gaze fixed on the window, Bain reached for her hand and clasped her fingers in his. The gesture surprised her, but his palm felt warm and inviting.

"What's happened to us?" he asked. "How did we get to this place?" He still didn't look at her, but he squeezed her fingers a bit tighter. "It's not just finances, the sale of the house. I'm talking about our sons. I thought I'd raised men who would flank my side as I charged into battle. Instead, well, I'm not sure I even want them in the vicinity when the going gets tough."

"It's not so bad. They mean well." Grace couldn't help herself. Although she'd harbored similar thoughts, somehow it seemed as though agreeing with him would make all the disappointment too real.

"Sweet Gracie, the eternal optimist. How dearly I love that about you." He squeezed her hand. "I told myself that if I ever became a parent, I just wanted to raise children who were hardworking, independent, and honest, but that what they did with their lives, their professions, their choice of spouses, all that stuff about where and how they chose to live, was up to them. I told myself I'd support them in those decisions. But it's much harder than I expected—harder to be supportive, I mean, harder not to be critical. It never occurred to me that I might be responsible for a person who lacked fundamental decency."

"Maybe it's our fault. Maybe we did something wrong."

Bain was silent. He took a sip of soup and ripped a roll in two. Grace waited, patiently. He was no doubt formulating his thoughts, and she didn't want to rush the conversation that she needed to have with him more than he even realized. Despite the context, she appreciated his candor. It relieved her of the doubts she'd had, the wondering she'd done, over whether her husband had lost any capacity to feel.

Bain opened a small plastic tub of butter and spread the contents on half the roll. "I don't think so. What could we have possibly done that wasn't right for them?"

Chapter Twenty

The early-morning light glittered on the surface of the water. A breeze rustled the long beach grass, and four piping plovers ran back and forth at the waterline, their movement so delicate that they left no trace of their presence imprinted in the sand. It wasn't yet six, but Grace had been awake for hours. This walk was her reward for the more taxing job that lay ahead: the organization of the attic in preparation for her yard sale.

"You're crazy," Bain had said when she suggested the idea. "Why do you want to spend some of our last days in this house sitting in the front yard selling stuff we don't want?"

"It's a waste to throw out perfectly good, usable objects. And we might make some money," she'd said, defending her plan. "The Warrens made several thousand dollars when they had one over Memorial Day," she'd added, remembering somebody's comment on the recent success.

Bain had shrugged. "It's your time."

Now she needed to sort through, throw out, pack to save, or plan to sell the contents of myriad boxes, trunks, cartons, and unidentifiable objects that they'd amassed over the last thirty years.

The plovers seemed to follow her, quickening their awkward scamper as her stride lengthened. She loved these particular birds. Other than the puffins that arrived on Mill Pond each December, there was no other creature that seemed to embody the Cape in the same way. They represented the fragility and beauty of this environment. That they now required protection to stave off extinction seemed emblematic of the destruction of natural resources everywhere on this exquisite elbow of land—the over-fishing, the overbuilding.

She chuckled. Bain would have quite a time if he heard her soapbox tirade on the disasters occurring in their midst. A good distraction, though. Focusing on the prob-lems and devastations in the external world was certainly easier than facing the carnage in her personal one.

She stopped and stared in disbelief. There, bent over, with a clam rake and a bucket, was Prissy. She couldn't see her face, but she knew the lean body, the baggy canvas coat, and the rubber boots. Until two months ago, she'd seen the same image framed by the same ocean backdrop nearly every day.

Her heartbeat quickened. She'd told herself again and again that she wanted this moment, this encounter. She wanted to know what had transpired between her friend and her brother. Prissy no doubt knew fears and dreams and fantasies that belonged to Ferris, and rightfully should be told to his sister. Only she knew what had hap-pened during their final conversation. Only she could confess to having smuggled in the alcohol that had turned lethal.

But now that the moment was here, Grace felt helpless. Maybe none of it mattered. Nothing could bring Ferris back. And could anyone, even his adoring sister, ever truly understand what drove him to such a place of pain that he couldn't go on? As she stood in the sand, over-whelmed by emotion, she silently prayed that Prissy would approach her first, would break the ice by acknowledging their distance and the destruction she'd caused, would offer up tidy explanations wrapped in twine that could ameliorate the hurt.

She stood still, watching, as the woman was consumed with her work. She raked and raked, reached down with her free hand and dug out clams, and threw them into the wire bucket without once straightening up to alleviate the strain on her back.

Grace moved closer, gathering her courage. She took a few more steps. As her shadow cast darkness on the wet sand, the clammer detected her presence and looked up.

"Oh no!" Grace exclaimed. The shock and surprise caused the exclamation quite unwittingly. The face was young, pretty, with a nose dotted with freckles, bright blue eyes, and plump lips that formed a natural pout.

"Are you okay?" the unfamiliar woman asked.

"Yes . . . yes," Grace stammered. She forced a smile. "I beg your pardon. Here I am, sneaking up on you. I thought you were someone else."

"No problem." The woman turned back to her work.

Grace hesitated for a moment before adding, "A friend of mine, an old friend, clams in this spot, and I haven't seen her in quite a while. I mistook you for her."

"Are you talking about Prissy?" the woman asked, reading her mind.

Grace nodded.

"I'd better get a new life if this one is aging me that fast. She's old enough to be my mother."

From their close proximity, it was readily apparent that the woman was no more than twenty. She had no lines on her forehead, and no crow's-feet around her eyes. The sun hadn't leathered her skin in the slightest. And Prissy was her own peer, a middle-aged woman. No wonder the girl was taken aback.

"So you know her?" Grace asked.

"For as long as I can remember."

"How?"

The clammer laughed. "She's been as much a part of my life as the roll of paper towels my mother kept in her kitchen. Prissy and Kody rented the cottage in the back of my parents' house. They were there before I was born. Probably because the place was so dilapidated, they were outside in the yard a lot. And they'd have meals with us when their oven gave out or the refrigerator was on the blink."

Grace didn't reply. Although Prissy had mentioned several times that she had a place in West Chatham, she'd never been invited to the house. She'd spent more time wondering about Kody than her friend's home, and hearing that it was a run-down rental fit with the image that she had conjured of a couple living close to the margin. It was the image that explained some of Prissy's attraction, her deviance, her betrayal. Ferris must have seemed very affluent. Despite his own modest means, he no doubt offered considerable luxury to his lover. She wondered how much of his last savings he'd squandered on hotel rooms or gifts. The thought made her shudder.

"My parents moved into an apartment a couple of years ago. You know that retirement place—or should I say assisted-living facility? Just at the intersection of Route Twenty-eight and Crowell Road?"

Grace nodded. When she'd first seen the advertisements, she'd briefly contemplated the possibility of making a home there for her and Bain. They could grow old with twenty-four-hour nursing and meals prepared in a common dining space. They'd have someone to care for them. But the last thing she wanted was to be surrounded by other elderly, infirm people. She didn't need such obvious reminders of the passage of time.

"When they moved into a unit there, they gave me the

house, and Prissy and Kody stayed on as my tenants. A bit irregular with the rent, but it helped me out." She laughed, throwing her head back. "Prissy was the one who suggested I take up clamming. Said the work was steady so long as nature cooperated."

"I see."

"Prissy had a way of talking about it as though it was better than it is, you know, she romanticized it. She spoke about a life on the ocean, a life living off the land, being self-employed, the independence. For a kid who hated school and dreaded the idea of getting dressed for an office every day, it seemed like a pretty good way to earn a living. And true to her word, she taught me almost everything I know, all the ins and outs of dealing with the retail markets, that sort of thing, kind of like a mentor. But then again, I think Prissy could have talked anyone into anything. She seemed so self-possessed, so much her own person. I really admire her."

This woman was remarkably perceptive and articulate. Perhaps her self-reliance had given her a particular kind of maturity. Grace felt inadequate by comparison. "She and I spent a lot of time in this very spot. She taught me to clam, too. I helped her," Grace said.

"Did she give you a cut?" The clammer eyed her suspiciously.

"Oh no, nothing like that. We just enjoyed each other's company."

"Oh." She wiped her hands on her waders, and then extended a hand. "I'm Emily, Emily Crocker."

Grace smiled and introduced herself.

"Grace Alcott, yeah. Prissy talked so much about you. You live in the gray house up there," she said, tilting her head in the right direction. "It's a very nice place you've got."

"Yes," she replied, without confessing that it was only

hers for a few weeks longer. "She's . . . Prissy's my son's godmother."

Emily laughed. "Oh yeah? I never thought of Prissy and religion walking hand in hand." A moment of silence passed, but she didn't return to her work.

"I haven't seen her recently. I wondered if she's gone away." Grace hoped the girl could not sense the anxiety in her question.

"She sure did. She and Kody left a while back. Just packed up that truck with its muffler dragging and its exhaust banging, and their belongings covered with a tarp. It was a sight. I told them they'd never get anywhere, but they were determined. Who knew they'd even make it to the Sagamore Bridge? But she bet me a buck they would, and I assume since they haven't shown up asking to move back in that they made it somewhere. I guess I owe her a dollar."

"Then your place is still empty?" It was only a thought.

"Yeah, if you know anyone, have them give me a call."

"And Kody, he left, too?"

"I'd say he didn't want to get left behind."

Her husband hadn't needed to run away, but if Grace was to venture a guess, he had no idea of the emotions behind his wife's decisions. "Did she say why? Why they were leaving?"

"Prissy?" Emily shook her head. "I've known her for a long time. And I can tell you this: She might give you every detail she can think of to help you rake a clam, but when it came to her emotions, her private life, forget it. She was as tight as one of these little buggers." She reached into her bucket and then extended her hand in Grace's direction. Seawater dripped from a muddied clam. Its shell was locked shut.

Oddly, Grace felt some relief in the words. At least the behavior was consistent. At least her failure to confide in

Grace wasn't due to an aberration of Grace's own personality. Everyone had been kept at bay, her secretive life, passions, and relationships carefully compartmentalized.

"Did she happen to mention where they were going?"

Emily scratched her thigh with a sandy hand. "No, she didn't. All she told me was that it was time to do some exploring. She'd worked hard her entire life. I got the feeling she wanted an adventure, to see the world. Who wouldn't want to bug out of here if they had the chance?"

"But what about Kody? What about his work?"

The girl made a face.

"The commercial fishing boat?"

"Kody? Work?" Comprehension passed over her face. "You didn't know him, did you?"

Grace shook her head. "This must seem so odd to you. I'm telling you that Prissy and I were friends, close friends, old friends, but I realize now there was a lot I haven't known."

"Join the club." Emily pushed her hair behind her ear, leaving a streak of muck on her cheek. "That was Prissy's way. And don't get me wrong. Kody can be a real sweetheart. You know, gentle and funny. But he couldn't hold a job. Or at least no kind of job he wanted. Prissy tried to get him to be a mail sorter, said the federal government offered good benefits, but I don't think he could manage."

The phrase seemed odd. "Was something wrong?" she asked tentatively.

"With his head, no, but with his body, yeah. Prissy had to do almost everything for him."

"Was that recent?"

"He's always been in a wheelchair, or at least since I've known him. He was paralyzed. I heard he had a motorcycle accident, but I was never told details, and it wasn't the kind of thing you could ask."

Grace had the sensation that she was on a carnival ride, a whirling, spinning, falling machine with g-forces so strong that they made it difficult to breathe. Kody was disabled. The floor dropped from underneath her, and centrifugal pressures were the only thing keeping her from slipping into an abyss. Had Prissy made up everything? Her mind raced, piecing together the bits of information she'd been given over the decades. Kody was the partial owner of a fishing boat. He was handy around the house. He was antisocial. He was as stable as an old couch. No quality was inconsistent with paralysis. But wasn't the overall impression a person made as much a part of the truth as actual factual detail? In that way, Prissy's omissions had been horribly deceptive and misleading.

She wondered if Ferris had known.

"Maybe she didn't want you to know. She was always kind of reserved about that. She didn't want people . . . you know . . . to feel sorry for her."

Their eyes met.

"How long ago did she leave?" Grace asked, although it was one answer she thought she knew.

Emily frowned, remembering. "A month or so, maybe a little longer. It was a typical Prissy maneuver. She told me about this spot, how great the clamming was. I'd been driving out to Morris Island, but there were more and more problems with parking, and this is a town landing. We'd talked about that before. Anyway, she suggested I take this place. It was only when I asked her where she was planning to clam that she told me she was leaving Chatham. The next day the truck was packed. Between you and me I'm a little pissed. She gave almost no notice after being a tenant for nearly forty years. But she did give me a couch and some dishes that she said she couldn't take with her. So I guess between the stuff and this spot, I ended up ahead of the game."

"Did she say when she might be back?" Despite the recent revelations — all of them — it was difficult for her to fathom that there had been no telephone call, no letter, no communication whatsoever.

This time the clammer looked puzzled. "Boy, you really were out of the loop. Far as I know, she's got no plans to return."

Grace looked away, feeling her eyes well with tears. She had disappeared. Although Grace had sensed this, hearing the confirmation hurt more. There could be no discussion, no apology, no attempt to understand, and certainly no rapprochement. Grace felt her complete and utter absence in the pit of her stomach.

"Knowing Prissy, I'll get a call one of these days to collect her winnings, the dollar I owe her. I'll let her know you were looking for her."

Grace forced a smile. "That's very kind. But I'd hate to bother her."

"No bother. Any message?"

"Well . . . um." Grace paused to think. "Just tell her that I hope her quest is meaningful, whatever it is and wherever it takes her. If that's not too much to remember."

Emily smiled. "I like that. It sounds poetic."

"Thanks," Grace said. "Let's just hope she knows what I mean." She turned to leave.

"Hey," Emily called after her.

Grace stopped.

"I'm sorry if I said too much. I have a tendency to ramble. Probably comes from living alone and working alone, too. The silence gets to me. Someone seems like they want to have a conversation, and the floodgates open.

Truth is, I should probably get a roommate. I didn't mean to overwhelm you."

Grace smiled. "No need to apologize. I appreciate your candor. And I hope we meet again."

Emily beamed. "Thanks. Me, too."

Chapter Twenty-one

I s Dr. Preston there?" Grace whispered into the receiver. Bain had left nearly an hour before to meet with their lawyer about the purchase and sale agreement on their home, the insidious document that would begin to assign rights in their dwelling to Mr. and Mrs. John J. Marx of Wellesley. Given that it was legal business, he'd insisted it wasn't necessary for her to accompany him. Even though he was several miles away in a conference room located in a modest office complex along Route 28, she still harbored the irrational fear that he could hear, and that her secret would be exposed.

But she had to make the call. Dr. Preston had telephoned nearly every day in the last week, and she couldn't run the risk that Bain would answer the telephone directly or question one of several messages that had been left on the machine to date, all formal, all proper, messages that revealed or disclosed nothing, but nonetheless left with a sense of urgency. The very fact of the calls was dangerous, and Bain's suspicions would no doubt be aroused even with his other preoccupations. No doctor would waste precious minutes leaving more than one message, not with how the insurance companies compensated him for his time.

Bain would have no choice but to conclude that there was either something horribly wrong with her health or that she was having a torrid affair with her Boston physician. And she didn't want either thought to pass through his mind.

"The doctor's not in at the moment." The female voice was raspy.

She heard the smack of chewing gum.

"Could you put me into his voice mail?" Grace's hands trembled as she gripped the telephone tighter. She wanted to leave a message, a personal one, and didn't want to have to explain or repeat herself to an administrative assistant scribbling on a *While You Were Out* pad.

"Yes, ma'am. But I can't tell you when he'll pick up those messages. Is this urgent?"

Grace paused a moment before answering, "No."

"Oh, well then, voice mail will be just fine." The woman sounded relieved. "Please hold while I transfer you."

The phone line beeped several times, and then Grace heard Dr. Preston. The voice startled her before she realized it was, truly, a recording. Impersonal and automatic. She was safe.

"You've reached Dr. Preston. I'm sorry that I am unable to take your call right now, but please leave your name, number, and a brief message after the tone, and I will get back to you as soon as possible."

She waited for the beep.

"Dr. Preston, this is Grace Alcott. I received your messages and appreciate your concern, but my mind is made up. I am not going to return to the hospital until . . ." She felt her face flush even as she stood alone in her house talking to a machine. Until what? Her incapacitation? Her death? She took a deep breath. When she continued, her words came slowly. "I'm feeling fine, really, better than ever, and whatever happens . . ." Her voice drifted off.

Focus, Grace, she told herself. She didn't want the tape to cut her off for leaving too lengthy a message. She didn't want to have to call back and get the gum-chewing assistant to put her through again. "Dr. Preston, I do want to handle the current situation in my own way." She would control the manner in which she died. Wasn't that some sort of God-given entitlement or constitutional right? Wasn't that one area where the rest of the world couldn't intervene? She wanted—needed—that to be true.

"I've made my decision, and I believe it is the best one under the circumstances. If you disagree, I'm sorry. But this is my choice." Her decision, yes; even the words made her feel stronger. "Please do not call the house anymore. I do not want Bain to be alarmed."

Her voice cracked as she pressed the receiver to her face. "I wish you all the best, health and happiness. Thank you . . . Thank you very much for your care."

She slammed down the telephone as though it had suddenly ignited, making it too hot to hold. Her heart pounded in her chest. She didn't know the details of the Hippocratic oath, and hadn't kept the copy of the Patient's Bill of Rights that the nurse-technician had given her when she'd had her fateful X-ray, but she did understand the only thing that mattered at the moment: He was her doctor and he'd have to honor her wishes, even if he disagreed. He had an obligation to maintain her privacy and secrecy.

She'd done it. Covering her face in her hands, she leaned against the wall and wept.

Chapter Twenty-two

Dust filled the air of the cramped space. Sunlight through the triangular window at one end of the attic was insufficient to illuminate the interior, so Grace worked by a bare-bulb lamp she'd rigged using two extension cords and a plug in the guest bathroom a full story below. Although she'd dreaded the task earlier that morning, now she relished having something to keep her mind occupied.

The array of worthless possessions formed a road map of her life. The Pucci slips she'd cherished, their elastic waistbands now frayed, were wrapped in a bundle beside several flattened purses, and a collection of Bain's old suspenders was at the bottom of a trunk. Baby clothes worn by Erin and then Hank mixed with old photographs and a broken wooden dog on a pull string. Paintings on dried and cracked paper were rolled and kept in place with rubber bands. Some were dated. Others were indecipherable. Had Hank or Erin made the art? Had it been a finger-painting project in kindergarten, or were the lines and colors sophisticated enough to have been done at an older age? She couldn't tell. She'd even come across her wedding dress, the lace yellowed, that she'd packed away in pink tissue in the hope that it would be worn again, a hope that had never come to pass. No doubt Sarah would have wanted a new one, a smart style of her own choosing with a brocade bodice and a flowing train.

Looking at the relics, the tangible memories, she regretted that all of Sarah's belongings had been donated to Goodwill just days after her death. Bain had wanted to purge the house, as if the elimination of tiny possessions could eliminate the enormous human loss. And she'd agreed. She'd even taken some comfort at the thought that a disadvantaged baby girl might benefit from the beautiful clothes, toys, and furniture. Now Grace hated that she had artifacts from only two of her three children, that there was nothing stored in the attic that had belonged to her daughter, and that despite her every hope, she wouldn't discover a bootie that Sarah had worn or a teddy bear that she'd embraced. No doubt those objects no longer existed.

Bent over, Grace half crawled to the next box, fiddled with the masking tape that had lost its adhesive years before, and opened the top. She reached in. Her hand found Erin's tennis trophy. The small metallic man poised in service position atop a column of gold and blue, his left arm extended and his right arm bent back with the racquet, his face lifted to the sky. The plaque on the faux-marble base read: WINNER. 14 AND UNDER BOYS' SINGLES. Erin had triumphed even though in the summer of 1988 he was still a few months shy of thirteen.

Grace remembered the day of the finals. She'd found a seat on one of many Adirondack chairs that overlooked the tennis courts of the Chatham Beach and Tennis Club. Erin and his opponent, Herbie Grant, were in the middle court. The sun was high and hot in the sky, but Erin had brushed off her attempts to apply sunscreen and taken his place on the service line, pulling down his baseball cap. It was a pro set, the first of eight games. She'd watched anxiously as Erin scrambled for each point, rushed the net, or tried to smash an overhead. She'd clapped at his victories and been careful not to applaud Herbie's mistakes. When Erin's beautiful crosscourt backhand ended the match, she'd jumped out of her seat with a surge of pride and excitement, and run down the steps to offer congratulations.

"What a wonderful job you did! That was fantastic!"

Erin, surrounded by his friends, had barely glanced in her direction.

She'd watched for several seconds as he laughed and joked with a red-haired girl and her pigtailed friend. Neither face was familiar. "Are you too tired to ride your bike home?" she'd asked. Without a response, he'd turned away from her and walked off the courts.

She'd spun around, not wanting to watch him leave. The signal was too obvious. There were still spectators on the porch. No doubt all had seen her failed attempt to interact with her son, to share in his victory.

Herbie sat on a bench, tying the lace of his sneaker. Neither Mr. nor Mrs. Grant was anywhere in sight. His tennis racquet lay on the ground at his feet beside a half-empty bottle of orange juice.

"Congratulations. You played beautifully," she'd offered to the runner-up. It was true. Just because Erin had won didn't mean this little boy hadn't put up a valiant struggle. He was a good player. His family should have been there to remind him of that.

Herbie smiled. "Thanks, Mrs. Alcott. And thanks for coming to watch."

What had become of the boy with his sweet face and curly red hair? She wondered whether Herbie had won the tournament the following year, or any of the years after that, and hoped he had.

Erin wouldn't care about the trophy, and probably wouldn't remember the details of his finals match. Perhaps she should send it to Herbie. She made a note to herself on a Post-it and stuck the yellow square to its base.

She reached into the box again and produced a package of papers, the typewritten collection of report cards from Hank's days at the Advent School. She skimmed the one on top.

> *Although Henry is quick to grasp the principles of geometry and consistently performs well on his exams, his attitude is, regrettably, a disruption to the class. He is sarcastic, disengaged, and often rude, all clear indications that he has difficulty with authority and direction. It is a shame that his comportment cannot rise to the level of his comprehension as he shows considerable promise in the area of mathematics.*

Mr. McFarland. She remembered the seventh-grade math teacher, the charming, handsome academic whose criticism of her son had been so devastating. She had been too ashamed to face the man directly and resisted his invitation for a conference to go over the obvious problems. Her solace had been that Hank had a new teacher the following year for algebra.

Beneath that bundle was a similar one marking Erin's academic record. He'd lacked his brother's intellect and struggled throughout high school with mediocre grades, incompletes, and one required session of summer school in order to be awarded a diploma with his class.

She remembered the apprehension over his graduation, the precariousness of his status. In his junior year, he'd been expelled from a middle-tier preparatory school for marijuana use after he'd been placed on probation for poor performance. He'd arrived home by Greyhound bus without ever calling to ask her to come get him. His duffel bag, stereo, and a box of albums were still in the hallway when Bain had returned from work. Bain had been livid, but in the quiet, controlled sort of way that she found infinitely more frightening than when his temper exploded in a passing fit. Yet even as his father told him that he was an embarrassment, that he'd squandered opportunities that most boys weren't given and that, perhaps, he didn't deserve, Erin had remained calm, seemingly unfazed. "They didn't discover half of what I'd done," he replied, as if to suggest he possessed a cleverness and cunning that his parents should admire.

"Don't expect us to take solace from that," Bain had retorted.

In Brookline, they'd found a small, private school for recalcitrant boys that was willing to admit him midyear. Overlooking the fact that the other students had long hair, dirty clothes, more serious drug problems, and broken homes, they had enrolled him without further discussion.

She wondered now whether she should save the clothes and report cards and artwork or add them to the growing pile of garbage. Would her sons want this evidence of their past conduct, the tangible reminders of a far-from-perfect record, the unsavory keepsakes? She couldn't imagine that they would, not now, not with how their lives had transpired. Hank would want to keep his transgressions out of Susan's sight, lest she arrive at the conclusion that her son might share his father's propensity for underachievement. As for Erin, he no doubt couldn't be bothered. Alone with his children, devastated by his wife's decision, he had no time for perusing memorabilia. He still hadn't even found the time to call home.

Quickly and efficiently, she shoved everything into a Hefty bag and cinched it closed.

It was almost noon and her task nearly completed. She'd organized everything. With Bain's help, she could drag the overstuffed trash bags down to the car. If he returned soon, they could get to the dump before it closed for the day.

She paused and wiped the perspiration from her brow. There was little air in the attic, and she needed a drink of water. But almost as soon as she'd made her way to the kitchen, she heard the front door open, followed by an array of footsteps and a mixture of voices. Kay's was unmistakable, but there were several others that she did not recognize.

She put her glass on the counter and hurried to the foyer. There stood the Realtor with Robin Marx along with three men and one woman whom Grace did not recognize.

Kay's eyes opened wide as she saw Grace. "Grace, what are you doing here?"

The question seemed to echo, and the thought occurred to her that instead of hours passing, she'd been up in the attic for weeks, undiscovered, and had only descended to find that the house had been sold with her in it. She'd been included in the asking price along with the sconces.

Grace scanned the row of faces that stared back at her as though she were a creature at a zoo. The unfamiliar woman resembled Robin in type: young, blond, and attractive. She stood with her thin ankles crossed and one hip jutting out, while she hugged several thick files to the front of her fitted jacket. Beside her a man with well-greased hair and a long thin face wore a seersucker suit and green loafers. He held a collection of shopping bags, each of which had fabrics printed on it and the name of a textile designer. His trousers had large cuffs, and Grace wondered what sort of fashion statement he was trying to make.

The other two men were older, less formal. One wore a baseball cap, a chambray shirt, and construction boots. The other had on a crisp striped oxford with rolled up sleeves, blue jeans, and an alligator belt. She could see the dark hair on his muscular forearms.

"I'm sorry," she replied, confused. "Did I forget something?"

"Well, we did leave a message." Kay chuckled, nervously. She wore the sort of half-irritated, half-alarmed expression that Grace remembered from the day the Marxes had first come to look at the house, the day that Bain and Grace hadn't left in time for the showing. That day they'd been delayed making love, but this time she had no such romantic excuse. What Grace wouldn't give to experience that morning all over again, the tenderness of Bain's caress and the blissful ignorance of impending buyers.

"Now that we're almost at closing, Mrs. Marx was eager to bring in her consultants, you know, to get a jump start on the project. She's certainly got the best. Bob Miller's architectural firm is in Boston. Victoria Errancrantz is an interior designer in Wellesley. And you must know Carson Andrews. He builds the best houses here in Chatham."

Except for the young man in the seersucker pants, each of the people nodded in turn as Kay doled out the compliments.

"I see," said Grace as she studied the entourage, the payroll of people descending upon her home. They had come to assess the problems, clean up the mess of the past decade, and restore this home to its original grandeur. They would redecorate and rearrange, paint and replace and redo to execute the Marxes' vision. It could become another status symbol in what she guessed was a rather large inventory.

"We haven't even signed a purchase and sale agreement," she mumbled. "And Bain isn't here. He's meeting with our lawyer now, but he's been gone quite some time. I'm not sure what's taking him so long. Perhaps there are complications." Her speech was hurried, and as she spoke she wanted the words to be true. Complications meant the deal might fall through, or delay the transaction long enough. Maybe Robin Marx wouldn't get this house after all. But she caught herself. All that a postponed sale would really mean is that Bain would be left with the responsibility of moving on his own. Whether she was with him or not, he couldn't afford to stay.

"An all-cash offer isn't likely to fall through, so don't you worry." Kay forced a second chuckle, louder this time. "We just need to get inside. Bob and Victoria need measurements. Don't worry, Grace, nobody's going to start tearing walls down."

"You're no bother to us," Robin added cheerily.

"You must be very excited about having a fresh start," piped up Victoria, uncrossing her ankles and taking a step past Grace.

Grace glared at the decorator. She knew it was rude, but for once she didn't care. The Alcotts were still the owners of record and the inhabitants of this house. An accepted offer—even one with no contingencies—hardly constituted a transfer of title. The closing was less than three weeks away. Robin and her team could hold off for another twenty-one days until the property was rightfully hers.

She wished Bain were home. He'd know how to handle this crowd. Although no doubt Bain would try to excuse her misconduct after the fact—*It's a stressful time for her,* she could hear him say—she wanted to call the police and have an officer come to arrest the trespassers. But she couldn't risk jeopardizing the sale.

The man in the construction boots removed his cap and

smiled. Even in her rage, she had to admit he had a nice face, with broad cheekbones, walnut eyes, and white teeth. "If you can, Mrs. Alcott, pretend we're not here. We'll try to stay out of your way."

"Shall we, then?" Kay said, extending her hand in the direction of the kitchen.

The group fell in line.

Somehow Grace found herself following. She felt drawn to the caravan. She wanted to know what they were going to say, what judgments they would pass on her home, and whether they would show any signs of appreciating all that had transpired, the lives that had been lived, within these walls.

Victoria stopped the group. "Alan, are you sure you've got both the Nina Campbells?"

The young man glanced down at his shopping bags. "Absolutely, Vic."

The decorator waved one arm overhead, a gesture that appeared as though she were about to throw a lasso. "I'm getting a feeling . . . I'm sensing that the damasks will work after all. It just goes to prove that you can't experience feng shui based on photographs alone, right?" She smiled at Robin. "I think the salmon-and-sage motif we discussed will work. Yes . . . Yes," she said as she twirled in a circle. "Sea and earth, fish and herb, it's perfect!"

"Do we want to start here or the kitchen?" Carson, the builder, asked, ignoring the unfolding drama. "Isn't that where you were talking about the addition?"

"Isn't this the library?" The architect looked confused. Kay nodded.

"Bookshelves, Bob, remember? We're certainly not keeping these," Victoria explained. "We're wanting warmth. Think English, you know, moldings, detail. Think Professor Higgins." Then she reached for Robin's arm and squeezed it. "Oh, I forgot to tell you I found the greatest place for leather-bound books, all gently worn of course to give that great patina to the spine. Some are real novels — I think they're sold in batches of mixed classics — and others actually hold VHS cassettes. You can hide your movies."

"Perfect," Robin replied. "I've been dying to get rid of Jay's ratty volumes. Would they work for the Wellesley study, too?"

"I'm not touching Jay's Wellesley study," Victoria said, feigning horror. "He'll see to it that my design work for you ends quickly."

"He'd never dream of doing such a thing. I'd divorce him in a heartbeat. Who wouldn't take a perfect library over a husband any day?"

The two women laughed, sharing a conspiratorial moment.

Grace looked at the simple white bookshelves filled with worn hardcovers and paperbacks that she and Bain had read over the years. These novels, biographies, histories, and memoirs comprised a road map of what had caught their interest at various stages in their life. She wondered what Bain would want to do with them. It hadn't occurred to her before this moment that they wouldn't be with him in his Florida condominium, reminders of the journey he'd had with her.

"I don't mean to rain on the parade," said Bob, "but you're talking about finish carpentry. That's probably months away. If we could focus big to small, I think it would help streamline this process."

"Absolutely." Robin smiled. "Believe me, Jay wants streamlined. This way."

They passed through the library, then the dining room, and moved into the kitchen. Robin and her team congregated around the island while Grace hung back by the threshold. Bob opened his briefcase, removed a clipboard

and measuring tape, and began to note various dimensions. Carson put down his pad and pen, and knocked on
the walls, commenting periodically about load bearings.

Victoria removed a leather-covered organizer from her
purse. She also produced several tiles, which she laid on
the island. Grace took a step closer so that she could look
at the squares of yellow, purple, and green vegetables.

"French Provincial," Victoria remarked. "Isn't the
aubergine divine? I'm thinking splashboard, splashboard,
splashboard. It'll capture a country feel and add some color."

"Mrs. Alcott, you don't have the original blueprints, do
you?"

Only when Bob repeated the question did she realize
he was addressing her. These people had been so oblivious
to her feelings that, standing alone, witnessing this inva-
sion, she'd almost forgotten she was visible.

"No," she said, "we don't." Then she added, "I'm not
sure we ever did."

Carson made a note to himself.

"What are you thinking of doing to our kitchen?" she
asked. Her voice was timid, and she didn't expect the
reaction she received. All stopped what they were doing,
turned, and stared at her. Was her question improper?
Perhaps it was the phrasing. Certainly the person who'd
lived her whole life in this house was entitled to ask, now,
wasn't she? She looked at Kay for help, but none was
offered. She felt perspiration on her forehead, but she
didn't dare move to wipe her brow. Wishing she could
disappear, she tried to think of a way to extricate herself.
The effort was a failure.

"What aren't we doing may be a better question,"
Robin finally said, and the group chuckled nervously.
"European appliances are a must. New cabinets and coun-
tertops are, too. We want to blow out that wall, and build
a proper breakfast nook with a banquette and bay

window. And I want to rip off that mudroom and make a family room—someplace for Jay's billiard table where I won't have to see it."

You need a mudroom, Grace wanted to shout. *Don't you understand about a house on the beach, about life on the ocean? It's different. You don't need high heels and matching handbags, fur coats or Palm Pilots. You need rubber boots and rain slickers and canvas hats, and a place to store the croquet set and the badminton.* The Marxes had no business in Chatham. They didn't belong.

Her home was big enough, bigger than any family of three needed. The Alcotts had been four and done just fine. If these people wanted a mansion, why buy an old shingled home? In fact, if they wanted to play billiards and wear leopard print, why bother leaving Wellesley at all?

"I'm trying to convince my husband that we need all-new windows."

"There's charm here," Bob said. "We don't want to lose the feel."

"Believe me, I can recognize charm when I see it, but nothing's operational. And Jay likes things to work." Robin walked over to one of the windows, unhinged the lock, and tried to pry it open. It wouldn't budge. "See?" She emphasized her point. "Whether Marvin or Pella are better, Carson, that's your call. Just don't give me Andersen. I want true divided light."

"The lady's a pro," Carson said, somewhat sarcastically.

"I've been through this before."

Bob nodded. The supplicant. Grace wondered whether he was paid by the hour.

Carson made a sweeping gesture toward the far wall. "You may be better off blowing the whole thing out and redoing this entire space. Then you'll get what you want."

"Easier to do from new than renovate," Victoria sang.

Robin nodded in agreement.

"What kind of permit approvals would we need for that?" Bob asked.

"The process is definitely a factor," Carson replied. "Especially given your timetable."

Robin had moved away from the island, joining Carson as he continued to knock on walls. She used her long, painted nails to tap, the pattering simulating mice. Bob stared out the small window to gauge what kind of a family room could be built between the house and the lot line. Victoria and Alan riffled through several different fabric books.

A wave of nausea washed over Grace, and she held on to the Formica countertop for balance. What was going on? Why were these strangers in her house, discussing blasting through walls and tearing out appliances? How could they be so unconcerned about her? Robin Marx was planning to move into a redefined space, one crafted without regard to expense. She would eliminate the shabbiness, the mildew, and the peeling paint. The premium was efficiency. History was ignored, legacy discarded. Everything would function with precision. Artificial book covers and after-the-fact moldings would define reality. This woman, her successful husband, and her healthy daughter would enjoy a multitude of impeccably decorated rooms and a magnificent view. No grapefruit-size lump ate at her flesh. Her million-dollar bank account could purchase as much underwear as she wanted. She would stay a member of American Express with all its attendant privileges.

Never before had Grace hated someone so completely.

What had happened to her? Grace admonished herself. She hated the venomous sensation of jealousy, the hot, acidic feel of envy. Was it only the house, or was it that Robin had everything she wanted, plus the health to enjoy it?

She wished at that moment that she'd followed Dr. Preston's advice. He'd wanted her to do tests, to find out information, to talk to Bain, and she'd refused, convincing herself that she had no future. She hadn't allowed herself to learn the truth because she was too fearful to find out. She hadn't been able to face the reality of bad news, or the public pressure that would attend it. Acknowledgment of cancer meant that conversations would have to take place. There might be confrontations, even arguments. Everyone would start some frantic search for closure, and she didn't want to end every telephone call as if it might be the last. So instead she'd blinked, closing her eyes to avoid seeing the possibilities. Ignorance, the shroud of mystery, was easier than mustering the courage to face her mortality.

What she hadn't anticipated was this bitterness. She'd never expected that she would resent others' happiness, health, or success. And she hated that more than anything. Her emotions were destroying her more quickly than the disease.

This all had to change.

She coughed to clear her throat. "If you're planning to tear off the kitchen, I'd recommend you put in a proper basement, at least under this portion of the house."

Everyone turned to stare at her. Was it disbelief frozen on their faces?

"I mean, if you're doing so much work already, you might want to think about the added benefit. There have been some problems over the years with just the crawl space."

Bob quickly scribbled something on his pad. "That's a great suggestion. We haven't even been thinking subterranean change."

"Let's put in a wine cellar!" Victoria shrieked. "Jay will love me for that idea."

Robin clapped her hands. "Brilliant."

Grace smiled. She'd made her contribution. It was just as well that the house be transformed into something different. It should move on, too.

❧

Bain reported that the paperwork was in order. In a matter of weeks, ownership would change hands. He'd contacted a real estate office in Palm Beach about a golf-course community. Actually, it was in West Palm, but the Realtor had assured him that the distinctions were disappearing. Highly desirable one- and two-bedroom units were still available, some with distant water views, and there might be some flexibility on the price since the development hadn't sold as quickly as anticipated. The Realtor promised to send brochures.

His announcements over, he'd gone upstairs to read.

Grace's fingers trembled as she dialed the Vermont exchange and counted the rings. After six, the answering machine picked up. Marley's voice on the greeting surprised her. It was a long recording, and contained something about a daily wisdom that was no doubt outdated. For a moment, Grace wondered what would happen to such calendar-specific, inspirational thoughts when the day ended. Then she tried to formulate a message to leave after the tone. *Sorry to hear your life has fallen apart. Mine has, too. But at least you're young. You're healthy. You've got great children. That's more than I can say.*

"Erin . . . it's your mother," she said tentatively when she heard a beep. "Hank told me about Marley. I'm sorry. I'm very, very sorry. I'm here . . . we're here if you want to talk."

After she'd hung up, she remembered something else, and redialed.

"Erin, it's your mother, and I'm sorry to bother you, again, to take up so much time on your machine. I just . . . I wish you were at home so we could speak. You're not alone. I want you to know that I love you."

Chapter Twenty-three

G race felt fortunate that the weather had cooperated. The day was mild but slightly overcast. Not everyone would feel the need to rush to the beach. She opened the cigar box that doubled as her cash register and checked the change. Aside from the collection of singles, twenty in fives, and a roll of quarters that constituted start-up money, she counted six twenties, five tens, a check for $133, and an assortment of loose change as well.

She'd arranged her wares in a semicircle: lamps, appliances, and other household bric-a-brac on a table, old clothes and several fur coats hung from wire hangers on a coatrack, jewelry and handbags displayed on a small side table, framed art propped against the side of the house, and furniture, including a wicker settee with one torn pillow and matching armchairs, arranged attractively on the grass. She hoped no one would notice the flaws, the nicks and chips, tears and faded patches, but if they did she was prepared to adjust her prices accordingly.

Her advertisement in the local papers had specifically said, *No Early Birds*. The kind ad agent, a woman whose voice made her sound elderly, had advised her on the appropriateness of including that direction. "Otherwise you'll get people knocking on your front door before you're even dressed. From what I hear, tag salers can be vultures."

Despite the prohibition, the first cars had pulled in more than ninety minutes before her yard sale officially started. Those people had surveyed the tables, walked through, and plucked their selections with surgical precision. Several Bakelite bracelets were the first sale of the day. A print from the Venice Biennale, some garden tools, a transferware platter, and two bicycles quickly followed. Although her advertisement had also specified *Cash Only*, an elderly man had convinced her to accept his personal check, drawn on a bank in Portsmouth, New Hampshire, as payment for a strand of freshwater pearls. "My wife has always wanted a set of these," he said, flashing a toothless grin. "We'll have been married forty-one years this November," he added, his voice full of pride. "And you know what she'll say when I give her this present?"

Grace didn't reply.

"She'll say, *You never stop surprising me.* That's right, that's exactly what she'll say." He chuckled. "The day I do is the day she should take me out back and shoot me."

The current lull in shoppers had allowed her to run inside for a cup of tea. She removed the tea bag, adjusted her folding chair so that from her seat she had an unobstructed view down the drive, and sat. She stared at the meniscus of the brownish yellow liquid. A brand called Wellness. As if a steeped bag of herbs would help.

A maroon Oldsmobile parked by the hand-printed sign at the end of the drive. A middle-aged couple alighted and approached Grace. The man wore a striped golf shirt and carried a Styrofoam coffee cup and a small paper bag stained with grease. His wife wore her hair tied in a colorful scarf, tight white pants, and a loose peach sweater. She proceeded to weave in and around each table, touching books, jewelry, the backs of chairs, everything and anything that her hand could reach. Grace watched, fascinated, wondering what would compel a total stranger to finger the used contents of a fifty-eight-year-old woman's house. Perhaps she was blind.

"Excuse me, but did you notice that one of these napkin rings is chipped?"

Grace looked up. A young, slender man in blue jeans and a Nike running jacket stood in front of her. Although he didn't strike her as the tag-sale type of shopper, he'd been browsing since before she'd gone inside for tea.

"See, right here." In one hand he held four porcelain napkin rings tied together with garden twine. She remembered buying them in a small town in Mexico decades before, a place they'd taken the boys for spring vacation. The trip had been a disappointment, the four-star hotel obviously mislabeled, and the beach dirty. But the vibrant colors of the napkin rings had caught her eye as she'd perused stands filled with local goods in the marketplace. Only when she got home did she notice that a small gold sticker marked MADE IN CHINA hadn't been removed from inside one of the rings.

"I'll give you a dollar for all four," the man said, without waiting for her reply. "You've got them priced here at fifty cents apiece, but, like I said, one's chipped, and what am I going to do with only three?"

"Why don't you take them as my gift?" Grace remarked.

The man looked confused. "I said I'd give you a dollar."

"I'd rather you just took them." She didn't want to haggle. She wanted the yard sale run on her own terms.

He stared briefly at the rings in his hand, then at her, and back at the rings. Dropping them on the table as if they'd become radioactive, he turned on his heels and quickly ran down the driveway.

"Thank you for stopping by," she called after him.

❧

It was nearly four o'clock, and nobody had come through in more than an hour. Despite the fact that much remained to be sold, Grace pulled the sign from the driveway. Her outdoor shop was closed. The dump would be the repository for all that remained. As she walked back up the drive, she surveyed the scattered objects, her belongings that had been fingered, studied, and rejected throughout the day. A rose-painted demitasse had fallen and broken into dozens of pieces. Whoever had knocked it off the table lacked the courage or generosity to confess to the transgression.

She collapsed into her folding chair and, inadvertently, sipped from her teacup. The long-cooled liquid tasted bitter.

"I don't know how you did this," Bain remarked from behind her. "I couldn't stand even looking out the window, watching people paw through our stuff."

A violation. She'd felt it, too, watching people pick up the remnants of her home, examine the objects, and then reject them or haggle over a dollar here, a quarter there. Other than the pearl purchaser, the buyers acted as though they had done her a favor, taking her belongings off her hands for a fraction of their value.

"It was too much to bring with you—with us," she corrected. "And it seemed a pity to have it go to waste." She handed him the cigar box, filled to overflowing. "Can you count it for me?" Her voice cracked. She felt tears burn her eyes.

He reached for the box, but paused before taking it. "No, you deserve the glory. You can count your booty."

She tried to smile but knew her expression looked forced.

"What's wrong?" he asked. When he furrowed his brow, his bushy eyebrows almost touched.

"Wrong? Nothing." She felt weary, sick. Should she tell him? How many more days could she continue to hide her secret? She'd harbored the notion that there would be one night when she would kiss him and drift off into eternal slumber, that she would never have to say good-bye or see his pain. But morning after morning she awoke to face another day, and, with it, the pressure to disclose the truth mounted. She knew she'd been acting strangely. And this yard sale was further evidence. All the effort and hours of work to sell no more than a few hundred dollars' worth of items when they could have given the valuables to the church, taken a tax deduction, and brought the rest in two trips to the dump. Her conduct hardly fit Bain's business-oriented model of rational economic behavior.

"Grace, tell me what's wrong?"

Willing the conversation to end, she didn't reply.

"I know how hard this move is for you. Believe me, it's killing me to see you like this."

Did he know? Could he tell? She knew the point of no return was drawing near. She imagined she could feel changes occurring in her body, her systems shutting down. But there was no good way to announce her disintegration to him. *I may be dying,* sounded too glib, too facile. She wondered if there was a book that could provide some guidance, a candy-coated solution packaged neatly in an $11.95 trade paperback, maybe even a large-print edition. She wished she had someone, something to tell her what to do.

But that was Bain's role. Throughout their life together, he'd been the guide. He'd played the part of adviser, leader, instructor. Without turning to him now, without trusting him with her secret, she had no one.

Grace cleared her throat. "I want to have a party."

"What?" Bain appeared confused by her non sequitur.

"A party. Once all the furniture is gone. Maybe the night before the closing. A celebration to mark the end of our years here. It will be a chance to say good-bye."

"In an empty house?"

"Please, Bain. Let me do this." She looked at the stuffed cigar box still in her hand. "We can use the proceeds from this yard sale to get some wonderful champagne. I'd like one more chance to fill the rooms of this house with life."

He glanced briefly toward the ocean, then leaned forward and kissed her cheek. She thought she saw his eyes water and his cheeks glow with moisture, but perhaps it was only the damp sea air.

"This house will always be full of your life," he said, his voice soft. "Jay Marx can't get rid of your spirit that easily. I suspect, my darling, that your ghost will haunt his family long after we've all joined the dearly departed. But if a party is what you want, go ahead." Shaking his head, he picked up a lamp, two bookends, and a blender that hadn't sold from one of the display tables, and loaded them into the trunk of his car. "What the hell. Let people think we're odd to entertain under the circumstances. We'll never have to see anyone again if we don't want to."

"Thank you," Grace murmured, although her voice was too quiet for him to hear.

❧

The sky was darkening as Bain wedged the last few items into the back of the car and squeezed the door shut. Exhausted, Grace lay down on the grass, feeling the newly cut blades against her bare ankles. He flopped down beside her, draped one arm across her torso, and closed his eyes. "You're a remarkable woman," he whispered.

"Let's see how well I did before we compliment me,"

she replied as she dumped the contents of the cigar box out on the lawn and began to tabulate the day's haul. First she separated the bills into neat piles. Then she moved on to the loose change. When she finished counting, she lay back flat, cradling her head in her hands and staring up at the sky. A flock of geese in V-formation flew overhead, and she watched the power of their flapping wings.

And then the most remarkable thought occurred to her. Could it be? She flipped through the reel of her life to confirm its truth, and laughed aloud at the realization that it was. This was the first money she'd ever made, the first cash that was solely derived from her efforts, labor, and organization. At fifty-eight, she could finally say that she'd earned something. Six hundred forty-three dollars and seventy-five cents suddenly felt like a million.

She propped herself up on her elbows and was about to share her discovery with Bain when she heard the popping, puttering sound of a muffler sorely in need of replacement. He did, too. They both stared in the direction of the noise.

A badly rusted Volvo station wagon pulled up to the house. The driver's-side door opened, and Erin climbed out. His hair was down to his shoulders, and he had the early growth of a beard. His wrinkled shirt hung out over his blue jeans. Seconds later, India and Deshawn tumbled out, scampered to their father, and hung on to his legs. He was barefoot. From inside the car, Grace heard a baby crying.

As she approached her son, she could see dark circles under his eyes. His cheekbones were decidedly more pronounced than the last time he'd visited. She extended her arms. "What a wonderful surprise!" She put her arms around Erin's neck and held him tight, feeling his ribs and the bones in his shoulders.

He buried his face and murmured, "I thought I could manage, could get through this, but I can't."

"Erin, I must say your timing is far from perfect," Grace heard Bain speak from behind her. "Did it occur to you that we're moving shortly? If you'd called—"

"Stop," she interrupted. Her forcefulness surprised her. "You're here now. And we're thrilled . . . thrilled to see all of you." She felt the soft touch of little hands on her body, as her grandchildren shifted their grasp from their father and clung to her instead. "Come inside," she said to Erin. "The children must be starving. You get your bags, and I'll get the baby."

"Are you sure this is okay?" he asked. "After I got your message, I thought—"

"Of course," she said without hesitation. "This is what home is for."

As she reached into the backseat, unbuckled Namid, and lifted his plump body into her arms, serenity washed through her. She kissed his cheeks and the top of his head, smelled the sweet, distinctive scent of baby skin, and whispered that everything would be just fine. Calling to India and Deshawn, she hurried toward the house, bouncing Namid on her hip to quiet his tears.

She would deal with Bain later. She knew he'd come around; he just needed a bit of time to process this unexpected turn of events. He was a man who liked order, and four houseguests—even family—at this particular time in their life hardly comported with his sense of that. But with the closing just two weeks away, there was nothing for them to do but enjoy their last days at home. Erin's company wouldn't disrupt that.

Besides, regardless of how Bain felt, for now she had to focus on the task at hand. Her son, whatever his faults, needed her, and her grandchildren did, too. And even though the tragic events saddened her, she relished the chance to mother again.

It was just the distraction she needed.

Chapter Twenty-four

T wo days had passed in a fleeting moment, so consumed was Grace with feeding, tending, and caring for India, Deshawn, and Namid. The older children seemed eager to accompany her on even the most mundane errands—carrying bags from the car to the dump, shopping for more butter, milk, and baby formula—and to find genuine pleasure in her company. They played Monopoly and hopscotch, flew kites, baked brownies from a mix, and made drip castles from wet sand. They told knock-knock jokes, blew air down their straws to make the juice bubble, and then collapsed on the floor in peals of laughter. Grace found herself giggling, too.

Although Namid was old enough to walk, he seemed content to watch the goings-on around him from the security of Grace's arms. He even smiled when she sang her out-of-tune rendition of "Down in the Valley." Erin mumbled apologetic thanks, an occasional comment, or a half-hearted instruction to one of his children. Mostly, though, he hovered like a shadow. He, too, seemed only to want her nearby.

Was it her tragedy or his that had made them more intimate? Had they all reached a tacit agreement to put the difficulties behind them? And why was it that this family had to fall apart for them to enjoy one another's company? Several times she'd almost raised the subject, wanting to

wonder aloud, but decided against it. An unspoken sweetness was better than none at all, and she refused to mourn
the years passed or lost. She couldn't look back.

On the third evening, Bain went to the Elliotts' for a
dinner party. Grace had welcomed the excuse of her
grandchildren to decline the invitation, and after feeding
India, Deshawn, and Namid, she surprised them with a
Dumbo videotape. Now three sets of legs stuck out from
the cushion of the sofa as they sat in front of the television
fascinated by the tale of the baby elephant ridiculed for
his oversize ears.

In the far end of the room, Erin sprawled on a love seat.
She joined him, picking his feet up, settling herself, and
allowing his legs to drop into her lap. They listened to the
sound track in the background.

"Am I allowed to ask about what happened?"

For seventy-two hours, she'd wondered whether Erin
would volunteer details of what had transpired, of the di-
sastrous course of events, but he'd said nothing.

"I don't mean to pry. I just wonder whether you'd like
to talk." She smiled. "I know it's not something you're
used to, at least with me."

He shrugged. "It's painfully short," he replied.

"Maybe short is worse," she offered. "There's no time to
prepare." Was she consoling him or herself? she wondered.

"I guess that's right." He began. It had been a day like
any other, until he announced that he'd made appointments for the three children to see the local pediatrician.
They needed checkups. Namid was behind in his vac-
cines, and the other children hadn't been examined in
more than a year. Marley objected vehemently. She'd
been furious, accusing him of undermining her and her
beliefs by adhering to Western medicine, but he knew her

concern was primarily selfish. He'd had to let their health insurance lapse, and they couldn't afford to pay.

"You should have called us," Grace interjected.

"I couldn't ask you and Dad for money. Not again. Not this time."

"But health insurance, Erin, you mustn't let that go."

He closed his eyes. "I know. I know I've made some very bad, some very stupid choices."

She rubbed his shin. "Go on," she coaxed.

Erin sighed, exhaling resignation and exhaustion. Then he continued. He'd insisted on the doctor's visit. He still had a little credit on a Visa, enough to cover the appointments so long as no one needed any extra tests or blood work. As Marley stood on the porch glaring at him, her hands on her hips in a posture of defiance, he'd loaded the children into the car and driven off. When he returned less than two hours later, she was gone. He found a brief note to that effect, as if he needed written confirmation. She'd taken her clothes and a few personal objects, but not much else. Not even a photograph as far as he could tell.

"She did manage to stop at the bank and empty what little there was in our savings. It wasn't much, three hundred bucks or so. And I haven't heard a word since. I've tried calling a couple of friends."

"Nobody knew anything?" Grace asked.

"No. They were all sympathetic. A few even brought over some casseroles and a beef stew. I guess they assumed with Marley out of the house, we didn't practice vegetarianism."

"The children need protein," Grace admonished.

"Now you're being a mom," Erin said, smiling. It was the first glimmer of happiness he'd displayed since he'd arrived.

"A grandmother," she corrected, teasing. "I learned

long ago that my children weren't about to follow my advice."

"Anyway, yesterday I tracked down a colleague of hers from the Healing Institute. That's the funky place where she got her degree. I knew there had been this woman named Paula whom she'd kind of befriended. I found Paula and we talked for a long time. I was pitiful, crying and begging for information. It wasn't pretty."

The image of her son in tears, searching for news of his wife, was painful. Why had Marley been so selfish?

"I think she just wanted to get me off the phone, but Paula finally confessed that there were rumors, rumors about Marley and her guru."

"Her what?"

"Teacher, inspirational leader, I don't know what you'd call him. She talked about him all the time, a guy named Yogi Far."

"What sort of a name is that?"

"Probably not the one he was born with. He specialized in solar healing."

This world was so bizarre, so foreign to everything she'd ever known.

"A sun-worshipper type. I should have seen it coming. Marley spoke of his power and intensity and conviction, his inner strength and emotional sensitivity. He apparently had all the characteristics that she reminded me again and again I lacked. I met the guy once. He was a lot older and looked like a freak. That gave me comfort. I figured all he could be was a mentor to her. I couldn't believe anyone would find him attractive . . . sexually, I mean."

They were quiet for a moment before Grace spoke. "But you don't know that anything happened between them. You don't know that Marley won't come home. Won't she miss the children?"

Erin shrugged and glanced toward the television.

"Coincidentally, Yogi the Bizar-ro left on some spiritual journey to Nepal the morning after Marley walked out. I have a feeling the pediatrician visit had nothing to do with it. It was just an excuse, and an opportunity to leave while we were all out of the house."

"Did Paula agree?"

"She didn't have to openly agree." He rubbed his eyes. "She did offer to buy Marley's healing table, though, which confirmed she didn't think Marley was coming back. I think she felt guilty. She offered me five hundred dollars, and came and got it right away. That saved me. It felt plenty good to get that ugly reminder out of our living room, and it's cash in my pocket. It covered gas and a few snacks I picked up for the kids on the road."

Five hundred dollars. Her son was living on what remained.

"It's weird to have nothing at all. Not that Marley and I ever had much. My days of luxury ended when I moved out of this place."

Grace wanted to remind him of all he did have, the nonmonetary components that were so much more important than savings accounts or credit cards, but she knew her forced optimism would sound unsympathetic. And she did know how he felt. As she glanced around the living room and saw the packing boxes lined up against the wall, she certainly understood loss. Disappearance, too. There seemed to be no way to prevent such monsters from intruding.

"I wish you'd told me. You know that the only reason I called the other day was because of Hank? He told us Marley had left."

"And he probably also told you that I was better off this way. He's been telling me that for years. Maybe he was right—I can hardly argue with him under the circumstances—but . . . well . . . how can anyone understand someone else's relationship?"

"It's very difficult," Grace replied. Her response sounded glib. "No doubt he just wanted you to be happy. We all do." In fact, that Hank and Erin even discussed each other's marriages was both a shock and a comfort. She'd never thought of the boys as close.

"But his version of happiness may not be mine. That's the trouble we have. He wants a sprawling stone-and-shingle mansion in the 'burbs, a Superbaby son, and . . . Susan." Erin grimaced, and Grace held back a laugh. "I'm not sure how to characterize her."

"She's a very good mother."

"Okay, there." He nodded for emphasis. "That's my point. You actually see something redeeming in her."

"Now, Erin."

"No . . . I know you're right. That's what I was saying, about coming to terms with, and accepting, each other's choices. I think about you and Dad. You are another story. Hank and I always thought you were miserable together. You seemed so . . . I don't know . . . beaten down by him. We fully expected a divorce, or that you'd have a torrid affair with someone who was gallant and kind." He laughed. "It took me a long time to understand that's just how you two are together—he's demanding and you go along with it. That's part of your connection, your bond."

His comment stung.

"Your father treats me very well. He treats all of us well. And he always has." Did she sound defensive? "I love him." It was the first time she'd acknowledged the fact aloud to anyone other than Bain himself.

"I know. I know that now."

There was a long pause. She wanted to get up and walk around. She felt nervous. But the weight of his legs on her lap kept her down.

"You and Marley have—you had—a very different sort of dynamic." Should she use the past tense? Was the marriage truly over? Despite Erin's story, it didn't seem possible.

"Maybe. But I don't think I was prepared for her. What I'd seen and learned was to be reserved, to *keep your cards close to your chest,* as Dad used to say. That was how you two interacted, as though it was a constant tea party with everyone on his best behavior. I guess it worked between the two of you—that formality—but it didn't work for me. I held the door open, and Marley thought I was a chauvinist pig. I didn't want to leave the kids to go on some sexual-exploration weekend with her, and she thought I lacked passion. I compromised, and she accused me of having no conviction. I walked away rather than have a fight, and she thought I was disengaged."

The ease with which he recited the list saddened Grace. He'd obviously gone over his perceived failings a thousand times.

"What she considered romance, I thought was craziness. I didn't know how to bridge the gap. I couldn't translate the model of what I'd seen in you and Dad and how I'd been raised into something that could work in my marriage. And yet I am totally drawn to her because she's so different, so animated, so . . . so alive."

The foreign, the exotic; she'd heard it before. Were she and Bain tied inextricably together because they were alike? She'd never thought of them as having the same emotional responses; in fact, quite the opposite. Bain had a temper. She'd struggled to keep everything inside, quiet. But she knew at one level Erin was right. She and Bain had respected each other's boundaries. That made their relationship seem distant. "Every marriage is different."

"But I didn't know how to be Marley's lover—her husband—since I'd spent my whole life as your son!" Erin raised his voice.

"Can you keep it down?" India called. His outburst had interrupted the poignant reuniting of Dumbo and his caged mother.

"Sorry," Grace replied. "We'll try to do better."

"We didn't know about confrontation. You never showed us, and I never understood what it was to invest enough emotionally in someone else. Until there's been that confrontation and you can see that everyone stays together anyway, that you can scream bloody murder and still love each other, that I could rip Marley's hair out one minute and still throw myself in front of a truck to protect her, that the love never changes or goes away . . . well . . . that's what we never got."

"Your father and I were always here for you."

"You gave me a roof over my head, the best sporting goods and school supplies, you recognized all the major milestones with appropriate celebration and reward. But you never made the emotional investment." He turned to stare at his children. Namid flapped his arms with excitement as Dumbo curled up against his mother. An enormous pink tear rolled down the elephant's face. "I wasn't Sarah."

Grace gasped. "I . . . that's not . . ." She stammered, searching for words, wanting to say something reassuring or comforting. Sarah had been dead a long time. Erin was her grown son, her family. And yet she still missed her daughter every single day. "What does that mean?"

"I felt as though you were going through the parental motions, but that your heart wasn't in it."

"Is this how Hank feels, too?" She needed to buy herself time to think.

"Hank?" Erin asked, as if the reference was foreign.

"Hank is . . . I can't speak for him. He's certainly got his share of demons."

"I loved you. I loved your brother. I did everything I could . . ." She let her sentence drift off. Had she? Maybe he was right. Maybe her emotional intensity had disappeared down the drain with that fatal bathwater. "I'm sorry. I don't know how I can make it up to you if that's the way you feel."

Erin reached for her hand. "What you're doing now . . . for all of us . . . is amazing. As for Hank, I'd bet his only issue with you and Dad at the moment has to do with the sale of this house."

"I'm not sure whether that's a curse or a blessing."

He squeezed her hand. "That's one I can answer."

She raised her eyebrows. "But I don't want you to." She squeezed back.

❧

The next morning Bain offered to take the children to the diner for breakfast.

"Are you sure?"

"Why not?" he asked, as though it were a daily occurrence. "Maybe then we'll play a round of miniature golf. It's about time we get those children adept at using a putter."

She didn't object, although she knew what was truly motivating him. The telephone had rung late the night before and had woken everyone up. Erin had answered, hopeful that it was Marley. Instead it was Hank. He'd been at a party. Someone from Chatham had been there, too, and relayed the information that Erin and his children had moved into the house on Sears Point. Hank was instantly—and not subtly—suspicious. He'd also obviously had too much to drink.

"Did you decide to let him take what he wanted before I appeared?"

"This is insanity. It's nearly midnight. And Erin's arrival had absolutely nothing to do with any objects," Bain explained when he got on the line.

If that was the case, Hank insisted that furniture, antiques, and art be divided in his presence. "I'll be down first thing in the morning."

Bain had hung up and pulled the pillow over his head with a sigh. "Maybe the Sagamore Bridge will collapse in the night," he muttered.

Now, with Hank's expected arrival less than an hour away, Bain preferred spilled orange juice, sticky syrup, and gooey scrambled eggs.

"We'll keep Namid with us," Erin offered.

"He doesn't like pancakes anyway," India said, slipping her small hand into her grandfather's palm. "Come on, let's go. You said if we didn't get there early, they might run out of doughnuts."

Bain laughed and patted her on the head. "This one doesn't miss a trick."

Erin and Grace watched the car drive away. "Do you think they'll be all right?" he asked as it disappeared around the bend.

"They'll be just fine. I'd say of the three adults here, he's got by far and away the best deal."

⟡

Hank and Erin busied themselves in the dining room, examining the silver candlesticks, several china sets, sterling napkin rings, crystal goblets, chargers, and other valuable tableware that Grace had arranged on the table. Despite the tense atmosphere the division caused, it made sense to give heirlooms to the boys now. Hank and Susan entertained. They could use the formal services. As for Erin, he could take his share to the nearest consignment shop.

After the dining room, they could move into the library, where an assortment of other objects awaited their perusal. There was even Bain's collection of lead soldiers. His one instruction was that the armies stayed intact.

In a morbid tribute to the article she'd read, she purchased round labels in red and blue. They could color-code what they wanted. That way she could pack and ship their new belongings so that nothing would break in transport. Both boys had been duly impressed with her organizational scheme.

Leaving them to make their decisions, she'd put Namid down for his nap. He'd fallen asleep before she'd finished *Goodnight Moon*, and so she sat in the rocking chair staring at his favorite page, the blank one. "Goodnight nobody," it said. She liked that page, too.

As she descended the stairs, she heard Hank's voice.

"This is mostly crap. Silver plate I think."

"I'd be surprised," said Erin. "I suspect in their heyday, they were buying up the best."

"Heyday? That era has come and gone. They sold off the good stuff. Look how they're liquidating this place."

"It's too big for just the two of them. This move makes sense."

"Oh, please." Hank sounded dismissive. "You think they *want* a condo in Florida? We both know that Mom would be buried in the backyard if there were any way to hold on to it. Dad's run through his money with no regard to us, our families, his legacy. He hasn't done squat for his grandchildren. Now he's just trying to save face."

"But if they're broke—"

"*Selfish* is a better word. Dad could get a job, something in town selling ties at the Puritan or bait at the tackle shop. Mom could, too. She's never worked a day in her life. But they'd prefer to wander around this broken-down place, marking their turf and waiting for a five o'clock cocktail hour."

"At their age, it's not easy."

"Oh, please. They're not so old. They're both mobile, healthy. Why not try to earn a living instead of wasting the few assets they've got? Plus it would be good for them to see how the real world operates. It might make them a little more tolerant."

"I'm not sure anything could take the need to be judgmental out of those two."

Grace strained to hear, but there was no discernible response. Then, after a moment, she could make out Hank's voice again. She leaned against the wall, knowing that her eavesdropping was wrong and yet unable to tear herself away or announce her presence.

"Remember the Elliott kids? Marcy and Cal?"

"On the corner of Battlefield?"

"Yeah. Cal lives up near me now, has a private investment business, gets to work out of his house. Susan and his wife have become friends. According to the wife, old man Elliott subdivided the property, and they're looking at millions. He did it for them, you know, to provide for the kids, the grandkids. No one will ever have to worry."

"Yeah, but the property is ruined."

"And with the proceeds they'll collect, they can buy something else."

"Maybe. But they won't have their family home, the home they grew up in."

"Neither will we."

"That's true."

She heard shuffling on the table.

"And I could sure use a million right now."

"Don't hold your breath. By the time they're dead, there'll be nothing left."

Grace stepped across the threshold as if a strong gust of wind had propelled her into the room. She felt a surge of anger, and she glared first at her younger son and then his brother. Even while picking over their parents' carcasses, they'd still managed to criticize, resent, and want more.

"How dare you," she said, softly. Adrenaline rushed through her, and her arms and hands started to tingle.

They both turned in her direction. "What is it?" Hank asked. He squinted slightly.

She crossed her arms in front of her chest.

"What?" he repeated, looking at Erin, then back at his mother.

"She heard us," Erin said, the confession of a co-conspirator.

Hank turned back to Grace but didn't say anything.

The color had drained out of Erin's face as though he was going to vomit or collapse. He took a step back from his brother, obviously trying to distance himself. She knew how much he hated to be caught.

A memory of Erin as a five-year-old flashed into her mind. A friend from his preschool had come to play, and, after lunch, she'd heard peals of laughter from his bedroom. When she'd gone to check, she discovered both boys with their size 4T pants down around their ankles. Before she'd said a word, they'd scrambled to pull up their underwear, embarrassed even at such a young age, instinctively knowing that she wouldn't approve.

"What are you doing, Erin?" she'd asked, shocked.

He'd hesitated before responding. "It's a butt club. We show our butts." Then he'd smiled with pride. "Mine's bigger."

She'd called the other mother and confessed her mortification, but the woman laughed and dismissed it as normal. "They're just being little boys." The pediatrician did, too. But a part of her had been unwilling to accept that this behavior was commonplace, and she'd resented that for years afterward she'd had to watch his every move when other children came to play.

Now Hank and Erin stood frozen, each still holding a sheet of colored labels. "I'm disgusted by both of you." There, she'd said it. The words couldn't be taken back even if she wanted them to be. With everything that she'd done for Erin and his children, he hadn't had the decency to come to her defense. "I've a good mind to give this all to Goodwill. At least it'll find someone who appreciates it."

"Don't make us into the enemy, Mom," Hank replied. His voice showed no hint of nerves or anger. It was flat. "I've told you how I feel before. You can't pretend to be shocked now."

"You have no right to tell me how I feel, or how I'm entitled to feel."

Erin moved to his mother and reached for her arm. His touch was weak, timid.

She pushed his hand away. "Why did you come here?"

"Erin came because he needed help, and I'm here to help you move," Hank answered for both of them.

"Help? You consider this help? I wouldn't congratulate myself if I were you."

"You just don't want to accept what I am doing. Every time I've tried to help, to offer suggestions, you and Dad just cut me off. You've never been willing to listen."

"Helping requires recognizing what the other person needs."

"I did. I do. You just refused to honor the fact that I've made my life in real estate. I know what I'm talking about. I'm experienced. But no, you'd rather consult with some guy in Chatham you've played golf with. Do you know how that feels? To be marginalized by your own parents? Meanwhile you're giving this house away."

Grace inhaled, feeling the hot air burn her lungs. Why was this happening? Why were her boys so angry? What had she done wrong? "The Realtor, who, by the way, happens to be a woman, is extremely competent. We've known her for years, and she's done a good job. And where we live is our business. How we spend our money is, too."

"That's not true. We're your sons. We have the right to know."

"Mom, Hank, stop. Both of you." Erin's efforts at reconciliation fell on deaf ears.

"You haven't shown the slightest concern for either of us," Grace continued, finding that the words spilled from her lips. "You never have. And maybe that's all right. Maybe children should never have to worry about their parents. But I can't remember the last time you called to see how we were, you know, a call for no reason, a call to let us know you were thinking about us."

"Why do you want to make this my fault?"

She looked at Hank, wanting his features to be familiar, his mind to be transparent. Instead she felt as though she'd dug a photograph of an ancestor out of a box, an image yellowed with age. She stared at the face, knowing she was related, that there was a blood connection, but having no idea who the person was.

"This is a family!" Hank exploded. "When are you going to acknowledge that?"

Grace felt tears well in her eyes. She didn't want to cry, not now, not in front of the boys. It seemed too pathetic to weep with her china services and candelabra as a backdrop. "When we all start to act like one." She took a deep breath to regain her composure. "All of us. Not Dad, not me. All of us."

"But a family doesn't need to act. It just is. That's what you don't get. You treat us like we're some meal you can cook to perfection. And when we don't respond the way you want, you make us feel rotten. Well, let me tell you something. And perhaps now, at this stage of the game, you'll finally listen. Erin and I aren't a soufflé. And you're not a master chef. We're your sons, for better or for worse." With that he threw his package of red stickers onto the table and walked out.

⌘

Bain dismissed the incident. "He's furious about the house and even more angry that we didn't list it with him. He'll get over it. It's a tense time for all of us." But Grace felt sick. She tried to reach him on his cell phone, but got no answer. Even Susan seemed reluctant to take a message, although she promised she'd tell him that his mother needed to speak to him.

"How about a walk?" Erin asked, tentatively. "Please? It's a beautiful afternoon, and even two rounds of miniature golf didn't tire India and Deshawn. They're eager to get out."

The children chased each other in a circle. Although she appreciated that they were able to amuse themselves with the most senseless of pastimes, just watching the energy expended was exhausting.

"I don't know if I can manage any more conversation, or should I say confrontation. Not with you."

"How about we talk about nothing?"

Grace smiled, feebly. Her nerves felt raw. "So I can report that the Odd Lots is having a sale on cranberry soda, and we can feel like we're communicating."

"Absolutely. We can even pick up a case if that's what you want. And I promise not to launch into a lecture on the dangers of aspartame."

Under those circumstances, she agreed. A walk would do her good.

The breeze had blown out the humidity. The children took off their shoes and frolicked, skipping stones and chasing seagulls. India brought a bucket and gathered feathers, sea glass, and even a dead horseshoe crab. "Look," she said, holding it up by its long tail. "Did you know it's related to the dinosaurs? That makes it a million billion years old. That's even older than you, Grandma."

"Thank you for noticing," Grace replied.

As the children played, she and Erin walked along in silence. She stared at the various footprints ahead of her in the sand. One set belonged to a pair of large boots with thick-tread soles. She liked the carefully delineated pattern of grooves left behind.

Erin carried Namid in a backpack. The baby's arms dangled, and he made various indecipherable noises, expressing his excitement. Then, pointing, he called out, "Bird." The word sounded like *bud*. Grace reached up to hold his hand, enveloping his small pudgy fingers in her palm. He smiled, and the sight warmed her. She wished every relationship were this easy.

"Can I break our agreement?" Erin asked after a while. "Our agreement not to talk."

She'd known he would, known the walk wouldn't be completely peaceful. It couldn't be. Not after all they'd been through, the showdown, Hank's fury. This was new territory for all of them, and having started something, they could not relax now. "Why not?" She rolled her eyes. "Bring it on."

He laughed, no doubt amused by his mother's colloquialism. "Maybe candor will do all of us a bit of good. I mean, going forward."

Grace forced a smile, wishing she hadn't let Hank leave. She should have followed him out, spoken to him before he got in his car and disappeared. "At the rate we're going, it's more likely that we'll flee to the four corners of the earth and won't have to put up with one another. An igloo on the North Pole actually sounds inviting. Peace, quiet, and polar bears."

"That works, too." He squeezed the back of her arm and turned to face her. "I just want to apologize. You have a right to be angry. I don't want the house sale to destroy us. It's just a building with some bedrooms and a pool. I need to remind myself that the memories don't get left behind when you and Dad move out."

"I wish your memories were happier. I somehow thought your childhood was idyllic, at least a lot of the time. I guess I was wrong. I never, ever meant to be judgmental." It was hardly a response to his comment, but the word—the accusation—had echoed in her mind for the last several hours. Judgmental seemed the worst possible quality in a parent, a mother, the person who was supposed to love unequivocally and unconditionally. Why had that been so hard for her?

He took her hand. "I guess I can't blame you when I've been such a fuckup. Excuse my language," he added.

"If you were little, I'd wash your mouth out with soap."

He paused for a moment and furrowed his brow. The expression reminded her of Bain. "Did you ever do that?"

"What?"

"Actually put a bar of soap in my mouth, scrub my tongue with Ivory. I remember you threatening it all the time, but I can't remember if it ever happened."

"Of course I didn't."

She closed her eyes, remembering holding a sudsy

white bar in her hand and shaking it at her son. He was in high school, but the language he'd used made him sound like a prison inmate or a gang member. She'd been shocked. As soap and water drops flew around her, he'd glared at her and walked away. "If you're so into it, wash your own mouth," he'd called from over his shoulder.

"Yeah, I guess I would remember," Erin said. "I probably would have been sick." He thought for a moment. "Then why did you threaten us?"

"Why?" She wasn't sure. She'd tried to assert some control. Manners were important, and part of that was proper language. "I didn't want you and Hank to curse or swear, or even use slang for that matter, and it seemed the appropriate punishment. But you two won in the end." The reality was that she couldn't have wrestled her fifteen-year-old son over the sink and stuffed a bar of soap into his mouth. Even if she'd had the mental fortitude to follow through on her threat, she didn't have the physical strength. "I was never very good at imposing my will on you two."

"Maybe we should have listened."

"That's kind of you to say." She wondered if his words were genuine.

"Look, Mom, don't think I don't hate myself for still turning to you and Dad for help. I'm nearly thirty. I don't want to be dependent. I'd like nothing better than to provide for my own kids the way Dad provided for us, give them a great education and a sense of security."

"It's harder now. Things are more expensive, more difficult. I know that. Maybe your father and I were luckier than I realized."

"Maybe Dad had more business talent than I give him credit for."

"We're fortunate for that, since he hasn't written that great American novel we've all been waiting for."

"Do you think he ever will?"

Grace looked at Erin, wondering what answer he'd prefer to hear. Would he feel better about himself if he knew his father had failed at something? Or would Erin seek inspiration from the idea that there was still time ahead for a man nearing his sixties to leave his mark on the world? "I'm not sure."

"Maybe Florida will inspire him."

"God help us if he's inspired by that culture."

"Is it another time zone?"

Grace shook her head. "Only another universe."

"And a plane ride. We'll have to work harder . . . you know . . . to stay in touch." His tone and expression were hopeful.

Erin was right. Real connection—the rarity of what it was and what it meant—was hard to maintain. It was how she'd felt about Ferris, her only sibling, with Prissy, the one friend with whom she'd been completely honest, and with Sarah, the child who transformed her into a mother. And it was the link she had with Bain. Maybe it was because they were similar, or maybe difference had formed their bond. In any event, it was a love that had endured. She knew that without her, Bain would be only partly alive.

Erin's comment was more profound than he realized. In a brief period of time, Bain would be alone. He would need his sons and the distraction of his lively grandchildren more than ever. He didn't have other family, and, in a new environment, he wouldn't have the attention of old friends. Erin and Hank—both boys—would have to grow up. But she didn't know how to relay the importance of that message without disclosing the truth. Her truth. The one she wouldn't give up. "Yes. It's not going to be—"

An array of voices interrupted her conversation. Turning around, Grace saw that India and Deshawn had found Emily, hard at work in Prissy's famous spot across from the town landing. She was talking to them, gesticulating with her rake, and showing off the contents of her bucket.

"I see you've met my grandchildren," Grace called out.

"I think we have some clammers in the making. They want a lesson."

"A noble profession," Grace responded. "I'm sure their father would approve. In fact, he may want to join you."

"Given the current status of my unemployment, anything that might bring in a buck or two is greatly appreciated," he said, humbly.

"And after all, your godmother was one of the very best," Grace reminded him.

With that she made the necessary introductions. Erin extended a hand, but Emily only held up her muddy palm.

"How about we dispense with formalities?" he offered.

"They don't do much good around here, anyway," Grace replied, as she took Namid from Erin's back. Together, they settled in the sand to watch Erin, India, and Deshawn learn the basics of digging, finding, and measuring a Chatham clam.

Chapter Twenty-five

Grace checked her list again. She'd ordered flowers—peonies were in season—five pounds of Wellfleet oysters, a case of champagne, a box of plastic flutes, and three dozen toile-print cocktail napkins. The card table that didn't sell at her yard sale would serve as a bar since the dining room table would be packed onto a moving truck. The day before, she'd sent out laser-printed invitations that the local stationer's store had done since there had been no time for engraving. Hank and Susan's included a handwritten personal note urging them to come. Five days of silence was too long.

All that was left was for her guests to RSVP, and for the movers to take away the furniture that remained. Then they could have a party.

Despite the Realtor's insistence that West Palm was the place to be, Bain had signed a lease on a two-bedroom apartment in Palm Beach. "A rental is better. We're not locked in," he'd explained. It was a modern high-rise, but it had a decent view of the Intracoastal and a balcony. Grace was relieved. Although she found herself more and more tired with each passing day, the end of this limbo was near. At least she would be able to help him get settled.

She looked up from the writing table and noticed him standing in the doorway. His eyes were red. She wondered how long he'd been there.

"I suspect we'll have about fifty people," she said, her voice cheerful. "It will be a wonderful chance to say good-bye."

He didn't reply.

"I'm only wondering about renting some chairs. Our friends aren't getting any younger. Do you think people can stand the whole time?"

Still he said nothing.

"Are you all right?" she asked.

"Is that what you're concerned about? Where guests are going to sit? What is this party anyway—a memorial service? You don't have to be like your mother. I'm perfectly capable of honoring you on my own. I could give you a thousand tributes, Grace."

Her heart pounded. She clenched her pen in her hand. "Why are you talking like this?" Her efforts at concealment sounded as pathetic and flimsy as they were.

Bain rested his hand on the doorknob. "Dr. Preston called me. He was apologetic, said he normally wouldn't speak to me, not directly, but apparently he's been calling you for weeks and gotten no response."

I did respond. I left him a message. I told him to stay away. She wanted to defend herself but no words came out. The room started to spin.

"He's worried. Very worried. I asked him why he was worried about *my* wife?" Bain reached into his pocket, pulled out a handkerchief, and then blew his nose. His gaze wandered beyond Grace and out the window at the still-covered pool. They hadn't bothered to open it for the summer, another effort to cut back on costs. The Marxes could bear that expense after they moved in. They were no doubt going to remodel it anyway, spend thousands on a complex mosaic tile pattern, or at least repaint the bottom. "Am I the last to know? Were you ever going to tell me?"

"Bain," she said, feebly.

"What's going on?"

"It's nothing."

"Then why?" Half lunging and half falling, he kneeled at her feet. "Is it cancer?"

"I . . . don't know." As she spoke, the three small words made her gag.

"Dr. Preston says you refuse to have any tests. He can't even confirm the diagnosis or ascertain the severity. He says you're giving up for no reason."

"No, not for no reason."

"Then why?"

She looked into his tear-filled eyes. He hadn't cried since Sarah's death. His businesses had collapsed; their home had fallen into disrepair; he'd been hurt and mistreated by his two sons. And he'd simply barreled ahead at full throttle, leaving no wake of emotions behind him. Now he looked shattered.

How could she possibly explain everything that had gone through her mind in the last several weeks? How could she articulate her realization that she'd made so many mistakes without seeming to blame him—fault him—at the same time? Maybe that was what she wanted to do. Because, after all, weren't they both responsible? Weren't their failures shared?

"I love you," she said.

He looked momentarily confused.

"I always have and I always will."

"That's not the point. Grace, you need to follow Dr. Preston's advice and do what needs to be done. You can't will this to go away," he pleaded.

"But I want you to understand that."

He paused, looked directly into her eyes, and gripped her knees. "I do. And it's more important to me than anything in the world."

She wished at this moment that she could draw on a higher power for guidance. She needed strength. She had conviction, but she wasn't at all sure she had the fortitude to convey it. Every ounce of her wanted to pick herself up out of her chair, excuse herself, and hide in her bedroom, ending any further discussion. That was the pattern she'd followed for the last fifty-eight years; it was the coping mechanism that worked, that made sense. And now she wondered if that avoidance had kept them together. If so, what would happen when she explained, asserted her own decision? This very conversation was what she'd been desperate to avoid.

"I don't want chemotherapy or operations or radiation. I don't want to be in the process of dying."

"You're not."

"No, Bain, don't dismiss this. I need you to listen. Really listen. Not just hear the words. Can you do that, do that for me?"

He nodded.

"I want to be me, here, alive, and then gone, with nothing in between."

"But if you're sick —"

She touched his lips with her finger to silence him.

"I'm fifty-eight. I look at my life and wonder what happened. I've accomplished almost nothing. I'm a mother and my children resent me. There probably isn't time to change that. Hank won't even speak to me."

"That'll pass. You know what a terrible temper he has."

"I'm a homemaker, to use a horribly old-fashioned term," she continued. "But my home will soon belong to someone else." She cupped his cheeks in her palms and felt the slight bristle on his skin. "But I've been your wife, and that is the one thing I'm proud of. The one thing I've done right. I don't want to ruin that now by an illness where you're left with bedpans and test tubes. I don't want to be sick, and I don't want you to nurse me."

"That's not fair."

"Bain, you said you'd listen. This is a decision I've made for me and for you, for us. But I've known it was going to be difficult. It's not our dynamic. I've gone along with everything you chose, all the decisions you made for both of us. Now it's my turn."

"This is not the time to try to even a score."

"That's not what I'm talking about and you know it."

"Grace!" he exclaimed. "I'm your husband. We were practically children when we met, and look at us now. Our own children are grown." He tried to smile momentarily, but then his expression grew serious again. "I can't imagine life without you. And if you're sick, you can be damn sure it's me who will take care of you. You're not being fair to me otherwise." He didn't bother to look away as the tears escaped his eyes. "I *want* to care for you. I want to be your nurse if you need one. I couldn't live with myself if I didn't."

She shook her head. "Palm Beach will be easier, easier for both of us. And you . . . you're not that old, Mr. Alcott. And you're still the handsomest man I know. There's a lot of life left."

"I don't want it without you."

His hands were dappled with age spots. His hair had thinned, his temples grayed. And yet she could picture him so easily, sitting on a blanket on the banks of the Charles River, eating her sandwiches and then kissing her. It was the kiss that had prevented her from protesting the war in Vietnam; the kiss that had set the course of her life.

"Aren't you scared?" she asked.

"Scared?"

"Of knowing. It's easier for me to just let whatever will

happen, happen. Then I can let my imagination go and hope for a Hollywood ending."

"The truth isn't scary. Whatever it is, whatever the outcome, knowing what we face means we can face it together. It's the demons that spin in our heads, the uncertainties that will haunt us. We'll never be able to just enjoy; we'll always wonder. Every day will be filled with panic and uncertainty and fear. The truth, no matter how bad, will give us freedom to be together. Please, Grace, I'll be right by your side."

"If I go back to the hospital, you and Dr. Preston will take over. I know that. I need that not to happen." She closed her eyes.

"It won't." He paused for a moment, thinking. "That morning, the morning the Marxes first came to look at the house, do you remember?"

She felt herself blush. "Of course."

"I've asked myself why we don't make love more."

She looked away. After all these years together, conversation about sex still embarrassed her.

"You're as beautiful to me now as you've ever been. In some ways, you're more beautiful. And after that morning—I guess I should say that night and the morning—I realized again how very lucky I am. I may not have shown you enough, or reminded you enough. Perhaps I should have held you in my arms every day and told you again and again. I don't know. But I want those days back, the days and nights that have passed without intimacy. I'm the luckiest man in the world. I'm lucky to have you. Lucky to hold you. Lucky to have you as my wife."

With that his shoulders shook and he buried his face in her lap. She didn't say a word, but gently rubbed the top of his head, feeling his hair and his skull beneath her fingertips. Time passed, she wasn't sure how long, without them speaking, but she couldn't bring herself to interrupt the silence that seemed to tie them together. The physical contact was more palliative than anything either of them could say.

Finally, he sat back on his heels and wiped his eyes. "Let's run the tests, get the diagnosis. Together. And then . . . then you can decide what you want to do. It will be your choice, not mine. I promise. I promise to respect whatever decision you make. I may try to dissuade you," he said, forcing a smile, "but I won't go back on my word." He slipped the thin gold band off his left finger. "Here," he said, holding it out to her. "Take this. It'll remind you of my promise, my commitment. That ring is everything to me. And if I can't be your husband and honor your wishes now, then I'm no good to either of us."

She held it in her palm. She remembered picking it out at a jeweler on Newbury Street. An elderly man had helped them make a selection. She'd been surprised that Bain had wanted a ring at all, the public branding of matrimony, but he'd insisted. She doubted he'd ever taken it off before this moment. She couldn't recall ever having seen him without it. Nicked and scratched, the thin ring had survived.

∽

Nobody questioned her when she made a series of calls, hastily canceling her even more hastily planned farewell party. She wasn't particularly surprised. As soon as news of the house sale had made its way through the tributaries of the community, her relationships had changed. Acquaintances were visibly distant; friends aloof, too. She wouldn't be entertaining. In Florida, Bain was hardly a resource for business connections, and the Alcotts would no longer pledge at St. Christopher's. So they had nothing to offer. There was nothing to be gained by maintaining an effort.

In some ways, Grace appreciated the distinct lack of interest. She couldn't have managed with lots of questions or more than idle curiosity. She had her response, which she left on countless answering machines. The party had been ill advised given everything she had to do with the move. "I don't know what I was thinking," she parroted breezily. She was sorry for the confusion and hoped she'd have an opportunity to say good-bye in person.

Only three people called her back to make arrangements for that to happen.

Chapter Twenty-six

T he conference room on the twenty-third floor of International Place had a spectacular view of Boston Harbor and the Federal Courthouse. Sun sparkled on the water. From her plush swivel chair, Grace watched a steel-hulled liner slowly making its way to dock while two sailboats, weaving in and out of commercial vessels and channel markers, raced to sea.

The chairs surrounding the polished granite table were filled. Bain and Bob Chadwick spoke in hushed tones. The Alcotts' lawyer, a legal version of a family practitioner with a small, unassuming office on Route 28, had driven up with them from Chatham. On the trip he'd explained somewhat apologetically that the Boston attorneys had done the bulk of the work. They'd even revised his draft of the deed.

Beside Bob sat Kay, who fiddled with a gaudy gold pin on the lapel of her pink suit with a faux-fur collar. The outfit, including her pink shoes, looked as though it had been purchased in its entirety off a window mannequin. Grace speculated that she'd spent part of her handsome commission in advance on a new wardrobe.

Robin Marx presided over one end of the table. She flipped through the pages of *Vogue* magazine, obviously bored by Kay's efforts at conversation. Then she checked her watch and her BlackBerry, hoping that someone or something would distract her.

Across the table from the Alcotts stretched a row of pin-striped suits. They each had a substantial pile of paperwork in front of them. A blond man named Mark fidgeted with his polka-dot bow tie. The partner, Chad Barker, scribbled notes on a yellow pad. The senior associate, Emma Watts, drummed the eraser end of her pencil against the table. The nervous gestures made Grace wonder what possible legal issues hadn't been addressed at this point. Hadn't this team of Juris Doctorates attended to every detail well in advance?

Jay Marx was on the telephone. One hand was shoved deep into the pocket of his wide-wale corduroy slacks. He paced back and forth in front of a credenza and intermittently uttered "Unacceptable" into the receiver. "Absolutely unacceptable."

In addition to the telephone, the credenza held platters piled with sandwiches, curled parsley garnish, and nearly two dozen cans of soda. Would they be here long enough to need nourishment or was the meal in place for another meeting in this conference room? Although her throat was dry and her stomach empty, the last thing she wanted following the sale of her home was a meal.

Jay paused for a moment. "Could someone get rid of that tuna? It smells like crap."

Emma buttoned her fitted jacket and nodded at Mark.

"Sorry, Mr. Marx," he said, jumping up. He grabbed the platter and disappeared out the door.

Bob Chadwick sat forward and cleared his throat. "We did say eleven. By my watch, it's twenty past. Shall we get this show on the road?"

Kay laughed nervously and recrossed her legs. "Yes. Yes, absolutely."

Without getting off the telephone, Jay raised one finger as a signal. He needed more time.

"Well, how about if Mr. Alcott begins looking at all that paperwork?" Bob asked. "I don't think I've even seen the final copies."

"I'm sure you'll find everything in order," Chad said. He was a handsome man in his midforties. When he'd introduced himself, his handshake had been extra firm. Now his potent sandalwood cologne filled the entire room.

Emma stopped her drumming. "We did overnight it to you."

"Well, since I needed to be here this morning, my paperwork and I must have passed on the Southeast Expressway," Bob replied. "Although of course you still can charge your client for premium mailing," he muttered.

Bain smiled, amused by the small-town versus city lawyer dig.

"Our mistake," Chad said, flashing a politician's smile. Then, turning to Bain, he said with a level of enthusiasm that seemed inappropriate, "Get your pen out. We'll need lots of signatures."

Grace watched as the papers were passed one by one to Bain and Bob. They conferred briefly over each document: the certification and indemnification regarding urea formaldehyde foam insulation, the municipal lien certificate, real estate tax credits, final water bill, settlement sheet, and Title V certificate. With his jaw set, Bain signed his name again and again. She watched the neat scrawl emerge from his fountain pen, the curves and letters with which she was so familiar. Not once did he look up or acknowledge her, less than an arm's reach away. To do so would make his task infinitely more difficult.

In many ways, her presence was extraneous. Grace had known every nook and cranny, creaky floorboard, cracked molding, and swollen cabinet; she'd planted every tulip bulb and holly bush, trimmed the *Rosa rugosa* and weeded the flowerbeds; she'd explored every inch of property around a house that had never been hers to begin with. Bain had held the property in his name and his alone. But he'd wanted her to come with him since they had to be in Boston anyway. In a few hours, they were boarding a plane for Florida. Even now their two overnight bags stood sentinel by the conference room door. He hadn't wanted her to wait, wandering around Faneuil Hall alone.

She swiveled her chair to glance out the window. Off in the distance, a jet escaped the runway at Logan and climbed into the sky.

Bain hadn't raised the subject of the medical tests in the last week. They'd agreed to postpone the decision until after the closing. Hospitals in Florida were perfectly adequate, and Dr. Preston could give referrals if she was willing to proceed.

Jay ended his call and sat beside his wife. He crossed his arms and leaned back. Watching his smug expression, Grace wondered whether he and his wife were as dreadful as she perceived them to be or whether jealousy and bitterness had clouded her perspective. Did they genuinely feel entitled to have others at their disposal or was that simply the impression they wanted to exude?

After Bain signed each document, Bob passed it to Chad, who placed it in front of Robin. With his pointer finger, he showed her where to affix her signature.

Jay smirked. "The first acquisition for the Robin Marx Corporation Limited," he said, teasingly. "Let's hope its CEO doesn't get any more grand ideas."

Emma giggled. The noise sounded silly.

Chad rested his hand on Jay's shoulder. "You're a good man."

Why did a corporation need a house in Chatham? Grace lacked financial acumen but she knew enough to know that Robin did, too. She'd even needed an outside consultant to come up with a salmon-and-sage theme. No doubt the arrangement was some sophisticated transaction devised by her husband and his lawyers, a way to pass off home improvements as business expenses or avoid taxes. That kind of scheming was why Jay and Robin could afford the house, could do all the repairs, could renovate and rebuild until it was unrecognizable. She and Bain were old school, nothing fancy, and look where they'd ended up.

"Let's sign over the deed and we're done here," Chad said.

The deed. Actual ownership.

"Where is my payment?" Bain asked.

"Right here." Chad handed a check to Bain. $1,170,000. The amount was printed electronically. It was the largest check Grace had ever seen.

Bain held it in both hands, studying it. As he squinted his eyes, he reminded her of a 7-Eleven clerk, trying to verify that a fifty-dollar bill wasn't counterfeit by looking for nearly invisible colored threads on one side. He didn't say a word.

"Is something wrong?" Chad asked after more than a few minutes of absolute silence had passed. "Must feel pretty great to hold that in your hands," he chuckled.

Bain looked at Chad and then at Jay. "This is not certified."

Jay scoffed.

"Please," Chad said, sarcastically. "It's drawn on Jay's private client funds account at Fleet." He turned to his client. "And what's the minimum balance you need for them to let you in?" He chuckled. "Frankly, it's better than certified."

"That may be true. But the purchase and sale agreement specifies a bank check." Bain's voice was firm.

Tuning in to the conversation, Bob reached into the pile of documents and pulled out the relevant one. He pushed it toward Chad, pointing to the pertinent paragraph. "Right there. Three-B. The balance of the purchase price is to be paid by bank or certified check."

"What exactly are you insinuating?" Jay rose from his chair.

"Nothing. I'm only asking for compliance with the terms of our agreement."

"I really find this insane," Chad said.

"Not insane. Insulting," Jay said, scowling.

"Sir," Bain said, deliberately. "I am neither making nor passing judgment. You and Mr. Gates may well be of comparable worth for all I know. But I am entitled to a certified check. Not a private client check or a business check or any other kind of check."

"What's going on?" Robin said, the pitch of her voice reflecting her sudden anxiety.

Grace felt similarly anxious. She'd been listening to the exchange, wondering about the rising level of animosity. Was Bain actually trying to stop the sale, or just to exert some control? Was he insisting on a technicality for a reason? She couldn't tell, and she couldn't let herself imagine the consequences. Horizons had to go. They couldn't hold on to the property.

As hard as it was for her to offer a solution, one did seem obvious. "Isn't there a branch nearby? Couldn't we get it certified now? We're in no hurry," she suggested.

All heads turned to stare at her.

"Perfect," Bain said, touching her forearm. "We'll wait."

"If you're going to insist, fine." Chad nodded at Emma. "Let's call over to the bank and let Barbara know we're on our way. She can expedite this process."

She rose from the table. Her skirt was substantially shorter than Grace would have found acceptable in a business environment, but she knew times had changed. Bain didn't seem to notice. His eyes were fixed on her. She couldn't read his expression.

"Mind if I have one of those sodas while we're waiting?" Bob asked. Without waiting for permission, he got up, moved to the credenza, and returned with a can of Coca-Cola and a small bag of Cape Cod Potato Chips. He tore it open and removed a kettle-boiled chip. The crunch seemed to echo.

Grace's palms felt cold and clammy. There was no reason to be apprehensive. People like the Marxes had plenty of money, had minions organizing their affairs. Orders could be executed instantly. Nothing was going to go wrong at this point.

They waited as the telephone conversation dragged on. Emma had turned her back to the room and now spoke in hushed tones, covering the receiver with her hand to muffle the conversation. Finally, she faced the table once again. "I see . . . Yes . . . Okay. Thank you for your assistance." She hung up.

"All right, then," Chad said. "Let's get this done as quickly as possible." He walked over and handed her the check.

She didn't take it. "The funds have not been transferred." Her voice was flat. "The check can't be certified today because the funds aren't there . . . yet."

"Not there!" Kay decided to enter the conversation now that it appeared her commission was in jeopardy.

"I can't believe this," Jay said. "I can't fucking believe it. You'll get your money. There's plenty of money. There must have been a delay somewhere, a glitch in the fucking fail-safe system. The wire transfer will clear by tomorrow, or Friday at the latest. I can assure you of that."

"I'm sorry. The house is not for sale."

Grace couldn't believe her ears. She would have thought she'd been dreaming, imagining, but the expression on the face of each Boston lawyer told her otherwise.

"You can't do that," Chad said. "This is not a material breach. We can close tomorrow."

Bob stood up and buttoned his jacket. "You were the ones who insisted on a time-is-of-the-essence provision. Not us. You're in breach."

Grace thought she saw the corners of Bain's mouth turn up. Bob had earned his fee.

"Grace, Bain, this is what you wanted. Who knows when another buyer might come along, if ever," Kay pleaded.

"The money is there. We're talking about a twenty-four-hour delay." Chad's voice bordered on shrill.

"Then I'll take a check drawn on this firm's account."

"What?" Chad exclaimed.

"No doubt you have more than adequate funds to cover it. And I'm sure Mr. Marx here is a very valuable client." Bain almost seemed amused. His eyes twinkled.

Chad cleared his throat. Grace thought his face looked flushed, but perhaps they were all overheating. "Uh . . . um . . . That's not possible. You're talking about a check for more than a million dollars. That would have to get approval from our management committee. It could never happen today."

No lawyer could look at Jay.

"What the fuck!" Jay shouted at Chad. "I give you shit-for-brains more business than you know what to do with. Let me tell you. There'll be none. There isn't a firm in town who wouldn't do this for me."

"Jay, please, let's be rational. You know I would if I could, but I can't authorize it—not for this sum and not on such short notice."

"Then find someone who can."

Chad slouched forward and held on to the edge of the conference table.

"It's a management decision," Emma parroted. "It's really beyond our control, as much as we'd love to help."

The blood had drained from Mark's face. He excused himself, exiting quickly.

"The condition of closing was a certified check. Now. At eleven A.M. The time you specified. Not sometime in the future. And certainly not sometime after we have transferred title to our house," Bain announced. "We did everything you asked. We even drove all the way up here when a closing in Chatham would have been substantially more convenient for both Mr. Chadwick and myself. All you had to do is make the money available, and it's not. Although under the circumstances I am quite sure you're not entitled to a return of your deposit, I'm instructing Kay to release the escrow back to you. I don't want your money. The deal is off."

Bob rose and reached for his briefcase. He'd known Bain long enough to know he wasn't likely to threaten and not follow through.

"Wait a moment," Robin said. "I don't understand. We're all set. I've got a decorator and a contractor and a landscaper meeting me this afternoon." She looked at her husband. "Who owns the house?"

"We do," Bain said without missing a beat. "And we plan to keep it that way."

❧

They stood by the elevator staring at the mahogany veneer and the marble plaque engraved with the name of the law firm. Other than Bob and a maintenance man polishing the brass on the doorknobs, they were alone.

Grace wondered if she were dreaming. Reaching into her pocket, she fumbled with her key chain. The house key was still there. Horizons was still home.

The ding of a bell announced the arrival of the elevator. It was empty. The three of them stepped inside.

"What will we do?" she asked. "We needed the sale."

Bain took her palms in his. "Let me tell you a little story," he replied. His voice was calm and gentle. "Many years back, in the fifties it was, there was a quarterback for the Detroit Lions, a man called Bobby Layne. He had a glorious career, was beloved by many, but alcohol and infidelities eventually tarnished his character and left him in some degree of disgrace. After he'd fallen into disrepute, he was interviewed. I remember reading it at the time. *How was he going to get by? How was he going to manage?* He was asked those questions again and again. He wasn't bitter or angry at how the crowds had turned on him. Instead he remarked that the goal of life was to run out of money and air at the same time." He rubbed the tops of her hands. "Maybe that's our goal, too, Gracie. All we need is enough to see us through."

Bob chuckled.

Then Bain leaned toward her and whispered, "Don't you worry. I'm going to keep you in your home forever."

Ten Days Later

Chapter Twenty-seven

From her bed Grace could see the first gray light of morning through the crack in the steely blue institutional curtains. The numbers of the digital clock showed 5:21. She pushed the button by her right hand, waited a moment, and then heard a groan and felt her head elevating as the metal frame shifted into position. She strained to hear traffic on the street below—even the sound of a siren would have been comforting, or a dog barking—but it was deathly quiet.

Her gaze shifted to the Naugahyde armchair next to the bed railing. Bain had fallen asleep there earlier in the evening, his fingers steepled in his lap and his chin resting on his chest. She'd been relieved to see him finally steal a moment of peace in what had been an arduous day in a very long week. Only when the nurse came in at nine to check her vital signs had he awoken, disoriented, and finally acquiesced to return to the hotel room for a few hours. "You can't sleep in a chair," she'd said, urging him to leave. "And you'll need a change of clothes. Please don't worry, I'll be fine."

"As long as you'll promise to call if you need anything," he'd instructed. He'd bent over and lowered his voice. "You can't be stoic anymore, Gracie." Then he'd kissed her, but barely. They'd brushed lips. He'd applied no pressure, as though she might break under even his gentle touch. "I'll be back," he assured her. "First thing."

He would return early. She fully expected that. Her surgery was scheduled for seven thirty.

For the last week, that period before she'd been admitted when blood work, X-rays, sonograms, and bone and lymph-node biopsies had been done, she'd stayed with him at the Ritz-Carlton, in the room he now occupied alone. It had windows overlooking Commonwealth Avenue, a cheery floral print on the bedspread and curtains, and a plush neutral carpet. In the drawer of the bedside table, she'd found several scenic postcards of Boston in a faux-leather folder along with some stationery and a ticket for the hotel's laundry service. She'd sat at the glass-topped desk and addressed them to her Chatham neighbors, her messages upbeat, as though she were taking a brief vacation before returning to her home on Sears Point. "We've decided not to sell," she'd written, "and are enjoying a few days in Boston. It has been a bit of a stressful time after all." The words gave her strength. Then she'd left her correspondence with the concierge on her way to the hospital. She liked that postage could be added to their room charge.

She would have preferred to be home from the moment they walked out of International Place, but Bain had insisted they find a hotel. Their furniture and possessions were en route to Florida. It would take a while to get them back. And he didn't want Grace to unpack, to set up house, not now. She needed to save her strength. They had bigger decisions to make.

So they'd said good-bye to Bob and checked into the Ritz with their overnight bags. They'd changed into the plush terry robes that they found in the closet, ordered supper early, and watched a movie. They'd spoken of nothing important, but laughed together at the romantic comedy. When it was over, they made love to each other, gently, tenderly, with the street lamps casting a glow across the room. She'd fallen asleep in his arms.

At her insistence, Bain had driven her to the Cape the next afternoon. She'd felt excited, rolling down her window as they drove across the Sagamore Bridge to breathe in the salty air and hear the distant sound of a motorboat speeding through the channel. The house was untouched. She'd walked through the empty rooms, comforted by every crack and imperfection, and relieved— overwhelmingly relieved—to be back. It was there, standing in her kitchen, watching the water seep from a leaky gasket on the faucet, that she'd finally agreed to proceed with Dr. Preston's recommendations and get the necessary tests performed immediately. She'd get to Dana Farber as soon as the arrangements could be made.

"I'm proud of you," Bain had said.

From then on, time had been a blur. Dr. Belafonte had been nothing like his name suggested. A pudgy man with thick folds under his chin, wire-rimmed glasses, and a black mustache, he wore a long white coat over his plaid pants and wedge-soled Earth shoes. Although he spoke in a slightly abrasive, nasal voice, he'd held her hand when he confirmed the diagnosis she'd known all along. Then he'd brought her a Dixie cup half filled with water. She'd studied the floral design stenciled around the cup as he'd explained what options she had. Bain hadn't said a word.

"I know it's a lot to process for both of you, and I also know that I'm unable to give you the assurances you want. But what do you think?" Dr. Belafonte had asked.

"It's Grace's decision," Bain had said, his voice cracking. "It has to be Grace's decision."

Sitting beside him, watching him fight back tears, she'd agreed to surgery. "I'd welcome it at this stage," she remembered herself saying. As she faced the doctor and listened to his explanation of what lay ahead, it struck her that the authority to act on her own was meaningless. Her life was in reference to Bain, as his was to her, and that degree of entanglement wasn't bad. She wasn't weak; she loved her husband. And he needed more than anything to believe they stood a chance. If she'd chosen to do nothing, she would force him to abandon his hope. Neither of them was ready for that.

Erin and the children drove down from Vermont, and Bain got them a room with a crib two floors below. India and Deshawn shared the bed, while their father slept on a pull-out couch. They went to the sea lion show at the aquarium, took a ride on the Swan Boats, feeding the ducks that swam alongside, and had tea at the Four Seasons with chocolate éclairs and strawberry shortcake. It might have been perfect—she might even have forgotten why they were all there—except that each moment felt so precious, so packed with activity and deliberate joy.

The last night they had dinner together at a pizza restaurant on Dartmouth Street. Grace nibbled on a bread stick and watched her grandchildren delight over the wood-burning stove and the Shirley Temples with maraschino cherries and twisted stirrers. Hank, Susan, and Henry had been invited to join them, but Susan had declined, promising to come to the hospital when the surgery was over. "We're all thinking of you," she'd said before hanging up. Hank hadn't come on the line.

Now the gray of dawn changed to the glory of early-morning sunshine. 6:23. 6:24. Grace watched the minute digit flip.

Slowly, she swung her legs to one side, stood up, and shuffled to the bathroom in the corner. The smell of Lysol greeted her as she opened the heavy door. The room had a safety railing, a sink with a mirror and fluorescent lights, and a toilet with a loud suction flush that reminded her of an airplane. What did happen to the urine—or worse— that was released into the atmosphere? It was one of many questions to which she had no answer.

She thought of the previous morning. Her last day of freedom, of wholeness. Only twenty-four hours had passed since her admission, but it seemed longer. She'd crossed the great chasm and couldn't retreat.

She thought of the moment she'd left the Ritz, wondering if she'd ever be well enough to return. She and Bain had ridden the elevator down to the well-appointed lobby. He'd carried her overnight bag. She'd clutched her purse to her chest, shivering beneath two layers of sweaters despite the warmth of July. Behind her two ladies had discussed their hair appointment at a nearby salon.

As the metal gates opened and she stepped out, she'd thought her heart would stop. Instead it had raced.

A tall, athletic woman in a long white skirt and a mustard-colored crochet top stood in the lobby. The figure was unmistakable even without a bucket or a rake or a floppy hat.

"Emily contacted me," Prissy had said. "Erin told her you were here."

"It's nice of you to come," Grace had replied.

Bain had offered to fetch the taxi, leaving them alone.

"We have a lot to talk about," Prissy had said.

"I suppose."

She crossed her arms in front of her chest. "Kody left me."

"I'm sorry." Then she added, "Truly."

Prissy didn't react to the sentiment. "We made it to Florida, Key West, I don't know if Emily told you that."

Grace shook her head.

"We'd been there about a month when I told him about Ferris. That was my mistake, but I felt he had to know.

That was it. He said he didn't want anyone to feel sorry for him, especially me. I'm not sure I ever did, but that's what he thought, that he'd been my charity case. It wasn't fair of him—to dismiss me like that, to dismiss everything we shared together—but he was adamant. I asked him to forgive me." Prissy paused, brushing a stray hair behind her ear. "Anyway, I wanted you to know that I'd been punished, too."

Grace pictured Ferris, wondering for a moment what he would think of her announcement. If Prissy had been honest with Kody sooner, and their marriage had ended, might Ferris still be alive? No, she told herself. It wouldn't have made a difference. That wouldn't have made Ferris happy. He'd wanted Prissy to choose him, actively and affirmatively, not because her first choice was unavailable. He'd wanted Prissy to make him feel special. Instead, she'd been selfish.

From the backseat of the taxi, she'd watched as Prissy, standing under the awning, got smaller and smaller in the distance.

Had she wanted to punish her? Probably so. Over the days and weeks, she'd felt hurt, betrayed, angry. Her dearest friend had stolen her brother. But at this moment of uncertainty in her life, all the conversations she'd expected to have before seemed pointless. Prissy had to live with herself and the consequences of her actions, her own private nightmare.

Now Grace shut the bathroom door behind her and turned the lock. In her trembling hand, she held a small paper bag.

Standing on the sterile tile floor, she took out the pair of red panties, snapped off the tag, and stepped into them. The fabric felt odd, unfamiliar. In the mirror she noticed that her pubic hair poked through the lace in the front. Was that supposed to happen? Even so, the underwear looked good, sexy. If she died on the operating table, she liked the idea that she would leave behind a surprise.

❧

Grace lay on a gurney, covered by a thin white blanket. The nurse insisted that Bain not push the stretcher to the pre-operating room, and so they were forced to wait in the hallway for transport to arrive. Nurses and doctors, orderlies and volunteers hurried past them, checking charts and pagers. Their rubber-soled shoes squeaked on the linoleum floor. She appreciated the commotion.

"It was supposed to be me," Bain said in a quiet voice. "I was supposed to go first, if we couldn't go together. That was how I'd organized the universe." He sniffled. "You're the one with the courage. You're the one with the strength. You have so many qualities I love, but I've admired you for that, for always being strong enough to go on regardless of what happened, for that inner fortitude more than anything else." He wiped his eyes with his free hand.

She'd never known. She hadn't thought of herself that way. She closed her eyes, thought of Sarah, then Erin and Hank. Her three children. "Do you think we learn too late?"

He looked confused. "To exploit my vulnerabilities?" He winked.

She knew his effort to seem lighthearted was herculean. "No, not that. I mean, do we learn when it's too late to change? I want to believe that even if we just have wisdom or insight for a fleeting moment, it's not a waste."

There was no opportunity for Bain to reply. At that moment, the orderly arrived, a young man in a blue cargo suit who looked as though he were part of a NASCAR pit crew. His nameplate read HAL. He smiled, his white teeth flashing from his dark skin. "All set?"

"Yes," she said.

Bain leaned over her and kissed her once and then again. Then he wrapped his arms under her, lifted her torso away from the gurney, and held her in an embrace.

As she tucked her hands beneath the blanket and allowed Hal to tighten the safety straps across her chest and legs, she thought of the smooth satin of her underwear. For a moment, she wanted to jump off the stretcher, pull up her hospital gown, and show Bain. Imagining the expression on his face, his shock perhaps, then his naughty grin of delight, made her laugh.

How much she wanted the time, that joy, another good run.

Hal glanced over at her. "You okay, ma'am?"

"Yes," she mumbled.

He unlocked the brakes and positioned the gurney toward the elevator. Ahead of her, a collection of people waited for its arrival. She stared at their backs, the white doctors' coats, green scrubs, street clothes. No one wore a blue-and-white oxford shirt or a blue blazer.

Panic gripped her. Bain wasn't among them. He was gone. He'd left his embrace in place of any parting words. She closed her eyes, trying to hold back the tears, and listened to the mumble of voices, the bits of disjointed conversation about a patient who had been discharged, a nurses' meeting, a lunch special.

The elevator doors opened, revealing a cavernous space inside. The crowd shuffled forward.

A bald patient pushing a bag of intravenous fluid on a metal pole bumped into the end of her stretcher. Turning toward her with a vacant stare, he muttered, "Excuse me." His complexion was yellowish gray.

"After you, sir," Hal replied.

The gurney shifted slightly.

If she'd been able to jump off at that moment, she would have, but the straps held her down. She couldn't get in, not now, not without Bain. Her heart pounded. Her hospital gown was clammy and matted against her chest.

Just then, she felt a hand on her shoulder. Even through the fabric, she could feel the heat of his palm, the strength of his fingers, his familiar touch.

Bain leaned forward. She smelled his skin, his breath. And then he whispered, so softly for a moment she thought she hadn't heard. But she didn't need the words. She knew what he was saying.

"Lead the way, my dearest Gracie. I'm right behind you."

Reading Group Guide

Discussion Questions

1. A recurring question in *Being Mrs. Alcott* is whether life unfolds as a result of accidents or choices. How do you think Grace ultimately interprets her own life?

2. There are three marriages featured in the novel: Grace and Bain, Prissy and Kody, and Erin and Marley. Are there any similarities? What does each marriage reveal about the nature of commitment?

3. Few parents would ever admit that they are disappointed in their children. Do you find Grace's criticisms of her sons realistic? If there is blame to place, do you think Grace, Bain, Hank, or Erin is at fault for the family's inability to communicate?

4. Inheritance in various forms is a complex part of the narrative. Grace ponders genetics and the age-old debate between nature and nurture, wondering what, if anything, her sons have inherited from her. Inherited wealth — or the lack thereof — shapes the relationship between Hank and his parents. What do you think the story reveals about what can and cannot be passed between generations? How do Grace, Bain, Ferris, Erin, and Hank reflect attitudes toward inherited traits or inherited wealth?

5. Eleanor Montgomery's stoicism is a point of contention between Ferris and Grace, and yet both siblings keep their personal pain secret in much the same way. Is this Eleanor's legacy? Is it the same one that Grace passes on to her own children?

6. Prissy's background differs substantially from the other major characters and yet part of her appeal is that she's different. What is her role in the novel? What does she reveal about Grace? Do you find her sympathetic?

7. How is "clamming" used as a metaphor?

8. The Cape Cod landscape is more than just the setting for this novel. How does it contribute to the feel/tone of the book? How does it illuminate the characters?

9. What is the author saying about the nostalgia of a "family home"? Is it the product of the imagination? Can memories be separated from the places in which they occurred? How do Grace, Bain, and Erin treat their memories—as sores or as solace?

10. Erin, even as an adult and father of his own children, is still heavily dependent upon his parents for financial and emotional support. Is there a time when children ever outgrow the need for a parent? Is Bain's anger justified or cruel?

11. Grace has deferred to Bain on many critical decisions throughout their life together and yet she comes to recognize Bain's tremendous dependence upon her. How do you interpret the last line?

Suggested Reading

I am a book lover. I like to hold them, read them, and gaze at the spines lined up on my There are so many wonderful books, both classics and contemporary, that it is hard for me to suggest any one in particular. But I offer the following recommendations, a small sampling of works that in my view make the world a richer place. The stories, characters, and settings have stayed with me long after I have closed the back cover.

- Louis Begley is one of my favorite authors. I recommend everything he's written, especially *Mistler's Exit* and *About Schmidt*. He captures the poignancy, humor, and pain of life in simple, lyrical prose.

- Kazuo Ishiguro's novel *When We Were Orphans* is an unbelievable story about the power of memory.

- *Up Country* by Nelson DeMille brilliantly captures the Vietnam landscape. His novel shows that the setting can inform the story in a vivid and dramatic way. Through fiction, he reveals the complexities and horrors of the Vietnam War.

- E. B. White's essay, "Death of a Pig," is what inspired me to try to write. He took the smallest occurrence—the raising of a pig on his farm—and used it to debate the most profound questions of life and death.

- *Truth and Beauty*, Ann Patchett's memoir of her friendship with the poet Lucy Grealy, is the best book I've read on the pain and reward of loving someone who is ill.

Nancy Geary on Nancy Geary

I've read Robert Frost's poem, "The Road Not Taken," more than a dozen times as part of every American poetry class I have attended in elementary school, high school, and college. It was one of my favorites, the familiar stanzas embracing a lack of convention and a celebration of risk.

I thought it could have been written for my mother.

She is an artist who created a magical world for my sister and me. Our life was full of adventures, projects, conversation, and stories, but decidedly lacking in basic necessities like heat and toilet paper. At one point, we had thirteen cats and nearly as many hamsters. For breakfast, we wore parkas over our nightgowns and ate cereal with the oven door open. I'd skip school when I wanted, and my mother and I would go to the Metropolitan Museum of Art, the Guggenheim, or the Whitney, or we'd rent a rowboat in Central Park and have a picnic. I'd skateboard down the hill outside our brownstone on Ninety-fifth Street and fly out onto Lexington Avenue while my mother stopped traffic. I missed a solid week of fourth grade to attend a festival of Katharine Hepburn films.

I remember opening the front door one afternoon to find an elderly man rolled up in white paper lying in the living room. My mother was photographing him. I stood and watched as she adjusted the lights, looked through her lens, rearranged a fold in the paper, and looked again. Finally, she noticed me. "I'm just experimenting a bit with death here. But I bought a lemon cake. We'll all have tea together in a few minutes." The old man looked up from the floor and smiled.

"Be original!" my mother always called to me as I climbed aboard the school bus. "Be special!" In our world, to be ordinary, normal, and average were the true sins.

Mundanity was a fate worse than death. A road other than the one less traveled was out of the question.

I read Frost's words again about the time that I'd finished my third novel, *Regrets Only*. I was thinking of an idea for a new book and sought inspiration, as I have before, in poetry. This time, though, the poem struck me in a way it hadn't before. The two roads diverged. His narrator took one. What would have happened if he'd taken the other? What if the road less traveled represented an alternate course? How much is a life shaped by the choices we each make when we come to that divergence in the path?

These questions haunted me over the next several weeks. I thought of my own life. I'd quit the practice of law to try to write. My decision was far from impulsive, yet I left behind four years of law school, six years of experience, and a partnership track. What would have happened to me if I'd continued to pursue a legal career? After I quit law, I'd enrolled in a memoir-writing course, where I met the woman who introduced me to my literary agent. What if the fiction class I'd intended to take hadn't been full? Would I have another agent or none at all? Would I ever have been published? Just after my first novel had been sold, my son was born and my husband and I separated. I had no particular place to go and no particular place I had to be. I drove south with my baby, my two dogs, and my computer. On a passing recommendation, I visited South Salem and fell in love with a farmhouse built in 1790. It has a thin river running behind the property and a moss-covered statue of St. Francis in the garden. I bought the place even though I didn't know a soul, hadn't known the town existed, and couldn't find the grocery store. But I made a choice that has shaped our lives for the past four years. What would have happened if we'd gone somewhere else? Where might we be?

Being Mrs. Alcott was written around this question of accident — or fate — versus choice — or free will. The novel spans the life of Grace Alcott, a woman for whom much has been beyond her control or not her choice. As she faces her mortality, she must come to terms with what she has done, what she has allowed to happen, what she has left to do, and what she wants to change. Like Frost's narrator, she reflects upon the journey she's taken and looks forward, having learned from the road she's traveled.